**"This case is going to be a hot potato,"
the district attorney said.**

"A brutal murder of a little boy in the town with the highest per-capita income in the whole damn state is bound to generate a lot of publicity and a lot of high emotions. I don't have to tell you that the folks in Oakwood are going to want a quick resolution of this thing. We want to make damn sure that whoever did this gets put away for a long, long time. This is definitely not a case where we want the perpetrator walking on a technicality."

Liz nodded. "Agreed. But where does that leave me?"

"Well, it's like this," the sheriff put in. "We realize that you folks don't get involved until we're ready to charge somebody, but seeing how this case is a little out of the ordinary, Harry and me were thinking that this might be a situation where we should deviate from our standard operating procedure just a tad."

"Meaning?" Liz prompted.

"Meaning we'd like you to get actively involved from the beginning of the investigation," the district attorney concluded.

Liz could feel her heart pumping harder . . .

NANCY KOPP

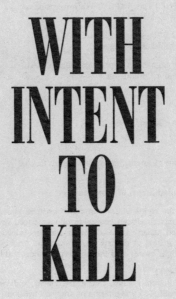

WITH INTENT TO KILL

A SIGNET BOOK

SIGNET
Published by the Penguin Group
Penguin Putnam Inc., 375 Hudson Street,
New York, New York 10014, U.S.A.
Penguin Books Ltd, 27 Wrights Lane,
London W8 5TZ, England
Penguin Books Australia Ltd, Ringwood,
Victoria, Australia
Penguin Books Canada Ltd, 10 Alcorn Avenue,
Toronto, Ontario, Canada M4V 3B2
Penguin Books (N.Z.) Ltd, 182–190 Wairau Road,
Auckland 10, New Zealand

Penguin Books Ltd, Registered Offices:
Harmondsworth, Middlesex, England

First published by Signet, an imprint of Dutton NAL,
a member of Penguin Putnam Inc.

First Printing, November, 1998
10 9 8 7 6 5 4 3 2 1

For Ann Muchin

Prologue

Detective Captain Jeff Gardner of the Horicon County, Wisconsin, Sheriff's Department had just finished washing and waxing his six-year-old blue Chevy when he heard the phone's insistent ringing. The forty-two-year-old detective mopped his sweaty underarms and chest with his gray sleeveless T-shirt, ran the shirt over his curly brown hair, and sprinted across the garage and up the two steps leading to the kitchen of his two-story colonial home.

It was twelve-thirty on a steamy Saturday afternoon in mid-June. Gardner had tried to bribe one of his sons into washing the car, but they'd both refused to bite. Sixteen-year-old Alex stooped to helping with car-related chores when he wanted to borrow one of the family's vehicles, but otherwise his time was pretty well consumed with his summer job stocking shelves at a local grocery store and thinking about girls. Fourteen-year-old Bill's passions were loud music and his junior high baseball team, of which he was the captain, and since he was still two years away from being able to get a driver's license, cars didn't hold that much attraction for him.

Gardner's wife, Julie, had left the house at dawn to report for her job as a nurse in the intensive care ward of the local hospital. Gardner had the day off and, finding himself home alone by mid-morning, he had decided to polish off a few odd jobs before the heat got any worse. He had finished all of them and was looking forward to taking a quick shower and spend-

ing the remainder of the afternoon vegged out in front
of the TV with a couple of beers. In his gut he was
afraid that the phone call would shoot that idea all
to hell.

Crossing the kitchen with long strides, Gardner
reached the phone and snatched up the receiver, the
sweaty T-shirt still clutched in his right hand. "Gardner," he barked.

"Afternoon, Jeff." The mellow voice of Andy
Young, the sheriff's department dispatcher, came over
the line. "They found a body over in Oakwood Hills
about a half hour ago. Thought you'd want to know
about it."

The T-shirt fell to the floor. Gardner had been expecting the call. For the past five days Oakwood Hills
had been the scene of the largest manhunt in the
county's history. Gardner himself had put in thirty
hours overtime and had volunteered to work today as
well, but the sheriff had told him to rest up for the
larger investigation to come.

After the first forty-eight hours had passed with no
sign of the missing person, everyone in the department
tacitly acknowledged they were probably dealing with
a homicide, and if that assumption proved to be true,
as the senior detective on the force, Gardner would
be in charge of the case. Of course, until there was
official word to the contrary, there was always a thread
of hope, albeit slender, that the outcome of the search
might be a happy one. As the call from dispatch had
proved, the only place you could be assured of happy
endings these days was in fairy tales. Score another
one for the bad guys, Gardner thought grimly.
"Thanks for the call, Andy. I'm on my way."

Gardner hurriedly showered, changed into clean
clothes, and fired up the Chevy for the twelve-mile
drive west to the site where the body had been found.
Thirty minutes after getting the call from dispatch, he
was at the scene reciting his impressions into a hand-
held dictaphone. "The body of a well-nourished white

male Caucasian child was discovered at twelve hundred hours on Saturday, June 15, by Deputy Ronald Hasslett of the Horicon County, Wisconsin, Sheriff's Department, with special assistance from K-9 Corps Officer Lady."

Gardner flicked his thumb down over the dictaphone's on/off switch and fought to control the strong emotions that engulfed him at the sight of this tiny corpse. After taking a couple of deep breaths, he switched the recorder on again and continued his narrative.

"The body was buried in a shallow grave in a heavily wooded area located in the northeast quadrant of the Village of Oakwood. The child had reddish-blond hair, was approximately thirty-eight inches tall, weighed about thirty-five pounds, and appears to have been about four years of age." Gardner paused again, then went on.

"The body shows marked signs of decomposition, consistent with the combined effects of the burial and the heavy rains and extreme heat of the past few days. There is massive trauma to the back of the head and large amounts of blood loss, leading to the conclusion that death was the result of a skull fracture. The body is fully clothed, and there are no outward signs of sexual molestation."

"Thank God for small favors. At least it doesn't look like a pervert got him."

Gardner again halted the dictaphone and turned to face the approaching bulky figure who had interrupted his soliloquy. "That's not much consolation in a case like this," Gardner said bitterly, "but I guess it's something." He had regained his composure now and was just damn angry that such a crime had occurred in his jurisdiction.

"Hell, yes," Sheriff Dan Isaacson's deep bass boomed out. "Believe me, the boy's daddy will take great comfort in it." The sheriff's voice held just a hint of a Southern drawl, which Gardner had always suspected must be contrived, since as far as he knew, his boss had never ventured south of Bloomington, Illinois, in his whole life.

"If you say so," Gardner replied, squinting up at the man mountain who now stood two paces away. Gardner was six feet tall, but next to the sheriff he looked like a choirboy. He glanced back at the small body, surrounded now by a buzzing mass of humanity: a full complement of deputies, forensics personnel, photographers, two members of the county medical examiner's staff, all measuring, probing, sifting, and cataloging the little boy's resting place and his remains.

The sheriff removed a red handkerchief from his back pocket and mopped his brow. "Christ almighty! This heat is sure oppressive. I was hopin' that rain would cool things off some."

"Guess we're just in for one of those summers," Gardner replied.

"Guess so." The sheriff motioned to where Deputy Hasslett was standing, talking animatedly to another officer. His German shepherd tracking dog, Lady, sat quietly beside him, panting from the heat but otherwise unaware of the excitement her find had caused. "That damn dog's turning out to be quite a hero, ain't she? This is the second find she's made this year." Several months earlier, Hasslett and Lady had helped locate a five-year-old deaf child who had wandered away from home.

Gardner nodded. "Yeah. She's sure earned her keep for this month. You'd better go buy her a great big juicy steak for a reward."

"I just might do that." The sheriff took a step forward and put his hand on Gardner's shoulder. "Say, Jeff, I don't suppose there's any way I could impose on you to go break the news to the boy's father?"

Gardner shook off the hand as though it contained an electrical charge. "Shit, no!" he exclaimed. "Bereavement calls aren't in my job description. Besides,

Dan," he added with just the hint of a smirk, "every now and then you've got to do something to justify the big raises you talk the county board into giving you every time you get yourself reelected."

The sheriff squinted against the sun, his dark eyes narrowing to little slits in his round face. "Would you maybe consider changing your mind if there was fifty bucks in it?" he cajoled.

"I wouldn't change my mind if you offered me five hundred bucks," Gardner shot back. "So you'd best haul your sorry ass back to your car and get it over with. I want to nose around here a little more, but I'll meet you back at the department later this afternoon to give you my quick and dirty impressions and my thoughts on what we ought to do next."

"All right," the sheriff said grudgingly as he turned to go. "I'm on my way. But I'll be honest with you. I'd sooner take a beating than have to pull this kind of duty."

As Gardner watched the sheriff make his way through the trees back toward the road, he nodded to himself. He was sure as hell glad he wouldn't have to be the one to inform Oakwood's most prominent citizen that his only child was dead.

PART ONE

Chapter 1

Liz Stanfeld was sure of one thing: it was too damn hot for a wedding.

That single thought kept repeating itself in her head, like her own private mantra, and it kept her spirits high throughout the long hours that she labored in the yard of her Oakwood, Wisconsin, home. As morning gave way to afternoon, through mowing, edging, weeding, digging, and planting, over and over she found herself offering up a heartfelt prayer of thanks to whatever force of nature was responsible for this sweltering heat. This was the day her ex-husband was getting remarried, and the temperature was downright unbearable.

Liz was on her hands and knees in one of the six flower beds in the backyard, pulling out the last remnants of spring's flowering bulbs and digging dozens of holes and filling them with salmon and white double impatiens. Sweat was running into her eyes, and she paused to shuck off her garden gloves in order to subdue several strands of dark brown hair that had escaped the loose ponytail into which she'd tied it that morning. She wiped her sweaty hands on her brown cotton shorts and pulled her oversized T-shirt down over her no longer svelte hips, then squinted up at the sun. She had purposely left her watch in the house, but she guessed it must be about two o'clock by now. The ceremony started at three.

Liz gleefully imagined the blushing bride being overcome by the heat and swooning. Of course, the girl was only twenty-three and an aerobics instructor, but what the hell, this was Liz's daydream and if she wanted swooning, by God, there would be swooning. And after all, Peter was thirty-eight and had always preferred cold weather. Liz envisioned him in his scratchy tux, sweating profusely. Let's think, she mused. What other horrors could she wish on the happy couple? Maybe Amanda's finger would swell so badly that Peter wouldn't be able to slip the ring on it. Maybe the air conditioning at the hotel would go on the fritz in the middle of the reception. Maybe Peter's BMW would overheat on the way to the airport. Why, the possibilities were absolutely endless.

Liz took a deep breath and replaced her gloves. She really didn't harbor any ill will toward her ex, she thought as she thrust her small spade fiercely into the soft earth and scooped out another plug of dirt. He was entitled to get on with his life, just as she had gotten on with hers. She would have preferred, however, that he not find eternal happiness with the blond Bennington graduate he'd begun screwing several months before their marriage fell apart. Of course, at the time Liz had been blissfully unaware of those activities. With hindsight, though, she had to admit that she should have suspected something was up.

It had been terribly out of character for Peter, who had always been a night owl, to suddenly take such an avid interest in exercising that he joined a six a.m. aerobics class. "To help stave off middle-aged spread," he'd told her. And the activity had seemed to do him a world of good. His disposition was better than it had been in years, and he'd dropped ten pounds within weeks. Fool that she was, Liz had encouraged him to continue with the classes. Little did she know that his weight loss and soaring spirits were largely the result of some one-on-one maneuvers between him and the pert instructor.

The announcement that Peter wanted a divorce had come completely out of left field. He'd unexpectedly called Liz one morning and asked if she were free for lunch. They had met at their favorite Italian restaurant, the place where they'd gotten engaged. Peter always did have a warped sense of humor. Over a nice glass of white wine and a delicious fettuccine Alfredo, as he'd passed the garlic bread, he had dropped the bombshell that after much soul-searching he'd decided he simply didn't want to be married anymore.

It was all rather civil—once Liz got used to the idea, that is. Oh, she had taken it hard at first, had yelled and threatened and questioned him about his motives, but through all her tantrums, Peter had stuck to his story that no, there was no one else, he just didn't want to be tied down. And sucker that she was, Liz had believed him, right up until the bright morning exactly one week after their divorce had become final when she'd opened the paper and on the society page had seen a photo of someone who looked startlingly like Peter looking down all starry-eyed at a ravishing young blond woman. With disbelief that had quickly turned to disgust, Liz had read that Mr. and Mrs. Reginald Thomas, of Milwaukee, Wisconsin, and West Palm Beach, Florida, were happy to announce the engagement of their daughter, Amanda Louise, to Peter Huntington, executive vice president of Huntington Construction Company, one of the Midwest's largest construction firms. A June 15 wedding in Milwaukee was planned.

As she had dropped the paper on the floor and raced to the bathroom, retching, Liz had thanked God she had followed her instincts and moved out of the city. It was difficult enough to cope with the situation from thirty miles away. If she'd stayed in Milwaukee, it would have been unbearable. Once it had become clear that Peter was intent on going through with the divorce, Liz had begun to reassess what she wanted out of life. Although she hadn't come up with a definite answer, she knew for sure that she didn't want the continued long hours and high pressure of her litigation partner's position at Harrigan and Gilchrist, Wisconsin's largest law firm. The property settlement she'd received in the divorce had ensured that at age thirty-five, she would never have to work again if she didn't want to, so to the great surprise of her friends and colleagues, she had resigned from Harrigan and taken a position as an assistant district attorney in the predominantly rural county of Horicon. While the new job paid only a fraction of her former partner's draw, it offered reasonable hours and little stress, thanks to the area's low crime rate. To complete her break with the past, she bought a stunning contemporary home in Oakwood, twelve miles west of Horicon's county seat.

After seventy-five years, during which Oakwood had remained an unincorporated wide space in the road with a general store, a blacksmith shop, and a tavern, the real estate boom and easy-money years of the late 1970s and early 1980s had put the community on the map. Young professionals, awash in cash and deploring the cramped spaces and lack of safety in their city neighborhoods, had flocked north to build their elegant homes.

The new urban settlers also proved to be good at town planning. The minimum lot size in the village was one acre, and Oakwood Hills, the area's premier address, boasted a two-acre minimum. A multitude of other deed restrictions also operated to keep out undesirables. The planning scheme had served its intended purpose—among its twenty-five hundred residents, Oakwood counted a Milwaukee Brewers shortstop, a Milwaukee Bucks guard and a United States senator. A quaint business district had sprung up on the southern end of town, with tony restaurants, an espresso bar, antique and gift stores, and a number of high-end specialty clothing shops.

For Liz, the move to Oakwood was an important step in putting her life back in order. She basked in her newfound independence and her new home. Gardening became a passion, and she was amazed at how much satisfaction could be derived from cutting the grass with her new Sears riding lawn mower or watching her flower beds deepen in beauty as the months passed.

Most of all, Liz loved Oakwood's friendly, small-town atmosphere. It seemed that everyone she met went out of their way to make her feel welcome. As a result, Liz felt a sense of belonging that had been sorely lacking in the city. She had recently been nominated to fill a vacancy on the planning commission, the village's most prestigious committee. She was touched that the village trustees thought enough of her to bestow such a coveted seat on a newcomer. She was eager to assume her duties so that she could give something back to the community and, by encouraging orderly growth, ensure that Oakwood would continue to offer a quality standard of living for future generations.

Liz was almost done planting the last of the six flats of impatiens when she heard a familiar voice behind her. "How many times have I told you to wear a hat when you're working out in the sun? All I can say is don't come crying to me when you get skin cancer."

"You know how much I hate hats." Liz turned and gave a little wave to her best friend, Esther McMillan, and her two children. Five-month-old Ariel rested comfortably in a Snugli attached to her mother's chest, while three-year-old Cameron trudged sturdily along under his own power. On leave from a tenured position as a history professor at a private college, Esther was tall, svelte, and blond, and Liz was certain her chum had somehow managed to look gorgeous even in the throes of labor. Dressed in lightweight cotton pastels, mother and children looked as if they had just stepped out of an Impressionist painting. Only Esther's sharp tongue belied her genteel bearing.

"I don't care if you despise hats," Esther scolded, adjusting her own floppy chapeau. "Have you ever seen someone in the advanced stages of melanoma? It's not a pretty sight."

Liz smiled. It was Esther who had encouraged her to make the move to Oakwood. During the dark days of the divorce, when their friends were dividing themselves up between her and Peter like so many pieces of china, Esther and her husband, Bob, had been the first to land solidly in Liz's column. Liz had been extremely gratified but also a bit surprised, since the McMillans' ties to Peter predated the marriage. Bob McMillan had been Peter's broker for years, and Liz knew that taking her side had cost Bob's firm a great deal of money. But the two of them had served as Liz's anchor through the whole sordid affair, always ready to lend a sympathetic ear, a shoulder to cry on, or a snifter of brandy.

The McMillans had moved to Oakwood Hills five years earlier, and when Liz had mentioned to Esther in passing that she, too, was thinking of leaving the city, Esther had immediately arranged for her friend to go through half a dozen houses that were for sale. Liz had made an offer on one of them the following day. While she occasionally had twinges of nostalgia for her historic home in the city, she quickly shrugged them off. She would create her own history here.

Liz stood up, brushing the dirt off her knees. "I'm all finished," she announced proudly, peeling off her gloves and tossing them on the ground. "Planted two hundred of those little suckers today. Not bad, huh?"

"Looks great," Esther agreed, extricating baby Ariel from the Snugli and setting her down in the grass. "I just hope the sun doesn't fry them before they've had a chance to take hold."

"They should be okay," Liz said, leaning down and tickling the baby's fat chin. "It's fairly well shaded here."

"I helped plant flowers yesterday," Cameron informed Liz gravely. "Big red ones."

"That was nice of you," Liz said, patting the little

boy on the head. "I'll bet your mommy was real proud of you."

"Mommy was thrilled," Esther laughed. "Especially when he got the bright idea that we could make the geraniums go much farther if he pulled each bud off and planted it separately. Luckily I caught him before he decimated my entire crop."

Liz worked her shoulders up and down. The long hours of crawling around on the ground had left her aching and sore. "Say," she said casually, "what time is it getting to be?"

Esther glanced down at her watch. "Quarter to three."

Liz nodded. "The quarry should be entering the church right about now."

Esther made a face. "Didn't I tell you to try to block the whole thing out of your mind? Peter is ancient history. He's not worth getting upset over."

"I know," Liz said hastily. "I haven't been dwelling on it. After all, there's nothing like gardening to help take out your frustrations. Why, this morning when I was using the clippers to chop off the last of the tulips, every time I made a cut I imagined I was slashing away at a different part of Peter's anatomy. It was great therapy."

"That's the spirit!" Esther congratulated her. "Say, why don't you let Bob and me take you to dinner tonight, to make sure you don't sink into the doldrums?"

"Thanks for the offer," Liz replied, "but Harry's taking me out."

"Oh," Esther said, the corners of her mouth turning down. "I see."

In his official capacity, Harry Washburn was the Horicon County District Attorney and Liz's boss. Unofficially, he and Liz had been dating for the past six months, much to Esther's dismay. Liz crossed her arms in front of her. "Let's not get into another one of *those* discussions," she said, her eyes narrowing. "I know you don't particularly like Harry, but he has a lot of nice qualities. He's kind, he's gentle, he's attentive—"

"So's my dog," Esther interrupted, "but that doesn't mean I want to date him." Seeing Liz's mouth turn down, she put up her hands in a defensive gesture. "Okay, okay. Sorry. If you're happy, I'm happy."

"I'm happy," Liz assured her.

"Good," Esther said, patting her friend on the shoulder. "It's your funeral. Well, have a nice dinner. I'll talk to you soon."

When the McMillan entourage had left, Liz returned her garden tools to the garage and tossed the empty plastic flower flats into a trash container before going in the house. She went up to her bedroom, stripped off her dirty clothes and tossed them into the hamper, then stood under a tepid shower for several minutes, until she felt her body temperature returning to normal. She lathered gobs of lotion on her sunburned skin, ran a brush through her hair, and pulled on a clean pair of shorts and a baggy top before walking barefoot back down to her bright, airy kitchen.

She opened up the refrigerator and for a long moment stared with disinterest at the half a dozen cans of mineral water lined up neatly on a shelf before wrinkling her nose and slamming the door again. She had gained fifteen pounds during the divorce, and while she had managed to shed about half of them, those last eight pounds seemed to be hanging on like an albatross around her middle. Still, she had put in a strenuous day, and she deserved a treat. She opened the freezer compartment and pulled out a half gallon of banana split ice cream. She set the carton down on a counter, pried off the lid, and began to eat out of the carton. That was one of the nice things about living alone. There was no one to scold you about your bad habits.

Liz had savored four or five spoonfuls when the portable phone on the nearby island squawked. She helped herself to one more delicious mouthful before padding across the bleached-oak floor to answer it.

"Well, Elizabeth, I'm surprised to find you home," a rather abrasive woman's voice announced.

Liz rolled her eyes. "If you didn't think I'd be home, Mother, why did you bother trying to call?"

The older woman ignored the sarcasm. "So, how are things going?"

"Fine," Liz replied noncommittally. Tucking the phone under her chin, she walked back to the counter, replaced the lid on the ice cream carton, and popped it back into the freezer. Then she opened the cupboard above the fridge and pulled out a bottle of Jack Daniel's. She got out a glass, poured a good inch of the liquor, hesitated a moment, poured in a bit more, and took a sip. It burned all the way down, yet was strangely refreshing. She took another swallow. The burning sensation eased a bit, and she began to feel more mellow.

"Well, I was just puttering around the house, and I got to thinking about you," her mother pressed on, "and, wondering how you were and, you know, wondering if you were all right—" There was a pregnant pause.

"Of course I'm all right," Liz said innocently. "What on earth would make you think I might not be all right?"

Mrs. Stanfeld expelled her breath loudly. "You know very well what I'm referring to," she retorted. "The wedding."

Liz took another sip of bourbon. "What makes you think I would give a damn about the wedding?" she said crossly. "I haven't given it one moment's thought."

"Well, I just thought you might be feeling a little down in the dumps today," her mother persisted. "And there would certainly be nothing unusual if you were feeling upset. After all, you were married to the man for seven years."

Liz could feel herself begin to do a slow burn. Mona Stanfeld had simply adored her son-in-law and could not understand how Liz had managed to let such a perfect husband get away without a fight. Liz often wished there had been some way her mom could have been awarded to Peter as part of the property settlement. "You got me, Ma!" Liz exclaimed, downing another swallow of booze. "I didn't want to tell you, but actually I'm so despondent and so anxious about what's happening that to find out I have someone standing by at the wedding as we speak, equipped with a cellular phone. We really shouldn't be tying up the line, because they're going to be calling any minute to give me a blow-by-blow description of the entire ceremony. I can't wait to find out who catches the bouquet."

"Really, Elizabeth," her mother said in a frosty tone. "There is no need to be impertinent."

Before Liz could respond, the call waiting signal cut in. Thank you, thank you, Liz silently mouthed to whatever god controlled the phone lines. "See, Ma? What'd I tell you? Here comes my call. Gotta go. Talk to you soon. Say hi to Pop. 'Bye." She clicked off before her mother could lob another retort and briskly answered the incoming call. "Liz Stanfeld."

"Liz?" a deep male voice asked. "I'm sorry to bother you at home—"

"That's all right, Harry," Liz cut in with a deep sigh, as she took another sip of bourbon. Then she frowned. "Say, you're not calling to cancel our dinner, are you?"

"No," Harry Washburn hastily replied. "We're still on for tonight. Actually, this is a business call."

"Oh?" Liz said curiously.

"Yes. I was hoping you'd be able to meet me down at the sheriff's department."

"No problem. What's up?"

"They found Jeremy Barker's body this afternoon."

"Oh, God!" Liz felt her stomach lurch. "I'm on my way." She dropped the phone back on the counter, tossed the rest of the bourbon down the sink, and hurried upstairs to change her clothes.

Chapter 2

Tom Barker was on automatic pilot as he pointed his car east on Highway 178, the road leading from Oakwood to Lakeview, the Horicon County seat. Later, when he replayed the events of that Saturday afternoon, he would not remember the drive. He would recall only the sheriff's brief visit to the house and then arriving at the medical examiner's suite in the basement of the Lakeview hospital. The intervening twenty minutes would be somewhere lost in space and time.

When the sheriff left the house, Tom was shaking so badly that he questioned whether he'd be able to make the drive by himself. He tried calling a woman friend to ask her to drive him, but when he was unable to reach her immediately he set off alone. He couldn't bear to wait a moment longer to see his son.

Fortunately, the black Lexus needed little guiding as it wended its way over the curvy road. It had taken Tom on this same journey many times in the last months of his wife's illness. It was hard for him to believe that Clarisse had already been gone a year and a half. It seemed like only weeks ago that she had still been with them. Through surgery, radiation, and chemotherapy, she had stoically battled the ovarian cancer that was diagnosed shortly after Jeremy's birth. Right up until the end, when the pain had become unbearable, she had fought with every ounce of her being to stay alive. For Tom and for their son.

After she was diagnosed, Clarisse had expressed her

profound regret that they hadn't started a family earlier. They had always agreed that they wanted two or three children, but they were both so busy with their careers—his as an insurance executive and hers as the manager of an exclusive jewelry store—that they kept putting it off. By the time Jeremy came along, they'd already been married eight years. Tom was thirty-eight and Clarisse thirty-five. There was still plenty of time for one or two more babies—or so they'd thought.

Clarisse had never really feared dying. What discomfited her the most was thinking that Jeremy would not remember her. "Don't let him forget me," she begged Tom quietly on her final day of life. "Promise me you'll help him remember."

"I promise," Tom said, tenderly stroking her face.

True to his word, Tom had spent a great deal of time talking to his son about his mother, showing him photographs, sharing the details of her life. The child seemed to enjoy the talks and was always enchanted with the photos of Clarisse. He'd point at the pictures and say "Mommy" so cheerfully that Tom would be moved to tears. And now Jeremy was dead, too. How would Tom ever find the strength to go on alone?

In the five days since Jeremy disappeared, the thought that he had been killed had flashed through Tom's mind countless times, and he believed he was prepared to accept that eventuality if it came to pass. But somehow actually hearing the words said was very different from just imagining them. As long as no one said it out loud, it was still possible that maybe, by some miracle, his son remained alive. Until Tom officially heard otherwise, a faint ember of hope still burned that Jeremy's captors would release him unharmed or perhaps would demand a ransom, which Tom would gladly pay. But all those hopes had turned to ashes as soon as Tom saw Sheriff Isaacson's car pull up to the gate.

As he passed the blue sign with the white sailboat announcing WELCOME TO LAKEVIEW—POPULATION

25,000, Tom unconsciously took his foot off the gas and let the car coast down to thirty-five. Was it only four and a half days ago that he'd gulped a quick cup of coffee and said good-bye to Jeremy before leaving for work? It was a hot, parched Tuesday morning, and the little boy had told him happily that he and Darlene, the loving, cheerful woman in her mid-fifties who had come to live with them during Clarisse's illness to serve as a combination nurse and nanny, were going to go swimming later that morning. Tom had told the boy how lucky he was to be able to spend the day loafing, and Jeremy had urged his dad to hurry home so the two of them could loaf together.

It was around two-thirty when a very distraught Darlene called, interrupting Tom in a meeting. She said that shortly before noon she and Jeremy were having lunch in the backyard, sitting at the white wrought iron table next to the pool. Darlene saw the UPS truck pull up to the front gate, which, as usual, was locked. She went inside, punched in the security code to open the gate, and then walked out to meet the truck and sign for the package. She came back in and put the package on the table in the kitchen. When she returned to the backyard moments later, Jeremy had vanished. His glass of orange juice was still half full, and part of his chicken salad sandwich remained on his plate.

Darlene anxiously searched the entire house and yard, and after failing to find the boy she ran the three hundred yards to the edge of the woods at the rear of the property, but she found no trace of him. It was as though the boy had disappeared into thin air. Frantic by this time, Darlene phoned the Oakwood police. They responded immediately, but after ninety minutes of unsuccessful searching they called the Horicon County Sheriff's Department for reinforcements.

As soon as he got Darlene's call, Tom had rushed home to join the search. Late in the afternoon the sheriff's department brought in a tracking dog, but by that time a fierce storm had blown up, severely hampering their efforts. The rain and high winds had continued unabated until Thursday evening, obliterating any clues that might have been left and making it impossible for the dog to follow a scent.

The sheriff's deputies had put a tap on Tom's phone in order to be able to trace any call demanding a ransom. No call ever came. The sheriff also placed the house under round-the-clock surveillance in case the perpetrator happened to come around to see the effects of what he had wrought. That effort, too, had been to no avail.

During the endless days and nights that followed, it crossed Tom's mind more than once how ironic it was that something like this could happen in Oakwood. He and Clarisse had moved there when she found out she was pregnant with Jeremy because they'd wanted a safe environment in which to raise their child. While there was an occasional burglary and once in a while some property damage caused by pranksters, the village had never been the site of a violent crime. A police force of five manning three squad cars kept busy patrolling the area, and each house got a drive-by at least once an hour. The officers were personable and handsomely paid, but they were simply not equipped to handle serious incidents, so once they'd assured themselves that Jeremy was truly missing and wasn't just playing a trick on his nanny, they quickly abdicated responsibility for the search to the larger and more experienced county sheriff's department.

For the first forty-eight hours after Jeremy disappeared, Tom had been convinced that ransom must be the motive for snatching his son. It was certainly no secret that Tom had money. His French manor home atop a hill was the former Parkhurst Brewery heirs' mansion, Oakwood's largest residence, and something of a tourist attraction. At the time he and Clarisse bought it, Tom had just been appointed president of Midwestern Mutual Life, Wisconsin's largest insurance company, whose corporate headquarters covered an entire square block in downtown Milwaukee. The Barkers had a cottage in Door County, which they visited on as many summer weekends as they could manage, but Tom knew his new position would require him to spend even longer hours at the office, and a new baby would make it doubly difficult to make the three-hour drive north. Oakwood seemed the perfect location, a place removed from the city but an easy commute away, where Jeremy could have plenty of room to play and where Tom could leave the pressures of his job far behind.

Jeremy had loved the house, especially the pool. He was already quite an accomplished swimmer. He was such a bright little boy, friendly and inquisitive. The sheriff's deputies had found no signs of a struggle, which led Tom to believe that the assailant must have rendered the child unconscious before snatching him. Jeremy was mature beyond his years, and he knew better than to voluntarily walk off with a grown-up he didn't know.

Darlene had become hysterical at the boy's disappearance and was still under heavy sedation at her daughter's home in Madison. Tom had not slept more than a few hours since Tuesday. He had wanted to join in the search, but the deputies tactfully discouraged it, saying he could do the most good by staying close to the phone. The ensuing days and nights had melded together until he had lost all sensation of time.

Tom stopped for a red light at the intersection of Lincoln and Sixth. When he had the green, he continued on Lincoln for two blocks before making a right on Sutherland. He pulled into the parking lot of the Lakeview Community Hospital and selected a parking place near a side door.

He put the car in park and gazed at the familiar red-brick building with glassy eyes. Lakeview was a quaint old town built on a hill overlooking Lake Michigan. During her numerous stays at the hospital, Clarisse had always requested a room on the top floor, facing the lake so that she could watch the sun rise over the water. With her cheery disposition she had been a staff favorite, and they had always obliged her, even if it meant playing musical rooms with several other patients.

The sheriff had told Tom that the morgue was in the basement, and he wanted to avoid going in the main entrance where a smiling receptionist would greet him and try to offer assistance in finding the room number of the person he wanted to visit. He cut the engine and removed the keys from the ignition, then sat very still, as though he were welded to the seat. He had a sudden urge to turn around and drive off somewhere. Anywhere, as long as it was away from here.

Tom caught a glimpse of himself in the rearview mirror and ran a trembling hand through his dark blond hair in an effort to tame it. His blue eyes were bloodshot and ringed with dark circles. His tan pants and tan and blue cotton shirt were rumpled. I look like shit, he thought. How very appropriate. He took a deep breath, then slowly got out of the car.

He walked the fifty yards to the side door feeling as though he had weights attached to his legs. Stepping inside, he spotted a stairway going down. He took the stairs slowly, one at a time, like a person who was unsure of his balance. A sign on the wall indicated that the morgue was straight ahead. He paused as he reached the double stainless steel doors, then took another deep breath, pushed open the doors, and stepped inside.

A young female aide in a white lab coat nodded sympathetically when he told her that he was looking for Dr. Carstensen. She led him silently down a short hallway and rapped quickly on the door to a small office. In a moment the door opened and a short, balding man of about fifty, also dressed in a white lab coat, stepped out. "Mr. Barker? Jim Carstensen," he said, extending his hand.

"Doctor," Tom replied hoarsely, giving the hand a firm shake.

"I'm very sorry for your loss," the medical examiner said.

"Thank you," Tom murmured. "Can I see him now?"

The doctor inclined his head. "Right this way." He stepped in front of Tom and led him through another set of doors into a large, windowless room. On one wall was what looked like a huge stainless steel refrigerator. Stopping in front of it, Dr. Carstensen turned to Tom and said tactfully, "I don't know if the sheriff mentioned that the body has undergone certain changes due to exposure to the elements."

Tom closed his eyes briefly and nodded. "I understand," he said.

"Good," the doctor said briskly. He opened the heavy door to the refrigerator and pulled out a gurney that contained a small form covered by a white sheet. Without further fanfare, the doctor gently folded the sheet back, uncovering the head and torso of the little body that lay beneath.

As Tom stepped forward, the stench caught him unaware and a wave of nausea swept over him. Fighting to regain his composure, he stared down at the child's face. The features had virtually melted away. This isn't Jeremy, Tom thought, his heart beating wildly. There must have been some mistake! Maybe his son was really still alive! Then Tom noticed the green and white Ninja Turtles T-shirt. Jeremy had been wearing it that last morning. Tom stretched out a trembling hand and gently stroked the small chest. "How did he die?"

Dr. Carstensen hesitated a moment before answering. "Repeated blunt force trauma to the back of the skull."

Tom felt his stomach lurch. "Do you think he suffered?" he asked hoarsely.

The doctor patted Tom's arm comfortingly. "In my opinion the initial blow would have rendered him unconscious. He would have had no cognitive recognition of what happened after that."

Tom heaved a sigh. "Thank God." Taking a deep breath, Tom took one last look at his son. Then he nodded at Dr. Carstensen and turned away. The doctor briskly replaced the sheet and rolled the gurney back into place.

When the two men had walked back to the doctor's office, Tom asked hesitantly, "When do you think you'll be able to release the body? I'll need to know what to tell people about the funeral."

"You could schedule it for Monday afternoon, if you'd like," the doctor replied kindly. "We'll be all finished with him by then."

Tom pursed his lips and nodded. "Monday. All right. Yes. That will be fine," he said disjointedly. "Thank you, Doctor."

"You're welcome, Mr. Barker," the doctor replied. "As I said, you have my sincere condolences."

Tom made his way back up the steps feeling as though he were struggling to find his way through a thick fog. As he emerged from the building and began walking toward the car, a tall, slender young woman with long reddish hair rushed to his side and embraced him.

"I came as soon as I got your message," Natalie Helprin, Tom's companion of the past six months, said breathlessly. "Why didn't you wait for me?"

As Tom opened his mouth to speak, his whole face contorted in agony.

"My poor darling," Natalie murmured, throwing her arms around him. "My poor, poor dear." Tom clung to her tightly and for the first time since the ordeal had begun on Tuesday, he broke down and sobbed.

Chapter 3

Liz pulled her blue Dodge Caravan into the sheriff's department parking lot. In the sixteen months she'd been with the district attorney's office, she had been careful to keep her home life in upscale Oakwood completely separate from her work life in middle-class Lakeview. That meant leaving her silver Jaguar XJS parked in the garage, her hand-tailored Italian suits hanging in the closet, and most of her good jewelry stashed safely in a drawer. While her colleagues knew Liz had come from a large law firm in the city, only DA Harry Washburn knew the full story about her background. It was difficult enough to gain acceptance at a new job without having to battle class prejudices too.

The Horicon County Sheriff's Department and jail were housed in a nondescript cement block building dating from the mid 1960s. Unlike most counties where the jails were bursting at the seams, Horicon had a relatively low incidence of jailable offenses; in fact, the county was able to pick up some additional revenue by leasing a few of its cells to neighboring counties that weren't so fortunate.

Liz wheeled the van into a parking space and got out, smoothing away the wrinkles in her blue linen skirt as she walked toward the building. She had topped the outfit with an oversized blue-and-rose blouse in an effort to hide the fact that the skirt was too tight to button at the top. One of these days, she thought grimly, she was going to get the rest of the weight off—somehow.

She walked up the five steps leading to the building's main entrance and stepped into a sterile lobby with dingy tan walls and a utilitarian gray linoleum floor. The uniformed female officer stationed at the reception window buzzed her through a security door leading to a group of offices. Liz found Sheriff Isaacson and District Attorney Harry Washburn waiting in the sheriff's corner office. Both men stood as she entered.

"Afternoon, Ms. Stanfeld," Sheriff Washburn said genially. "My, aren't you lookin' pretty today."

"Hello, Sheriff," Liz replied. She didn't particularly care for Isaacson. From what she'd seen, his department was a bit heavy on brownnosing local officials and a bit lax on protocol.

"Thanks for coming, Liz," the district attorney said. A tall, lanky man in his late forties, Harry Washburn had spent ten years in private practice with a small firm in Lakeview before running for the county's top prosecutor spot a dozen years earlier against a crotchety but popular twenty-five-year incumbent who pleabargained ninety percent of all cases filed. Washburn had campaigned on a platform of change, and to everyone's surprise—including his own—he had won by a narrow margin. He had lived up to his campaign promises and proved himself to be a tough, no-nonsense prosecutor who wasn't afraid to see the inside of a courtroom. The number of cases pleabargained dropped to twenty-five percent, and conviction rates soared.

Washburn was now on the short list of candidates for U.S. attorney for the Eastern District of Wisconsin, a prestigious position that would double his current salary and offer him the opportunity to prosecute high-profile federal offenses. Those in the know gave Washburn the inside track for the job, since he was on a first-name basis with the U.S. senator who lived in Oakwood—and who happened to be a member of the selection committee.

The district attorney was divorced and had two grown children. He and Liz had started dating about six months earlier. It was Liz's first relationship since her divorce. At a time when she'd been feeling slightly frumpy and a bit over the hill in the wake of her ex's impending marriage to a younger woman, Washburn made Liz feel attractive and helped her regain her sense of self-worth. She had been very hesitant about getting romantically involved with her boss, but Harry's easygoing manner and persistence had finally worn her down. As far as they knew, they had been successful in keeping the rest of the office in the dark about their personal lives. Their relationship was comfortable, if not extremely passionate.

"Have a seat," the sheriff said, settling his bulk into his padded vinyl chair and gesturing toward the two empty seats in front of his desk.

Liz chose the one next to Washburn. She noticed that in spite of the heat Harry looked cool and unruffled in black pants and a black-and-white-check shirt. "So they found Jeremy," she said, shaking her head sadly.

The sheriff nodded. "Yup. I had to break the news to his daddy earlier this afternoon. That's one part of this job I could sure do without. Harry tells me you live in Oakwood. Do you know Tom Barker?"

Liz shook her head. "No. I've driven by his house, but I've never met the man. How did Jeremy die?"

"The back of his head was smashed in," the sheriff replied.

"Jesus!" Liz exclaimed. The air conditioning in the office was turned up full blast, and she shivered a bit. "Who would do something like that to a little boy?"

"Well, ma'am, the truth of the matter is that right now we have no idea," the sheriff said. "Would you like some coffee or a soda?"

Liz shook her head, then looked quizzically from

the sheriff to Washburn. "You don't have a suspect? Then why am I here?"

The sheriff motioned to Washburn to field an answer. "Dan and I have been talking it over," Washburn said, turning to face Liz. His dark brown hair was just starting to gray at the temples, and in Liz's eyes this made him look very distinguished. "I guess there's no question in anybody's mind that this case is going to be a hot potato. A brutal murder of a little boy in the town with the highest per capita income in the whole damn state is bound to generate a lot of publicity and a lot of high emotions. I don't have to tell you that the folks in Oakwood are going to want a quick resolution of this thing. We want to make damn sure that whoever did this gets put away for a long, long time. This is definitely not a case where we want the perpetrator walking on a technicality."

Liz nodded. "Agreed, but where does that leave me?"

"Well, it's like this," the sheriff chimed in. "We realize that usually you folks don't get involved until we're ready to charge somebody, but seeing as how this case is a little out of the ordinary, Harry and me were thinking that this might be a situation where we should deviate from our standard operating procedure just a tad."

"Meaning?" Liz prompted.

"Meaning we'd like you to get actively involved from the beginning of the investigation," Washburn concluded.

Liz could feel her heart pumping harder. She'd never prosecuted a homicide. This would be a plum assignment. Then she frowned. "What do you mean by 'actively involved'? I'm not an investigator."

"No, no, you're misunderstanding us," Washburn cut in. "You wouldn't be investigating, merely acting as a backup, as needed, on any legal points."

"Hell, yes," the sheriff seconded. "The investigation is in mighty fine hands. I've assigned my very best man to the case. Ah! Speak of the devil! Here he is now."

Liz looked up as a tall, well-built man with curly brown hair stepped into the office. She recognized Jeff Gardner from previous cases she had worked on. "Come in, Jeff. Come in," the sheriff exhorted. "We were just talkin' about you."

"Recommending me for a big pay raise, I hope," Jeff said, leaning against the doorjamb.

" 'Fraid not," the sheriff chuckled. "Have a seat. I assume you know District Attorney Washburn and his ace assistant Liz Stanfeld?"

"Yes, I've had the pleasure," Jeff replied, settling into the chair next to Liz. He glanced over at her. He remembered her all right. He had testified in a couple of cases that she'd prosecuted. He'd thought she was bossy and inflexible.

Liz briefly met Jeff's gaze, then looked away. This assignment was going to be even tougher than she'd originally thought. Gardner was well known as the darling of the sheriff's department, but she'd found him to be cavalier and disrespectful of anyone in authority, particularly women.

"Good afternoon, counselors," Jeff said genially. "To what do we owe this double honor?"

"We've just been going over some background in the Barker case," the sheriff explained. "Speaking of which—did your search turn up anything?"

"Yes, as a matter of fact, it did," Jeff said, casually crossing his right leg over his left. There was nothing like a homicide investigation to get the old adrenaline pumping. Horicon County saw only a handful of murders each year, and while Jeff wasn't nearly so crass as to ever admit he looked forward to someone getting killed, and while child murders were probably the most heinous crime known to man, Jeff had to admit that an occasional murder *did* help break the monotony of having to investigate an endless string of bicycle thefts.

"We found a pair of men's glasses about twenty yards from Jeremy's body," Jeff explained. "As luck would have it, the name of the optometrist who prescribed them was in one of the bows. Dr. Gerhardt. Local guy. I've already talked to him, and he agreed—somewhat reluctantly—to try to figure out who the owner was."

"Good job," the sheriff praised.

"Don't break out the champagne just yet," Jeff cautioned. "It's a real long shot that the glasses will end up having any connection to the murder. But for the moment it's the only clue we've got, so I guess we'll have to run with it. How did your talk with the father go?"

"As well as could be expected," the sheriff replied. "The poor fellow was pretty shook up. Losing a child is probably the worst thing a parent can face."

"It's a bitch," Jeff agreed. He looked at Liz and Washburn again. "So, you two are just here shooting the breeze?" he asked.

"No, Jeff," the sheriff replied, shifting a bit uncomfortably in his chair. "It's like this. This here is going to be a very high-profile situation, with Tom Barker's son being killed and all, so Harry and me thought it would be a good idea to have Ms. Stanfeld get involved in the case right from the get go."

"And just what does that mean?" Jeff asked, frowning. He was starting to get an uneasy feeling in the pit of his stomach about the reason for the two prosecutors' presence.

"It means we think she should be kept fully briefed on all aspects of the case and she should perhaps participate in interviews with key witnesses," Washburn put it.

"The hell she will!" Jeff pounded his fist on the arm of his chair.

Liz sat back in her seat as though she'd been punched, completely stunned by Gardner's outburst.

"Since when do we take orders from the district

attorney?" Jeff railed. "Dan, what's going on here? Don't tell me you agreed to this horseshit?"

"Calm down, son," the sheriff said soothingly. "Me and Harry gave this some careful thought, and we both feel Ms. Stanfeld can offer a valuable perspective on the case."

"I don't believe this!" Jeff stood up and began pacing back and forth in front of the window. "Dan already knows more than he cares to about my work habits, but let me spell out a few things for you two," he said, glaring at Washburn and Liz. "It's very simple. I'm a loner. I work solo whenever possible. Occasionally I am forced to partner up with someone, but when I do it's someone of *my* choice, someone I've worked with before, someone whose capabilities I know. I do *not* work with strangers, and I sure as hell am not going to have someone with no law enforcement background telling me how to run my investigation!"

"Now just hold your horses, Jeff—" the sheriff began.

Liz's face was flushed with anger. "May I please say something?" she interrupted in a sharp tone of voice, "Or am I expected to sit around the rest of the afternoon while the three of you talk about me as if I wasn't even here?"

The sheriff and Washburn looked properly chastened. Jeff stared at her defiantly.

Liz shot Jeff an icy glance and continued. "First of all, Detective, let me assure you uncategorically that I did not ask for this assignment. And believe me, if your performance here today is any indication of how you work, I should have my head examined for not racing out of here and telling you to go straight to hell!"

She tossed her head defiantly and went on. "Unfortunately, the sheriff and District Attorney Washburn are right. This is going to be a touchy case. The press is going to be crawling all over Horicon County. The

Barkers' neighbors are understandably going to be very antsy about the situation. While I agree with you that it's unusual to involve someone from the DA's office at this stage, I think there are a whole host of reasons why this case should be an exception to the rule. Now let me assure you that I have no intention of trying to tell you how or who to investigate—''

"And just what do you think your role *should* be?" Jeff interrupted.

"Well—" Liz paused a moment, then echoed what Washburn had said earlier. "For starters, perhaps we should discuss the case on a daily basis, and I think I'd like to sit in on key witness interviews."

"To do what?" Jeff shot back. "Hold up cue cards with the Miranda warnings on them in case I have a memory lapse?"

"No," Liz replied through clenched teeth. "to make sure there aren't any screwups."

"That's bullshit! I don't screw up cases. At least not those where I'm left alone to do my thing."

"All right, all right. That's enough. Time out." The sheriff held up his hands. "This is getting us nowhere. Why don't you two kiss and make up—metaphorically speaking, of course," he said, chuckling. "I know this isn't exactly a marriage made in heaven for either of you, but I'm sure once you get used to each other, it'll work out just fine."

"That's right," Washburn agreed. "Why don't you try to work out some kind of protocol to get the ball rolling?"

Liz turned to Washburn and frowned. She'd like to get the ball rolling and bounce it right off that smart-ass detective's head. Washburn gave her a look that urged appeasement. She sighed and turned back to Gardner. "Where do you anticipate starting your investigation?"

"I've already started the investigation," Jeff answered with exaggerated patience, "by talking to the optometrist. As far as other witnesses, I talked to the father and the nanny earlier in the week, but I'll want to hit both of them again. I hear the nanny is under doctor's care over in Madison, so I'll probably take a run over there tomorrow. I guess the funeral is tentatively scheduled for Monday afternoon, so I'll either try to catch the dad on the way home tomorrow or, if he's really not feeling up to it, hold off on him until Monday night."

Liz nodded thoughtfully. "I'd like to sit in on both of those interviews if you don't mind."

"I *do* mind," Jeff countered, "but it sounds like I don't have much of a choice. I'll set up the interview with the nanny and give you a call."

Liz reached into her purse and pulled out a business card. "Here's my phone number."

Jeff made no effort to reach for the proffered card. "I'll find you. I'm a detective, remember?"

As Liz and Washburn got up and walked toward the door, Jeff was leaning close to Sheriff Isaacson. Liz heard him say, "Jesus Christ, Dan! Is this your idea of a bad joke?" Liz kept walking. She had no inclination to stick around to hear the sheriff's response.

Washburn walked Liz over to her van. When they reached it, she wheeled around to face him. "Thanks a lot for all the support you gave me in there."

"You seemed perfectly capable of defending yourself," Washburn chuckled.

"I don't know if I should thank you for giving me this assignment or punch you in the face," she said ruefully.

"A simple thank-you would suffice," Washburn replied.

Liz rolled her eyes. "Sounds like it's going to be quite an experience working with Sam Spade." Then she added seriously, "Tell me something, Harry. Why me? I've never done a homicide. Is it just because I live in Oakwood? Am I supposed to keep the restless natives at bay?"

Washburn put his hand on her shoulder. "You're the best damn trial lawyer in the office," he said. "Next to me, of course," he added with a smile. "I meant what I said in there, Liz. This is one case where we don't want the bastard who did this walking out on a technicality. You're the best person for the job, and your status as an Oakwood resident was not the deciding factor; it's merely an added bonus."

"If you say so," Liz said, squeezing his hand. "So what time are you picking me up for dinner?"

"Eight o'clock on the dot. In the meantime, I'll expect you to work up a fierce appetite for steak and tails and to have a powerful thirst for champagne." He opened her car door and she climbed in.

"See you at eight," Liz said, slamming the door behind her. As she started the van and headed back along Highway 178 toward Oakwood, she glanced at the clock. It was five-thirty. Amazing. More than two hours had passed without her giving a thought to Peter's nuptials. Maybe this case was just what she needed to get her out of the blue funk she'd been wallowing in for months. Too bad it took such a gruesome event to get her life back on track. Still, the thought of prosecuting Jeremy's murderer and putting him away for life was heady stuff. She cranked up the blower to the air conditioner and sped toward home, already planning the opening statement she would make to the jury at the trial.

Chapter 4

Liz and Washburn were barely even out of earshot when Jeff unleashed the full force of his anger at Sheriff Dan Isaacson, calling him every pejorative term he could think of for a full five minutes. The sheriff, who had known Jeff since he was a confused twenty-year-old trying to figure out what direction his life should take, bore the tirade in good humor. When Jeff finally stood before him, red-faced but momentarily silent, Isaacson got up out of his chair, slapped the younger man soundly on the back, and advised him to go home, have a few stiff drinks, and get a good night's sleep. "Believe me, son, this case is gonna be tough enough without your aggravatin' the situation. Do yourself a favor and try to get along with the lady. Things could always be worse," he said with a sly wink. "Hell, from where I was sittin' she looked mighty easy on the eyes."

Before Jeff left, his boss spilled the beans about Liz's status as an Oakwood resident and her rumored relationship with Harry Washburn. In Jeff's mind, those two tidbits spoke volumes about why Liz had been assigned to the case and served only to increase his ire. The fact that the DA happened to be boinking the woman was no reason to let her horn in on Jeff's investigation.

The detective drove home like a man possessed. His wife, a petite blond woman of forty, was in the kitchen making tuna salad when he burst in. Slamming the door behind him, he savagely jerked the refrigerator door open and yanked out a can of beer. After knowing Jeff for thirty years and being married to him for eighteen, Julie Gardner paid little attention to her husband's frequent bouts of anger. For all his growling, Jeff was really a soft touch, and she knew that if you kept quiet and let him growl, his bad moods would dissolve as quickly as they'd arisen.

"I heard they found Jeremy Barker's body," Julie said, spooning a bit more mayonnaise into the salad.

Jeff popped the top off the beer can, slumped into a chair at the table and took a long swallow, then wiped his hand over his mouth. "Yup. Ron Hasslett's goddamn dog found him. Story of my life. Upstaged by a dumb animal." He took another gulp of beer. "Then to give the day some comic relief, Dan and the goddamn district attorney decided it'd be a good idea to assign an assistant DA to bird-dog every move I make in the goddamn case. Seems she's a rich bitch who lives in Oakwood, and she also happens to be Harry Washburn's main squeeze. Can you imagine?" he snorted. "Twenty-one years at the goddamn department—half of my goddamn life, and seven medals of commendation besides—and just because the kid of one of the county's richest residents gets whacked, all of a sudden somebody decides I'm not fit to do my job and I need a goddamn woman looking over my shoulder, making sure I don't belch when I'm interviewing all the muckety mucks over in Oakwood. I have to tell you, Jules, if we weren't lookin' at college tuition for the boys in a couple of years, I would've told Dan to stick the job up his goddamn ass." With that, he finished his beer and savagely crumpled the can and hurled it across the room into the wastebasket.

Julie gave the salad another toss and then slipped it into the refrigerator. "This probably isn't a good time to bring it up," she said, sitting down across from her husband, "but Alma Henkel announced her retirement today, and I'm thinking of applying for her position." Alma was one of the supervising nurses at the hospital. "It'd mean I wouldn't get stuck with so many swing shifts," Julie went on, "and the salary would be about ten thousand more than I get now. So, what do you think? Should I go for it?"

"You already make more money than I do," Jeff said flibly, "so what's a few grand more between friends? I don't know, Jules," he said with a shrug. "What do *you* think?"

"I think you should have another beer," Julie replied pragmatically. "It might improve your mood."

Jeff took his wife's advice, and while after two more beers and a light supper with her and the kids he was still not pleased with the situation, at least he was focused enough to be able to spend a couple of hours making phone calls to gather information about the case. He phoned Liz at six-thirty Sunday morning.

"Rise and shine," he said brightly as Liz's groggy voice came on the line. "Are you ready to go to work?"

The heavy meal and champagne that Liz and Harry had enjoyed the night before had left her feeling bloated and slightly queasy. "Work?" she replied blankly. "Now?"

"Well, not right this minute," Jeff replied. "I arranged an interview with Darlene Powell in Madison at ten, and Tom Barker said he'll see us this afternoon. Should I pick you up?"

"Ah . . . no," Liz said hurriedly. She didn't want to tell him where she lived. "I'll meet you at the sheriff's department at eight-thirty."

"Suit yourself," Jeff said. "I'll be there with bells on."

They made the ninety-minute trip to Madison largely in silence. Liz spent most of the drive staring out the window. From time to time Jeff caught himself glancing over at her. Dan had been right about one thing: she wasn't bad-looking. Her dark hair was thick and shiny, her eyes deep green, her skin clear, her cheekbones high. It looked like she was carrying a few extra pounds around the hips, but her blue cotton sleeveless dress was flattering, and from what he could see, she definitely had nice breasts. He could understand what Washburn saw in her. Jeff briefly smiled to himself and looked back at the road. He was happily married and had never been unfaithful to Julie, but there was no law against looking.

In Madison, Darlene Powell's daughter met them at the door and quietly warned them that her mother still blamed herself for what had happened to Jeremy and remained under sedation. The daughter then ushered them into a small but comfortable living room, where Darlene was seated on a cream-colored sofa. The woman was neatly dressed in white cotton slacks and a floral blouse, her hair was fashionably styled and her face lightly made up, but her eyes betrayed the fact that she was distraught. They continually opened and closed, then darted around the room, then stared straight ahead blankly. As gently as he could, Jeff led her through the events of the morning that Jeremy disappeared. In a halting voice, Darlene repeated the same story she had told when she'd called to report the boy missing.

"Jeremy loved being outdoors, and if the weather was nice, he and I would spend at least part of the day in the backyard, by the pool. The Barker property was very secure," the woman added quickly, as though she were afraid her interviewers might think it was inadvisable to allow a little boy to spend time outdoors. "The front yard was bounded by a ten-foot-high fence, and the gate to the driveway was always locked, so whoever took Jeremy must have come from the woods." Darlene stopped abruptly and brought one fist up to her mouth, struggling to hold back tears.

"How long was Jeremy out of your sight when you went to get the UPS package?" Jeff asked gently.

"Five minutes at most. It might have been even less."

"Did Jeremy know not to talk to strangers?"

"Oh, yes. I never worried about leaving him alone briefly because he was very bright and very articulate. I read him stories about strangers trying to entice children into going with them, and I'm sure he knew better than to fall for such a trick. That's why I think he must have been overpowered. He would've yelled for help if he'd had the chance." She began to cry.

Through more gentle probing from Jeff, the woman said she had never noticed anyone standing in the woods and watching the house. She did see people walking there from time to time, but she assumed they were village residents, and it had never occurred to her to make note of the people or report them to the police. Most folks in Oakwood valued their privacy, just as the Barkers did. Sometimes she and Jeremy walked in the woods, too, though they never went in very far. The woods covered more than five hundred acres, and Darlene was slightly claustrophobic and worried about getting lost.

"Mrs. Powell, do you have any idea who might have kidnapped Jeremy?"

The woman shook her head.

"Are you aware whether Tom Barker ever received any threatening phone calls or letters?"

"Not that I'm aware of. I just don't understand how anyone could harm that child," she concluded. "He was such a sweet little boy. What kind of monster would want to hurt such an innocent little creature?" Her face contorted with grief, and she put her hands over her face and began to sob in earnest.

Jeff stood up, signaling that it was time to go. Liz, too, got to her feet. Jeff thanked Darlene for talking to them and told her to call him if she remembered anything else. Liz also murmured her thanks and then patted the older woman gently on the arm and said, "I know how difficult this must be for you, Mrs. Powell, but please don't be so hard on yourself. There's nothing more you could have done." Darlene lowered her hands and looked up at Liz through her tears. Liz's words seemed to have soothed her, and the woman swallowed hard and nodded.

It was after noon and Jeff's stomach was growling on the drive back to Oakwood, so he suggested they stop at the Pine Cone, a truck stop restaurant midway between Madison and Milwaukee, for a bite to eat. He ravenously chowed down a double cheeseburger, fries, and a Coke while Liz daintily nibbled at a broiled chicken breast sandwich and sipped a glass of iced tea. "Watching your weight, huh?" Jeff queried.

Liz ignored him. After locking horns with the man the day before, she'd told herself she would try to remain civil, and it seemed that the best way to accomplish that was not to say anything.

"So, how do you like living in Oakwood?" Jeff asked jovially as he twirled a french fry in ketchup and popped it in his mouth.

Liz frowned. How the hell did he know where she lived?

"Oh, I know all your dirty little secrets," Jeff said airily. "But don't worry. I won't tell a soul." As Liz scowled and took another bite of her sandwich, Jeff laughed heartily to himself. That ought to make her squirm a bit.

As they continued on toward Oakwood after leaving the restaurant, Jeff again tried to bait her. "So, I'll bet seeing how a real investigation works is a little different from reading Nancy Drew mysteries, isn't it?"

"Look," Liz said in a firm voice as she turned to face him, "let's get something straight here. I can understand your being somewhat less than ecstatic about having me tag along with you. As I already told you, I didn't ask for this assignment, but now that I've got it, I intend to see it through. So if your devious little mind has been thinking that maybe you can bully me or make me so angry that I pull out of the case, you've got another guess coming."

"Wait just a minute—" Jeff said indignantly.

"No. You wait," Liz interrupted. "I'm not finished. I meant what I said yesterday. I have no intention of invading your territory. I know this is your case and I'm just an observer, so there's absolutely no reason for you to feel threatened by my presence. You just do your thing and pretend I'm not even here."

"That's gonna be a hell of a lot easier said than done," Jeff mumbled. They completed the rest of the drive to Oakwood without any further conversation.

Jeff pulled his Chevy up to the gate of Tom Barker's mansion and, rolling down the window, leaned out and pressed the button on the security call box located on one of the stone pillars. Seconds later a buzzer sounded and the lock on the gate slipped open. Once inside Barker's driveway, Jeff pulled the Chevy in behind Tom's black Lexus. Tom was waiting at the massive oak door as they came up the walk. He gravely shook hands with both of them, then ushered them into the house.

Jeff had briefly been inside the French manor home while the search for Jeremy had been going on, but as he followed Tom and Liz down the wide center hallway leading from the foyer to the back of the house, he was again struck by its size and splendor. Everywhere he looked were massive rooms with twelve-foot ceilings, ornate woodwork, crystal chandeliers, hand-painted murals on the walls. It was rumored that Barker had paid a cool three million for the place. Holy shit! Jeff thought. How could a guy his age afford something like that?

Jeff and Julie had bought a fairly modest house twelve years earlier. Since then they'd refinanced twice, once to finish off a rec room in the basement and once to remodel the kitchen, so they still owed nearly as much as they'd paid for it. Every month it seemed like they had to scrape to come up with the money for the mortgage payment. The two of them could have been pretty well set by now, but nobody ever told you how damn expensive it was to have kids. Both boys had part-time jobs, and Jeff insisted they pay for some of their own clothes and recreational activities, but just feeding them cost a bundle. The two of them ate like sumo wrestlers. Once in a while on a Sunday when he and Julie had nothing else to do, they'd go through some open houses as a lark. It was always a rude awakening to see how much housing cost these days. It looked as though they'd be stuck in their present home the rest of their lives.

Liz, too, let out a gasp of astonishment as she surveyed the home. It was absolutely magnificent. She was accustomed to fine architecture and furnishings, but she had never seen such lush and tasteful decorating in the Midwest.

Tom led them to a solarium at the back of the house. Its banks of floor-to-ceiling windows overlooked the pool, the spacious backyard, and the woods beyond. Tom sat down on a blue-and-rose-striped sofa. Jeff and Liz each chose a matching chair facing him. Jeff looked around. Evidently this was the room the family spent the most time in, and the lack of live-in help was already starting to show. There were kids' toys and books all over. A man's shirt was thrown carelessly over a chair. Several plates and cups were stacked haphazardly on a low table in front of the sofa where Tom sat.

The events of the past week had taken their toll on Tom as well. Jeff knew Barker was his age, forty-two, but it looked like he'd aged ten years since the day Jeremy disappeared.

"Have you ever noticed anyone watching the house, either from the woods or from the street?" Jeff asked.

Tom rubbed his hands over his bloodshot eyes. "Not really," he replied. "As I'm sure you know, all of Oakwood—and particularly the Hills—has become a kind of tourist attraction, so we do get a fair number of people driving around, looking at the houses, especially on weekends. But I can't say I've ever noticed the same car coming back or seen anyone who looked suspicious."

"Did Jeremy ever mention anyone approaching the house or trying to talk to him?"

"No. Both Darlene and I had warned him about talking to strangers."

Jeff nodded. "Did you ever get any threatening or obscene phone calls?"

"No."

"How about weird mail?"

"No."

"Do you know of any reason somebody would want to harm you? A business rival, for instance?"

"No," Tom replied in a more curt tone. "Look, I feel like I've already gone over this with half the people in your department. I don't know of anyone who'd hate me enough to commit murder."

"Midwestern Mutual handles only life insurance, right?" Liz asked.

"Yes."

"Has the company denied any large claims recently?"

"What does that have to do with anything?" Tom asked incredulously, turning to face her. "You can't seriously believe that a disgruntled policyholder killed Jeremy?"

"I know some of our questions might seem repetitious or off the wall," Jeff said, "but statistically speaking, the odds are the killer is someone who knew you, either personally or professionally. So it could prove helpful if you could get us a list of claims that were denied."

"All right," Tom replied in a more even tone. "How far back would you like me to check?"

"Let's start with three years," Jeff said. "And just have your people look for denials over a certain dollar amount, say three hundred thousand dollars. We can probably assume that someone wouldn't resort to such drastic measures over a smaller amount of money."

"I'll put someone right on it," Tom said. "I should be able to have some information in a couple of days."

"I hate to belabor the point," Jeff went on, "but are you quite certain you don't have any enemies? People at your company whose toes you might've stepped on in moving up the ladder, guys that you always cleaned out at poker, neighbors you got in a fight with—anybody at all?"

Tom threw up his hands. "Look, sometimes I'm an SOB around the office, and I'm sure any number of my subordnates have periodically wished I'd drop dead, but for the life of me I don't see what any of that has to do with Jeremy."

"There are a lot of sick puppies out there," Jeff said patiently. "We just don't want to rule anybody out." He got to his feet. "Well, we won't intrude on you any longer. I know this is a very difficult time for you, and we appreciate your taking the time to talk to us. We'll keep in touch as things develop."

Tom, too, stood up. "You're not going to be able to find the person who did this, are you?" he demanded. "Since my wife died a year and a half ago, Jeremy was all I had left in the world. And now he's gone, too, and some son of a bitch is going to get away with killing him."

Filled with compassion for the pain the man must be feeling, Liz quickly crossed the short distance to where Tom was standing and put her hand on his arm. "We'll find him," she assured him as she looked into his eyes. "And after we find him, we'll make sure he's put away for a long, long time."

Although Tom remained highly skeptical, his face softened a bit. God, he's handsome, Liz thought involuntarily. "I'll let you know what I find out about the claims that were denied," Tom said in a more even tone.

Jeff did a slow burn all the way back to Lakeview. While he held his tongue, he took out his frustrations by driving much too fast on the curvy road. Liz, too, endured the ride in silence, but braced herself in her seat, prepared for the definite possibility they might land in the ditch. It wasn't until Jeff brought the car to a screeching halt next to her van in the sheriff's department parking lot that she spoke up.

"What the hell's the matter with you? Are you trying to kill us both?" she shouted.

"You reneged on our deal," Jeff shouted back. "I thought you were just going to sit there and observe. The next thing I know, you're asking Barker a bunch of questions, and worse than that, you go and promise him that *we* are going to find the murderer. Jesus!" he snapped. "The first thing you've got to learn about this business is never, ever make promises you can't keep! You can't go around getting people's hopes up."

"But you saw how upset he was. He's all torn up inside. For God's sake, the poor man needs some reason to be hopeful," Liz countered.

"Shit!" Jeff spat back. "All you accomplished is that now Barker is gonna be calling me every half hour wondering if *we've* cracked the case yet. It's bad enough to have you tagging along after me, but you're gonna have to learn to keep your mouth shut!"

Liz unfastened her seat belt and bolted out of the car. "You can go to hell!" she shouted, slamming the car door as hard as she could.

"Bitch!" Jeff mouthed back as he stomped on the gas. He squealed out of the parking lot, leaving Liz standing there, angrily shaking her fist at the departing car.

Chapter 5

Liz switched the phone receiver to her other ear and raised her voice. "No, you wait a minute, Mr. Wilson. We had a deal. You assured me your client would plead guilty to one count of armed robbery and testify against his codefendant if I agreed to recommend a three-year sentence. I went along with that—rather reluctantly, I might add—because it was a first offense and I thought if your guy was willing to cooperate with us and testify he should get something in return. Now you're telling me he's changed his mind. Obviously that's his prerogative, but there's no way in hell I'm going to agree to continue the trial. Either your client goes along with the deal we worked out or I'll see you both in court on August 1. There's no room for further discussion on this one." She angrily slammed down the receiver and leaned back in her desk chair. This job used to be low stress. What the hell had happened?

Liz jotted a few notes on a legal pad, ripped the page off the pad, and walked over to a file cabinet, where she shoved it into the appropriate folder. She then crossed to the window of her office, which was on the third floor of the Horicon County Courthouse, and looked out to the east. It was a clear day, and the waters of Lake Michigan were blue and calm, with a myriad of sailboats. She stood there for a moment, rubbing the heel of her hand over the back of her neck. She wished she had time to go for a walk on the beach. Better yet, she wished she could go home and work in the garden. Her roses were coming into bloom, and she loved to be outside so she could enjoy their delicious scent. She glanced up at the clock on the wall. Two o'clock. She supposed she'd have to somehow settle down and try to get some more work done, but her heart just wasn't in it.

It was Wednesday, four days after Jeremy Barker's body had been found, and the case was weighing heavily on her mind. Dr. Carstensen's autopsy had revealed that the boy had died of multiple blows to the head inflicted by a blunt object like a pipe or a piece of wood. Based on his examination of the stomach contents, the doctor opined that the child had probably died within minutes of his abduction. Just thinking about it sent chills running down Liz's spine.

Jeff Gardner had called her first thing Monday morning to ask if she wanted to accompany him to the funeral. "Are you going?" she asked. "What for?"

"Why, it's a well-known fact that murderers often go to their victims' funerals," Jeff said flippantly. "Occasionally they become so distraught when they realize what they've done that they throw themselves into the grave on top of the coffin. I love it when that happens. It's so easy to make an arrest."

"I think I'll pass," Liz said. "You can call me after you've got the guy in custody."

Although neither one had mentioned their row of the previous afternoon, the friction between the two of them virtually crackled over the phone line. Liz had serious doubts that they would ever be able to forge a satisfactory working relationship.

As Liz had expected, Harry's assigning her to the case had not set well with a couple of the more senior assistant DA's, who felt she was infringing on their territory. Harry had handled that matter deftly by calling an office meeting early on Monday at which he announced that he'd put Liz in charge of the Barker case and that he expected everyone to give her whatever backup or support she might need. While he had made it clear that his choice was not open to debate, he was powerless to stop people from bitching about it behind his back.

Although Liz had known Jeremy's murder was newsworthy, she hadn't been prepared for the scope of media coverage it had generated. Television stations from six states broadcast footage of the funeral. The receptionist at the DA's office was kept busy answering calls from print media all over the country. Luckily, Harry had taken full responsibility for dealing with the press. He was virtually unflappable and managed to remain cordial but noncommittal when answering reporters' inquiries. Privately, though, he had confided to her that the case had him a little on edge.

Harry hadn't come out and said so, but Liz knew he was hoping that a quick arrest and conviction would enhance his chances of getting the nod for the U.S. attorney position. He had let it slip that Senator Kilpatrick, an Oakwood resident and a member of the committee appointed to select the new U.S. attorney, had called, expressing his concern about the case. Liz felt a tremendous amount of pressure to see the matter brought to a rapid conclusion, and the fact that the success of the investigation rested so heavily on Jeff Gardner was very unsettling.

Tom Barker had called Liz Tuesday afternoon with the names of five people who had had large insurance claims denied on the basis of fraud. She had immediately passed the names on to Jeff, who said he'd check them out.

Liz returned to her desk and sat down. Although she'd had a big sandwich at noon, she was already hungry again. She opened her bottom desk drawer, where she kept a large box of rye crackers, then abruptly slammed the drawer shut again. Willpower, she scolded herself. She opened her top drawer and took out a stick of gum, unwrapped it and popped it in her mouth. She tried to proofread a complaint charging someone with driving after revocation but found her mind wandering.

Part of the reason for her bad mood was a phone conversation she'd had with Esther the night before. Liz had called to pry some information out of her friend about Peter's wedding. She'd been certain that by this time Esther would have spoken to someone who had attended, and she decided that hearing the gruesome details was preferable to imagining what might have happened.

"Oh, all right. If you insist," Esther had finally said irritably. "I did talk to Molly Caldwell this morning, and she said, quote, It was a lovely affair. Amanda's dress was absolutely stunning, and Peter never looked so handsome, unquote. There. Are you happy now?"

"What did her dress look like?"

"Old-fashioned. High neck, acres of lace and pearls, and a long train."

"How many attendants?"

"Six. Seems a bit excessive, don't you think? After all, this *is* Peter's second trip to the altar."

"What were they wearing?" Liz asked.

"Rose strapless satin gowns, tightly fitted at the waist and full skirts. Flowers in their hair. They carried roses and baby's breath." She made a retching sound. "It's enough to make you lose your lunch."

"How many guests?"

"What do you think I am, a gossip columnist?" Esther complained. "I think you've heard enough."

"Tell me how many guests," Liz persisted.

"Oh, all right," Esther grumbled. "Four hundred."

"What did they serve at the dinner?"

"Choice of filet mignon or salmon."

"Where are they going on their honeymoon?"

"Paris," Esther snorted. "You know, you really got a raw deal, only getting as far as San Francisco on *your* honeymoon. Peter must be getting extravagant in his old age."

"Do you know any other details worth passing along?" Liz queried.

"No," Esther said firmly. "Now, will you please try to forget that Peter ever existed? You know you really are much better off without him."

"Financially, anyway," Liz said airily. "Sure, I'll forget all about the happy couple until six months from now, when they announce word of their impending parenthood. Let's see. I think if the kid's a boy they should name him Chip and if it's a girl, Muffy. What do you think, Es? Aren't those adorable names?"

"What I think is that if you had a more interesting companion than an old geezer like Harry, you'd get over this unhealthy fascination with your former husband."

"Thanks for the info," Liz said, ignoring the comment about Washburn. "I'll expect updates as you receive them."

"Oh, no!" Esther shot back. "This is positively the first and last news bulletin you're getting from me. If you want further details, you're going to have to call the *Journal-Sentinel* and bribe the society editor."

"Okay," Liz said genially, confident that in a few days she'd be able to cajole her friend into disclosing some more nuggets. "Let's change the subject. What do you know about Tom Barker?"

"I've met him a couple times. He's one of Bob's clients."

"How did his wife die?"

"Slowly and painfully, of cancer. Ovarian, I think. I know Tom was devastated."

"Do you know if Tom has had any female companions since his wife passed away?"

"Now you're talking!" Esther teased. "The two of you would make a dynamite couple. I'll help you ditch Harry and see if I can talk Bob into putting in a good word for you with Tom."

"Really, Esther," Liz protested, "my interest is purely professional. It's always helpful to have background information whenever you're working on a case."

"Well, I've heard that he's been seen out and about with Natalie Helprin."

"Who's she?"

"My God, woman, where have you been? She owns Natalie's, the chicest women's shop in Oakwood."

"Is that the new place on Main Street next to Starbucks Coffee?"

"The same. The clothes are very avant-garde and hideously expensive. And she doesn't carry anything larger than a size ten."

"I knew there was a good reason why I hadn't been in the place," Liz said crossly. "None of the damn stuff would fit me anyhow. So what's old Nat like?"

"She's an absolute bitch," Esther replied without hesitation. "The last time I was in there she fired one of the salesgirls for some very minor faux pas, right in front of a store full of customers. She turned me off so much that I walked out and made up my mind I'd never go back."

"Sounds like a delightful person. What do you suppose Tom sees in her?"

"Aside from the fact that she's about twenty-nine and absolutely drop-dead gorgeous, I can't think of a single thing. I'm sure you'd know her if you saw her. She does her own modeling for most of her ads."

"Does she live in town?"

"No, she lives in Milwaukee, but she's probably got her sights set on snagging Tom and moving up in the world."

"Can't wait to meet her," Liz said.

"Just be careful you don't get scratched," Esther advised. "From the looks of her, she's got sharp claws."

"There was no sign of a woman's presence at Barker's house when we were there Sunday," Liz mused. "The place was kind of a mess. If the relationship was serious, I would have expected her to be there helping out."

"Well, I wouldn't," Esther replied. "Natalie definitely doesn't look like the type who does windows. If you'd like, I can ask around and see if anyone has any dirt on her."

"Do that," Liz said. "And let me know what you find out."

Now Liz shook her head to rid herself of memories of both Peter and Tom Barker and stared down at the page in front of her. The words seemed blurred, and she chomped down on her gum so fiercely that she bit her tongue. "Shit!" she mumbled. She took the gum out of her mouth, wrapped it in a scrap of paper, and tossed it into the wastebasket. The hell with willpower. She opened her bottom drawer again and pulled out the box of crackers. She took out half a dozen and set them on the desk. As she ate the first one, she went back to reading the complaint. This time it seemed to be in focus. See, she thought to herself, gnawing on a second cracker. She really had needed some nourishment. Maybe she had low blood sugar.

"Too many carbohydrates can really put on the pounds," a cheerful voice announced.

Liz looked up and saw Jeff standing in the doorway. "Didn't anyone ever tell you it's common courtesy to knock before walking into someone's office?" she said irritably as she covered the remaining crackers with a piece of paper.

"Yeah, they told me, but it's much more fun sneaking up on people. You never know what you might catch them doing." He sauntered over toward her desk and, without waiting to be asked, sat down in the chair in front of it. "Have you seen the posters?" he asked.

"What posters?"

"The ones offering a fifty-thousand-dollar reward for information leading to the capture of Jeremy's killer," Jeff replied, reaching over and snatching a cracker out from under the paper. "They're nicely done, with a big picture of the kid in the center. The whole town's plastered with them," he went on as he popped the cracker into his mouth.

"Who's putting up the money?"

"A group called Friends of Jeremy. Apparently it's a group of Barker's neighbors."

Liz slapped his hand away as he reached for another cracker. "What's wrong with offering a reward?" she asked crossly. "It seems to me that anything that might induce a witness to come forward is worth a shot."

"There's nothing wrong with offering a reward," Jeff said, leaning back so the front legs of the chair came off the floor. "It just really sticks in my craw how you rich people seem to think you can work miracles if you just throw enough filthy lucre around."

"Did you have some reason for coming here other than to piss me off?" Liz growled. "Because if that was your goal, I'd say you've accomplished it quite nicely and you could leave now."

Jeff leaned back further so that the chair tipped precariously. Just as it was about to go over backward, he leaned forward, causing the front legs to land on the vinyl floor with a resounding crash. "Now that you mention it, there was something else I wanted to tell you. The optometrist was able to trace the glasses we found near Jeremy's body."

"And?" Liz asked eagerly.

"And they belong to a seventeen-year-old named Frankie Snipes." He reached into his pocket and pulled out a scrap of paper. "I did some checking. Frankie lives right here in Lakeview and has a juvenile record as long as your arm. Petty theft, breaking and entering, shoplifting, the whole gamut of small property crimes. He was waived into adult court for a burglary last year. He got six months in jail. The sentence was stayed and he's on three years' probation. No record of violent crimes, at least not any that he's been caught for. I just talked to his probation agent, and she says Frankie missed an appointment with her last week on the very day Jeremy went missing. He didn't show up at his job that day either. The PO went to talk to him about it and he got real defensive. Wouldn't give her a straight answer about why he hadn't come in or where he'd been."

"Sure sounds like a viable suspect to me," Liz said, unable to keep the excitement out of her voice. "Do you know where to find him?"

"Is the Pope Catholic?" Jeff smirked, helping himself to another cracker. "Of course I know where to find him. From the way you're starting to salivate, I take it you'd like to accompany me to have a little chat with Frankie."

Liz got to her feet, her eyes shining. "Let's go nail the bastard."

Chapter 6

They caught up with Frankie Snipes at his job at a home construction site on the north side of Lakeview. One of the laborers directed them to the job foreman, a heavily muscled man in his late forties named Joe Grundal.

"Frankie in some kind of trouble?" Grundal asked warily as Jeff displayed his badge.

"We just want to ask him a few questions," Jeff replied easily.

Grundal nodded skeptically. "I know Frankie's had his share of scrapes, but at heart he's really a pretty decent kid."

"Is he a good worker?" Jeff asked.

"Hell of a worker." Grundal paused a moment before adding, "That is, when he decides to show up."

"Bit unreliable, is he?"

Grundal shrugged. "Let's just say Frankie marches to his own drummer." He sighed. "It's not all his fault, though. His old man is the biggest drunk in the county. And his mother runs a close second."

"What does his father do for a living?" Liz asked. A hot wind was causing the fine dirt and sand at the site to swirl around like a mini tornado. She could feel pieces of grit stinging her in the face, and the heels of her black leather pumps sank into the loose soil.

"Works at the Simmons mattress factory—when he's sober enough to remember to go in."

"I hear Frankie didn't come to work last Tuesday," Jeff said. "That would've been the eleventh."

Grundal nodded. "That's right. I already told Frankie's PO about it. He didn't show up on Tuesday and then we couldn't work Wednesday or Thursday because of the rain, so the next time I saw him was Friday."

"Did he tell you where he'd been on Tuesday?"

Grundal shook his head. "Frankie pretty much keeps to himself and don't volunteer any more than he has to."

"Hey, Joe!" a voice yelled from across the way. "We need you over here."

"Coming!" Grundal yelled back. "Frankie's the one over there in the yellow T-shirt," he said, pointing. "Go easy on him, will ya? The kid doesn't get many breaks."

"Sure thing," Jeff replied. "Thanks for your help."

Liz and Jeff picked their way carefully through the debris strewn around the lot over to a tall, thin youth who was standing in the box of a pickup truck, tossing bags of cement to the ground. He was dressed in tattered blue jeans and a filthy yellow T-shirt and had stringy, shoulder-length black hair and three earrings in his left ear.

"Frankie Snipes?" Jeff called out as they approached.

"Who wants to know?" the boy asked as he turned to scowl at them.

"Detective Jeff Gardner. Horicon County Sheriff's Department," Jeff said, holding up his shield. "And this is Assistant District Attorney Liz Stanfeld."

Liz squinted up at the youth and was immediately struck by the eeriness of the boy's eyes. They were deep-set and almost black in color. Evil eyes, Liz thought to herself.

Frankie's scowl deepened. "I s'pose you're here to deliver papers saying they're gonna revoke my probation." He tossed another bag of cement to the ground. For a slight young man, he appeared to be extremely strong.

"And what makes you think that?" Jeff asked.

" 'Cause that Watson bitch was pretty pissed off at me last time I talked to her."

"I take it you're referring to your probation officer, Miss Alice Watson."

"Yeah, yeah," Frankie snorted. "Fuckin' bitch."

"Hey, pal. Watch your language," Jeff admonished. "There's a lady present."

Frankie's dark eyes briefly looked down at Liz with disdain, then he went back to his methodical handling of the cement bags.

"Miss Watson is concerned about you," Jeff said. "Says you missed your appointment with her last Tuesday."

Frankie merely set his jaw and kept on working.

"We hear you didn't show up for work that day either," Jeff continued. "Would you like to tell us where you were?"

In response, Frankie fiercely hefted another bag over the side of the truck. Jeff had to jump back to keep it from landing on his feet. In the process, he stepped down hard on Liz's ankle and nearly knocked her off balance. She gritted her teeth to keep from crying out. Jeff quickly turned. "Sorry," he apologized. Liz said nothing, but her eyes were flashing.

Frankie chuckled at the incident. "I don't have to talk to you," he said brashly. "You ain't read me my rights."

Jeff stepped forward again and flashed the youth a sardonic grin. "I would think that a smart guy with as long a record as you've got would know that *Miranda* only applies to custodial interrogations. You're not in custody, Frankie. So far this is just a friendly little chat, but if you'd like to keep it that way, I'd strongly suggest you tell me where you were last Tuesday."

Frankie surveyed Jeff up and down, then spat on the ground. "I went fishin' up to Bass Creek," he said, turning his back to reach for another bag.

Bass Creek was a small stream about five miles

north of Lakeview. "How'd you get there?" Jeff asked.

"Bike."

"What time did you head out of town?"

"Right after I got up. 'Bout ten-thirty."

"How come you got up so late? Did you over-sleep?"

Frankie spat again. "I was hung over. That's why I didn't come to work. See, I've come in late before and Joe Grundal told me if I can't be on the job at seven when the rest of the crew starts I shouldn't bother comin' at all. So when I woke up late Tuesday, feelin' like shit, I decided I needed a day off anyway, so I went fishin'."

"Alone?"

Frankie gave a curt nod.

"Was anybody else fishing at the creek that day?"

Frankie paused, a bag in his hand. "Yeah. I seen a couple old guys across the way from me."

"Do you know who they were?"

"Nope."

"Did you talk to 'em at all?"

Frankie shook his head.

"Did they see you?"

Frankie shrugged. "I dunno. They was pretty busy drinkin' beer."

The boy gave Liz the evil eye again, and she could feel the hair on the back of her neck begin to stand up.

"How long did you stay up to the creek?" Jeff asked.

"Till afternoon sometime."

"Can you be a little more specific?"

Frankie shook his head. "Nope. I don't wear a watch. I stayed there a while, but I wasn't catchin' nothin', and then the wind started to come up and I figured maybe it was gonna storm and I didn't wanna get caught in the rain on my bike, so I headed back to town."

"Where'd you go then?"

"Stopped into Smitty's Bar down on Front Street and played a couple games of pool."

Liz frowned. She'd have to make a note to get the Lakeview police to have a word with Smitty about his policy on carding underage patrons.

"Who'd you play with?" Jeff asked.

Frankie shrugged. "Coupla the regulars. George Clovis and Pat Wiganowski."

"Do you wear glasses, Frankie?"

Frankie's eyes narrowed at the abrupt change in the line of questioning. "Yeah," he said hesitantly.

"Have you got your glasses with you today?"

Frankie shook his head.

"Why not?"

"I lost 'em coupla weeks ago."

"Where did you lose them?"

"I dunno," the youth said impatiently, throwing another bag to the ground.

"Well, when did you notice they were missing?"

"My old man told me I could use his car one night. I mostly only wear glasses when I drive. I don't need 'em to see things close up. And when I went to go out that night, I couldn't find 'em."

"Who's your eye doctor?"

Frankie thought a moment. "Gerhardt. Over on Main Street."

"Did you order a new pair of glasses?"

Frankie shook his head.

"Why not?"

"Ain't got the money," he spat. "That's why not. I told my old man I wanted a new pair, but he said if I was so goddamn careless as to lose them, I'd have to pay for new ones myself. I got an old pair at home that I can see pretty good with, so I just been wearin' them. After I get some money saved up I'll probably spring for new ones."

"Do you ever drive through Oakwood, Frankie?"

Was it Liz's imagination or did Frankie's eyes darken even more when he heard the question?

"My old man hardly ever lets me take the car. Mostly I just ride my bike."

"So have you ever ridden your bike through Oakwood?"

The boy snorted. "What the hell would I wanna go there for? All that's there is a bunch of rich snooty bastards who'd probably turn their dogs on somebody like me."

Jeff turned to Liz and tried halfheartedly to suppress a smile. She shot him a dirty look.

"So you're saying you've never been to Oakwood."

"Well, sure, I've been through there a couple times," Frankie said irritably. "Sometimes on a Sunday my ma likes to go for a drive and look at all the rich people's houses."

"Have you been through there lately?"

"Nah. Ain't been there for six months or more."

"Ever hear of a guy named Tom Barker?"

"Nope."

"Do you keep up on the news?"

"Not no more than I have to."

"Did you hear about the little boy they found murdered over in Oakwood?"

"Yeah."

"His name was Jeremy Barker. Tom Barker was his dad."

Frankie's eyes narrowed to tiny slits. He dropped the bag he was holding and stared down at Jeff. "Shit! Is that what you been drivin' at, man? You think I had somethin' to do with killin' that kid?"

"I don't know, Frankie," Jeff said in an even tone. "You tell me. *Did* you have anything to do with it?"

"Fuck no! And I ain't talkin' to you no more," Frankie said, his voice increasing in volume. "You wanna arrest me and try to pin some murder rap on me, you go ahead. But I ain't sayin' another word to you without my lawyer. You call up Fred Haynes at the PD's office. That's who defended me the last time I got busted. I ain't sayin' nothing else till Fred gets here." He jumped off the end gate of the truck and started to walk away.

"That's all right, Frankie," Jeff said, as he and Liz started to follow the youth. "We were all done for today anyhow. But I'm gonna do some checking on the story you told me, and if I find out that things didn't happen just the way you said they did, I'll be back. And believe me, the next time I'm not gonna be nearly so friendly. You just keep in mind what happens to people who lie to the police. It ain't no walk in the park."

Frankie turned abruptly and gave Jeff the finger. "Fuck off, cop!" he shouted, then turned again and sprinted away.

"Nice kid," Jeff said as he and Liz made their way back to the car. "There's nothing that ails him that a good caning wouldn't cure."

"He sure got agitated when you mentioned the murder," Liz said.

"There's no crime in that," Jeff snorted. "You'd get the same reaction out of ninety-five percent of the population if you implied they might've had something to do with a murder. Hell, I'd be willing to bet I could even get a rise out of you if I showed up at your door without warning and gave you the third degree."

"Well, he's got no alibi for the day Jeremy disappeared," Liz persisted.

"Sure he does," Jeff retorted. "Didn't you hear what he said about the two old guys he saw fishing?"

"Don't tell me you believed him?" Liz asked irritably.

Jeff shrugged. "I don't know what I believe yet."

"Well, what are you gonna do?"

"I'm going to check out his story," Jeff said patiently as they reached the car.

"How?"

"Talk to the guys at Smitty's and nose around up

by Bass Creek to see if I can find a couple of drunks who remember seeing a punk kid in the area last week."

"I don't believe this!" Liz said incredulously as she tried to brush the grime off her clothes before getting into the car. She couldn't wait to go home and take a long shower. "His glasses were found at the scene, and he's got a half-assed alibi. Why don't you take him down to the department for some additional questioning? You might be able to shake something out of him, and at least then you'd know where he is. What if he tries to run off?"

"He's not gonna run off."

"How can you be so sure of that?" Liz asked as she got in the car and slammed the door.

Jeff shrugged. "I just am. It's pretty clear this job is the best thing that's happened in his miserable life. He can earn some bucks here, and money is his ticket out of the shitty life he's been living." He started the engine and pulled away from the curb. "Don't worry. I guarantee I'll be able to find Frankie Snipes again if we need him."

Chapter 7

Liz took a sip of beer and looked across the table at Harry Washburn. "You know, after working with Jeff Gardner for four days, I think I'm beginning to understand how people are driven to commit murder. I swear, I was so frustrated with him this afternoon that I would've liked to punch him out."

It was early evening on the day Jeff and Liz had interviewed Frankie Snipes, and Liz and Harry were having dinner at a German restaurant on the north side of Milwaukee. "It's rather curious you feel that way," Harry said, taking a bite of red cabbage, "because Dan Isaacson never stops singing Gardner's praises."

"Well, that just helps prove my case. Dan Isaacson doesn't strike me as someone who'd have particularly good judgment. I know you're on good terms with him, but frankly I don't think the man is any great shakes as a sheriff."

"Oh?" Harry asked. "Why not?"

"He's too much of a good ol' boy politician to suit me, and unfortunately Horicon County is still full of enough of his kind to keep getting him reelected."

"Don't forget," Harry reminded her, "I belong to the same party as Dan, and I've managed to get myself reelected quite a few times, too."

"You've been reelected because you've done a good job and you're the best man for the position. Just like you're the best man for the U.S. attorney's slot, which is why you're going to get that appointment," she added, smiling at him. "I just hope that one of these years at election time Dan Isaacson will find himself facing a viable candidate."

"Dan's been in office over twenty years, and he's got quite a temper if he's pushed far enough," Harry said, signaling the waiter to bring two more beers. "I hope I'm not anywhere within twenty miles of him the day he finds out he's got any type of real opposition."

"Wouldn't that be something?" Liz agreed. She took another sip of beer and smiled at Harry. Although her friend Esther thought Harry was as bland as vanilla pudding, Liz truly enjoyed his company. He was thoughtful and caring and knew how a woman liked to be treated. True, as Esther liked to point out, he wasn't as handsome as Peter or as witty, nor was he well-to-do. But to Liz, that was the whole point. She had been deeply hurt by her ex-husband's desertion, and she wanted no part of any man who remotely resembled him.

"So I take it your day with Detective Gardner didn't go well," Harry said.

"That man is positively loathsome," Liz exclaimed. "When we go out to interview someone, he excludes me from conversations and acts like I'm not even there. When I try to say something or offer my opinion, he makes fun of me. I knew he was going to cause problems the minute I realized he'd been assigned to the case. The two jury trials where I had him testify were among the most nerve-racking experiences I've had as a DA. The man refuses to take direction. On the first case I remember telling him over and over not to volunteer any information when he was being cross-examined. He got very indignant and said he'd testified dozens of times and knew the score. So what does he do about ninety seconds into cross? He shoots his damn mouth off, volunteers a bunch of unnecessary stuff, and almost blows the case for me!" She made a growling sound. "I still get pissed off just thinking about it."

Harry smiled. "And what did he do today that particularly bothered you?"

"He flatly refused to consider the notion that Frankie Snipes might be the person who killed Jeremy."

"And you think Frankie did it?"

Liz cocked her head to one side. "Of course, I don't know for sure," she admitted, "but I'd say there's a damn good possibility. His glasses were found at the scene. He missed both work and an appointment with his probation officer the day Jeremy disappeared."

"All that's merely circumstantial evidence, of course," Harry put in.

The waiter brought the beers, and Liz took another sip. "Yes, but there's more. You're probably going to think I'm overreacting, but there was something about Frankie, about the way he looked, the way he acted. It's hard to describe it, but—" She searched for the right words. "He just had a bad aura."

"Aura?" Washburn asked with amusement. "You mean like his karma was bad?"

"Stop making fun of me!" Liz scolded. "Yeah, for lack of a better term, the kid's got lousy karma. He's a bad potato, a rotten apple, a guttersnipe. Get the picture?"

"Guttersnipe," Washburn chuckled. "Haven't heard that term in a while. That brings back memories. My mother used to call really low-class, degenerate people guttersnipes. In Mom's book, the only thing worse than being a guttersnipe was being riffraff. If she called you that, you were really the scum of the earth."

"Well, trust me, Harry. Your mom wouldn't have touched old Frankie with a ten-foot pole." She took another swallow of beer. "I know I shouldn't drink this stuff 'cause it's just empty calories," she said ruefully, "but it sure does taste great on a hot night."

"As I've told you before, you should stop worrying

about your weight," Harry said. "In my opinion you look just fine. So, finish telling me about Frankie."

"It was his eyes that really spooked me," Liz explained. "Normal people don't have eyes like that."

"Like what?"

"You know how when you look at pictures of Charles Manson, his eyes are like a couple of dark, bottomless pits? Well, that's how Frankie's eyes looked. Like he ought to be playing the lead in the movie version of Stephen King's latest novel."

"That bad, huh?" Washburn smiled.

"Listen," Liz said earnestly. "Whoever killed Jeremy hit him repeatedly in the back of the head with something like a piece of pipe. The first blow probably killed him, but the bastard just kept on hitting him over and over again until the back of his head was completely smashed in. It would take a very cold-blooded maniac to do that to a little boy. And looking at Frankie Snipes's eyes made me believe he was that cold-blooded."

"You realize that's an awful accusation to level at a seventeen-year-old." Washburn finished the last of his food and pushed his plate away.

"Frankie is seventeen going on forty," Liz retorted. "He's got a long juvenile record and last year got waived into adult court for the first time. It's a classic situation of a kid starting out with small crimes, petty theft, breaking and entering, and then working his way up the ladder. Property crimes probably weren't giving him much of a thrill anymore and he decided to try something heavy-duty."

"There's nothing much more heavy-duty than murdering a child," Washburn agreed.

"And the act itself is risk-free," Liz said. "A four-year-old can't exactly fight back."

"But Detective Gardner doesn't share your views about Frankie."

Liz shook her head. "I can't believe he really thinks the kid's alibi is going to hold up. I think he just likes to bug the shit out of me. Hopefully when I get to the office tomorrow morning there'll be a message saying he's bringing Frankie in for further questioning. You have to admit, it's certainly warranted. To me, the fact that Frankie's glasses were found near the body is definitely enough to make him our prime suspect."

"It'd sure be nice to get an arrest soon," Washburn agreed. "But what if Gardner doesn't come around to your way of thinking?"

"Then I'll just have to try to put some pressure on him until he does. Or maybe you could use your influence with the sheriff."

"Maybe," Washburn said doubtfully. "Although in my experience Dan doesn't take too kindly to advice on how to run his department. I take it Gardner doesn't have any other possible suspects waiting in the wings?"

"Hardly," Liz said with disdain. "He still makes like it might turn out to be one of the disgruntled insurance policyholders, but I just can't see it. If a person was that upset over not being able to collect Granny's death benefit, wouldn't they just burst into Midwestern Mutual's offices with a gun and blow away Tom Barker or someone on his staff?"

"Even after many years in the business, I still don't profess to understand the criminal mind," Washburn admitted.

"I don't either, but there's no question Jeremy was killed by a real sicko, and it doesn't look like it was a spur-of-the-moment deal. We're talking definite intent to kill. I think whoever did it planned the whole thing, scoped out the house, knew the boy and his nanny regularly went out in the backyard, and then sat back in the woods and waited for the nanny to be called away so they could swoop in and grab the kid."

"And none of the neighbors saw anything?"

Liz shook her head. "Barker's house sits on five acres on top of a hill. Unless someone else had been walking in the woods at the time, there'd be no way for anybody to see what was happening in the backyard."

"This is a weird case by Horicon County standards," Washburn said, running his index finger around the rim of his beer glass. "As you well know, we don't have many murders here, and those we do get tend to have an obvious suspect provided for our convenience. Business partner who got cheated. Jilted husband. Guy whose best buddy stole his girl. A nice, clean, obvious motive. I guess I'd rather believe Gardner's theory that a Midwestern Mutual policyholder killed Jeremy; at least then we'd have a motive, weak though it may be. But let's say you're right and Frankie did it. *Why* did he do it? It doesn't sound like there's any connection between him and Barker."

"There doesn't *always* have to be a motive—or at least not one that logical people would understand," Liz replied. "Sociopaths kill because the act is exciting. It gives them pleasure. If Frankie falls in that category, he wouldn't need a reason."

"But you just said the murder was premeditated. The killer lay in wait so he could catch the child alone. That means he specifically wanted to kill Jeremy. It wouldn't have been good enough to clobber some other little boy who might have come skipping through the woods. How does that fit in with your sociopath theory?"

"I don't know," Liz admitted, "but those are all things we could maybe find out, if Jeff Gardner were willing to pursue the matter."

Harry nodded. "How's Tom Barker holding up?"

"Pretty well, considering. I spoke to him again briefly today. He's working through a lot of anger, and he's understandably concerned that the killer might get away with it. He wants to make sure we're keeping him updated on all developments, so he's called me a couple times, and Gardner says he's called him every day." She brushed a piece of hair off her forehead. "Now it makes perfect sense to me that a father should be concerned enough to want to make sure that everything possible is being done to catch the killer, but of course Detective Gardner doesn't see it that way. He apparently believes it's an inconvenience to have to deal with bereaved parents."

Harry signaled the waiter for the check. "Sounds to me like the detective has some unresolved problems in the area of interpersonal relationships. I hope he doesn't give you too much trouble."

"Don't worry," Liz assured him. "I'm not going to let him get the best of me."

Later on, when Washburn had driven Liz home and they were walking in the front door, the phone began to ring.

"Christ!" Liz grumbled as she headed for the living room. "What do you want to bet it's Detective Gardner calling to say he's found a Franciscan monk who will swear that he and Frankie were deep in prayer at the time Jeremy was killed?"

"I guess we'll never know if you don't talk to him," Washburn said with a smile.

"Liz Stanfeld," she snapped as she picked up the phone.

"Really, Elizabeth, what kind of way is that to answer the phone? You're in your own home now, not giving criminals the third degree."

Liz plopped down on the couch and rolled her eyes. "Thank you for pointing that out, Mother," she said with mock patience. "Sometimes I get so wrapped up in what I'm doing that I forget where I am."

Harry smiled, then sat down next to her and put his arm around her.

"Did I catch you at a bad time?" Mona Stanfeld asked.

"As a matter of fact, I was doing some research on a new case," Liz said. Washburn leaned over and began to kiss her neck.

"Oh, well, then, I won't keep you long. What kind of case is it?"

"The Barker child murder," Liz said, holding the phone in one hand and stroking Washburn's hair with the other. "I'm sure you read about it in the paper."

"Oh, my! Your first murder! Congratulations! Your superiors must be very pleased with your performance to assign you such an important case."

"Yes, I think it's fair to say that my superiors are *very* pleased with my performance," Liz said, biting her lip to keep from laughing. "But then, of course, I do go out of my way to make their lives just as pleasant as I can." Washburn put one hand on her leg. "Listen, Mom," Liz said quickly, "I really can't talk long. Did you want something in particular?"

"No. Not really," her mother said innocently. "I just like to keep in touch with my children, that's all. Of course, I never have to call Marlon. He's so punctual. Calls me every Monday and Thursday like clockwork. All the way from Connecticut."

"Well, Marlon always was much more organized than I was. I guess that's why he became a CPA." Harry's hand slid up under her skirt, and Liz let out a small moan.

"Elizabeth? Is something wrong?" her mother asked with concern.

"No. Everything's absolutely fine," Liz assured her. She'd have to take quick action to get the woman off the phone before she launched into another game of twenty questions about Peter's wedding. "But I really have to get back to my research project now." She reached down and touched Harry's crotch. "It's a big one and it might take me the better part of the night to really get on top of it. But I promise I'll call you tomorrow."

"All right. Don't stay up too late."

"I won't. 'Bye, Mom. Say hi to Pop."

"Good night, Elizabeth."

Liz dropped the receiver back in the cradle, then

turned her attention back to Washburn. "That was very naughty of you, Harry," she said, rubbing his cheeks with her hands. "What on earth would Mother say if she knew?"

Washburn's fingers worked to unbutton her blouse. "I'll make you a deal. I won't tell her if you won't."

"Fair enough," Liz said as she slid over onto his lap. "Now, come here. It's time for me to get started on that big project of yours."

Chapter 8

Jeff spent the next day following up on Frankie Snipes's alibi.

In midmorning he set off for Bass Creek to see if he could track down Frankie's drunken fishermen. Jeff's dad had liked to fish and had done his best to instill a love of the pastime in his son, but the effort had been to no avail. Even as a kid, Jeff had always thought it was a damn stupid way to spend your time. The weather never seemed to cooperate, so you were always either freezing your ass off or getting burned to a crisp. Even at its best, the fishing around Lakeview was never much good. And if you were lucky enough to catch something, you had to clean and scale the damn things. Jeff didn't even like to eat fish that much, and if he was occasionally overcome with a burning desire for trout or catfish, the area was awash in good restaurants that would bring the critters to you on a platter without any muss or fuss on your part.

Since Jeff thought the pursuit was one of the dumbest hobbies ever invented, its popularity always amazed him. He pulled the Chevy over to the side of the narrow township road that ran next to the creek, behind half a dozen other vehicles, then got out and walked down to the stream, where he found ten people standing or sitting patiently, their lines in the water. There were several teenagers, a couple guys his age, and three old-timers.

When scouting for general information, Jeff didn't identify himself as a sheriff's deputy unless he was pressed. He'd learned over the years that while the average citizen is open and friendly and likes to feel he's being helpful, that same average joe will clam up tighter than a drum if he knows he's being questioned by a police officer. Jeff suspected this phenomenon arose from the fact that deep down nearly everyone is harboring some kind of guilty secret and there's always a fear that Officer Friendly just may be coming to ticket you for rolling through that stop sign on a deserted street at two o'clock last Wednesday morning.

The fishermen were a loquacious group, and no one bothered to ask why Jeff was so interested in finding out whether any of them had noticed a tall, skinny, dark-haired teenager with a punk look who might've arrived by bicycle late on Tuesday morning ten days earlier. Most members of the group were sporadic fishermen who had decided the rise in the creek brought about by recent rains might make it worth the time to try their luck. Two of the old codgers said they fished fairly regularly, but Bass Creek wasn't their usual venue. No one admitted to knowing two older gentlemen who enjoyed a beer chaser with their morning fishing. One of the old guys did volunteer that there was another fishing spot about a mile upstream and suggested that Jeff might want to try there.

Jeff thanked them and drove to the second site. The only inhabitants there were a grandfather and his two young grandsons. The grandpa said it was his first fishing excursion of the year, and that he really wasn't much of a fisherman but he was baby-sitting for the day and was trying to humor the boys.

"You're a man after my own heart," Jeff said. "Nice talkin' to you. Good luck."

As he turned to walk back toward the car, Jeff heard one of the boys yell, "Grandpa, Grandpa! I think I got somethin'!"

Jeff turned back and watched while Grandpa took the boy's pole and reeled in a trout. "That's a beauty,

Larry," the old man said, congratulating the child. "I'll bet she'll make mighty fine eating." Then the old man deftly removed the hook from the fish's mouth and clubbed it over the head.

That's another thing I hated about fishing, Jeff thought with a shudder as he turned again and headed for the car.

It was just after noon when he arrived at Smitty's Bar. It was one of Lakeview's older watering holes, located just south of downtown. While northern Lakeview, where Jeff lived, was the city's more prosperous area, the south side was decidedly blue-collar. The interior of Smitty's was clean and well maintained, with an attractive old oak bar, but its furnishings were rather spartan. It was a far cry from the fern bars that had sprung up in and around Oakwood.

Jeff walked in and took a seat at the middle of the bar. There were a few people sitting at small square formica tables and a couple of guys who looked like heavy drinkers on the side of the bar nearest the door. "Do you serve food here?" Jeff asked.

"Sure do," replied the bartender, a short, stocky man about Jeff's age with a friendly smile.

"I'll have a cheeseburger and an order of onion rings."

"Get you something to drink while you wait?"

"Yeah. Gimme an MGD."

"Comin' right up," the bartender said cheerfully.

"You own the place?" Jeff asked, looking around.

"Yup," the bartender replied, setting a bottle of beer and a glass down in front of Jeff. "Samuel T. Smith, at your service. They call me Smitty. And you are—?"

"Jeff Gardner. I'm a detective with the sheriff's department." Jeff's general rule about not volunteering his identify didn't hold with barkeeps. They were in the business of sizing people up and had a well-developed radar system for spotting phonies, so the best strategy was to play it straight with them and hope they'd do the same with you.

Smitty's eyebrows rose just a bit, but he said nothing.

"Do you know a kid named Frankie Snipes?" Jeff asked, pouring some beer into the glass.

Smitty held up his hands in a defensive gesture. "Look, if you're here to give me a lecture about not allowing underage kids in the place, I admit I look the other way when it comes to Frankie, but I swear he's the only one I let in, and I never serve him liquor." He reached for a rag and wiped the top of the bar. "It's just that the kid loves to play pool and with the problems he's had in the past, well, I figure I'm doin' him and the community a favor by keeping him off the streets."

Jeff took a swallow of beer. "I'm not here to cause you any trouble. I'm just looking for a little information about Frankie."

"Why? Is he in hot water again?"

"Not really," Jeff fudged. "He missed an appointment with his probation officer last week, and we're doing some routine checking."

"Things must be slow at the sheriff's department if they've got detectives chasing after every juvenile who misses one appointment," Smitty said pointedly.

Jeff shrugged. "Keeps me out of trouble. How often does Frankie come in?"

"Once or twice a week on average," Smitty replied. "He's been workin' construction this summer, and sometimes he'll ride his bike down here when he's finished. I'll give him a can of pop and he'll shoot a few games of pool and then leave. He never causes any problems. I think it makes him feel important that some of the guys will play with him. He sure as hell doesn't get much support at home."

"I hear his old man's a drunk."

"Calling him a drunk is too good for him," Smitty snorted. "The guy's a Grade A Number One asshole.

Beats up on Frankie's ma pretty regular, and I think he punches the kid around a good bit, too."

"I hear the same story about a lot of delinquents," Jeff said, pouring some more beer into his glass. "It's a shame people like that have kids."

"It sure is," Smitty agreed, placing a basket containing Jeff's food in front of him. "I known Frankie's got a pretty hefty record for a kid his age, but I really think the reason he stole stuff is it was the only way he could figure out how to have nice things. His old man spends every cent on booze and won't give the boy a plugged nickel. Frankie saw all his classmates having fancy bikes and running shoes and the whole schmear and knew he'd never be able to have stuff like that unless he took it. I think all that's changed, though, since he got the construction job. I can tell it's done him a lot of good to get a regular paycheck. It's taught him some responsibility."

"Good burger," Jeff said, licking his fingers. "It was a week ago Tuesday—that was the eleventh—that Frankie missed the appointment with his PO. He says he came in here that afternoon. Do you remember seeing him that day?"

Smitty scratched the top of his head. "Sounds about right. I think he was in just once last week. Then I didn't see him again till day before yesterday."

"Did he seem to be acting weird at all when he was in here last week?"

Smitty paused a moment to think, then said, "Not that I remember, no. He seemed normal. Now that I think about it, he was in earlier than usual, and I asked him why. He said he took the day off."

Jeff poured some catsup on his onion rings. "Frankie says he played pool with two guys named George Clovis and Pat Wiganowski. Would you know where I could find either of them?"

"Wiganowski works at the FS mill, a couple miles south of town. Clovis drives for a delivery service, so it's hard tellin' where he'd be this afternoon, but he lives up on Spring Street."

Jeff finished the last of the onion rings and nodded. "Thanks for the information."

Smitty turned to look at a calendar hanging on the wall, then turned back to Jeff and frowned. "A week ago Tuesday was the day that Barker kid was snatched, wasn't it? You don't think Frankie had anything to do with that, do you?"

Jeff shook his head. "Nah. Like I told you, I'm just doin' some checking."

"Yeah," Smitty said skeptically. "Look, for what it's worth, Frankie isn't the violent type. He's got a temper when he's pushed too far or when people make fun of him, but he wouldn't hurt a little boy. I'd bet money on that."

Jeff got up and put a ten on the bar.

"One more thing," Smitty said, putting his hand on Jeff's arm.

"What's that?"

"If you can help it, don't let Frankie's old man get word that you're investigating him," he said confidentially. "The bastard would probably beat the shit out of the poor kid."

"I hear you," Jeff said, nodding. "Thanks again."

Pat Wiganowski confirmed that he and George Clovis had played pool with Frankie on Tuesday the eleventh and that there had been nothing unusual about the boy's behavior that day. "Hell, no!" Wiganowski said over the noise of the mill behind them as it turned corn and oats into ground feed for cattle. "The kid was in real good humor. 'Course there was no reason not to be. The little son of a bitch won eight bucks off me that afternoon."

"Have you ever known Frankie to have any violent tendencies?" Jeff asked.

Wiganowski shook his head. "No. I know he's been in some scrapes, but George and me kinda look after him and he's sort of adopted us as second parents.

I've never met his old man, but George tells me the guy shoulda been put out of his misery years ago. Anyway, we're good to Frankie and he appreciates it."

Jeff got home at five o'clock. Julie was in the kitchen taking dishes out of the dishwater. The sounds of rap music could be heard wafting down from upstairs. "I take it the kids are home," he said, taking a can of beer out of the refrigerator and sitting down at the table.

"Bill is, but he's going over to Steve Wagner's for supper," Julie replied. "Alex is working a double shift. Somebody called in sick and the manager asked him if he'd be willing to stay."

Jeff took a swallow of beer and nodded. "How was your day?"

"Pretty uneventful for once," she said, stretching to put some glasses on a high shelf. "There was an accident south of town around eleven and they brought two people in, but luckily they just needed some stitches. What would you like to do for supper? Feel like going out for fish?"

Jeff wrinkled his nose. "Not tonight, thanks. I had my fill of fish this morning." He briefly told her about his day. "This job's getting to me, Jules," he sighed. "It's just no fun anymore. Lately I've been wondering why I've stuck with it so long. There's nowhere left for me to advance. I'm at the top of my pay grade. All I've got to look forward to is cost-of-living raises."

"I thought Dan promised that when he retires you're going to be his handpicked successor," Julie teased.

"Bullshit! Dan's never gonna retire. Besides, I'm not cut out to be sheriff. All that bureaucratic crap would drive me bonkers."

"For what it's worth," Julie said, "I've decided to apply for Alma's job. I think I've got a decent shot of getting it, and if I do, well—I guess what I'm saying is, if you want to switch jobs, I'd be able to take up some of the slack financially."

"You already do more than your share financially," Jeff said, patting her on the rear, "but I'll admit I've been thinking that once this case is over maybe I should reevaluate what I want to do with the rest of my life. That is, *if* I ever solve this one."

"So you don't think Frankie did it," Julie said, putting the last of the dishes away and sitting down next to him.

Jeff took another swallow of beer and shrugged again. "I don't know what to think. He could have done it. I wasn't able to verify his fishing alibi. And Frankie sure acted like he had a chip on his shoulder when I was questioning him, but with his record it's understandable that he isn't exactly gonna view a cop as being a friend. And so far, everybody I've talked to who knows him says that in spite of his record, he's really not a bad kid." He ran his finger around the rim of the can. "So as much as I'd love to make an arrest, my gut is telling me Frankie's not our boy."

"If it wasn't Frankie, then I wonder who—" Julie mused.

"You and me both, sweetheart." The rap music suddenly increased dramatically in volume to the point that Jeff's beer can vibrated on the table. "Bill, turn that damn noise down right now!" Jeff shouted. The din subsided again. "Jesus!" Jeff sputtered. "Who invented that shit anyway? That's not music. They just holler a bunch of dirty words at the top of their lungs."

Julie shrugged philosophically. "Remember, our parents said our music was crap."

"The Beatles and the Beach Boys were not crap. That"—he motioned toward the second floor—"is unmitigated, unrefined, unadulterated crap!"

"Speaking of our parents," Julie said, "your mother called just before you got home."

Jeff rolled his eyes. His widowed mother also lived in Lakeview. "What did she want this time? No, don't tell me. Her big toe started throbbing again and she's sure it's cancerous and she wanted you to make an appointment for her to have her leg amputated before it spreads."

"Jeff! Don't make fun of your mother," Julie protested. "I agree she's turned into something of a hypochondriac the last few years, but that happens to a lot of older people. No, she called today because she's back on the kick that she should take out a reverse mortgage on her house."

"Oh, God!" Jeff exclaimed, slapping his hand to his forehead. "Where does she get those hairbrained ideas? Some banker must be filling her full of that garbage. I thought we'd convinced her that it was a stupid idea because she doesn't need any extra money now."

"I know," Julie sighed, "and I told her that again, but she's afraid she *might* need money sometime, and she thinks it'd be a good idea to have it in reserve."

"Did you explain that a reverse mortgage means she won't own her house free and clear anymore? All my life she kept pounding it into my head that it was some kind of a sin to owe money on things. What's got into her all of a sudden?"

"I think where this all started is that her friend Nina Summers did a reverse mortgage and now your mom thinks maybe she's missing something by not having one, too."

"Jesus!" Jeff finished his beer. "I'll call her tomorrow and go over it one more time," he said with resignation. "My mind's in enough of a muddle right now that if I called her tonight we'd probably just get into another argument."

"Tomorrow's soon enough," Julie agreed. "After all, it's the weekend and I don't think any banks are open, so she wouldn't be able to go ahead with any paperwork till next week." She got up and looked in the refrigerator. "How about making steaks on the grill? I could thaw a couple out in the microwave."

"Sounds good," Jeff replied.

"So what happens next with your investigation?" Julie asked as she took a package of meat out of the freezer compartment.

"I'm gonna keep trying to chase down Frankie's alibi, and in the meantime I'll check out the disgruntled policyholders." He went to the refrigerator and helped himself to another beer. "But I don't think that angle's gonna pan out either."

"Any other bright ideas?"

"Not at the moment," Jeff admitted, popping the top on the can. "Except I think I'll nose around Oakwood some more. Who knows, maybe I'll hit it lucky and find that one of Barker's neighbors suddenly remembers seeing something." He took another swallow of beer. "All I know is I'd better come up with something fast or that snaggletoothed assistant DA is gonna have my head on a block."

Chapter 9

Jeff pulled his Chevy into the parking lot of the Oakwood municipal building. Holy shit! he thought as he searched for a parking spot. The place looked like a luxury-car dealership. There were BMW's, Infinitis, Jaguars, Mercedes, and Lexus, with a few high-priced American jobs thrown in for good measure. The total value of the vehicles probably exceeded the GNP of some developing nations. He didn't see Liz's van and idly wondered which car might be hers. He had taken a quick drive past her house on the way over. Pretty snazzy digs for an assistant DA. She no doubt had a set of wheels to match.

He eased the Chevy into a space next to a red Dodge Viper. Better not scratch that baby with the door, he thought as he got out of the car. With a teenage boy driver in the house, his insurance rates were high enough. His agent would probably cancel him out if he harmed one of these beauties.

It was a Tuesday evening, exactly two weeks since Jeremy Barker had disappeared. Liz had called him the previous day to tell him that Oakwood's mayor, an investment banker named Stuart Althorp, had invited her to a town board meeting to address the local citizenry about the status of the investigation and to assuage their fears about the safety of their fair village. She had told Althorp that she'd feel more comfortable if Jeff were the one to field questions about the case. Althorp had termed that a capital idea. Jeff had termed it a damn nuisance and had wanted to bow out, but Sheriff Isaacson had convinced him it would be good PR for the department. So here he was, much against his better judgment.

As he walked across the parking lot, his radar was operating on full power, and he felt as though he were making his way through a mine field. To him this was alien territory, and he didn't trust any of these people, including Liz. While inviting him to the meeting, she had managed to get in some jabs about why he hadn't yet brought Frankie Snipes in for further questioning. He had told her patiently that he was still checking out Frankie's story. He'd made two more trips up to Bass Creek but still hadn't stumbled across the drunken fishermen. Liz had encouraged him, pleasantly but firmly, to try to speed things up. He had resisted the impulse to tell her to go to hell. Tom Barker had also called with similar inquiries. Jeff felt like telling them all to sit back and wait like good girls and boys and when he was ready to make an arrest he'd pump smoke out of the sheriff's department chimney, like they did at the Vatican when they elected a new pope.

He walked up the sidewalk of the attractive red-brick building that also housed Oakwood's police and fire departments and entered the front door. A sign directed newcomers that the village board meeting was to the left. Following the sound of voices, Jeff came to the doorway of a large room filled with folding chairs. As he glanced around him, he did a double take. I've got a feeling we're not in Kansas anymore, Toto, he muttered under his breath.

While Lakeview's city hall was a dilapidated building with ugly gray cement block walls and dirty linoleum, this place looked like the boardroom of a Fortune 500 company. The walls were painted a soft pink and were dotted with what looked to Jeff's uninitiated eye like original artwork. A white marble floor gleamed underfoot, while soft track lighting overhead cast a rosy glow. Along the back wall was a table filled with soft drinks and mineral water and another laden with trays of cheese and sausage, crackers and veggies. People were walking around, mingling and making small talk, carrying paper plates and plastic glasses. *This* was a village board meeting? Maybe he'd stumbled into a garden party by mistake.

But no, this must be the right place. He spotted Liz standing near the front of the room, talking animatedly to a stunning woman with long blond hair and a tall dark-haired man. Even at a distance, he could tell there was something about Liz that was different. He looked closer and frowned. She was dressed to the nines.

He'd never seen her in anything but fairly casual clothes, even in court. Tonight she was wearing a mint-green-and-white suit with a white blouse. The skirt was slim and had a large slit up the back that revealed quite a shapely pair of legs. White snakeskin heels and a small white leather bag completed her ensemble.

Taking his eyes off Liz for a moment, Jeff looked around him and scrutinized the apparel of the other people in the room. Most of them would have been dressed appropriately for dining out at a first-class restaurant. The majority of the men wore light gray suits with either red or yellow print ties. The women favored either short-sleeved floral dresses that fell bellow the knee or short, starkly simple linen numbers accented with large, colorful jewelry. Jeff looked down at his navy cotton slacks, navy and white sport shirt, and tan crepe-soled shoes and felt terribly out of place.

Son of a bitch! he thought as he looked back at Liz. She'd set him up! She could have warned him to dress up, but no—she probably wanted him to look like a fool. Step right up, ladies and gentlemen, and see the poor, pathetic hayseed detective who's been assigned to this important case. Now I ask you, does this man look smart enough to catch a killer? Of course he doesn't. I rest my case. As Jeff's eyebrows knitted together in a deep frown, Liz caught his eye and waved. He grimly made his way toward the front of the room.

"There you are," Liz said cheerfully, touching Jeff's arm. He angrily pulled away, but she didn't seem to notice. "These are my good friends Esther and Bob McMillan," she prattled on. "Bob is one of the village trustees."

Jeff somehow managed to shake hands with the attractive couple and mumble a few words of greeting.

"Would you like something to drink?" Esther asked him.

"No, thank you," Jeff answered curtly.

"I think they're just about ready to start," Liz said. "You'd better go find yourself a seat, Es. I want to introduce Jeff to Stuart before things get rolling." Jeff followed her to the table at the head of the room. Seated in the center was an intense-looking man in his mid-forties, his brown hair streaked liberally with gray. "Stuart, this is Detective Jeff Gardner. Jeff, Stuart Althorp, Oakwood's mayor."

Jeff extended his hand. Althorp had a strong grip. "We appreciate your coming tonight, Detective. As you can well imagine, our residents are very concerned about what happened to Jeremy."

"It's a concern shared by the entire county," Jeff replied evenly. What the hell gave these rich upstarts the idea they'd cornered the market on compassion?

"Let's sit down here at the end," Liz suggested. "Stuart tells me they've got a couple of other matters to take up before they get to us."

They took their seats, and Jeff stared down at the table, trying to rein in his anger. The noise level in the room remained high as neighbors caught up on each other's summer plans and new yacht purchases. Suddenly a hush fell over the hall. Jeff looked up and saw Tom Barker entering the room, followed closely by a stunning redhead in a short, clinging yellow knit dress. "Who's the woman?" he whispered to Liz.

"That must be Natalie Helprin," Liz whispered back. "Barker's girlfriend."

"The guy's got good taste," Jeff murmured. Barker was looking considerably more chipper than the last time Jeff had seen him, but then with a babe like that on your arm, who wouldn't be? Barker put his hand on Natalie's elbow and guided her to a seat near the front.

Althorp called the meeting to order. Besides Bob McMillan, there were five other trustees and a village clerk at the head table. The discussion on the couple of other matters took the better part of thirty minutes. A lively debate developed on whether or not to grant a building permit to an out-of-towner who wanted to open a children's clothing store. Jeff tried to tune the whole thing out by doing deep breathing exercises, but he found he still picked up snatches of the conversation. Those against granting the permit were afraid the clothing to be sold at the store might be of "inferior quality," "discount merchandise," or just plain "cheap." Horrors, Jeff thought glumly. A fate worse than death. Discount merchandise in Oakwood. The applicant's lawyer assured the assembled multitude that the proposed clothing line would, in fact, be "up-scale." Once this happy information was received, the permit was unanimously approved.

Althorp pounded his gavel on the table. "As all of you know, since our last meeting, Jeremy Barker, the four-year-old son of Tom Barker, was abducted from his home and brutally murdered. Tom is with us to-night and I'd just like to say, Tom, you have our very deepest sympathies on your loss, and if there is anything any of us can do to make this difficult time a bit easier for you, please don't hesitate to call on us."

Barker nodded in response and mouthed, "Thank you." Jeff saw Natalie squeeze his hand.

"As most of you also know," Althorp went on, "a

group of village residents has established a fund to reward persons coming forward with information leading to the capture of Jeremy's killer. Any of you who have not yet contributed to that fund may do so by contacting Marty Lawrence, the fund's treasurer.''

Althorp turned toward Liz and Jeff. "In a related matter, we are honored tonight to have with us Assistant District Attorney Liz Stanfeld, an Oakwood resident and a nominee to fill the current vacancy on our planning commission. Ms. Stanfeld will be responsible for prosecuting the case once an arrest has been made. Also with us is Detective Captain Jeff Gardner of the Horicon County Sheriff's Department, who is leading the investigation. I asked them to come and address any concerns you might have about the safety of our village. With that, I'll turn the floor over to Liz Stanfeld.''

Liz inclined her head. "Thank you, Stuart. Detective Gardner and I appreciate the opportunity to come here and speak to you tonight.''

Speak for yourself, lady, Jeff thought.

"District Attorney Washburn asked me to tell you that he would have liked to be here tonight as well, but unfortunately he had a previous commitment in Milwaukee that prevented him from attending.''

No doubt sucking up to the hoi polloi, hoping they'll help him get a big political appointment, Jeff thought, rolling his eyes.

"As an Oakwood resident, I share your horror that such a heinous crime could have occurred in our village. I want to assure you that the investigation into Jeremy Barker's murder is proceeding on schedule—''

Whatever the hell that means, Jeff's private commentary went on.

"—and all of us working on the case hope for an early arrest.''

Yeah, just as soon as we figure out who did it with practically no leads.

"Now, for some additional comments, I'll turn the floor over to Detective Gardner."

Jeff cleared his throat. Show time. "Good evening, ladies and gentlemen. On behalf of myself and the entire Horicon County Sheriff's Department, I'd like to thank you for having me here tonight. As far as safety is concerned, we have every reason to believe that what happened to Jeremy Barker was an isolated incident and not part of some master plan to wreak havoc on your community. Your local police department has stepped up its patrol of the area, and the sheriff's department has also assigned one squad car to assist in additional patrol duties. While you should, of course, continue to exercise caution in caring for your families' safety, there is no reason to panic. In spite of what happened, we firmly believe that Oakwood remains a safe community."

He shifted in his chair and continued. "What this means is that you should remain alert. Watch for suspicious behavior, suspicious individuals, or suspicious vehicles, and report them promptly, either to your local police department or to the sheriff's department by dialing 911."

He ran his tongue around his lips, wishing now he'd taken a can of soda. "As far as Jeremy Barker's murder is concerned, I am not at liberty to discuss any details of an ongoing investigation. However, let me reiterate what Ms. Stanfeld said. The sheriff's department is working very hard on cracking the case, and we are doing everything in our power to see that Jeremy's killer is apprehended and swiftly brought to trial." He paused for a moment. "I guess that's all I have."

"Thank you, Detective Gardner," Mayor Althorp said. "Are there any questions from the floor?"

A hand immediately went up in the back of the room. "Yes, sir," Jeff said.

The questioner, a tall blond man, shouted, "Isn't it

true that the prime suspect in the investigation is a Lakeview teenager with a lengthy criminal record?"

Jeff felt like he'd been hit in the head with a fifty-pound block of ice. He clenched his jaw and shot Liz a withering glance. Son of a bitch! She must have blabbed to someone about Frankie!

"I'm sorry, sir," Jeff replied through clenched teeth, "but as I said, I can't divulge specific information about the case. If anyone has any questions relating to safety concerns, I'd be happy to answer them."

Another man jumped to his feet. "Detective Gardner, Oakwood people have a right to know what they're up against. I realize you're not a resident here, but for those of us who are, Oakwood is a very special community, and we don't want to see it spoiled by criminals making their way over here from the eastern portion of the county. I want to know what steps the sheriff's department has taken to make sure that what happened to Jeremy Barker doesn't happen to any other village child."

There were murmurs of "Yes" and "We want an arrest" and "What *is* the department doing?" from the audience. Christ, Jeff thought, these refined people were starting to sound like a lynch mob. For two cents he would have liked to vault over the table, run down into the crowd, and pound the shit out of two or three of them. Instead, he took a deep breath and said in an artificially calm voice, "As was mentioned earlier, the sheriff's department, along with your local police, has increased both the frequency and the visibility of patrols through the village. Those patrols, along with the excellent neighborhood watch program already in place here, are the best way to assure that Oakwood does not become the site of other violent crimes."

"That's not good enough—" a woman protested.

Fortunately for Jeff, Mayor Althorp cut them off. "Thank you all for your comments, but I'm afraid it's time to move on to the next item on our agenda. I'd again like to thank both Ms. Stanfeld and Detective Gardner for taking the time to be with us tonight."

Jeff nodded politely to Althorp, then got up and walked resolutely out of the hall. He picked up speed when he got outside and was already halfway to his car when Liz caught up to him.

"Hey, wait a minute!" she hollered. "I want to talk to you."

Jeff wheeled around. "Well, the feeling is *not* mutual," he snarled.

He could see the look of hurt and surprise on her face. "What's the matter?" she asked.

"Don't try to be cute. You know damn well what's the matter!" He pointed back toward the building. "That dog and pony show you invited me to turned out to be more than I bargained for. You forgot to tell me I'd be playing the part of a horse's ass!"

Liz opened her mouth to say something, but Jeff cut her off. "Who do you think you are, leaking information about the case?"

Liz's face was flushed. "I didn't leak anything!" she exclaimed. "I was just as surprised as you were when those people started talking."

"If they didn't hear it from you, where *did* they hear it?" Jeff demanded.

"I don't know, but I promise that tomorrow I'm going to get to the bottom of it."

"I don't believe you!" Jeff shouted.

"Why not?"

"Because you're one of them."

"One of what?" Liz asked incredulously.

"One of that bunch of rich phonies in there who thinks your shit don't stink." Jeff railed at her.

"You don't know anything about me!" Liz shouted back.

"Sure I do. I swung by your house on the way over here tonight. Pretty fancy. I'd estimate that if you're lucky, maybe your salary would cover your real estate taxes and a few outfits like the one you've got on. Or maybe your boyfriend helps you out. 'Course, I know what his salary is too, so I guess if he is helping you financially, he must be on the take big time."

"What am I supposed to do?" Liz sputtered. "Apologize to you for having resources besides my salary?"

"You people are all alike," Jeff said with disgust. "You're born with a silver spoon in your mouth, and from that day on you expect perks just 'cause you've got money. You make me sick, the whole lot of you." He turned to leave.

Liz caught him by the arm. "What are you suggesting, that Jeremy Barker deserved to die because his dad is rich? Even you can't really be that callous. You know as well as I do that every person deserves equal treatment under the law. Rich or poor. It's not fair to deny Jeremy a thorough investigation just because he didn't come from a family like Frankie Snipes's."

"You have no idea what it means to be poor," Jeff said angrily. "My grandparents owned a farm right here in what's now downtown Oakwood. They lost it in the Depression."

"Oh, I see," Liz said sarcastically. "Is that why you've got such a chip on your shoulder? What am I supposed to do, feel guilty and offer you my house to make up for all the bad things that ever happened to the Gardner family?"

"No," Jeff shot back. His disdain for the monied class had far deeper roots than Grandpa Rudy Gardner's misfortunes, but he wasn't about to share his innermost feelings with Liz. "My point is that my people made a living with their hands. People like you have no idea what that's like."

"I know what it is to work hard for not much money," Liz retorted. "My family was comfortable, but we sure as hell weren't rich. I baby-sat and worked as a waitress and sold shoes in a department store and was expected to contribute toward my clothes and my schooling. So don't think you cornered the market on learning the American work ethic."

"And I suppose you sold so many shoes that as a bonus the shoe company bought you that shack you live in."

Liz's eyes were flashing. "Listen, you jerk! It's really none of your damn business, but for your information I got my money the old-fashioned way—I divorced a very rich son of a bitch to get it!"

Jeff's mouth dropped open.

Liz continued. "Now will you please stop treating me like I'm the enemy? We'd be much farther ahead if we both realized we're working for the same side."

"I'll make you a deal," he said in a calmer voice. "I'll believe you're on my side when you tell me who leaked the info about Frankie."

"I already told you I don't know," she protested.

"Well, you either find out by tomorrow or I want you off this case!" Jeff gave her one more piercing glance before turning on his heel and stalking off to his car.

Chapter 10

After Jeff marched off, leaving her standing alone in the parking lot, Liz went back inside the municipal building. Althorp had just rung the gavel down on the meeting, and people were milling about and chatting. A crowd had gathered around Tom Barker and his companion, and Liz dutifully waited in line to talk to them.

When it was finally Liz's turn, Tom turned to her and said, "I've been wanting to speak to you. Oh, forgive my manners. This is Natalie Helprin. Nat, Liz Stanfeld."

"How you do?" Natalie gave Liz a limp handshake, scrutinized her closely, then stood there with her head slightly cocked as if to signal she was not impressed with what she saw.

"It's nice to meet you," Liz said. You snooty bitch, she added silently. Esther sure had you pegged right.

"Did Detective Gardner leave?" Tom asked, glancing around the room.

"Yes, he had some other business to attend to," Liz replied. Like trying to figure out how to get her off the case.

"Is it true you have a suspect?" Tom asked, his brows knit together in a deep frown. "Why didn't someone tell me? I thought I made it clear that I wanted to be kept abreast of any leads in the case."

Liz chose her words carefully. "I'm sorry, but as Detective Gardner said, it would be improper for either of us to comment on the particulars of the investigation, except to say that it is still ongoing and we hope it will be possible to make an arrest soon."

"Why not cut the bullshit!" Natalie exclaimed. "From all the comments tonight, it's obvious you know who did it. Why are you stalling on making an arrest?"

"Nat—" Tom put a restraining hand on her arm.

Liz could feel the blood rushing to her face. "I don't know where those people got their information, but the case is not as open and shut as they seem to think. I know the waiting must be agony," she said, directing her comments to Tom, "but these matters can't be rushed and I simply can't give you a precise timetable for when to expect an arrest." Jesus, what was happening? She was actually defending Jeff. This was quite a turnabout.

"I hope for your sake—and Detective Gardner's—that an arrest occurs sooner rather than later," Natalie said, staring at Liz defiantly.

As Liz stared back, wondering if she should tell the bitch that there were laws against threatening public officials, the person in charge of handling the reward fund that had been established on Jeremy's behalf came up and told Tom he'd like a word with him. "I'll expect to hear from either you or Detective Gardner very soon," Tom said to Liz as he turned and followed the other man. Natalie tagged behind, strutting like a model waltzing down a runway.

Esther and her husband joined Liz moments later. "Well, what do you think?" Esther asked with amusement.

Liz clenched her jaw. "The woman is definitely in the running for the Leona Helmsley Personality Plus award," she snarled. "Tom sure doesn't strike me as the type who would put up with a bitch like that, but she's obviously got a hold on him. She must really be something in the sack."

"If it's just sex he cares about, he'd be better off

buying himself an inflatable woman," Esther offered. "Besides, it'd be bound to have a better personality."

"You're the epitome of tact, as always, my dear," Bob McMillan chided. He took Liz's hand. "Thanks so much for coming. Oh, and I wanted to let you know that I have it on good authority that the planning commission should be meeting sometime in the next few weeks to confirm your appointment. You'll be setting policy for Oakwood before you know it."

"I'm looking forward to it," Liz said sincerely. "Now, if you'll excuse me, I think I'll say good-bye to the mayor and call it a night."

Liz went home soon after that, and in spite of dosing herself liberally with Jack Daniel's, spent a restless night. The leak in the investigation really upset her. Jeff had seemed sincerely shaken by the whole thing, so he couldn't be the culprit. The more she thought about it, the more she suspected Sheriff Isaacson. She never had trusted that man. After all, a person who faked a Southern drawl would probably stoop to anything. She arrived at the courthouse early the next morning, eager to share her theory with Harry.

She was sitting in his office when he arrived at eight, whistling the chorus to "Oklahoma." "You're in a good mood," Liz said as he took off his navy sports jacket and hung it behind his door. "I take it your talk went well."

Harry nodded, sat down in his chair, and looked at the schedule of cases pending for that day. "It went very well. I met a couple of your old colleagues who offered to put in a good word for me on the nomination."

"Who's that?"

"John Christensen and George Rector." He finished skimming the schedule and set it on the corner of his desk. "How was the village board meeting?"

"Not so hot, I'm afraid." She told him what had happened. "It was very embarrassing, especially for Jeff," she said, drumming her fingers on the arm of her chair. "Dan Isaacson must be behind it, and I think you should confront him about it right away. It could screw up our whole case if he leaks information prematurely."

"Maybe you shouldn't be so quick to accuse Dan," Harry said quietly.

"Well, of course it must be him! Who else could it be?" She looked at Harry. His face appeared flushed, and he was fidgeting with a paper clip. Liz's eyes widened in astonishment and she felt a cold chill go through her. "You didn't!" she exclaimed.

There was an embarrassed pause. "There's really a simple explanation," Harry said, averting his gaze. "You see, I was talking to Senator Kilpatrick the other day and the Frankie Snipes lead just happened to come up. The senator must have mentioned it to some of his constituents."

Liz's stomach was churning. "Harry, how could you? What if it turns out Frankie didn't do it?"

Harry swallowed hard. "In that case, I guess I'll just have to accept the consequences. If it's any consolation, I didn't divulge Frankie's name—just a general description."

"For Christ's sake, why did you divulge anything?"

Harry sighed. "The senator was concerned. I guess maybe I was overly anxious to assure him that the investigation was proceeding smoothly. I'm sorry," he added contritely.

"You're sorry!?" Liz jumped up and angrily began pacing in front of the desk. "It's possible you just fucked up the entire case and all you can say is you're sorry?"

Harry quickly came around the desk and reached out to put his hand on Liz's shoulder. "Liz, please. If I'd had any idea—"

"Spare me," she said, angrily moving away and walking toward the door. When she reached it, she turned and said in an acrid tone, "I guess I didn't realize the federal appointment meant so much to you that you'd be willing to compromise your integrity to get it." She strode briskly out of the room, slamming the door hard behind her.

Jeff didn't have a restful night, either. In fact, he tossed and turned and thrashed around so violently that finally, around two in the morning, Julie gave him a sharp jab in the ribs with her elbow and reminded him that she was working the early shift and needed her sleep. She suggested that if he was going to keep those antics up all night, it might be more restful for both of them if he'd go downstairs and sleep on the couch. He managed to settle down a bit after that, but his sleep had been fitful.

He stayed in bed in the morning until long after Julie and both boys had left the house. Around nine-thirty he dragged himself out, showered, shaved, and dressed. After downing a bowl of cornflakes and two cups of coffee, he decided to make one last trip to Bass Creek. If he didn't find the two drunks this time, he'd have to give up on that angle and try to figure out some other way to convince Liz why they shouldn't arrest Frankie.

The first fishing spot contained two older men and a teenage couple, none of whom knew Frankie or the drunks. Jeff thanked them and moved on to the second site. As he parked the car and crossed the road on his way down to the creek, he could hear voices. "You dumb son of a bitch! You just dumped over the whole bait bucket!"

"I didn't neither," a slurred voice replied.

"You did, too! Look. All our bait's layin' out on the ground."

"What's it doin' on the ground? It's s'posed to be in the bucket. Ya better pick it back up."

As Jeff sprinted the last fifty yards through the trees and down the bank, he saw two men who appeared to be in their sixties, sitting at water's edge. One wore striped bib overalls with no shirt underneath. The other was dressed in tattered blue jeans and a faded white T-shirt. Each held a fishing pole in one hand and a can of beer in the other.

"How are they biting this morning, fellas?" Jeff called in a cheery voice as he approached.

"Pretty goddamn good," bib overalls replied, taking a big swallow of beer.

"Yeah," his sidekick chimed in. "We caught ourselves some beauties. 'Course we threw 'em all back in. Catchin' fish is the fun part, but fish all taste like shit." He chugged some of his beer.

"You fellows come here often?" Jeff asked, sitting down beside them.

"Nah, not often," bib overalls answered. "Just ever once in a while."

"Were you up here a couple weeks ago?"

"When was we here last, Kenny?" bib overalls asked.

"Prob'ly 'bout then," his buddy agreed. "I 'member it was right before we had all that rain. Fishin' was no damn good that day. Creek was too low."

"By any chance do you remember seeing a teenager here fishing that day? Tall, skinny kid with long black hair?"

Bib overalls put down his beer can and scratched his head. "I dunno," he began, then he suddenly slapped one hand on his thigh. "Yeah, now that you mention it, I do 'member him. Was wearing a buncha them damn earrings. 'Member that, Kenny? The straggly-haired kid with them earrings? The one we figured must be a fairy?"

"Oh, sure!" his companion agreed amiably, wiping beer off his chin. "Didn't look like the fishin' type."

"Do you remember what time of day you saw him?"

"Close to noon, most likely," bib overalls said. "I'd reckon we'd been here 'bout an hour before he come."

"Did you talk to him at all?" Jeff asked.

"Nah." Bib overalls waved his hand. "We could tell he wasn't nobody we wanted to talk to."

"How long was he here?"

"I dunno. Couple hours, I guess. He stuck with it longer than I'd expect from somebody what looked like that."

"Where are you fellows from?" Jeff asked.

"Stockton," bib overalls replied, referring to a small town about a mile north of the creek. "Me and Kenny walk down here when we feel like it."

"Do you mind telling me your names?"

"Hell, no. We don't mind a bit. I'm Wally Jenkins and this here's Kenny Pederson."

"Well, it's been nice talking to you two," Jeff said, getting to his feet. "Good luck fishing."

As he walked up the bank, he heard Wally say, "That guy was kinda nosey, wasn't he?"

"Yeah, he sure was," Kenny agreed. "Wonder what all that was about."

You guys don't know it, Jeff thought to himself as he walked back to the car with a broad smile on his face, but you just saved Frankie Snipes's ass.

Jeff was waiting in Liz's office when she got back from lunch. From the expression on her face, he could tell she was in a foul mood.

"So how was the rest of the meeting?" he asked. "Did they hang me in absentia?"

"No," Liz said, as she sat down in her chair. "But Tom Barker wanted to know if it was true we had a suspect."

"What did you tell him?"

"That I wasn't at liberty to discuss it and, basically, that he'd have to keep his shirt on and wait for the investigation to run its course."

"What was his reaction to that?"

"He took it fairly well, but for a minute there I thought his girlfriend was going to attack me."

"I would've liked to see that," Jeff chuckled. "So, did you find out who leaked the story about Frankie?"

Liz looked at him, tight-lipped, and nodded. She had calmed down a bit but was still furious with Harry.

"It was your boyfriend, wasn't it?"

Liz's mouth dropped open. "How did you know that?" she demanded.

"I keep trying to tell you I'm a hell of a good detective. You just aren't paying attention."

"Well, if you're such a good detective, why don't you hurry up and find some proof that Frankie did it so we can arrest him?" Liz said curtly.

"Sorry," Jeff said, shaking his head. "No can do."

"Why not?" Liz asked, frowning.

" 'Cause he didn't do it." Jeff got up from the chair and stood in front of her desk. "I found the two drunken fisherman this morning. They look like a couple of hayseeds out of an old *Andy Griffith Show* rerun, but they definitely remember seeing someone matching Frankie's description right before we had all that rain. So if you were counting on having a big party to celebrate Frankie's arrest, I guess you'd better cancel the cake."

Liz groaned. "So how did Frankie's glasses wind up next to Jeremy's body?" she demanded.

"I don't know," Jeff replied. "Maybe the real killer planted them there. Maybe a bird carried them in all the way from Lakeview. What I do know is Frankie didn't drop 'em there—at least not the day of the murder."

Liz balled her right hand up into a fist and slammed it down hard on the desk. "What is with you?" she hissed. "Why in the hell did you feel you had to make it your life's work to find evidence that would get Frankie off the hook? You're not working for the public defender's office, you know. In case you've forgotten, our job here is to make an arrest and prosecute someone."

"You're wrong," Jeff shot back, pointing his index

finger at her. "Our job is to arrest and prosecute the person who did it. And the fact that Frankie Snipes is out of the running for that particular honor doesn't make a damn bit of difference."

"It sure as hell does!" Liz shouted, jumping up from her chair and staring him in the face. "It means we're back to square one. No evidence and no suspect."

"Hey, chill out," Jeff said cheerfully. "In this business you win some and you lose some, but I've got a feeling something will turn up eventually. In fact, I'd lay odds on it."

"You can take your odds and stick 'em where the sun don't shine," Liz snarled. "Now get out of here and don't come back until you've found some evidence."

"Yes, ma'am." Jeff made a courtly bow and swept out of the office.

While deciding what to do next, Jeff stopped at the sheriff's department to check his messages. Among the day's callers was a Joanne Johnson with an Oakwood phone number. "Did this woman say what she wanted?" Jeff asked the bright young receptionist who'd taken the call.

"No. Just that no one else could help her; she needed to speak with you."

Jeff's lower lip curled downward, and he briefly considered tossing the message into the wastebasket. Ms. Johnson had probably gotten the word that a teenage psycho from Lakeview was responsible for Jeremy's death and was calling to berate Jeff for dragging his feet on making the arrest. Oh, hell, he thought, reaching for the phone. He'd no doubt be getting a lot of these calls. He might as well get some practice handling them.

Joanne Johnson had a quiet, breathy voice. Jeff guessed she must be in her thirties.

"Ms. Johnson? This is Detective Jeff Gardner. I had a message that you called."

There was a pause. "Oh, yes. I did. Thank you for calling back. I was at the meeting last night and heard your talk—"

Oh, shit. Here it comes. "Yes?" Jeff prompted.

Another pause. "Detective, do you suppose it would be possible for you to come to our house this evening? You see, I believe my son has some information about the murder."

Jeff could feel the hair on the back of his neck stand up. "What kind of information?"

"I think it would be best if Nate and I discussed that with you in person."

"All right." Jeff grabbed a pen. "What's your address?"

"817 Ravenswood Drive."

"Would six o'clock be okay?"

"Six would be fine."

"Great. I'll see you then."

Jeff stared down at the address, then rubbed his middle finger over the bridge of his nose. He tried to tell himself not to get his hopes up, but his heart was racing. This could be the break he'd been waiting for. He smiled and nodded. Just half an hour ago he'd told Liz that he was sure something would turn up. With a little bit of luck, she just might have her damn evidence even sooner than he'd thought.

Chapter 11

It was ten minutes to eight and Liz was kneeling in a flower bed in front of her house, pulling weeds from around a stand of lilies, when she heard a car squeal its tires around the corner to the south and accelerate up her street. "Damn crazy drivers," she muttered. As she turned around to get a look at the hot-rodder, Jeff pulled his Chevy into the driveway and came to a screeching halt next to her Jaguar. "Christ," Liz grumbled as she sat back on her haunches. She was hot and tired, and she'd seen enough of that man in the last few days to last her a lifetime. What the hell did he want now?

Jeff got out of his car and eyed the Jaguar with obvious admiration. "A Jag, huh?" he said as he walked toward her. "Guess your ex-husband must've gotten the Rolls."

Liz's eyes narrowed as he approached. He was wearing tan dress slacks, a white shirt, yellow striped tie, and a light brown silk jacket. In his right hand he carried a small tape recorder. "What's the occasion?" Liz asked sarcastically. "Are you on your way to another funeral?"

"After seeing how all the swells were dressed last night, I decided to turn over a new leaf," he replied flippantly.

Liz was in no mood for games. "What do you want?" she asked pointedly.

"I've got something here that I think might interest

you," Jeff replied, holding up the tape recorder. "Can we go inside?"

Liz eyed him quizzically. "Sure." She stood up and wiped the dirt off her hands, then led the way into the house.

As they sat down at the round oak table in the kitchen, Jeff explained the telephone call he'd received from Joanne Johnson. "She's probably about your age. Her husband up and left her and their thirteen-year-old son, Nate, last month, and she hasn't quite gotten her act together yet, but she's a nice woman. They live in the Hills, about a mile from Barker's place." He went on to explain that when he arrived, Mrs. Johnson was obviously struggling with the decision whether or not to let her son talk to him. "She sat there wringing her hands and saying nothing for about five minutes. I was starting to feel damn awkward. Finally she said she had to go through with it because she was at the meeting last night and heard we had a suspect from Lakeview and she couldn't allow an innocent person to be prosecuted for Jeremy's murder."

"Then what happened?" Liz prompted.

"She called Nate down from upstairs. He's a shy, good-looking kid. He'll be in eighth grade this fall. And—well, let's let him tell the story." Jeff flipped on the tape recorder.

"Go ahead, Nate," a woman's voice said soothingly. "Just tell the detective what you told me this morning."

"Um, I have this friend named Greg Saunders," a soft, boyish voice explained. "He's thirteen, same as me. He lives a couple houses up from here. We've been friends for about five years, ever since his family moved here." Nate paused. "We used to do a lot of stuff together, but the last six months or so I haven't seen Greg so much 'cause he started hanging around with some older kids."

"How much older?" Jeff's voice interjected.

"Just a year. They were eighth graders this past year. We were in seventh. But they acted a lot older than that."

"In what way?"

"Um, well, they swore a lot. They made raunchy phone calls to people. I've heard they stole stuff. And sometimes they bullied younger kids."

"What were their names, Nate?"

"There's about six of them that hang out together, but the one Greg really thought was cool is Brent Tompkins."

"Do all these kids live in Oakwood?"

"Yeah."

"Okay, Nate. Sorry to interrupt you. You were saying that Greg started hanging around with this Brent and didn't spend much time with you anymore."

"Yeah." The boy's voice sounded sad. "I felt bummed out about it, 'cause we used to be pretty tight. We had a couple of fights on account of it. I told Greg that Brent didn't really like him. He just let him hang around like you'd let an old dog follow you home. Sometimes Brent would make Greg do stuff for him."

"What kind of stuff?"

"Oh, things like write phony absentee excuses, stuff like that. Greg wanted Brent and the other older kids to like him, so he'd do most anything Brent asked."

There was another pause. "Have you talked to Greg recently?" Jeff asked gently.

Nate sighed. "Yeah. A week ago. I hadn't seen him since school got out. I'd called him a couple times but he sounded kinda weird and always said he was busy. But one day last week I didn't have anything to do, so I thought I'd try again. I called and he said he'd come over. I was surprised, but I was glad too. I missed doin' stuff with him."

"And did Greg come over?"

"Yeah. He rode his bike down."

"Then what happened?" Jeff asked softly.

"He was acting real weird, kinda spooky like, you know—like he was afraid of something. And I kept asking him what was wrong and he kept saying nothin'. But I just kept asking and finally he told me."

"What did he tell you?"

There was a long pause. "Go ahead, Nate," his mother urged. "Tell him what Greg said."

Nate swallowed hard. "He said he knew what happened to Jeremy Barker. That he knew who killed him."

Liz gasped and reached over to turn off the recorder. "Is this for real?" she asked in astonishment.

"Why don't you judge for yourself?" Jeff said, switching the machine back on.

"Can you tell me about it?" Jeff asked Nate.

Another deep breath. "Greg said that the day after Jeremy went missing, Brent had called him and said he wanted to talk about something. Greg went over to the Tompkinses' house, and Brent told him that for a long time he'd been planning to play a trick on Tom Barker."

"What kind of trick?"

"He was gonna make it look like Jeremy had been kidnapped."

"Did Brent say why he wanted to do that?"

"Yeah. He told Greg that Barker had really pissed him off a couple times. I guess Brent had rode his bike on Barker's lawn or somethin' and Barker hollered at him and called him a little bastard. Brent's got a bad temper and he doesn't like to be yelled at, so I guess he got the idea he'd get back at Barker by pretending to snatch his kid."

"And how was Brent going to accomplish this?"

"He told Greg he'd been watching Barker's house from the woods with binoculars. He said most days the kid and his nanny would sit in the backyard by the pool for quite a while. Sometimes the nanny would go inside for a few minutes and the kid would be out there alone. Brent said he figured one day when the nanny went inside, he'd run down through the lawn and bring the kid back into the woods with him. Then he'd hide Jeremy until Barker got real nervous and then he'd let him go."

"And did Brent follow through on this plan?"

"Yeah. He told Greg he was watching the house and when he saw the UPS truck pull in and he saw the nanny go inside, he ran down to where the kid was sitting by the pool."

"Did Brent take Jeremy against his will?"

"No, he tricked him. He told Jeremy there were horses in the woods and asked if Jeremy wanted to go see them. I guess the kid got real excited and took right off with Brent."

"What happened after Brent and Jeremy reached the woods?"

"They started walking deeper into the woods. Brent was holding Jeremy's hand. Then I guess Jeremy must've realized there weren't any horses and he got scared and started to scream." Nate paused.

"Then what happened, son?"

Another pause. "It's all right, Nate," the boy's mother said. "You can tell him."

Nate took a deep breath. "Well, Brent told Greg that he panicked. He thought the kid was gonna run away and ruin his plan, so before he knew what he was doing, Brent picked up a tree limb or something and started hitting Jeremy over the head with it to shut him up."

"Oh, my God!" Liz said hoarsely. Jeff motioned toward the recorder, indicating that the story wasn't over.

"What happened next?"

"Jeremy was laying real still on the ground. Brent shook him to try and wake him up." Nate paused and swallowed hard. "But he was already dead."

Liz's face contorted in anger.

"And then?" Jeff prompted.

"I guess Brent panicked over what he'd done, so he buried the body."

"Is that everything that Greg told you?" Jeff asked gently.

Nate sniffled. "Yeah. Except that Brent threatened to kill Greg if he ever told anybody about it. Greg's not going to get in trouble for this, is he?" he asked anxiously. "He's my friend. I don't want him to get in trouble. When he told me about this, he made me promise not to tell anybody. You're not going to tell him that I told you, are you? He's real scared of Brent. Greg won't get hurt, will he?"

Jeff flicked the tape recorder off and turned to Liz. She was sitting very still, staring at him, a horrified expression on her face. "Well, what do you think?" he prodded.

Liz put her hands to her cheeks. "Oh, my God! I don't know what to think. Do you believe that's what happened?"

"I believe Nate related exactly what Greg told him."

Liz drew in her breath, then exhaled. "I can't believe a fourteen-year-old is responsible for Jeremy's death."

"Why not? Frankie Snipes is only seventeen, and you were only too happy to believe he was a killer," Jeff chided.

Liz ignored the dig. "If this story is true, Brent didn't intend to kill Jeremy."

"But he did intend to kidnap him, and he killed him in the course of committing that crime."

"And in this state a person is assumed to intend the natural and probable consequences of their acts," Liz continued the analysis.

"Exactly. So we're still looking at some degree of intentional homicide."

Liz nodded. "Assuming, again, that what Greg told Nate was the truth."

"I guess that's what we need to find out, isn't it? Do you know Greg Saunders's parents?"

"I've met them," Liz replied. "They live right next to my friend Esther. I think they were at the meeting last night."

"Ever met the Tompkinses?"

"No."

"Well, this might be a good time to get acquainted."

Liz looked at him soberly. "I think I'd like to pass. This turn of events is making me feel very uneasy."

"Oh, no, you don't!" Jeff exclaimed. "I need you. This is one time your connection to this lovely village is going to come in very handy."

Liz hesitated, then pushed back her chair. "Okay," she said with resignation. "Give me about fifteen minutes to clean up."

"Take your time," Jeff said as she headed for the stairs. "And if you don't mind a friendly piece of advice, could you maybe wear something along the line of what you had on last night? We want to come across like a couple of neighbors dropping by for a friendly chat."

Liz nodded dumbly.

She returned a short time later wearing a dark rose suit and white silk blouse. She'd added her Rolex watch, a diamond tennis bracelet, and large gold earrings with a sunburst design for good measure. "How's this?" she asked.

"Perfect," Jeff answered, nodding approvingly. "If I were a teenage boy, I'd spill my guts out to you in a minute. Let's go."

As they walked out the front door, Jeff said, "Would you mind if we took your car? It'll make a better first impression than if we drive up in my beater."

"Sure," Liz replied automatically. "Why don't you drive? The keys are in it. I feel a little bit shaky right now."

"Whatever you say." Jeff slid into the driver's seat,

wishing that his first experience behind the wheel of a Jag could have taken place under happier circumstances. He started the engine, then turned to her. "You realize that if what Nate says turns out to be true, it's gonna turn this nice, quiet little community on its ear." Liz frowned and he continued. "I mean, how many of those self-righteous people at the meeting last night do you suppose would've been calling for swift and firm justice if they'd thought the perpetrator was one of their own favorite sons?"

As the import of what he'd said slowly penetrated Liz's consciousness, she began to feel very queasy and had to fight the impulse to run back into the house.

Jeff leaned over and patted her arm. "I'm sure glad you don't think like that." When she didn't respond, he grinned sardonically, shifted the car into reverse, and pressing his foot to the floor, laid rubber the entire length of the driveway.

Chapter 12

"How are we going to play this?" Liz asked in a worried tone as Jeff wheeled the Jag into the Tompkinses' driveway.

"We tell them our prime suspect just got ruled out and we're going door to door in the neighborhood talking to people to make sure no one saw anything suspicious around the time Jeremy disappeared."

"What if they check with other neighbors and find out they're the only ones we've interviewed?"

"They won't, because first thing tomorrow morning I'll be beating a path up and down these streets talking to a whole bunch of people to corroborate our story."

"Okay," Liz said warily, "but how are we going to draw the kids into the questioning?"

"Don't worry. I'll handle it," Jeff said confidently as he cut the engine. "Just follow my lead. And can you maybe try not to act so nervous? One look at your face and they're gonna suspect something and clam right up on us."

"I can't help how I look. I *am* nervous," Liz admitted. "I don't know how you can deal with heavy-duty stuff like questioning children. I'd make a lousy cop."

"That's the most sensible comment I've heard from you yet!" Jeff exclaimed. "Come on, let's go," he said, opening the car door.

"Relax," he said as they made their way up the sidewalk. "I guarantee we aren't gonna have any big scenes tonight. We're just gathering information. All you gotta do is sit there and look like you're deeply fascinated by everything I say. I'll take care of the rest."

Liz could feel her heart pounding wildly as Jeff rang the doorbell. Moments later the heavy door was opened a crack by a tall, dark-haired man in his forties.

"Martin Tompkins?" Jeff asked.

"Yes?" the man replied, peering out at them suspiciously. "Can I help you?"

"Detective Jeff Gardner, Horicon County Sheriff's Department," Jeff said, displaying his badge. "This is Assistant District Attorney Liz Stanfeld. She's one of your neighbors—lives over on Charing Cross Road. We're in charge of the Jeremy Barker murder investigation, and well, frankly," he said sorrowfully, "so far all we've been able to come up with is a bunch of dead ends, so we're trying to talk to as many Oakwood Hills residents as we can to see if maybe somebody might have seen something the day the boy disappeared."

"My wife and I were already interviewed by another deputy the day after the boy's disappearance," Tompkins said curtly, making no move to admit them.

"I realize that, sir," Jeff said apologetically, in a tone that would have done Lieutenant Columbo proud, "but as I said, we're not making much headway in the case. For a time we thought we had a suspect, but that person was ruled out today, so now Ms. Stanfeld and I are reinterviewing folks up here in the Hills. Would you mind if we came in? I promise it won't take long and you'd be doing us a big favor."

Tompkins frowned but after a moment opened the door wide. "All right," he said with obvious reluctance. "Come in." Jeff and Liz followed him down an enormous marble-tiled hallway into a den furnished in masculine burgundies and greens. "Have a seat," Tompkins said, motioning to a wine-colored leather chesterfield sofa. "I'll call my wife."

"Thank you, sir. We appreciate it," Jeff said as the

two of them sat down. "Oh, by the way, I meant to ask you—do you and your wife live here alone?"

Tompkins paused in the doorway and turned back to face them. "No," he replied with obvious wariness. "We have two children. Why do you ask?"

"Well, if you don't mind, sir, I'd appreciate it if they could join us. You see, we are really making an effort to talk to *all* Oakwood Hills residents, regardless of their age."

Tompkins's frown deepened. "I assure you, Detective, my children have no information that could possibly be of use."

"You're probably right, sir," Jeff agreed, "but there's always the chance they might've unwittingly heard or seen something and not even realized its importance. We'll only take a few minutes of their time. Please?"

Tompkins's jaw clenched, but he finally said, "Oh, all right. If you insist. I'll get them."

After the man had left the room, Liz turned to Jeff. He put his finger to his lips. "Don't say anything," he cautioned her under his breath, "and for God's sake stop gripping the arm of the damn couch like it was a life raft. Remember: act casual."

Liz nodded and reluctantly relinquished her grip on the sofa. The waistband of her skirt was too tight, and she squirmed uncomfortably. She folded her hands demurely in her lap and took several deep breaths. If she got through this without fainting or having a heart attack, it would be a miracle.

A short time later Tompkins returned, flanked by a tall, auburn-haired woman dressed in a striking yellow shorts outfit, a red-haired girl of about eleven, and a tall, handsome, dark-haired teenage boy. "Detective Gardner, Ms. Stanfeld—my wife, Maureen, our daughter, Bridget, and our son, Brent."

There were murmured hellos all around. Liz found it nearly impossible to keep from staring at Brent.

Was it really possible that this attractive youth had taken a child's life?

Bridget and her mother sat on chairs facing Jeff and Liz. Tompkins and Brent remained standing, Tompkins leaning against the back of his wife's chair and Brent near a window, his arms crossed disinterestedly in front of him.

Jeff reiterated the reason for their presence for the benefit of the new arrivals. "Did any of you notice any unusual activity in the neighborhood, say, in the week prior to Jeremy's disappearance?"

Mrs. Tompkins nervously cleared her throat. "It's a pretty quiet neighborhood," she offered.

Jeff nodded. "How about you, Bridget?"

"No," the girl answered in a soft voice. "I don't remember anything unusual happening that week."

"Brent?"

The youth met Jeff's gaze evenly. He appeared to be mulling the question over, then he shrugged. "Nope. 'Fraid I can't help you either, Officer." He had a deep voice for one so young. Liz felt a shiver run down her spine.

"Were any of you home on Tuesday the eleventh?"

"I was at work," Tompkins replied gruffly.

"Where do you work?" Liz asked politely, figuring she'd better say something before the Tompkinses began to wonder why the hell Jeff had brought her along.

"I own and manage the Chosey Gallery on Juniper Drive."

"And where were you the day of Jeremy's disappearance, Mrs. Tompkins?" Liz asked.

Mrs. Tompkins cleared her throat again. "Bridget and I were at the club taking a tennis lesson." Was it just Liz's imagination, or was the woman's voice shaking just a bit?

"How about you, Brent? Were you home that day?" Jeff inquired.

"Off and on," the boy said.

"Were you here by yourself?"

"Part of the time."

"And the rest of the time?"

"My friend Greg Saunders walked down that morning, right after Mom and Bridget left. We watched a couple movies, made ourselves a sandwich, and went for a swim in the pool."

"I've got a son your age," Jeff said. "He's really into those kick-boxing movies. You know the ones I mean? With that French star—oh, what's his name?"

"Jean-Claude Van Damme," Brent said.

"Yeah. That's the guy. You like his movies?"

Brent smiled condescendingly. "No, not really. I'm not into all that gratuitous violence. Greg and I like to watch classics. You know, *Casablanca, Citizen Kane,* stuff like that."

"Wish I could get my boys to show an interest in that stuff," Jeff said, shaking his head. "Do you remember what time Greg left here that day?"

Brent shrugged. "I don't know exactly. I guess somewhere around two or two-thirty. I remember he was already gone by the time Mom and Bridget came back."

Jeff nodded again. "And you're how far from the Barker property—three or four houses?"

"Four," Tompkins cut in as though he didn't want his son answering any more questions.

"Can you see the house from here?"

"In the winter you can," Tompkins said. "In the summer there's too much foliage."

"Brent, do you know Tom Barker?"

The boy shrugged again. "Yeah, sort of. I mean, I know who he is when I see him, but I don't think I've ever talked to him. The man's got good taste in cars, though. Drives a black Lexus."

"Yeah, that's a pretty nice machine, isn't it?" Jeff said. "So I guess if you and Greg didn't venture any farther than your swimming pool, you didn't see any activity at the Barker house that day?"

"Nope." Brent shook his head. " 'Fraid I didn't."

"I told you we wouldn't be of any help to you," Tompkins said smugly.

"Well, we want to thank you folks for your time, anyway," Jeff said, standing up. Liz gratefully followed suit. Jeff walked to the door of the den, then turned back to face the Tompkins family so abruptly that he almost stomped on Liz's foot. "I don't mind telling you all that this case is turning out to be a mighty tough one," he said ruefully. "We don't see many homicides up here in Horicon County—we can thank the Lord for that—but I've handled a few in my day and the trail on this one is gettin' colder all the time. I sure do hope we come up with some clues soon. It'd be a damn shame if the person who snuffed out that poor little boy's life wasn't brought to justice. Well, it's been a pleasure talkin' to you folks. Good night."

As they slid into the Jaguar and Jeff started the engine, he turned to Liz. "Well, what'd you think?"

Liz shook her head in wonder. "I think you deserve an Oscar for that performance, pardner. I was afraid if we stuck around much longer you'd start yodeling or something. Don't you think you were carrying the dopey-small-town-cop routine just a little too far?"

"Nah," Jeff replied confidently as he drove around the circular driveway and headed back out to the street. "Never underestimate people's belief in their inherent superiority over policemen. And that goes double for the kind of people that live in this neck of the woods. Present company excepted, of course," he added hastily. "Besides," he chuckled, "I haven't worked for Dan Isaacson for twenty years for nothing. Somehow it seems that folks around here really go for Southern accents. Reminds 'em of pecan pie and mint juleps and makes 'em trust you so much they hardly notice you've painted 'em right into a corner. Now tell me: Was it my imagination or did you get the feeling old man Tompkins was hiding something?"

"I don't know about that," Liz replied, "but I thought the mother seemed rather nervous."

"What'd you think of Brent?"

"I'm not sure," Liz admitted. "He seemed a little too brash to suit me. Belittling your son's taste in movies and all."

"Fooled you, too, didn't I?" Jeff snickered as he came to a corner and made a hard right. "My kid wouldn't be caught dead watching that kick-boxing shit. *I'm* the only one in my household who thinks Van Damme is a pretty awesome dude. Any other thoughts?"

"Yeah. Brent claimed he was with Greg the day of the murder, but Greg didn't mention that fact to Nate. Do you suppose Brent was telling the truth about that or is he just using Greg as an alibi?"

"I don't know," Jeff replied as he braked sharply and pulled into another driveway. "But maybe we'll know more after we've talked to the Saunders family."

Teresa Saunders, a petite woman with short, dark hair and delicate features, greeted them warmly and graciously ushered them off the front entryway into a cheerful three-season porch furnished in white wicker and colorful chintz. After seeing that Liz and Jeff were seated in comfortable chairs, she obligingly fetched her husband, Donald, and their sons, Greg and eight-year-old Pat.

While they waited for the family to assemble, a large, furry Akita sauntered into the room, walked straight over to Liz, and stuck his nose in her lap. "Bear, get away from there!" Teresa Saunders scolded as she returned. "You'll get her all hairy."

"It's okay," Liz said weakly, petting the dog's enormous head. "He's not hurting anything." Because she had met the Saunderses before, she felt like a traitor sitting here in their home, questioning their son about a murder. She wished the interview were over.

Jeff went through the same preliminaries and posed the same questions. Mr. Saunders was the general manager of a BMW dealership on the north side of Milwaukee. Mrs. Saunders did some freelance interior design work out of her home. She had been in Milwaukee having lunch with a new client the day Jeremy disappeared. Pat had been at a Boy Scout day camp.

"And how about you, Greg? What exciting things were you up to that day?" Jeff asked.

As Nate Johnson had said, Greg Saunders was small for his age. Obviously a latecomer to puberty, he looked more like eleven than thirteen. He had fine blond hair and pale blue eyes. He was seated next to his mother on a wicker sofa and turned to her when Jeff posed his question. Only when she had given him a smile and a reassuring nod did he answer. A mama's boy, eh? Jeff thought to himself. That might come in handy somewhere down the road.

"I was here in the morning," Greg said in a quiet voice. "I played some CDs for a while. And then later on I rode my bike down to Brent Tompkins's house."

Liz's ears perked up and she stopped petting the dog. So Greg and Brent had apparently been together that day. But Brent had said his friend walked down to the house. Who was telling the truth? The dog nudged her with his nose, and she resumed her stroking.

"About what time was that?"

"Around ten or so, I guess."

"How long did you stay at Brent's?"

"Till sometime in the afternoon."

"What'd you do?"

"We watched some movies Brent had picked up at Video Station."

"The VCR is sure a great invention, isn't it?" Jeff said enthusiastically. "Why, my kids just love those action movies. Schwarzenegger, Van Damme. You like that kind of stuff?"

Greg nodded tentatively. "Brent and I watched *Terminator 2* that day," he volunteered.

Liz felt a prickly sensation on the back of her neck. Another small inconsistency.

"Did you do anything else besides watch movies?"

"Yeah. We had somethin' to eat and then we swam for a while."

"I guess you probably weren't paying much attention to traffic going by or anything when you were swimming, but did you happen to notice any strange cars—or maybe people walking that didn't look like they belonged here?"

The boy shook his head. "No. Not that I remember."

Jeff nodded. "Everybody we've talked to so far has told us the same thing," he said ruefully. "I know it's like lookin' for a needle in a haystack, but I keep hopin' if we talk to enough people we might come across somebody who did see something that day. I sure pray that happens because it'd be a real tragedy if the person who killed that little boy in cold blood weren't caught and punished for what he did."

Jeff's gaze focused squarely on Greg as he spoke. "This whole thing has been a nightmare for Jeremy's dad. I can sure feel for him. I've got two boys of my own, and I can't begin to imagine the pain a father must feel when he loses a child like that. To think that some animal beat that precious little boy's skull right to a pulp. My, oh, my, what is this world comin' to?"

As Jeff stood up to go, Liz gently pushed the dog aside and got to her feet. She then carefully turned and caught a glimpse of Greg's face. The boy had turned ashen and his lower lip seemed to tremble. Before she could observe any more, Jeff had taken her firmly by the arm and was pulling her toward the door. "Thank you, folks," he said in his newly acquired drawl. "We appreciate your takin' the time to talk to us. 'Night now."

"What was the meaning of dragging me out of there

like a sack of flour?" Liz complained as they headed out of the driveway.

"You almost gave the whole thing away by staring at the kid!" Jeff fumed. "I told you to play it casual."

"And I told you I'm not used to this spy stuff!" she retorted angrily.

"All right, all right," he said in an effort at reconciliation. "Well, now that you've seen both kids, what do you think?"

Liz leaned back in her seat and closed her eyes momentarily as she gathered her thoughts. When she opened them again, she turned to Jeff and said, "I think it's clear Greg is very frightened."

"There's no doubt about that," Jeff agreed. "But what struck me more is the difference in character between the two kids. Brent is brash and self-assured, while Greg's this little mouse. Do you really believe that if Brent killed Jeremy he'd be so stricken with conscience that he'd run to someone like Greg to confess?"

"What are you saying?" Liz asked. "Surely you don't think Greg was involved with the murder too." The horror of that possibility made her shudder.

Jeff turned to her, his eyes bright with determination. He was on the scent of the killer now and his adrenaline had kicked in. "I'm not sure yet," he said. "But if it's the last thing either of us does, we're going to find out what really happened. Whoever killed Jeremy is not going to get away with it—not while I have breath left in my body." He gunned the Jag's engine furiously and squealed out of the driveway.

PART TWO

Chapter 13

Liz arrived at work early the next morning. She hadn't slept well again, and she felt exhausted, yet at the same time keyed up with the knowledge that the case was on the verge of breaking wide open. At eight she phoned Tom Barker and set up an eleven o'clock meeting in Milwaukee. Tom was understandably curious about what she wanted, but she managed to be evasive, telling him only that she had a few points she needed to go over with him.

She was listlessly drinking her fourth cup of coffee of the morning, wishing she had a couple of chocolate donuts to go with it, when Harry knocked briefly, then stepped inside her office and closed the door behind him. "Hi," he said.

Liz glanced up at him. His expression was wary. "Hi," she replied.

"You're all dressed up today," he commented, noticing her black and white suit. "Going someplace?"

Liz nodded. "I have a meeting later this morning. Have a seat."

Harry dutifully sat down, shifted uncomfortably in the chair, then cleared his throat. "I want to apologize again for what happened," he said quietly. "It was wrong of me to divulge any information to the senator. Believe me, I didn't do it intentionally. We were just having a friendly conversation and he kept pressing me for answers and—well, I guess somehow it just slipped out. I had no idea he'd pass the information on to anyone else." He looked at her hopefully. "Will you forgive me?"

"I don't know."

"Please," Harry begged.

Liz pursed her lips, then nodded. "I guess I can try. But don't ever do something like that again."

Harry smiled, obviously relieved. "I promise."

Liz took a sip of coffee. "There were some big developments in the case yesterday," she said.

"Really?" Harry exclaimed. "That's great! What happened?"

"Well, it's kind of a good news, bad news thing," Liz replied evenly. "Part of the bad news is Frankie Snipes was excluded as a suspect. Jeff found two alibi witnesses who'll vouch for Frankie's whereabouts at the time Jeremy was killed."

"And the good news?"

"The good news is we're pretty sure we know who did it."

Harry frowned. "If you know who did it, why aren't you showing a little more enthusiasm?"

Liz looked him in the eye. "Because this is where the other part of the bad news comes in." She took a deep breath before continuing. "The killer is apparently a fourteen-year-old boy from Oakwood."

Harry's mouth dropped open. "You can't be serious!"

Liz nodded. "I'm dead serious."

"Oh, Christ! What did we do to deserve this?" Harry got up and began to pace back and forth in front of her desk. "Are you positive you're not mistaken? Remember, up until yesterday you were ready to swear out a complaint for Frankie's arrest."

Liz shook her head. "I don't think there's any mistake. Last night Jeff and I interviewed the fourteen-year-old as well as a thirteen-year-old friend. It was very low-key. Jeff just asked a lot of general questions about where they were the day of the murder. The two kids claim they were together, but their stories don't completely jibe."

"Do you think the thirteen-year-old had any involvement in Jeremy's death?"

"I don't know what to think," Liz admitted. "The thirteen-year-old told another friend that the older boy had confessed he'd kidnapped Jeremy but that he didn't intend to kill him. The older boy has a real attitude about him—a sort of braggadocio you don't normally see in someone that age. And the thirteen-year-old got very spooked when Jeff mentioned how poor little Jeremy had been beaten to death."

Harry stopped pacing for a moment. "What was the motive for the kidnapping?"

"Supposedly Tom Barker caught the fourteen-year-old on his property, swore at him, and ran him off the place. I'm meeting with Barker at eleven to see if he can corroborate that."

"Jesus!" Harry exclaimed, leaning against a file cabinet. "The shit has really hit the fan this time, hasn't it?"

Liz nodded. "I'm afraid so."

Harry sat down again. "Look, Liz," he said earnestly, "do me a favor and take this thing nice and slow. At the moment all you've got is double hearsay, and that's not admissible in court. You've got to have something a lot more concrete than that. We can't go off half cocked and start arresting kids unless we're absolutely sure we have a case. Otherwise the county's gonna have lawsuits coming out of its ears. Those Oakwood people are not gonna take this lying down."

"Believe me, I've thought of that," Liz replied. "And I'm afraid the fact that they've heard we had a suspect from Lakeview is going to make matters all the worse. The people at the town meeting were out for blood, thinking an outsider killed Jeremy. I hate to think what they're gonna do when they find out one of their own kids is the killer."

Harry put his hands over his face. "Boy, I really

fucked things up royally, didn't I?" He pondered the situation a moment, then raised his head and said, "Look, I know I stuck my foot in it by talking to the senator, but that's now water over the dam. What we have to do now is try to contain the damage, and I think the best way to do that is to wait until we're sure we have an airtight case before making an arrest. If we do that, people in Oakwood will be more apt to think they're being treated fairly. If we act in haste, there's bound to be trouble."

Liz sighed. "Let's not fool ourselves. There's going to be trouble no matter how we handle this." She took another sip of coffee. It was cold. She set the cup down and wrapped both hands around the rim. "Harry, I want you to know I'd be willing to resign from the case."

He sat back in his chair, a look of obvious surprise on his face. "Why on earth would you want to do that?"

"I didn't say I *wanted* to do it. I said I'd be willing to."

"You still haven't told me why."

"Because prosecuting a juvenile is bound to be an unpopular move and the office is going to take a lot of heat for it."

"Does that bother you?" Harry asked.

Liz drew in a long breath before replying. "To some extent it does, yes," she answered honestly. "I mean, we're talking about a kid from a good family who's practically my neighbor. I'd be lying if I didn't admit that things would've been much simpler if Frankie Snipes *had* been the killer." She paused and sucked in her cheeks, then continued. "But when I offered to resign, I wasn't thinking of myself."

"Oh?" Harry asked quizzically.

Liz shook her head. "Surely you must realize that charging a minor from Oakwood with murder might cost you some important political allies. If I stay on the case, I'm not going to cut this kid any slack. I just wanted to give you the opportunity to replace me with someone else who might not mind having you behind the scenes calling the shots."

"You know very well I don't run my office that way," Harry said indignantly. "Once I assign a case, it's up to the assistant to handle it as he or she sees fit. The fact that I'm in the running for a federal appointment doesn't change that one iota." He shifted in his chair and continued in a more even tone. "As I told you right from the start, I chose you for this case because you're a good lawyer. It doesn't make any difference to me whether you're prosecuting Frankie Snipes or a kid from Oakwood or Senator Kilpatrick himself, so long as Jeremy Barker's killer is caught and punished."

"Just so long as we understand one another," Liz said.

"We do," Harry assured her. He stood up and walked toward the door. "Now, let's not have any more talk of resigning. It's your case. You run with it. If you want advice, I'll always be available. And if you don't, well, then I'll stay the hell out of your way." He paused a moment, then added, "If you don't mind, I *would* appreciate it if you'd keep me posted on what's happening so I can help keep the press and sundry angry citizens at bay."

"Sure thing."

He paused in the doorway, his hand on the knob. "Look, we've both had a rough couple of days," he said quietly, turning back to face her. "You had every right to be upset with me, but I'd like to make amends. How about coming over to the house around seven? I could grill steaks."

Liz truly wasn't in the mood, but she didn't have the heart to turn him down. "Okay. See you at seven."

Harry gave her a quick smile. "Good luck," he said, opening the door and quickly walking out into the hall.

"Thanks." As he vanished, Liz murmured to herself, "I'm gonna need it."

Chapter 14

Tom Barker's office atop the Midwestern Mutual building was much like his house—cavernous and elegant but still somehow managing to retain a human scale and a personal touch.

Glancing around her at the lavish surroundings, Liz felt a fleeting pang of regret at having left private practice. She'd had many CEO clients with plush offices similar to this. She remembered what it was like to attend meetings in conference rooms where the walls were adorned with genuine Impressionist paintings and coffee was poured from Georgian silver urns. She had ultimately eschewed that way of life as frivolous, but there was something to be said for a career that didn't require her to meet with the distraught parents of murdered children.

After Liz had settled into a deeply padded chair in front of Tom's cherry desk and declined his offer of coffee, Tom leaned back in his chair. He was dressed in a light gray suit, and the sunlight pouring in through the bank of windows behind him picked up the golden highlights in his hair.

As Tom looked at her expectantly, he waved his hand over the tall stacks of paper covering his desk. "As you can see, I'm snowed under here, so I do hope your visit means there have been some new developments in the case." His voice held more than a hint of skepticism.

Liz ran her tongue over her lips. She had rehearsed what she was going to say to him endlessly on the drive down, but somehow no matter how perfect your lines might sound when you were alone, it was always much tougher to deliver them to a live audience.

Jeff had strongly cautioned her not to tell Barker about Brent and Greg. He had urged her to ask general questions and give only noncommittal responses to any inquiries Tom might pose. While Liz knew this was standard operating procedure, as she looked into Tom Barker's face she thought, Dammit, this man is in pain. His little boy was murdered and he deserves to hear the truth about who did it. It was all she could do to keep from blurting out the whole story and all the sordid details.

Realizing that Tom was staring at her, she finally managed to say, "We've had a couple of leads." Seeing his face light up, she immediately put her hands up and said, "It's nothing definite yet, but I wanted to ask you a few things."

"Ask away."

"Have you had occasion to chase anyone off your property—say, in the last six weeks?"

Tom immediately shook his head.

"Are you sure about that?"

"Yes, I'm sure. You mean someone in a car?"

"Not necessarily. How about someone on foot or on a bicycle?"

Tom shook his head again. "No. As I mentioned the day you and Detective Gardner came by the house, the front gate is virtually always locked."

"You're certain you never yelled at someone riding a bicycle on your driveway or on the lawn?"

"I'm positive," Tom answered. "Why do you ask? Is that how Jeremy was taken, by someone on a bike?"

Liz shook her head. "No."

"Please tell me," he said in a soft, urgent voice. "I have to know. Do you have a suspect?"

Liz momentarily closed her eyes, battling with herself. Should she tell him or not? Then she opened her eyes again and looked at him and knew the answer. "Yes," she said quietly.

"Who is it?"

"A teenage boy from Oakwood."

Tom's head snapped back as though he'd been sucker punched. "No," he said with a low moan. "It can't be!" Then he leaned forward again. "Who is it?"

Here Liz drew the line. "I'm afraid I can't tell you that just yet, but he supposedly said he wanted to teach you a lesson because you'd caught him on your property with his bike and called him a little bastard."

"That's a damn lie!" Tom exclaimed. "What else did he say?"

"Apparently he told another boy he was just going to hide Jeremy in the woods for a few hours so you'd get worried, and then he would release him unharmed. I don't know why things got out of hand."

"What about the suspect who was mentioned at the village board meeting—the boy from Lakeview?"

"There *was* such a suspect for a time," Liz conceded, "but Detective Gardner found two witnesses who will back up his alibi for the time of Jeremy's disappearance. We stumbled onto the Oakwood boy because of a phone call the detective received from a concerned Oakwood parent."

"When will you be making an arrest?"

"Soon, I hope." Liz replied. "Detective Gardner wants to track down as much evidence as he can before the entire village realizes what's going on. Once word of an arrest gets out, people are likely to clam up and refuse to cooperate with us."

Tom stared at her, a puzzled look on his face. "I don't understand. How could anyone not want to help catch Jeremy's killer?"

"I'm sure everyone in the village wants to catch the killer," Liz assured him, "but it would be a lot more palatable for them if the killer was an outsider, if you know what I mean."

Tom paused a moment to reflect on what she'd said,

then a light went on. "Oh, I see the problem," he said, rubbing his palms over his cheeks. "It's one of those situations where we have seen the enemy and he is us."

"Exactly," Liz said. "And a lot of people are going to be unable or unwilling to admit that one of their neighbors could have done such a dreadful thing."

"But you're sure you're going to be able to prove it, aren't you?" he asked, his voice rising. "This person isn't going to get away with murdering Jeremy?"

"We'll prove it," she said, fervently hoping that Jeff never got wind of this conversation. She stood up. "Well, now that you've heard my news, I'd better let you get back to work."

Tom got up too and came around his desk to stand in front of her. "Can I buy you lunch?" he asked.

Liz shook her head. "Thank you for offering, but I have a one o'clock court appearance, so I really have to get back to the office." She extended her hand. From his close proximity, she could smell Tom's expensive cologne.

After giving Liz's hand a firm shake, Tom cleared his throat. "Ah—" he stammered just a bit, "it appears as though I may have underestimated both you and Detective Gardner. And if my behavior in our earlier meetings seemed a bit boorish, well—I apologize."

"There's no need for apologies," Liz said. "I'd say you've done an admirable job of maintaining your composure. Good-bye," she said, patting his arm. "I'll be in touch."

"Good-bye."

As she pulled the Jag out of the building's underground parking ramp, Liz briefly considered making a quick stop at her old law firm. She still kept in touch with several people there. She didn't often make it into the city during business hours, and she knew they'd be pleased to see her. But at the last minute she zoomed past the turnoff, deciding she really wasn't in the mood for socializing.

She rolled down the windows and reveled at the feel of the warm breeze ruffling her hair. Driving fast, she headed north, then east, then north again when she hit Lake Drive. As she came to the 5000 block, she checked her rearview mirror to make sure there was no traffic, then abruptly slowed. There it was, just ahead. Her former house. She hadn't been past it in more than a year. She gave the yard a quick glance to make sure neither Peter nor Amanda was lurking anywhere about, then slowed the Jag to a crawl.

The place still looked damn good, Liz thought ruefully. Of course, what had she expected? The house had been built by master craftsmen in the twenties. It was hardly going to topple into disrepair simply because she'd had the audacity to move out. And after all, Peter was in the construction business and had always made sure the property was meticulously maintained. Her eyes lingered on the copper roof, the brick driveway. Yes, everything was just as she'd left it. She idly wondered whether Amanda had made any changes to the interior. Mummy was no doubt handling the redecorating. Probably had Mario Buatta flying in from the coast to work on the job. The though of the entire house awash in chintz was enough to make her gag.

A car was coming up behind her now, and she quickly pressed the accelerator to the floor and took off. She'd seen enough. She glanced at the clock. It was after twelve, and she was famished. Heading west again, she saw a McDonald's and pulled into the drive-through lane, intending to order a hamburger and a large strawberry shake. There was a long line of cars ahead of her, and as she waited she thought about Harry.

She'd always known theirs was not destined to be a grand passion, but she'd thought she had outgrown that phase. She had been madly, hopelessly in love with Peter, and what had it gotten her? A broken heart, that's what. Harry was endearing—or at least she'd thought so until his faux pas about Frankie Snipes—and he made her feel attractive and cherished. She had thought that was what she wanted at this stage in her life, and she'd honestly believed that Harry was the type of man she could feel comfortable with for a long time. So why did she suddenly feel so confused?

As she pulled up a car length, her thoughts inexplicably turned to Tom Barker. Now there was a handsome man. Much better-looking than Harry. Maybe better-looking even than Peter, who, in the days of her foolish youth, she had believed resembled a Greek god. She'd be willing to bet someone like that could inspire real passion in a woman. No one would ever describe Tom Barker as bland as vanilla pudding.

Stop that! Liz chastised herself, moving up another car length. Why was she having such crazy thoughts? What she needed right now was stability and order, and those were things Harry could provide. Besides, Tom was already involved with someone. Oh, boy, was he ever! Liz groaned slightly as she thought of Natalie Helprin. What was it Esther had said? That Natalie had sharp claws and would undoubtedly use them if Liz started to look like she had designs on Tom. Liz shook her head emphatically. Absolutely not. There was no way she was going to give Tom Barker a second thought. She would banish him from her mind completely, starting right now. Liz finally reached the drive-up window. "May I take your order?" a cute black teenager called out.

"Yes," Liz replied, ignoring her rumbling stomach. When it came to food, she'd been a little short on willpower lately, but suddenly—as an image of Natalie Helprin's perfect size four figure popped into her mind—she seemed able to conjure some up without any effort at all. "I'll have a large diet Coke."

Chapter 15

Jeff and two other deputies spent the morning making the rounds of Oakwood Hills homes, asking residents where they had been and if they had seen anything unusual the day of Jeremy's murder. As Jeff had expected, they didn't learn anything useful, but in case the Tomkinses or the Saunderes mentioned to their friends over cocktails at the club that they'd been visited by the police, they would find they hadn't been singled out for special treatment.

Shortly before noon, Jeff instructed the other two officers to continue their questioning while he headed back toward Lakeview to pick up a court order entitling him to go through Brent's and Greg's school records. For the hell of it he decided to swing past the Tompkins house on his way out of town. As he approached it, he saw a lone bicyclist coming toward him. He braked and saw that it was Greg Saunders. Hot damn! he thought. What perfect timing! He slowed the car even further and rolled down the window. "Hi, Greg," he called out cheerfully. "Nice day for a ride, isn't it?"

A look of sheer terror came over Greg's face as he recognized who was sitting behind the wheel of the faded blue car, and the bike tipped precariously, nearly causing him to lose his balance. The boy sharply activated the hand brake, then dragged his feet, coming to a stop about ten yards from the Tomkinses' driveway.

"You and Brent going to watch some more movies today?" Jeff asked genially.

Greg looked down at the ground, unable to make eye contact with the detective. He gripped the handlebars so tightly that his knuckles were white. He swallowed hard, then shrugged his shoulders. "Ah . . . I dunno . . . maybe," he said haltingly, his eyes still averted.

"Well, you boys have a good time," Jeff said, giving a small wave as he rolled up the window and slowly drove off. As he glanced in the rearview mirror, he could see Greg nervously watching the Chevy make its way up the street. The boy then looked at the Tomkinses' driveway and back at the Chevy before pedaling his bike hastily up the drive. Bet there'll be some interesting conversation going on there this afternoon, Jeff thought to himself.

After picking up the court order, Jeff stopped at a favorite greasy spoon for a roast pork sandwich, an order of onion rings, and a Coke. By one-thirty he was walking in the front door of Oakwood Junior High School.

Like virtually every other structure in town, the school was new and radiated wealth and good breeding, from its immaculately maintained grounds to its gleaming tile floors. Jeff's lower lip curled down as he thought of the spartan old high school his sons attended in Lakeview. At least it managed to instill its students with the basics, like how to read and write and that it wasn't nice to kill people.

After identifying himself to a middle-aged, frizzy-haired secretary, Jeff found himself ushered into the spacious office of principal Harlan T. Richards. Richards was a tall, slender man of about fifty with a shiny bald head and half glasses perched at the end of his nose. In spite of the fact that it was eighty-five degrees outside, the man was dressed in itchy tweeds. Jeff remembered having a principal who looked like that when he was in school. They'd called him Chrome

Dome. He'd been fired for fondling little girls. This guy looked like his taste probably ran more toward little boys.

"What can I do for you, Detective?" Richards asked in a somewhat high-pitched voice.

Jeff plopped the court order in the middle of Richards's meticulous desk. The wall behind him was filled with framed diplomas and awards of merit. Richards didn't look smart enough to have earned all those honors. Maybe he'd bought the plaques at garage sales and whited out the original owners' names and replaced them with his own. "I need to take a look at the records on two of your students," Jeff said conversationally.

Richards carefully picked up the document by its edges, as though he were afraid its print might emit a caustic substance. Peering through his half glasses, he scanned the order, frowned, then looked back up at Jeff. "May I ask what this pertains to?" he asked in a caustic tone.

"No, you may not," Jeff answered brightly, then chuckled to himself, *You didn't say Mother may I, you asshole.*

"This is highly irregular—" Richards began.

"There's nothing irregular about it," Jeff interrupted. "I serve order like this all the time. Of course, if you think I might have forged Judge Rogers's signature, feel free to call him up and ask him if he actually signed it this morning." He made a show of checking his watch. " 'Course at this time of day the judge *is* usually still in chambers sucking on his private stock of vodka and he *does* get rather testy when he's disturbed, but hey, if you want to call, be my guest."

Richards's frown deepened, but he picked up the phone and barked instructions to his secretary. "Go down to the guidance department office and bring back the files on Brent Tompkins and Gregory Saunders." He slammed the phone down and glared across the desk.

Ignoring the older man's obvious animosity, Jeff pulled a small notepad and pen out of his pocket and plunged ahead. "How long have you been the principal here?"

Richards hesitated a moment, then apparently decided the most prudent course of action would be to supply this inferior creature with succinct answers. "Four years," he replied in a clipped tone.

"What is your background?"

Richards sat up straighter in his leather chair. "I have a Ph.D. from Brown," he announced proudly. "I was associated with various private schools in Vermont and Massachusetts before coming here."

An Eastern blueblood, Jeff thought contemptuously. The man had spent his whole damn career catering to upper-class brats. What he needed was to have a bunch of inner city hoodlums bused into Oakwood to shake things up a bit in his neat little world.

"How many students do you have in junior high?"

"Approximately two hundred seventy-five."

"That's a nice, intimate little group," Jeff commented. "In a school this size I imagine you have a chance to get to know most of the kids personally."

"I pride myself on being able to identify most of the students by name," Richards said smugly.

"So you are personally acquainted with Greg and Brent?"

Richards eyed Jeff warily. "Yes."

"Would you characterize them as good students?"

"Yes."

"Exceptionally good students?"

Richards paused. "Brent is exceptional. He has won virtually every award the school offers. I would classify Greg as a bit above average—by Oakwood district standards, you understand. When judged by statewide norms, both boys would be considered outstanding."

Oakwood standards, Jeff thought bitterly. What the hell made these people think that the earth revolved around them?

"Have you had any disciplinary problems with either of the boys?" Jeff asked.

Richards shook his head adamantly. "None."

"Would you describe either of them as aggressive?"

"In what respect?"

Jeff shrugged. "In any respect."

Richards stroked his chin thoughtfully. "We encourage our students to be aggressive academically, so to some extent I suppose both would fit into that mold. As I mentioned, Brent is by far the superior intellect of the two, so I guess I would have to say that he is more aggressive scholastically than Greg."

"What about other types of aggression?"

Richards frowned again. "I'm afraid I don't understand your question."

"Has either of the boys demonstrated any signs of physical aggression? Have they ever bullied other students?"

Richards shook his head. "Not to my knowledge."

"Have any of their teachers ever reported having disciplinary problems with them?"

"I don't believe so."

"If there were any such reports, would the students' files reflect them?"

There was a slight hesitation. "Yes, of course."

There was a light knock on the door, and the frizzy-haired secretary entered carrying two files. She briskly crossed the room and placed them on Richards's desk.

"Thank you, Mary," Richards said. The secretary nodded in response and walked out. Richards picked up the files. "Well, here you are, Detective. I trust that any information you might desire about the two students will be contained in these."

Jeff took the proffered files. "Just a couple more questions. Do you know whether Greg and Brent are close friends?"

Richards shrugged. "I really couldn't say. I guess I've seen the two of them walking together from time to time, but as you probably know, Brent is a year older and in my opinion substantially more mature than Greg. I would doubt that theirs is a particularly close friendship."

Jeff nodded. "Do you happen to know whether Brent does have any close friends?"

"We pride ourselves on the fact that all of our students coexist harmoniously," Richards said in an imperious tone.

La-de-da, Jeff thought, rolling his eyes. With all the time the bozo spent priding himself on this and that, it was a wonder there were enough hours in the day left to run the school. "Yes, of course, but surely in the two years Brent spent here you had the opportunity to observe his choice of companions."

Richards pursed his lips. He was clearly struggling with how much information he should reveal to this upstart officer. "I have noticed Brent in the company of four or five young men on a somewhat regular basis."

"Do you recall their names?"

Richards hesitated.

"Look," Jeff said airily. "I can't make you tell me anything if you don't want to, but if you don't answer my question I guarantee I'll be back here tomorrow with an order authorizing me to look at the records on all of your students. And if I have to go that route, it'll mean you'll probably be tripping over me every day for the next three weeks." He paused in order to give Richards a chance to absorb that information. "On the other hand," he continued, "if you give me some names now you might not have to look at my ugly mug again after today. It's completely up to you."

Richards drew in a deep breath and said in a staccato tone, "Josh Mahoney, Chad Elliott, Taylor Huff, Dillon Freeman."

Jeff smiled as he jotted the names down on his pad. "I thank you, sir. You are a man of good judgment." He stood up. "Now, if you could direct me to someplace where I can go through these files in private and have access to a copy machine, I will darken your door no longer."

Richards stood up, clearly grateful that the interview was over. "There is a small conference room just down the hall that should suit your needs. Right this way."

"Oh, just one more thing," Jeff said. "It would be in your best interest if you didn't mention my visit to anyone, particularly the boys' parents. If I hear that there's been a leak, I'm going to have to assume it came from you—and I will be *very* unhappy. *Capisce?*"

Richards scowled but nodded. "I understand. Follow me."

An hour later Jeff had finished combing through the records and photocopying pertinent parts. Richards's depiction of the boys had been accurate. Greg was a good student, earning A's and B's. Brent had an outstanding academic record, garnering all A's in both of his junior high years, with the exception of a B in social studies during his first semester as a seventh grader. Greg's IQ was listed as 118, Brent's as 150. He was a smart little bastard, Jeff thought ruefully. It was a damn shame he couldn't have put those brains to better use. Neither boy's file contained any bad conduct reports.

Jeff sat there for a moment staring down at the files. Almost as an afterthought, he jotted down the names of all of the boys' teachers. It might be interesting to see if all of them would give the kids such glowing reports. Filled with fresh resolve to do whatever was necessary to see Brent punished for what he'd done, Jeff scooped up the files and headed back toward the main office, pondering what would be the best way to coerce old Richards into furnishing him with a list of faculty addresses and phone numbers. There had to be somebody out there who could blow the whistle on Brent's pure-as-snow reputation.

Chapter 16

"Get the paperwork on Brent ready to go," Jeff ordered as he charged into Liz's office at four-thirty that afternoon.

She looked up from the statute book she'd been studying. Her stomach was still growling, and her conversation with Harry and the trip to Milwaukee had left her feeling tired and confused. "What did you say?" she asked, rubbing her eyes wearily.

"You heard me," Jeff said, settling into a chair. "I want the delinquency petition typed ASAP."

Liz sat up straighter in her chair. "You mean we're ready to file charges?"

"Not quite," he said, tipping the chair back, "but we will be soon, and I want that baby ready to go by tomorrow morning."

Liz frowned. "What's the big hurry all of a sudden? Are you expecting some sort of breakthrough tonight? No, don't tell me," she said, pushing her hair behind her ears. "I suppose you think Brent's conscience will finally get the better of him, and when you get home you'll discover him weeping on your doorstep, begging you to arrest him."

"With the cast of characters we've got to work with, anything is possible," Jeff replied, bringing the chair's front legs back to earth. "And for your information, it just so happens that I *may* have a breakthrough tonight. I talked to the Oakwood Junior High principal. Lovely man." He rolled his eyes. "Jesus, what a prick! To hear him tell it, Brent ought to be elevated to sainthood. His school records don't reflect what a smarmy little monster he really is, but I got a list of all his teachers' names and I'm going to burn up the phone lines tonight to see if I can't get a more candid assessment of him."

"That's all well and good," Liz said, "but you still haven't explained the urgency to get the delinquency papers ready."

"Because it's only a matter of time before the kid squeals to mommy and daddy that he's in hot water. Oh, I don't think for a minute he's going to admit he killed Jeremy," Jeff added hastily upon seeing the expression of doubt come over her face. "I expect he'll concoct some story about how the police are so anxious to crack the case that they've stooped to fabricating a story that involves our hero."

He swung his left leg over his right. "At that point, Mommy and Daddy Tompkins, being the true-blue, All-American people that they are, will probably herd said innocent babe on the first available plane to Switzerland, where they'll demand political asylum for him. In the meantime, you and I will be sitting here doing some fast talking to try to convince people we're *not* really totally incompetent and we'll spend the next five years of our lives trying to get the little shithead back to the U.S. of A. That, in a nutshell, is why we need to have the fucking papers signed, sealed, and hot to trot."

"Your imagination is running away with you," Liz said disgustedly, getting up from her desk and walking over toward the window. "I'll admit I was concerned that Frankie Snipes might leave town, but you're talking about a kid from a solid, respectable family. He's not going anyplace."

"He might, goddamnit!" Jeff exclaimed, suddenly getting agitated. "Unlike the Snipeses, Oakwood families have the resources to spirit the kids far away and keep them there indefinitely. Believe me, when people with money are faced with a crisis situation, they'll pull every string imaginable to get themselves out of it."

"Since when did you become such an expert on people with money?" Liz asked skeptically.

Jeff hesitated just a fraction of a second before replying vehemently, "Since I was twenty years old and a drunk driver killed my old man."

Liz's mouth dropped open.

"The drunk turned out to be a fat cat from Chicago," Jeff continued. "He hired a big-name lawyer and they worked out a deal where he pleaded to reckless driving, paid a fine, and went on his merry way."

Liz grimaced. "Didn't your mother file a civil wrongful death action against him?"

Jeff snorted. "Oh, sure, she got a settlement from his insurance company, but we didn't give a damn about the money. All we wanted was to see him punished for what he did." His nostrils flared as he continued. "You can be sure if the situation had been reversed and my old man had been the one that was drunk he would've rotted in prison. But because the guy had big bucks, he got off scot-free." He paused and stared Liz square in the eye. "So that's why I want those papers ready to go tomorrow."

Jeff's eyes were bright with anger. Liz held his glance for a moment, then swallowed hard and looked away. "I'm so sorry," she said softly. "I had no idea. I'll get someone to stay late to do the paperwork." She jotted some notes on a piece of paper.

Jeff took a deep breath and exhaled. The tension he'd felt was dissipating. "Good girl," he said in a much calmer tone of voice. "We'll want to charge both first-degree intentional homicide and kidnapping."

Liz looked up again. "Let's get one thing straight," she said in an effort to lighten up the conversation again. "I'm the prosecutor here. You're the detective. You don't tell me how to do my job, and I don't tell you how to do yours. Got that?"

"Okay, okay," Jeff said, raising his hands in a gesture of surrender. "I was just thinking out loud. How did your meeting with Barker go?"

"Unfruitful," she replied. "He's positive he never chased anybody off the property because the gate's never open, so nobody can get in." She ripped the page of notes off the pad.

Jeff nodded thoughtfully. "I'm not a bit surprised. That story seemed pretty lame. So," he said casually, "did you spill the beans to Barker that our prime suspect is his very own neighbor?"

Liz could feel the color rising to her face, but she managed to keep her voice steady as she lied. "No, of course I didn't tell him."

"Good." Jeff smiled to himself. He'd bet next week's salary that she *had* told, but there was probably no harm in it. Tom Barker didn't look like the vigilante type who'd go out and buy a .357 Magnum and blow Brent away before he'd received a fair trial.

Jeff pulled his notepad out of his pocket. "The principal gave me a list of Brent's close friends. I'm going to have to talk to them at some point, but I'd just as soon wait till after the arrest. I don't want to alert any more people than I have to until he's safely in custody. Let's see—we've got Josh, Chad, Taylor, and Dillion," he read from his notes. "Jesus!" he shuddered. "It's no damn wonder kids these days turn out to be delinquent, saddled with candy-ass names like those. If my wife had wanted to name our kids somethin' squirrelly, I woulda divorced her."

Liz raised her eyebrows. "And what, pray tell, are your children's names?"

"Bill and Alex," he replied proudly. "Nice, normal, old-fashioned names. Just like Elizabeth," he added generously. "That's a good old name."

Liz shrugged. "I've never cared for it myself."

"Why not?" Jeff asked, surprised. "Oh, let me guess. I'll bet you were named after a doddering old maiden aunt who had blue hair and farted in public."

Liz chuckled in spite of herself. "Hardly."

"No? Let me think." He scratched his head. "Don't tell me you were named after Lizzie Borden? So that's where you get your cantankerous streak."

"I am *not* cantankerous!" she shot back. "For your information, I was named after Elizabeth Taylor."

"No shit!" Jeff exclaimed, scrutinizing her closely. "Well, you don't have violet eyes, but if you don't mind my saying so, you and she *do* both have—" He cupped his hands in front of his chest.

"Honestly!" Liz threw up her hands. "Have you no shame?"

"Nope," he replied. "None at all. So, tell me. How did you manage to get yourself named after Madame Taylor?"

"In her younger days my mother was a movie star groupie," Liz replied ruefully. "She named my brother Marlon—you know, as in Brando." She rolled her eyes. "Mom couldn't wait to tell everyone we met about our namesakes. Of course we were mortified. To this day, she's the only person who calls me Elizabeth. I always introduce myself as Liz. And Marlon goes by Mike.

"I *was* able to get back at Mom a little bit when I told her I was getting a divorce," Liz smiled. "She was horrified and carried on like I was the town hussy or something. So I reminded her that when her idol was my age she was already on husband number five, and I said if she'd wanted me to be the type of woman who deep-sixed her career in favor of being a wife and mother, maybe she should've named me after Grace Kelly."

She laughed at the memory, then stopped and looked at Jeff seriously. "I don't know why I told you that. I never tell anyone. And if you so much as breathe a word of it, so help me, I'll dig out my Lizzie Borden ax from behind the woodshed and come after you."

"Don't worry," Jeff assured her in a serious tone. "I never tell anyone the story about my old man either, so now we're even." He stood up. "You get to work on the papers and I'll start ringing up the teachers."

"Do you want any help with that?"

Jeff shook his head. "I think I'd better handle all the investigating from here on in. We're getting to the point now where whoever talks to these witnesses may have to testify in court about what they said, and you can't prosecute the case and be a witness too."

Liz nodded. She would never admit it to him, but in the last few days she'd discovered that investigating was not her cup of tea. She was more than willing to stick to handling the legal side of the case.

"I'll talk to you in the morning." He turned to leave.

"Jeff?" Liz called as he walked toward the door.

He turned back. "Yeah?"

"I'm glad you told me about your father."

Jeff gave a small nod. "I am, too. Good-bye, Elizabeth."

"Get out of here," she laughed.

Liz gathered her notes and stood up. After she got one of the secretaries started on typing the delinquency petition that would authorize them to take Brent into custody, she would swing by Harry's office and tell him she might have to take a rain check on dinner. She felt a slight twinge of guilt as she realized how little the change of plans upset her. Then she squared her shoulders and tossed back her hair. The hell with guilt. Until Brent was safely behind bars, this case was her number one priority. Harry would surely understand that. And if he didn't—well, that was his problem, not hers.

Chapter 17

Jeff hurried back to the sheriff's department, eager to tackle the job of contacting the teachers on his list. He had foolishly assumed he would be able to just pick up the phone and talk to most of them. However, he'd failed to take into account that it was summer vacation, a time when reaching out and touching someone in the education profession was no easy task, particularly in a district like Oakwood that paid its teachers handsomely enough to enable them to take extended European vacations.

After the fourth answering machine cheerfully informed him that Mr. Smithers was not at home and to please leave a message after the tone, he decided to take a more personal approach. He fired up the Chevy and started tracking down the teachers' homes. Even if no one was around, with a little luck a sympathetic neighbor might be willing to provide him with a current phone number or otherwise divulge the absent one's whereabouts.

He stumbled across his first live quarry around six, in the person of Lucille Schmerse, a gray-haired, middle-aged math teacher. She had just pulled into her driveway and was unloading bags of groceries from her car when Jeff arrived. He introduced himself and helped her heft the last three parcels into the kitchen of her raised ranch home.

"Thank you," she said gratefully, pausing a moment to catch her breath before she began unpacking the bags. "When I bought this house I thought I was getting a real bargain. Now I understand why the last owners wanted to get rid of it. All those steps probably ruined their knees." She opened the refrigerator and began to unpack two cartons of eggs. "Have a seat," she said, gesturing toward the padded oak chairs around the kitchen table. "So, what can I do for you, Detective?"

Jeff accepted the invitation to sit down. "I wanted to ask you a few questions about two of your students—Greg Saunders and Brent Tompkins," he replied. "It has to do with an investigation I'm conducting."

The woman frowned just a bit, then answered brightly, "They're nice boys. I enjoyed having them both in my class—especially Brent. He's so sharp that it was a real challenge trying to find enough extra assignments to keep him from getting bored."

Jeff nodded. "You're not the first person who's mentioned that. Did he ever present any type of disciplinary problem?"

"Brent?" The woman slammed the refrigerator door shut and turned to him, a look of obvious surprise on her face. "Never. He was a model student, in both seventh and eighth grades. I only wish there were more like him."

Yeah, a few more boys like that and Oakwood's surplus population problem would be solved for decades to come, Jeff thought sarcastically. "What about Greg?" he asked.

She shrugged. "Quiet boy. Bit above-average student. Nothing to write home about."

"Did you ever hear any of the other teachers complain about Brent's behavior?"

The woman shook her head. "Can't say that I did."

Jeff thanked her for her time and moved on. Two hours later he was back at the department mulling over how little he'd discovered. According to everyone he'd spoken to, Greg Saunders was a quiet, unassuming, run-of-the-mill student. Brent Tompkins, however, virtually deserved to be nominated for a medal of honor.

"Brent is the smartest boy I've seen in over twenty years of teaching." Yeah, smart enough to kill a four-year-old and almost get away with it.

"Brent has unlimited potential. I have no doubt he'll go far in this world." If Jeff had his way, the little scumbag would get a one-way trip to Waupun Correctional Institution.

"Brent is a born leader." That's for sure. If Jeff's hunch was correct, he was leading poor Greg down the road to ruin right along with him by forcing the younger boy to be a party to a cover-up of Jeremy's murder.

Jeff took a long swallow from a can of Pepsi he'd gotten from a vending machine in the lounge, wishing it were beer, and looked up at the clock. It was after eight. He was starting to get a headache and debated whether he shouldn't call it quits for now and start in again in the morning. As he was considering this option, a vision of Brent securely tucked away in some safe harbor and sneering at him flashed through his mind and he emitted a loud growling sound. No, goddamn it, there was too much at stake. He would try one or two more numbers.

The next name on his list was Philip Barry, an English teacher who'd had Brent as a student in seventh grade but had terminated his employment with the district, after only one year, at the end of that term. Although the school's records still listed a Lakeview apartment address for him, the landlord said he'd left town a year ago. The man was able to provide Jeff with a forwarding address in Seattle. Fully expecting a repeat of his previous conversations, Jeff dialed the number.

"Hello," a curt, deep voice came on the line.

"Philip Barry?" Jeff asked.

"Yeah. Who's this?"

"Mr. Barry, this is Detective Captain Jeff Gardner

of the Horicon County, Wisconsin, Sheriff's Department. I was wondering if you'd be willing to answer a couple of questions about one of your former students, Brent Tompkins."

Without so much as a moment's hesitation, Barry responded, "So the little bastard finally got caught."

Jeff nearly dropped the receiver. "Excuse me, sir," he said, clearing his throat. "What did you say? Caught at what?"

"Well, I guess you'll have to tell me that, Detective," Barry said wryly. "But frankly, nothing you could say would surprise me."

Jeff's heart was pounding. He fought to keep his voice calm. "And why is that?"

"Because as far as I'm concerned, that kid is bad news."

Jeff's hand was shaking as he picked up his pen. He could scarcely believe his good luck. "Could you elaborate on that a bit, sir?"

"Sure," Barry replied without hesitation. "Brent was in my seventh-grade English class. It was an advanced class for students who'd gotten the highest scores in language skills on the standardized tests that were given the previous year. The first couple months of school I was very impressed with the kid. He had a vocabulary far superior to any of his classmates. He showed a real flair for writing short stories and poems, and he wasn't shy like so many seventh graders are."

"From your tone, I take it something happened to change the high opinion you had of him," Jeff put in.

"It was a gradual thing," Barry replied. "The first incident I remember was shortly before Thanksgiving. I'd divided the class into six groups. Each was to write a ten-minute play having something to do with Thanksgiving and then act it out for the class. Brent, as usual, was his group's leader, and I suspect he wrote the entire play himself and doled out the parts to the other students. Of course, he claimed the biggest role for himself. The play was a very dark piece about the first Thanksgiving feast between the Pilgrims and the Indians. Brent played an Indian chief. I thought the thing was very well done until the end. After the meal was over, one of the Pilgrims said something derogatory to the chief, whereupon the chief scalped him."

Barry paused a moment, recalling the details. "It was all so unexpected, and it happened very fast. One minute everything was going along peacefully and the next Brent had this poor boy, who was much smaller than he, down on the ground and was beating him savagely. The kid was screaming bloody murder, and it took me a second to realize this was *not* part of the script. I ran across the room and pulled Brent off, and he looked at me with the coldest eyes I've ever seen and laughed and said something like, 'Sorry. Guess I got a little carried away. Acting is really a blast, isn't it?' "

"Was the other boy hurt?" Jeff asked.

"He was mostly just scared out of his wits," Barry replied.

"Did you say anything to Brent about the incident?"

"You bet. I had him stay after class. Once everyone else had left, I told him his behavior had been completely inappropriate and I hoped nothing like that would happen again."

"What was his response?"

"He just shrugged and said, 'I told you I was sorry.' "

"Were there other incidents after this?" Jeff asked.

Barry sighed. "Yes, and they seemed to escalate. In December I saw him knock a smaller boy down out on the playground. I ran over to see what was going on, and Brent said they were just fooling around. The smaller boy was crying but refused my offer to take Brent to the principal.

"After the first of the year, during an exam, I caught him passing answers to another student. That time I *did* march him up to the principal's office."

"What happened?"

"Not a damn thing," Barry spat back. "I told Richards about the earlier incidents and said I thought the kid had a serious problem and was in need of counseling. Brent claimed the piece of paper had just fallen out of his notebook onto the floor and that the other student was in the midst of picking it up and handing it back when I caught them. The principal bought Brent's story and told me I had a suspicious mind."

"I met Richards," Jeff told him. "I can believe he'd say that. Was there anything else?"

"Yeah. Around Easter I caught him rifling through my desk early in the morning. My door was always locked, so he must've managed to break in somehow. He claimed the door was already unlocked and that he was just looking for a pen because his had run out of ink. I reported that to Richards, too, but it didn't get me anywhere." He paused a moment. "Those were the high points. I think there were more episodes, but frankly I've tried to put Brent Tompkins out of my mind, so those are the only ones that I can think of right now."

"Did you ever talk to Brent's parents?"

"I tried. When it became clear I wasn't going to get anywhere with the principal, I sent the parents a letter asking them to call me to set up a meeting."

"Did you keep a copy of the letter or any of your reports to Richards?"

"No, I'm afraid not," Barry replied. "I tossed everything when I moved."

"So what happened? Did you meet the parents?"

Barry snorted. "Hardly. Brent's old man had his secretary call me with the message that he had talked to the principal and no meeting would be necessary. It was shortly after that I gave notice I would not be renewing my contract with the Oakwood School District."

"This is dynamite!" Jeff exclaimed. "I went through Brent's entire file, and there's no mention of any disciplinary problems. And when I asked Richards about it, he vehemently denied that Brent had ever been in any trouble. Are you telling me he falsified the records?"

"You bet," Barry said assuredly.

"Why would he do that?"

"The same reason he's done most things throughout his miserable time on this earth: money. He's pulling down eighty grand a year for what's gotta be the cushiest principal's job in the state. He knows which side his bread is buttered on. Most of the parents have donated large sums of money to the school. My guess is old man Tompkins threatened to send his kids to a different school and maybe encourage some of his neighbors to do the same unless Richards agreed to gloss over Brent's little transgressions. God, am I ever glad to be out of that rat's nest." He paused a moment, then said, "Say, I've been doing all the talking here. How's about telling me why our boy is being investigated?"

Jeff didn't hesitate. "We have reason to believe he beat a four-year-old child to death."

"Oh, shit!" Barry exclaimed.

"Yeah," Jeff agreed. "My sentiments exactly."

"Can you prove he did it?"

Jeff sighed. "All we've got right now is hearsay, but we're working on it."

Jeff looked over the notes he'd scrawled during his conversation with Barry and said, "I've talked to several of Brent's other teachers, and they all swear he walked on water. Why do you suppose you're the only one who saw his dark side?"

Barry considered for a moment before answering. "I think I was the only teacher in that whole damn school who ever challenged him. That's another reason I didn't fit in there. Almost all of my colleagues had spent their whole careers at Oakwood Junior High. They didn't want to make waves. If they had a smart student like Brent, they'd smile at him and pat him on the back and let him slough off all he wanted. I, on the other hand, was an outsider, a young upstart from the West Coast. I had no history with these kids. I didn't give a shit how brilliant they were, I expected each of them to put out one hundred percent effort. Brent clearly resented that. Maybe that's why I saw a side of him that no one else did."

"Did you ever discuss your problems with Brent with the other faculty members?"

"Nah," Barry said dismissively. "I didn't really get along very well with most of them. They thought I was a wild-eyed radical. Oakwood is a pretty conservative place. A lot of those people probably had pictures of Richard Nixon in their houses."

"Listen, would you be willing to come back here and testify at the trial? The county would pay your expenses."

"When would you need me?" Barry's tone was a bit wary.

"If things go according to plan, probably sometime this fall."

Barry hesitated a moment, then snorted. "Oh, what the hell. Why not? I consider it my civic duty to do whatever I can to protect society from the likes of Brent Tompkins."

"That's great," Jeff said enthusiastically. "Oh, just one more thing. Was it your idea to leave your job or were you let go?"

"I left voluntarily, but I'd pissed off so many people that I was only one step ahead of the sheriff."

"I really appreciate your help, man," Jeff said after giving Barry his address and phone number. "I'll be in touch." Smiling broadly, he eagerly reset the phone and immediately called Liz to tell her the good news.

Liz was skeptical of Jeff's sudden good fortune in locating Barry. "The man sounds too good to be true."

"What do you mean?" Jeff asked indignantly.

"I want you to go back to the school and check out his personnel file. You'd better make sure he's not hiding something. I don't want it to come out at trial that our key credibility witness was caught fondling little girls in the hallway."

Grumbling under his breath that Liz was a hard-ass, Jeff grudgingly agreed to give his new star witness a thorough background check.

As Liz hung up the phone, she found herself torn by conflicting emotions. She knew that Jeff's conversation with Barry probably marked a turning point in the case. Now that they had corroboration that Brent wasn't all lily-white, the case would proceed at warp speed. Jeff was going to pay another call on Greg Saunders in the morning, and if he could get Greg to crack, Brent could be in custody by tomorrow night. While Liz was elated that the prosecution of Jeremy's killer would finally get under way, deep down she knew this was going to be the most difficult case of her career.

She got up and went to the kitchen to get something to drink while she tried to sort out her thoughts. She took a can of diet soda out of the refrigerator, popped the top, and sat down at the kitchen table.

For starters, she knew Harry was not going to be pleased at this turn of events. While he had accepted her begging off from dinner with a modicum of grace, he had been clearly unhappy that Jeff was pushing to make the arrest as quickly as possible.

"You've got to take your time and make sure you're going to be able to prove your case," Harry had said. "You can't hang your hat on double hearsay."

"So you've said," Liz had replied. "Jeff seems to think that if he talks to Greg Saunders once more, he can get him to tell the truth."

"Dealing with juveniles is always a tricky situation," Harry had cautioned. "If you lean on them too hard, their lawyers will hollar harassment or coercion, and the next thing you know, some judge will have ruled that their confession is inadmissible.''

"Jeff is well aware of that," Liz had assured him.

"I must say you've certainly done an about-face with respect to Detective Gardner," Harry had said in a louder voice, shaking his head in wonder. "It seems like only yesterday you were telling me that you felt like strangling him, and now you're extolling his virtues."

"I misjudged him," Liz had said evenly. "He's a good detective, and he's one hundred percent committed to helping us get a conviction. I think the least we can do is give him some support."

"Just be careful, Liz," Harry had said in a quieter tone. "I know you handled some high-profile civil cases while you were at Harringan, but believe me, they were all pikers compared to this one." Liz had given him a wary look as he continued. "This is going to be the most high-profile case this county has ever seen. You probably thought Jeremy's murder generated a lot of publicity, but when you arrest an Oakwood teenager, all hell is gonna break loose. We're gonna have the press crawling all over this place, watching our every move. They're bound to pick up on the fact that you live in Oakwood, so you'd better get used to being asked a bunch of inane questions about how you feel about prosecuting a young boy who also happens to be your neighbor." He paused and looked her straight in the eye. "I don't know what your response would be to a question like that, but I'd strongly suggest you give it some serious thought before you find yourself cornered."

Liz took a drink of soda and pushed the can back and forth over the tabletop. She hadn't yet come up with a response. The truth was that as much as she wanted to secure a conviction of the person responsible for Jeremy's death, it did bother her that the killer was an affluent young man from the town in which she'd chosen to build a new life for herself. She hated to admit it, but she knew that if the evidence had supported it, she could have prosecuted a fourteen-year-old boy from Lakeview without feeling the slightest remorse. But the fact that Brent came from an upper-crust family altered the balance of the entire criminal process.

Liz walked over to the window and gazed out at the brilliant sunset. Though she had never articulated the notion before this, she now realized that one of the reasons she had been so enthusiastic about prosecuting this case was that it would give her the opportunity to do something positive for her newly adopted community. It seemed only fair that she, as an Oakwood resident, be the one to see to it that Jeremy Barker's killer was justly punished for what he did. But now, although she still firmly believed that Brent deserved punishment, she also knew the boy's prosecution might very well polarize the community, and she found that fact extremely troubling.

"It would have been so much easier if Frankie Snipes had been the killer," she murmured aloud. Then she caught herself and shook her head firmly. She had to stop thinking like that. That was bullshit. Lots of murderers came from good families in quiet little towns. That was no reason to go soft on Brent. She'd just have to keep reminding herself that she was a prosecutor first and an Oakwood resident second. It was her job to see that the state exacted its lawful revenge for Jeremy's murder. She clenched her jaw. It wasn't going to be easy, but damnit, she was determined to show everyone that Harry Washburn had picked the right person to handle the job.

Chapter 18

Jeff was awake a good portion of the night, trying to decide what tack to take with Greg Saunders. Questioning juveniles was always tough. If you talked to them out of the presence of their parents and they happened to confess to some foul deed, the parents would hire a hot shot attorney who'd swear up and down that the kid had been badgered into making a statement. If you questioned them with a parent on hand, mommy or daddy would almost inevitably shut the little darling's mouth before he could spill his guts. Either way it was a delicate operation.

Jeff knew his best chance for success lay in finding Greg home alone with his mother. Teresa Saunders had looked like a soft touch and, more important, she and Greg seemed to be close. Maybe if Jeff played on the mother's sympathies and didn't come on too strong, he might just get Greg to open up. At least it was worth a shot.

Jeff was up early the next morning. He took extra pains with his appearance, topping black slacks, a white shirt, and a red floral tie with a black and cream tweed jacket. He would never really look like he fit in with the Oakwood crowd, he thought ruefully as he straightened the tie, but at least maybe no one would mistake him for a shoe salesman.

He drove slowly, giving Mr. Saunders ample time to depart for another tough day in the BMW salt mines. It was nine-fifteen when he approached the house. All three garage doors were down. Had Saunders left or not? Jeff hesitated for a moment, then pulled into the driveway.

As he rang the bell, he heard the dog begin to bark, then footsteps rapidly approaching. Unless Saunders was walking on his tippytoes, they were not loud enough for a man. The door opened and Greg appeared, the family's furry dog close on his heels.

The boy looked even younger and more terrified than on the two previous occasions that Jeff had seen him, and his mouth gaped open when he saw the detective. "Good morning, Greg," Jeff said pleasantly. "How you doin' today?"

Greg merely ran his tongue nervously around his lips.

"Is your mom home?"

The boy shook his head. "N-no," he stammered. "I'm here alone."

Jeff debated his next move for a fraction of a second. Should he come back later or take a chance questioning the youth without an adult present? What the hell. He was here now. Might as well go for it.

"Would you mind if I came in for a minute?" Jeff asked smoothly. "I'd like to go over a couple of things with you."

Greg hesitated a moment, then turned and led Jeff to the kitchen, which was at the rear of the house. The detective took a seat in one of the black-lacquered chairs. Greg sat down at the opposite end of the table. The boy was dressed in a blue tank top and cutoffs. The dog sat down beside him, his nose tickling Greg's bare leg.

Jeff felt a twinge of regret for what he had to do next, but it quickly passed. Jeremy Barker's death had to be avenged, no matter what the consequences might be for this boy.

"It's like this," Jeff said, focusing his gaze squarely on the youth. "Since Ms. Stanfeld and I were here the other night, I've been talkin' to a whole bunch of your neighbors and—well—I'm happy to say that they've given me a couple of leads.''

Greg sat quietly, staring at the floor. He expressed no outward interest in this news.

''Those leads make me pretty darn sure that someone here in Oakwood saw something the day little Jeremy disappeared that he or she hasn't told us yet.'' Jeff paused and pretended to stare unconcernedly up at the ceiling. ''You know, this kind of thing happens all the time in murder investigations. People see something but are afraid to tell us about it. Can't say as I blame 'em much. Murderers are pretty scary people. But it's important for folks to remember that the only way to make sure the bad guys are put away where they can't do more harm is to come forward and tell us what they know.''

Jeff looked back at his audience and found that Greg was growing more agitated by the minute. He was still looking down at the floor and was also fidgeting with a loose piece of thread on the seam of his pants. Perhaps it was time for Jeff to turn up the heat a little.

''So, Greg, I'll bet you and Brent spent some time talkin' about the murder yesterday, didn't you?''

The boy continued to stare at the floor and mumbled something unintelligible.

''What was that?''

''Not really,'' Greg said in a tiny voice.

''No?'' Jeff said loudly. ''Why, I find that hard to believe. My two boys are constantly trying to outsmart me when it comes to solving cases. You sure you and Brent didn't jawbone about it just a little bit?''

The youth wet his lips again. ''Maybe a little,'' he admitted weakly.

''I thought so,'' Jeff said pleasantly. ''I know most of the boys your age that I've talked to have been real interested in the case. There sure are a lot of nice kids in this neighborhood.'' He paused a moment as though he were trying to recall their names. ''Let's see, there's Taylor Huff, Dillon Freeman, Josh Mahoney, Nate Johnson—"

At the mention of Nate's name, Greg involuntarily emitted a small yelp as though the dog had nipped him.

"Is something wrong, son?" Jeff asked with mock concern.

The boy bit his lip and gave his head a nervous shake.

"I don't know if I mentioned it the other night," Jeff went on in an even tone, "but little Jeremy was beaten over the head with a blunt object. Coulda been a piece of a tree limb or the flat part of an axe, something on that order. The coroner says the first blow more than likely killed the tyke, but whoever did it just kept beatin' on him till his skull was completely smashed in."

Jeff reached into his inside coat pocket and pulled out a small white envelope that contained some pictures. "Just take a look at this," he said, removing the top one. "Now you tell me. Isn't it a crying shame that something like that had to happen here in Oakwood?" He casually tossed the photo across the table.

The closeup of how Jeremy Barker's head had looked when he was pulled from his shallow grave seemed to have a spellbinding effect on Greg. He stared at it, then leaned forward to get a better look, then reached out a shaky hand as if he intended to pull it closer. Just as his fingers were about to make contact, his whole body snapped back and he began to tremble violently.

"It's a powerful picture, isn't it?" Jeff said in a low, even tone. "And seeing the body for real was even more powerful. I'll tell you, that's the kind of image that can stay with a guy for the rest of his life."

Greg crossed his arms in front of him in a futile effort to stop himself from shaking.

"You know, sometimes in cases like this I've gotten my best leads just by talkin' to people and finding out their theories on what might have happened," Jeff went on. "How about if you and I try that right now? Let's see. Where should we start?" He snapped his fingers. "I've got an idea. Why don't you tell me what you and Brent think might have happened to Jeremy. I'm sure you've given it some thought."

The boy was fighting hard to stay in control. He hugged himself tighter and mumbled something.

"What's that? You say you don't know what happened? Well nobody knows for sure, except the killer, of course. But let's just try to think this through. Let's pretend you were going to kidnap a little boy. How would you convince him to come along with you? Let's think." Jeff paused a moment, then slapped his hand on his knee. "I know. Maybe you could tell the kid you know where there are some horses and you could offer to take him to them. Do you suppose that would work?"

Greg began to bounce his right foot up and down.

"I'll bet that'd work real good. Little kids just love horses. Then after you've lured him into the woods with you, let's say the kid realizes you lied about the horses and starts to scream. What do you think your friend Brent might do if he were faced with a situation like that?"

The look of sheer terror on Greg's face made Jeff realize that he'd gone too far. If he pushed the boy any harder now, he'd surely be accused of harassment and any information he got wouldn't be admissible in court. He made a show of looking at his watch. "Damn. I'm gonna be late for an appointment. I'd better get going." He pushed back his chair and stood up. "Is your mom gonna be home later this morning?"

Greg gave a small nod.

"Good. I might just stop back to see her later. It's been nice talkin' to you." He briskly walked to the front door and let himself out. As he got in the car, he could see the boy furtively peeking out through the lace window curtain.

Jeff gritted his teeth as he started the engine. He was so close he could taste it. He wanted to go back in the house and throttle the truth out of that boy, but he knew the situation called for restraint. As he regretfully put the car in reverse and backed out of the driveway, he could still see the small face in the window.

Chapter 19

"Slow down," Liz scolded as she rushed to make notes during a phone call from Jeff an hour later. "Philip Barry's personnel file said what?"

"That he received a termination notice from the school board in March," Jeff replied bitterly. "The reasons given for non-renewal were insubordination and failure to comply with school policies. The son of a bitch lied to me! There goes his credibility, all shot to hell."

Jeff had gone to the school after leaving the Saunders residence, thinking he would be able to clear up at least one loose end in the case before again trying to break Greg down. Instead, he'd been slapped with yet another defeat.

"I hate to say I told you so," Liz said, "but I thought he sounded too good to be true."

"Does this mean we can't use him as a witness?"

"Well—" Liz hesitated. "Talk to Barry and find out his side of the story. I suppose it's possible there's some mistake. But if the records are correct, it's definitely not good for us to present a witness to impeach Brent's character who has bad character himself. We could probably still use him as a witness, but I think I'd want to hold him in reserve for use on rebuttal. He'll do a lot less damage that way." She paused a moment, then said, "I don't like to state the obvious, but this development makes it even more crucial that you get Greg to tell us what Brent told him."

"I'll get Greg to talk," Jeff growled. "If it's the last thing I do, I'll get him to talk."

"Well, you'd better take it easy with that kid," Liz cautioned. "It sounds like you're on shaky ground already. The next thing you know his parents are going to be suing the county for causing psychological damage to a minor."

"I know what I'm doing," Jeff said brashly.

"I hope so," Liz said, "because we're too close now to have things screwed up by your pigheadedness."

"I'll call you back as soon as I've got Greg's statement," Jeff retorted, slamming down the phone.

When Jeff rang the Saunderses' bell this time, it was Teresa who answered the door. She was dressed in white shorts and a T-shirt that read CANCUN. "Why, hello, Detective," she said cordially. "What can I do for you?" She was obviously blissfully unaware of his earlier visit.

"Hello, ma'am. I was wondering if I might have a word with you."

"Of course. Come in."

As Jeff followed her back to the kitchen, he asked, "Would Greg happen to be home?"

"Yes, he's upstairs," Teresa replied, turning to face him. "Would you like me to get him?"

"Yes, I would. The fact is, ma'am, I was here earlier this morning, talking to Greg. I guess he must not have mentioned it to you."

Teresa looked perplexed. "No, he didn't. Just a moment. I'll get him."

As Jeff sat at the kitchen table, he could hear her raised voice coming from upstairs. Not surprisingly, Greg wasn't eager to continue his discussion with the detective. After a few minutes the boy reluctantly entered the kitchen, his mother close behind.

Mother and son took seats next to each other, across the table from Jeff. Jeff could see that the boy's face was flushed and his eyes were red. It was obvious he'd been crying.

Teresa, too, had clearly noticed her son's distress. "What's this all about, Detective?" she asked, an edge to her voice now. "You said you were here earlier."

Jeff nodded. "Yes, ma'am, I was." He pursed his lips, then plunged ahead, deciding perhaps it was time for some honesty on his part. "You see, we have reason to believe that Greg has some information about Jeremy Barker's murder."

"That's absurd," Teresa said. "Greg doesn't know anything about that child's death."

"I'd like to hear that from Greg," Jeff replied quietly.

Teresa frowned, but was beginning to look nervous. "All right," she said anxiously as she turned to her son. "Greg, please tell the detective you don't know anything about that little boy."

As he'd done earlier, Greg stared at the floor. "Please, son," Jeff said softly. "I think you'd feel a lot better if you told me what you know."

The boy remained silent.

"Please," Jeff urged. "We know Brent formed a plan to kidnap Jeremy. Did he tell you why he wanted to do that?"

Teresa put a hand on her son's arm. "Greg, do you know something about this?"

After a long period of silence, Greg nodded and said haltingly, "Brent said he wanted to get even with Tom Barker for calling him a bastard one time when Brent went on his property."

Jeff leaned forward eagerly. "He thought if he pretended to kidnap Jeremy, it'd even the score with Barker?"

"I guess so."

"So Brent came up with the idea of luring Jeremy out of yard with the story about the horses?"

Greg nodded again.

"Had Brent been watching the house from the woods that day?"

Another nod.

"What went wrong when Brent got Jeremy into the woods that made him start hitting him?"

Greg's face contorted and he began to sob. Teresa immediately moved closer and put her arms around her son. "I think that's enough questions," she said.

Jeff ignored her. "What happened, Greg? What went wrong?"

"I couldn't stop him," Greg blurted out. "It happened so fast. All of a sudden he just started hitting him."

Teresa gasped in horror, and Jeff felt a chill run down his spine. The detective took a deep breath. "You were there, weren't you?" he asked quietly. "You saw the whole thing."

Greg gave another nod and then buried his face in his mother's shoulder.

"That's enough," Teresa said in a louder voice. "Don't you think maybe we should talk to an attorney?"

"Please," Jeff implored her, "let the boy finish. It'll be to his benefit, I promise." When Teresa made no response, Jeff pressed on. "Were you with Brent during the whole incident?"

Greg sniffed and nodded.

"Did you play any role in luring Jeremy out of the yard?"

Another nod.

"Can you tell me about it?"

In a small voice, Greg said, "Brent called me that morning and said I should meet him in the woods. When I got there, he told me what he was gonna do."

"You knew nothing about the plan before?"

Greg shook his head. "I thought it was a joke, so I said I'd help."

"What were you supposed to do?"

Greg wiped his eyes with his sleeve. "Get Jeremy from the yard into the woods."

"Why couldn't Brent do this himself? Why did he need you?"

"Brent said I looked more like a kid and Jeremy wouldn't be so afraid of me."

"How did you accomplish it?"

Greg swallowed hard. "We saw the UPS truck coming up the street and Brent told me to get ready. As soon as the nanny walked into the house, I ran down into the yard."

"Wasn't Jeremy afraid of you?"

Greg shook his head. "He was surprised to see me at first, but as soon as I told him about the horses he got real excited and ran right back to the woods with me."

"What happened when Jeremy saw Brent?"

"He said, 'Who's that?' and I told him Brent was the guy who was gonna take us to the horses."

"Then what happened?"

"Brent had told me which direction to go, so I took Jeremy by the hand and started walking." The boy suddenly broke off his narrative.

"And then?"

Greg closed his eyes.

"Please, son. Tell me what happened."

Greg's answer came in a voice so low that Jeff had to strain to hear it. "The next thing I knew, Brent had hit Jeremy over the head with a shovel."

Teresa Saunders gasped, and she turned so pale that for a moment Jeff thought she might faint. Greg opened his eyes and stared at the wall in front of him. He licked his lips as though he was parched.

"Where did Brent get the shovel?" Jeff asked.

"I don't know. He musta had it hid there someplace."

"What happened then?"

"Jeremy fell down and was out cold." The boy was

breathing hard now, as he recalled what had happened.

"What did you do then?" Jeff prompted.

"I hollered, 'Hey, what are you doing?' but Brent didn't answer me. He just kept hitting him over and over." Greg put his hands over his eyes. His mother held him tightly.

"What were you doing during this time?"

"Just standing there. I felt like I weighed a thousand pounds and I couldn't move my legs."

"What did Brent do then?"

Greg swallowed hard. "He took a plastic bag out of his pocket and put it over Jeremy's head."

"Why did he do that?"

"There was a lot of blood and he didn't want to get any on him. He handed me the shovel and made me carry it."

"And then?"

"He picked Jeremy up and started walking deeper into the woods."

"How did he know when to stop?"

"He must've picked out the spot earlier, 'cause he walked fast like he knew right where he was going." Another long pause.

"We're almost done, son," Jeff said. "You're doin' great. What happened then?"

"All of a sudden he dropped Jeremy on the ground and said, 'gimme the shovel.' I gave it to him and he dug a hole. He took the bag off Jeremy's head and put it inside another bag he had with him and stuck the whole wad in his pocket. Then he rolled the body into the hole and covered it up with dirt and brush."

"Did you see him do anything else?"

Greg nodded again. "He took a pair of men's glasses out of his pocket and tossed them into the woods. He said 'That's a clue to help the police find the killer.' "

"Did he say where he got the glasses?"

"He took 'em off a table at the McDonald's in Lakeview."

"Did he know whose they were?"

Greg shook his head. "No. He just told me it was some lowlife that belonged in jail."

"Son, did Brent say anything to you before you left the woods that day?"

There was yet another long pause before the boy nodded again. "Yeah. He said if I ever told anybody what had happened, he'd kill me, too."

Teresa Saunders cried out and clutched her son even tighter.

Jeff took a deep breath, then exhaled loudly. "Thank you so much, Greg. I know how hard this was for you, but what you did today was very, very brave." He stood up. "I'll leave you two alone now."

He was halfway to the front door when Teresa Saunders caught up with him. She put her hand on his arm. "What's going to happen to him? You promised it'd be in his best interests to talk to you. What are you going to do now?" she asked in a hoarse whisper as she anxiously searched Jeff's face for some assurance that this nightmare was not going to ruin her son's life.

Unfortunately, Jeff could make no such promises. "I'll be back within a couple of hours. In the meantime, I'd appreciate it if you and Greg didn't leave the house and if you didn't have any contact with anyone in the Tompkins family."

Teresa made an anguished, keening sound and let go of Jeff's arm.

"I'm truly sorry," Jeff said. "Are you going to be all right?"

Mrs. Saunders made no reply. As Jeff watched the tears run down her face, he found himself with a lump in his throat, and he quickly turned and saw himself out.

Chapter 20

"Why the hell is it taking so long to get those petitions finalized?" Jeff asked crossly as he paced back and forth in front of Liz's desk. Forty-five minutes had passed since he'd left the Saunders residence, and he was nervous as a cat. Every minute that ticked by seemed like an hour. He wouldn't be able to relax until both Brent and Greg were safely in custody.

"They'll be ready in a minute," Liz said grimly. Greg's involvement in the crime had hit her hard. It had been bad enough to think Brent had killed Jeremy. The realization that a second youth had been involved, albeit unwillingly, was devastating.

"Sorry," Jeff said, pausing by the window. "I'm just anxious to get this show on the road."

"We're all anxious," Harry Washburn, who was standing by the door, agreed. "Let's go over the Saunders boy's confession one more time," he said to Jeff in a voice heavily laced with concern. "I have to tell you I'm still afraid that the Saunderses' attorneys might be able to get it thrown out."

"On what basis?" Jeff asked with mock patience.

"You didn't read him his rights—" Harry began.

"It wasn't a custodial interrogation," Jeff cut in. "It was a nice little chat around the kitchen table between me, Greg, and his mom. Greg could've gotten up and left the room or his mother could've ordered me out of the house at any time. No judge is gonna throw the confession out for failure to Mirandize."

"The mother asked for a lawyer," Liz said quietly.

"She did not ask for a lawyer," Jeff protested. "She said, 'Don't you think maybe we should talk to an attorney?'"

"And you didn't answer her," Liz pointed out. "You just bulled ahead with the interrogation."

"I didn't have to answer her. According to the most recent Supreme Court case, her comment did not constitute a request for counsel."

"Well, I'd feel a lot better about it if you'd had him sign a statement," Harry put in.

"Jesus! Whose side are you on here?" Jeff shouted. He could feel himself turning red in the face. "There's no damn way Mrs. Saunders would've allowed the kid to sign anything. Once Greg started spilling the beans, things happened pretty fast. But you can bet your sweet ass if I'd whipped out a pen and paper and said to Greg, 'Hey kid, not so fast. I need to write down this confession you're making and when I'm finished you'll have to sign it in triplicate and initial each page,' the mother would've snapped to her senses and called in the militia."

Jeff paused to catch his breath. He ran his hand through his hair and said, "Believe me, I was just praying the kid would spit the whole story out as fast as he could while the mother was still trying to figure out what the hell was happening."

"I still would feel more comfortable if we had something in writing." Harry persisted. "Especially since their attorneys may agree that you unfairly badgered the boy by speaking to him outside the presence of his parents and you also appealed to his prurient interests by showing him that photo of Jeremy."

"Look!" Jeff exclaimed. "He confessed of his own free will. There was no coercion. I guarantee there'll be no problem getting the statement into evidence."

"He's probably right, Harry," Liz admitted.

"Thank you," Jeff said, giving her a curt nod.

"Very well," Harry said grudgingly. "But I still don't like it."

There was a knock at the door. "Come in," Liz called.

A young secretary entered. "Here they are," she said, handing each of them a set of documents.

"Thanks, Mary," Liz said.

Moments later the three of them were eagerly scanning the papers. Jeff read aloud as Liz and Harry followed along on their copies.

Summons and Petition for Determination of Status—Alleged Delinquent Child.

In the interest of Brent Tompkins, a person under the age of 18.

TO THE CIRCUIT COURT OF HORICON COUNTY, CHILDREN'S DIVISION:

Elizabeth A. Stanfield, an assistant district attorney for Horicon County, hereby states on information and belief that the child named above is delinquent in the community in that:

COUNT 1: KIDNAPPING

On June 11 of this year, in the Town of Oakwood, Horicon County, Wisconsin, Brent Tompkins did, as a party to a crime, by deceit induce Jeremy Barker, age four, to go from one place to another with intent to cause him to be secretly confined or imprisoned against his will, contrary to Wisconsin Statutes sections 940.31(1)(c) and 939.05.

COUNT 2: FIRST-DEGREE INTENTIONAL HOMICIDE BY USE OF DANGEROUS WEAPON

On June 11 of this year, in the Town of Oakwood, Horicon County, Wisconsin, Brent Tompkins, with intent to kill, did, as a party to a crime, kill Jeremy Barker by use of a dangerous weapon, contrary to Wisconsin Statutes 940.01(1), 939.63, and 939.05.

An identical petition had been prepared for Greg Saunders.

"Is there really any merit in adding the enhancer for using 'a dangerous weapon'?" Harry cut in. "After all, young Tompkins didn't use a gun or a knife. It just strikes me as being overkill."

"Hell, no, it's not overkill," Jeff protested. "We need to show 'em that we mean business, and the best way to do that is to hit them with everything we've got. If picking your nose was a crime, I'd charge them with that, too."

"I agree with Jeff," Liz spoke up. "The statute doesn't limit 'dangerous weapons' to knives and guns. The metal part of a shovel certainly qualifies, particularly when it's used to hit a four-year-old over the head."

"All right, all right," Harry said grudgingly. "Leave it in."

"Thank you, Liz," Jeff said, smiling smugly. "I'm glad you agree with me."

"I agree with you on that point," Liz said, "but I'm having second thoughts about charging Greg with first-degree murder. I believe him when he said he didn't know what Brent had in mind when he agreed to help lure Jeremy into the woods."

"Jesus Christ!" Jeff exploded, throwing up his hands in exasperation. "Are you two ever a couple of pansies!" He began to pace back and forth in the small office. "A four-year-old boy was murdered in cold blood. What do I have to do to convince you guys that this is serious business? *We* should be the ones locked up if we don't charge them both with first degree." He took a deep breath and continued in a calmer voice, "There'll be plenty of time for plea-bargaining Greg's charges down later—that is, provided his parents agree that he should testify against Brent. But if you start out with a two-bit charge, you won't have any leverage to get Greg to cooperate."

"There's no need to get hostile," Harry said, tossing his copy of the documents on Liz's desk and settling into a chair. "These look all right," he said grudgingly. "I guess we're ready to move."

"I'll run upstairs and get them filed and get a judge to sign the arrest warrants," Liz said, heading for the door. "And I'll see if I can set up the boys' initial

appearance for tomorrow morning." She smiled ruefully. "Whoever's assigned to this thing is gonna love
having to come to work on a Saturday."

Jeff frowned. "What's the hurry? The rule that you
have to hold a custody hearing for juveniles within
twenty-four hours of their arrest doesn't apply on
weekends. We don't need to do anything until Monday. Personally, I think a weekend in the slammer
would do those boys a world of good."

There was a moment of awkward silence, then Liz
said, "Harry and I decided it'd be best to hold the
hearing as quickly as possible. It puts the burden on
them to hire counsel and come up with an initial strategy overnight. That could work to our advantage."

"Shit!" Jeff grumbled. "Well, then, what about the
petition asking that Brent be waived into adult court?
Why not drop that on him tomorrow at the hearing?
Might throw a little chill into him."

"I think we've got enough to worry about for
today," Liz replied. "We'll tackle the waiver petition
next week."

"We'd better think long and hard before we make
that move," Harry said, his face tightening with
concern.

"What do you mean?" Jeff asked in astonishment.
"The little bastard is fourteen. The law says he deserves to be tried as an adult."

"No one in this county has ever been waived into
adult court at that age," Harry replied.

"No fourteen-year-old in the history of this county
has ever committed murder," Jeff shot back.

"Will you two stop it!" Liz exhorted, her hand on
the doorknob. Her head was pounding, and she fervently wished this day were over. "I'll be right back.
Try not to get into a brawl while I'm gone."

While they waited for Liz to return, Harry sat impassively in his chair, staring at the wall, while Jeff
continued to pace. Christ, that Washburn was a tight-
ass, Jeff thought contemptuously. What the hell could

Liz possibly see in him? He hoped to God that Washburn didn't try to take control of the case. At least Liz would listen to reason—most of the time, that is.

Moments later, Liz breezed back into the office. "Good news," she said, handing the papers to Jeff. "The custody hearing is scheduled for ten o'clock tomorrow morning. We drew Judge Franchetta. I think she'll be sympathetic to our way of thinking."

"Great," Jeff said, heading for the door. "I'm on my way."

"Hey," Harry called after him. "You *are* planning on calling young Tomkins's parents before you swoop in and pick the kid up?"

Jeff swung around again. "Why the hell would I want to do that?" he asked incredulously. "That'd be an invitation for them to clear out of town. I might as well call the airport and charter a plane for them."

"This is an extraordinary case," Harry said quietly but firmly. "We're dealing with respectable families here, and I think we owe the parents a courtesy call."

"Shit!" Jeff spat again.

Liz nodded. "Do it," she said.

Jeff gritted his teeth. "All right, I'll do it," he said to Harry bitterly. "But if I get to Oakwood and find that the little birdie has flown the coop, Jeremy's blood will be on your hands!"

Chapter 21

Jeff placed the call to Martin Tompkins from one of the two squad cars dispatched to take the boys into custody. He waited until they were halfway to Oakwood before making the call. He'd be a good boy and follow the DA's instructions to notify Tompkins that an arrest was imminent, but nobody had told him he had to make contact in time for Daddy to get home to try to obstruct Junior's arrest.

Jeff had already alerted jail personnel to prepare two cells for the new arrivals. State law preferred that juvenile offenders be housed in a facility separate from that of adult criminals. Horicon County had no separate secure detention for juveniles, so the law allowed holding children in jail, so long as they were kept separate from the adult offenders and had adequate round-the-clock supervision.

Jeff's phone call to the Chosey Gallery was answered by a haughty-sounding woman with a pinched, nasal tone. "Martin Tompkins, please," Jeff barked. "This is Detective Jeff Gardner. I'm with the sheriff's department. He'll remember me. I was at his house a couple nights ago."

"I'm sorry, sir," the woman replied in an aristocratic tone, "but Mr. Tompkins is with an artist and can't be disturbed."

"I don't care if he's with Leonardo da Vinci," Jeff snapped back. "Get him to the damn phone. Tell him it's about his son."

A moment later Tompkins's concerned voice came

over the line. "What's this about, Detective? Did something happen to Brent?"

Teresa Saunders must have heeded his counsel not to tip off the Tompkinses, Jeff thought with satisfaction. Good for her. "No, but something's about to happen," Jeff replied. "I'm in a squad car on my way to your house to take Brent into custody."

"For what?" Tompkins exclaimed.

"For the first-degree intentional homicide of Jeremy Barker," Jeff said coolly. "In case you'd like to be on hand for the occasion, we should be there in about ten minutes." He disconnected the call before Tompkins had the opportunity to retort.

Old Marty must have really put the pedal to the metal, Jeff mused, as the squad pulled into the Tompkins' driveway. A brown Mercedes was already parked in front of the garage. Jeff and the two uniformed officers with him walked briskly up to the front door. Jeff rang the bell.

Moments later the door was opened by the scowling patriarch of the family. "What is the meaning of this?" Tompkins demanded. "This is an outrage!"

"No, sir," Jeff replied calmly, handing the man a copy of the warrant and delinquency petition. "This is an arrest." He peered inside and spied Brent down the hallway. "There he is," he said to the uniformed officers.

Pushing their way past the elder Tompkins, the three officers marched inside. They stopped about three feet from where Brent was standing unconcerned, his arms crossed in front of him. The youth was wearing white shorts and a red T-shirt. "Brent," Jeff said, staring the youth in the face, "you are under arrest for the kidnapping and first-degree murder of Jeremy Barker. Officer Skilton will now advise you of your rights."

One of the uniforms stepped forward. "You have the right to remain silent . . ." As the young deputy quickly went through the litany of Miranda warnings,

Brent continued to stare at Jeff, his face devoid of expression, while his father stood nearby, shouting, "You'll be hearing from my lawyer. . . . I hope the county has its insurance coverage up-to-date, because I intend to sue for false arrest." No one paid him any mind.

As Officer Skilton put his hand on Brent's arm and guided him toward the front door, the boy turned back and gave Jeff a defiant "fuck you" glance. Jeff had to take a deep breath to resist the impulse to rush after the kid and punch his lights out.

It wasn't until Brent was out the door that Jeff noticed the array of suitcases stacked in the living room. "Someone planning a trip?" he asked Tompkins *père*.

"Yes, my wife and the children were planning to leave for Cape Cod tomorrow," Tompkins snapped, "until you swooped in here like the Gestapo and took my son away. Where are they taking him?"

"To the sheriff's department," Jeff replied, thanking his lucky stars they hadn't delayed a day in making the arrest. "You'll have to drive down in your own vehicle. It'll take about an hour to process him, but you'll be able to see him after that." He motioned toward the papers Tompkins was still clutching in his hand. "You'll notice it says in there that there's a hearing scheduled for ten tomorrow morning. At that time the judge will decide whether to keep Brent in custody. I guess I'll probably see you then." He turned and left the house, leaving Tompkins standing there open-mouthed.

As the squad car carrying Brent pulled out of the drive, a second squad car took its place. Jeff climbed in the front seat of that vehicle and directed the officer driving how to reach the Saunders house.

Teresa Saunders had evidently called her husband, since he was the one who opened the door. As Jeff and the other officer stepped inside, Jeff saw Teresa and Greg sitting close together on the wicker chaise in the sunroom. Greg had changed his clothes and was now wearing tan pants and a blue shirt. Teresa had her arm around the boy's shoulders. It was obvious they had both been crying.

"It's time to go, Greg," Jeff said gently.

Teresa's jaw trembled, and she looked up at Jeff with eyes that reminded him of a frightened deer. She and Greg both shakily got to their feet.

"Where are you taking him?" Mr. Saunders asked.

"To the sheriff's department," Jeff replied. He repeated what he'd told Tompkins about allowing an hour for processing and about the hearing the following morning.

"Don't worry," Jeff said to the anguished parents. "We'll take real good care of him. I'll see to it myself." He took Greg by the hand and led him out to the car.

Liz sat at her desk, clutching the phone receiver tightly as she waited for Tom Barker's secretary to pull him out of a meeting so she could tell him about the arrests.

"Liz, what is it?" Tom sounded breathless, as though he had sprinted back to his office to take the call. "Have you had a break in the case?"

"As a matter of fact, we have. Detective Gardner is in the process of arresting two people right now."

"Two!" Tom exclaimed. "Who are they?"

"One is the fourteen-year-old boy I mentioned to you the other day." She paused a moment before adding, "And the other is a thirteen-year-old accomplice."

"What are their names?"

"Brent Tompkins and Greg Saunders."

"Jesus! I know the Tompkins family. They live just down the street." Liz heard him take a deep breath, then exhale heavily. "What happens next?"

"There will be an initial appearance tomorrow morning."

"What time should I be there?"

"The judge hasn't set the exact time yet. I'll call

you later to discuss the logistics. I just wanted to tell you about the arrests before word gets out to the media."

"I appreciate that. I'll tell my secretary to put you through immediately whenever you call back. I want to be kept up-up-date on everything, down to the smallest detail."

"Will do," Liz promised.

"I don't know how to thank you," Tom said in a voice choked with emotion. "This is a fantastic development. I was beginning to doubt the case would ever be solved, but there's going to be justice for Jeremy after all."

Liz hung up the phone and sat quietly at her desk, waves of conflicting emotions washing over her. She knew she should be happy the killers had been arrested. But the task of prosecuting not one but two young teens from her hometown for murder both saddened and revolted her. And as an image of Greg Saunders and his mother flashed through her mind, a single tear ran down Liz's cheek.

Chapter 22

Shortly before ten the next morning, Liz sipped a glass of ice water and looked around her at the cast of characters assembled in Judge Franchetta's courtroom for the hearing to decide whether Brent and Greg should remain in custody pending further proceedings in the case. Considering the fact that this would be her first murder prosecution, Liz felt surprisingly calm. She fully expected the judge to release both boys into their parents' custody, so she viewed this hearing as the perfect opportunity to size up her adversaries and see them in action.

Knowing that she would be facing a couple of high-rolling attorneys from the city, Liz had dressed up. Happily she had lost two pounds in the last two days, so the waist on her royal blue linen dress was only a smidgeon too snug, and with the long matching jacket no one would ever notice.

The Tompkins and Saunders families had wasted no time procuring the best defense attorneys money could buy. To represent Brent, the Tompkinses had hired Paul Versey, the fifty-five-year-old founding partner of Versey, Stiglitz, and Rosenberg, Milwaukee's premier criminal defense firm. Although Liz had never met the man personally, she had seen his shining countenance on television numerous times and witnessed his wild shouting and gesticulating as he proclaimed his client's innocence and decried the underhanded tactics of the police and the DA's office.

Versey was tall and stocky, with a ruddy face and

a bulbous nose. He would have been bald if it weren't for the fact that he let his sparse fringe of hair grow and then carefully combed it over his naked pate and secured it in place with a liberal dose of hair spray. The resulting effect looked more like a spiderweb than a head of hair. He always wore hand-tailored suits in dark colors—black, navy, or pinstripe—perhaps in a futile attempt to minimize his bulk. The color du jour was navy. A navy and red paisley tie and matching pocket square completed his ensemble.

The Saunderses had chosen a more low-key attorney to represent Greg. Charles Bennett was in his late forties, of medium height and build, with dark hair just starting to turn gray and a neatly clipped moustache. He wore a light brown summerweight suit. Both he and Versey were accompanied by a young, eager-looking associate.

Liz knew that in their initial meetings, the attorneys would have advised each of their new clients not to have any contact with the other child's family, and the schism between the two groups was already visible. The Tompkins team was huddled together in one corner of the courtroom, with Versey, the quarterback, at the center, calling their next play. In the opposite corner Teresa and Martin Saunders sat close together, holding hands, as Bennett spoke to them quietly.

The prosecution's team would consist of just Liz and Jeff. Harry had asked Liz if there was any reason for him to attend the hearing, and he had seemed very relieved when she said no. Tom Barker had wanted to attend, but Liz talked him out of it.

In a phone conversation late the previous afternoon, Tom had pleaded with her to let him come to the hearing. "Can't you understand? It's important that I be there every step of the way so I feel like I'm a part of the whole process. Please don't shut me out!"

"You're going to be such an important witness that I want to hold you in reserve," she'd explained. "At the trial you're going to testify very eloquently about

Jeremy: what a wonderful boy he was, how much he meant to you. What's going to make your story all the more touching is the pain and outrage you're going to feel when you confront those two boys face-to-face. It's also going to shake them up to have to see you. If you start coming to hearings at this early stage, you'll get accustomed to seeing each other and the shock factor will be gone. I know it must seem heartless, but trust me, it's for the best."

Tom had reluctantly agreed but had insisted that Liz allow him to wait in her office so he would be able to get a full report the moment the judge had ruled. She'd had to sneak him in via a back stairway because the courthouse was swarming with press. After the arrests Harry had issued a terse statement saying that two juveniles had been taken into custody in connection with the Barker slaying. Newspeople had converged on the building minutes later, and some had remained camped out there all night. Juvenile proceedings were closed to the public, but the persistent media folk peppered everyone who so much as walked by with questions, hoping someone might let some tidbit slip.

At five minutes to ten the Tompkins and Saunders entourages took their seats. At three minutes to, Jeff breezed into the courtroom, sat down next to Liz, and poured himself a glass of water. "Where were you?" Liz asked in a low voice. "I was beginning to think you weren't coming."

"I was down at the jail, making sure all of the paperwork was up-to-date," he replied, taking a sip of water. "In a case like this we've got to be sure to dot every *i*."

"How did the kids enjoy their stay in the slammer?"

"Apparently Greg cried most of the night. Brent read a book, ate a big dinner, and was asleep by nine-thirty." Jeff shook his head. "I'm convinced that kid's the real Rosemary's baby."

"Did your search turn up anything?" she asked. The

previous evening, Jeff had executed a search warrant for Brent's room, hoping to find some evidence of the crime.

"Nada," Jeff shook his head ruefully. " 'Course I really didn't expect to find a bloody shovel under his bed. The kid's got quite the setup. His own computer and color laser printer, a home theater–size TV and VCR, and a stereo system that my boys would say is 'to die for.' "

"He'd better enjoy that stuff while he can," Liz murmured. "He's going to have quite a culture shock once he gets to a correctional institution."

"Now you're talkin'!" Jeff said enthusiastically.

Liz took one last sip of water and shifted in her seat.

At ten o'clock sharp the judge entered the courtroom through a rear door. Louise Franchetta, Horicon County's only female judge, was an imposing figure, six feet tall and rawboned. If she were to dress in men's clothing she could easily pass for a linebacker. She was in her late forties, wore her light brown hair cropped short, and used little makeup. Her entire being exuded an attitude of self-confidence. One look at her, and it was obvious the lady tolerated no bullshit in her courtroom. Liz liked Franchetta a lot and was happy she'd drawn this assignment.

"All rise," the bailiff commanded. Everyone in the courtroom obediently got to their feet. "The Circuit Court for Horicon County, Wisconsin, Judge Louise Franchetta presiding, is now in session. Your silence is commanded."

"You may be seated," the judge boomed in a deep voice. "This is a custody hearing in two juvenile matters: *In the Interest of Brent Tompkins* and *In the Interest of Gregory Saunders.*" She nodded to the bailiff. "Would you bring the boys in, please."

Moments later, the bailiff led the two boys into the room. Two uniformed deputies followed close behind. Liz could hear both sets of parents draw in their breath sharply as their offspring came into view. Both youths looked as if they were dressed for a formal occasion. Greg wore black slacks, a white shirt and floral tie, and a tweed sport coat, while Brent, in his gray pinstripe suit, looked like he'd stepped out of the pages of *GQ*. The night in jail obviously hadn't agreed with Greg—he walked with a shuffling gait, his head down. Brent, on the other hand, walk with a spring in his step and breezily looked around the room as if he didn't have a care in the world. I'm going to see him locked up if it's the last thing I do, Liz thought grimly, clenching her teeth.

When the boys had been seated next to their respective attorneys, Judge Franchetta called for the appearances.

Liz got to her feet. "Assistant District Attorney Liz Stanfeld for the prosecution, your honor."

Versey made a show of slowly pushing back his chair and rising like a king from his throne. "If it please the court, my name is Paul Versey of the firm of Versey, Stiglitz, and Rosenberg. I am appearing on behalf of Brent Tompkins. My co-counsel," he said, gesturing magnanimously toward the bespectacled young man sitting next to him, "is Joseph Untermeier."

"Thank you, Mr. Versey. It's a pleasure to have you with us," the judge said with what seemed to Liz just a hint of sarcasm She nodded at Bennett. "And for the other juvenile—"

"Charles Bennett and Bruce Hayward, representing Greg Saunders, Your Honor."

"Very well." The judge referred to some notes, then addressed the boys and their counsel. "Brent, Greg, before we begin the custody hearing, I am required to advise you and your parents of the allegations that have been made against you. You have both been charged with kidnapping and first-degree intentional homicide by use of a dangerous weapon. You both have the right to counsel, regardless of your ability to pay. You have the right to remain silent, and you have the right to confront, cross-examine, and present witnesses on your own behalf."

The judge paused and flipped through the papers in front of her. Turning to Brent, she went on, "Brent, in view of the fact that you are fourteen years of age, the state is entitled to ask that you be waived to adult court. If you are waived, you will be tried as an adult and will be subject to the adult penalties for the charges, which in this case would be twenty years in prison for the kidnapping charge, life in prison for the charge of first-degree intentional homicide, and an additional five years in prison for the use of a dangerous weapon." She turned to Liz. "We will now proceed with the custody hearing. Ms. Stanfeld, you have the floor."

"Thank you, Your Honor," Liz said, standing up again. "I would like to call Detective Captain Jeff Gardner to the stand."

Before Jeff could even get out of his seat, both Versey and Bennett were shouting objections.

"Don't you think you're being a bit premature, gentlemen?" the judge asked caustically. "The witness hasn't been sworn in yet. What seems to be your problem?"

Bennett beat Versey to the punch. "Your Honor, to the extent Detective Gardner will be recounting an alleged conversation he had with Greg Saunders, we object on the ground of hearsay."

"Overruled," the judge said immediately. She looked at them sternly. "Gentlemen, although neither of you has been in my court before, your reputations have preceded you. Surely experienced counsel such as yourselves are well aware that the rules of evidence are not binding at hearings such as this. I am bound to admit all testimony having reasonable probative value, and that includes hearsay evidence, so long as it has demonstrable circumstantial guarantees of trustworthiness. Now having heard that, does either of you have any other objections at this point?"

Both counsel meekly murmured, "No."

"Good," the judge replied. "In that case, perhaps we can have Detective Gardner sworn in."

Liz quickly had Jeff describe his background with the department and his role in heading the search for Jeremy Barker's killer. She then led him to Greg's confession.

"Objection!" Versey bounced up again like a huge cork. "Relevance. This is a custody hearing. The pertinent inquiry here is whether there is a valid reason to keep these boys incarcerated. There is no need to get into the merits of the case at this point."

"This line of questioning *is* relevant," Liz replied. "It tends to show that there is a reasonable basis for the serious allegations against the boys, thus demonstrating that they have an incentive to run away rather than stay and face the consequences of their acts."

"The objection is overruled," the judge said. "Let's move on."

As Jeff described his previous day's visit to the Saunders home, Greg sat motionless, staring down at his lap. Brent, on the other hand, stared Jeff directly in the eye.

"And then what did Greg say?" Liz prompted as Jeff reached the part of his narrative where little Jeremy had been lured into the woods.

"He said, the next thing he knew Brent had hit Jeremy over the head with a shovel. Jeremy fell down on the ground and Brent kept hitting him, over and over."

Liz could hear a gasp coming from the area where Brent's mother was sitting. She casually glanced at the two boys. Greg's head dropped even lower, and he appeared to be crying. Brent turned and glared at Greg, his eyes dark and menacing. Liz had Jeff summarize the rest of Greg's statement. "Thank you," she said. "I have no further questions."

Both defense attorneys declined the opportunity to

cross-examine Jeff. "Thank you, Detective," the judge said. "You may step down."

Bennett and Versey each put their respective client's fathers on the stand to discuss their status as upstanding citizens, their long-standing ties to the community, and the substantial amount of assets they would be willing to pledge as bail in order to have their boys released from custody.

The judge then called on Liz to make a brief closing statement. "Given the serious nature of the crimes with which these boys have been charged," Liz said, "once they are given their freedom, the call of the open road may become all too appealing. For that reason, the state requests that they remain in secure custody. In the alternative, Your Honor, if the boys are released, we would ask that bail be set in the among of five hundred thousand dollars."

After Bennett and Versey had reiterated their clients' testimony, Judge Franchetta announced her ruling. "The law favors releasing juveniles from custody whenever feasible. Even so, I see some problems doing that here. As Ms. Stanfeld aptly pointed out, these boys are charged with crimes of a most serious nature, and I must admit that I feel some trepidation about releasing them into the community."

The judge shifted in her chair and continued. "That said, I am somewhat reluctantly going to take the parents at their word that they will be able to control these two young men and keep them from absconding. It is the order of this court that Brent Tompkins and Greg Saunders be released into their parents' custody forthwith, upon the posting of five hundred thousand dollars bail for each boy. Their release is conditioned on the fact that they not travel further than a one-hundred-mile radius of their homes during the pendency of this action and that they have no contact with the Barker family." While sighs of joyous relief could be heard coming from the Saunders corner,

Versey and the Tompkinses seemed less pleased with the ruling.

"If I might have a word, Your Honor," Versey said, getting to his feet.

"Yes, Mr. Versey," Judge Franchetta replied tersely. "What is it? Are you unhappy with the amount of bail?"

"No, Your Honor," Versey replied. "Not at all. It is the condition that my client not travel further than one hundred miles from home that we find troubling. You see, each summer my client and his family visit an aged grandparent in Massachusetts. We would respectfully request that Brent be given permission to leave the state for two weeks for that purpose."

"Your request is denied," the judge said immediately, her eyes flashing. "My ruling stands. I would suggest that this might be a good year for the aged grandparent to visit Wisconsin."

Versey nodded and sat down. He was clearly pouting.

The judge went on. "I strongly caution Brent, Greg, and their parents of the dire consequences they will face—in the form of criminal charges—if these boys are so much as five minutes late for any scheduled court appearances. Oh, and while I'm admonishing people, just one more thing," she said sternly. "As you all know, juvenile matters are not public, and we must all do whatever we can to ensure that the privacy of the children who come before this court and that of their families is protected. Anyone who divulges any information that would identify either of these boys or their families will be subject to contempt of court." Banging her gavel on the bench, she said, "Court is adjourned."

Brent and Greg were immediately enveloped in the arms of their parents. Jeff turned to Liz and shrugged. "You called this one right," he said ruefully. "I don't like having them on the loose, but I guess there's not much we can do."

Liz leaned over and patted him on the arm. "What I need you to do is get me some more dirt on Brent," she said in a low voice. "We still need a motive."

"If it's out there, I'll find it," Jeff assured her as he pushed back his chair. He motioned toward the Tompkinses. "Can you believe it? That little bastard was giving me the evil eye the whole time I was testifying. He's starting to give me the creeps."

"What I can't believe is that Versey had the chutzpah to ask the judge to let Brent leave the state," Liz said, grimacing. "I've never heard anything so outrageous."

Liz picked up her file and sprinted back to the DA's office with her head down, pretending not to hear the litany of questions reporters were throwing at her. Once she had safely gained the outer office, she slowed her pace, then opened the door to her own digs and stepped inside. Tom Barker was standing by the window. He looked at her eagerly as she entered. "Well?' he asked.

Liz shook her head. "The judge released them to their parents' custody," she said as she dropped the file on her desk. "She did order that the kids not have any contact with you. Sorry," she said ruefully. "I wish we could've kept them locked up."

Tom quickly walked over to her. "There's nothing to be sorry about. Believe me, I'm just grateful that you found out who did it."

"You'll have to thank Detective Gardner for that," Liz said, looking up at him.

"Well, since he's not here right now, I'll thank you instead." Tom reached out and gave her a quick hug. "Good work, counselor."

"Thanks," Liz said.

This one-on-one contact with people was what she liked best about her job. It was a far cry from the years she spent toiling away on civil litigation cases. There, most of her clients had been megacorporations—impersonal, faceless entities. The only way she could ever be sure they were pleased with her services was if they paid her bill promptly. Getting immediate, positive feedback from a live person was much more satisfying. And, Liz had to admit, having the live person tall and handsome was definitely an added bonus.

Chapter 23

"You've really put Oakwood on the map," Esther teased. "You can't pick up a newspaper anywhere in the state without seeing your name. The chamber of commerce ought to consider making you the village spokesperson."

It was the Wednesday evening following Greg and Brent's initial court appearance, and the two women were methodically picking black raspberries in Liz's backyard. Both of Esther's kids had colds and had been left home in their father's care. "It's so good for Bob to bond with the children when they're cranky," Esther had cheerfully informed Liz when she arrived. "Builds character for all of them."

The previous day Liz had filed the petition asking that Brent be waived into adult court, and several local television stations had asked her to make a brief statement about the proceedings that would follow. Harry was normally only too happy to deal with reporters, but in this instance the waiver petition had been filed over his reservations and, wanting to keep a low profile, he had left Liz to face the media lions alone.

"God, some of those reporters are rude," Liz said, shaking her head ruefully, "and some ask the stupidest questions. I had to bite my tongue to keep from telling them all to go to hell."

"You sounded very articulate," Esther assured her, reaching for another cluster of berries. "Versey came across like a real blowhard. And I thought the TV clip of you last night was great. Cameron was watching with me at six o'clock, and he spotted you right away."

"It's sure true what they say about TV making you look ten pounds heavier," Liz lamented. "I looked like a baby whale."

"You did not," Esther replied. "A baby dolphin, maybe," she added with a mischievous grin. "But a whale, never."

Liz stuck out her tongue. "My mother saw that clip, too," she said, filling one gallon pail and reaching for another. "She was very impressed. Of course, as you know, it doesn't take much to impress her. 'Elizabeth,' " she said, mimicking her mother's voice. " 'I was so proud of you. Your father would have been proud of you, too, if he'd seen you, but he was working late as usual and I wasn't able to figure out how to program the VCR to record it for him, so he just had to take my word for it.' " Liz rolled her eyes. "She also said she always knew I had 'stage presence,' whatever the hell that means. I think in her mind the fact that I was on TV for a whole twenty seconds justifies her naming me after a movie star." Liz thrust one arm high overhead as though she were ready to lead a charge. "Today a short news clip. Tomorrow a feature film costarring Tom Cruise."

"How about a real-life production starring Tom Barker?"

Just as Tom's name was mentioned, Liz stumbled and kicked over the full bucket of berries, spilling many of them onto the ground. "Now look what you made me do!" she exclaimed crossly, as she squatted down to pick them up.

"Aha! Just as I thought," Esther said triumphantly. "Admit it. You've got the hots for the guy."

"I do not!" Liz snapped as she stood up again. "And in case you hadn't noticed, he's already spoken for. In fact, at this very moment, he and the divine Natalie are in Door County for a long Fourth of July weekend. As we speak, they're probably getting ready to embark on a moonlight nude swim."

"Believe me," Esther said fervently, "if you were interested in him, his relationship with that bimbo would be merely a minor impediment. So how do you know they're in Door County?"

"Because he called me yesterday to give me his phone number so that I could call him if anything related to the case broke while he was gone. He wants to be sure he's involved every step of the way."

"I think he just likes to talk to you," Esther said smugly.

"And I think you have an overactive imagination," Liz shot back.

"I don't know why you're being so coy," Esther persisted. "The man's a hunk. Trying to land him would certainly be a more noble pursuit than wasting your time with Hapless Harry."

Liz raised her eyebrows. "How many times do I have to tell you: there's nothing wrong with Harry."

"I suppose not, if you like your men bland and sexless," Esther said drolly. "But you used to prefer guys with a little more spark."

"I know all about spark," Liz shot back. "Peter had so much of it he went out and lit a fire in some other woman's bed. So if Harry is bland—which I'm not conceding, by the way—then I say what's wrong with that? Now, if you don't mind, I think this conversation has gone far enough." She peered at the raspberry bush. "It looks like we've got all the ripe ones. Let's go in the house. The mosquitoes are starting to bite."

Fifteen minutes later, as the two women were sitting in Liz's family room sipping gin and tonics, Esther said, "You seem crankier than usual tonight. Do you just have a bad case of PMS or is there something you're not telling me?"

Liz took a sip of her drink, then nodded. "I wasn't going to tell you, but I got some hate mail."

"No!" Esther exclaimed. "What kind of hate mail?"

"Two different letters, one two days ago and one yesterday. They both had Oakwood postmarks and were in the same format, so I assume the same person sent them both."

"What did they look like?"

"Like you sometimes see in movies where they cut words out of newspaper and glue them onto a piece of paper."

"What did they say?" Esther prompted.

"They were short and sweet. The first one said 'Traitor go home.' The second one said 'We don't need your kind of people in Oakwood.' "

"Where are they? Can I see them?"

Liz shook her head. "I burned them."

"You burned them!" Esther exclaimed incredulously. "Why did you do that?"

"Because they upset me, and I didn't want them around."

"But don't you think you should have shown them to the detective?"

"What for?"

"Maybe he could have traced them."

"Oh, Esther, you've seen too many spy movies," Liz scoffed. "There would have been no way to trace them, and after all, it's not like whoever did it was threatening my life."

"Who would do such a childish, hateful thing?" Esther demanded.

Liz shrugged. "It could be anybody in town. I guess I'd better get used to it—there will probably be a lot more of the same before this case is over." She stirred her drink with her finger. "I know I probably overreacted and that it was just somebody venting their spleen about what they see as an injustice in the criminal system, but I have to tell you it bothered me a lot. I guess I'm just not used to being involved in cases where everything is so damn personal."

"It goes without saying that it's a sad thing those

young boys are being prosecuted, but why should any-body take it out on you? You're just doing your job."

"I know, but when somebody's friend or neighbor is arrested for murder, their first instinct is to believe it's all a mistake, that the cops must have screwed up."

"Why is that?"

"Because nobody wants to admit that someone they're close to could actually have committed such a heinous act. It's easier to remain in denial and try to come up with some other explanation for what's happened."

"That doesn't make any sense," Esther said, frowning.

"Sure it does," Liz explained patiently. "Think about it a minute. If I were arrested for murder, would you believe I did it?"

"Of course not! You wouldn't hurt a flea."

Liz gave her friend a wry smile. "See—you've just proved my point. You would refuse to accept the fact that I could kill someone because you think you know me and if it actually turns out that I did the deed, then that makes you a very lousy judge of character, doesn't it?"

Esther looked skeptical.

"Oakwood is a small, close-knit community," Liz continued. "And let's face it, nearly everyone who lives here thinks of themselves as being a little bit better than your average citizen. So it stands to reason most people in town are going to have a tough time accepting that someone in their midst—and a teenager to boot—would be capable of murdering a child."

"That's an awfully bleak picture of humanity you're painting," Esther protested. "I can't believe the whole town thinks Brent and Greg are angels and that you and the sheriff's department are ogres who are trying to railroad them."

"I hope you're right," Liz said thoughtfully. "I've been so happy living here. I couldn't stand the thought of having to move."

"Of course you won't have to move!" Esther exclaimed. "How can you even think such a thing? Just because one sicko sends you a couple of childish messages doesn't mean the whole town is ready to tar and feather you. I'm sure most people understand the awkward situation you're in having to prosecute your fellow townspeople, and most respect you for it. Look, if the people here weren't behind you they wouldn't be adding you to the planning commission in ten days, now would they?"

Liz nodded halfheartedly. "Like I said, I'm probably overreacting. Will you do me a favor, though, and let me know if you hear any rumblings in the community?"

"Sure thing." Esther replied. She finished her drink and stood up. "Ready for a refill? Because I could sure use one."

Liz nodded. "Why not?"

Esther went to the kitchen and freshened the drinks. "Here you go," she said, handing Liz the glass. "I'm glad to hear you're not duking it out with the detective anymore," Esther commented as she settled back into her seat.

Liz nodded. "Yeah. We seem to have reached an accommodation." She smiled. "This sounds funny, when you think how much I despised the guy at first, but I'm actually starting to like him. That story he told me about his father getting killed helped me see where he's coming from. I can understand how having something like that happen to your family would haunt you all your life."

"That's good," Esther said. "You've got enough to worry about in the case without having a running battle with the chief investigator. So," she said smoothly, "let's get back to the question of what you should do about the divine Mr. Barker?"

"Absolutely nothing," Liz replied immediately, leaning back against the couch cushions. "Aside from the fact that I've told you six times I'm not interested, it's not good to get involved with clients."

"Now's a fine time to worry about etiquette," Esther shot back. "I wish you would have consulted Emily Post before you took up with your boss."

Liz furrowed her brow. "What do I have to say to convince you that I have no designs on Tom?"

"If that's true, you must be the only female in the state who doesn't. How can you not be attracted to someone who's that handsome and fabulously wealthy?"

"I've already had one man with those attributes. And after that experience, one was more than enough, thank you."

"What Peter did to you sucked," Esther said. "But you can't let that bad experience ruin the rest of your life. You've got too much going for you to waste your time with someone like Harry."

"Harry is a good companion," Liz put in.

"If you want a companion, we'll drive down to Pet World tomorrow and buy you one," Esther said sarcastically. "I'm sorry," she said, seeing Liz's face fall. "That was mean. But tell me the truth. Do you love Harry?"

"I don't want to love anyone," Liz replied without hesitation.

Esther sighed. "What kind of thing is that to say? Liz, listen to me. You quit your job and moved to Oakwood to start a new life, right? Well, the way you're living now is only half a life." Liz opened her mouth to protest, but Esther cut her off. "I kept thinking this was just a phase and you'd snap out of it, but you haven't. I mean, take a good look at yourself. You go to the office, you come home and work yourself into a lather in that damn yard of yours, and for fun you see Harry. You've cut off contact with most of your friends in the city and you haven't made any friends here. Now tell me honestly, don't you think you deserve more?"

Liz looked away. Although she was loath to admit it, Esther's remarks were hitting close to home. Esther plunged on. "I'm worried about you. You can't give up on passion, on excitement, just because Peter turned out to be a snake. There are some damn good men out there, and I think Tom Barker might just be one of them, if you'd give him a chance."

There was a long pause, then Liz looked at her friend and said quietly, "I hear what you're saying, and I appreciate your concern, but I think my life is complicated enough right now. Even assuming I was interested in Tom Barker—and I'm not saying I am, mind you—I really don't think this would be the best time for me to decide to start chasing after a guy who has given absolutely no indication he even knows I'm alive outside of the professional context and who is involved with a woman that looks like she eats barbed wire for breakfast. I tend to think it's more important for me to devote my energies to making sure Brent gets what he deserves and not getting run out of Oakwood on a rail. I couldn't possibly consider embarking on a personal relationship with anyone until this case is over."

Esther nodded. "You're right, of course." Then she sat forward in her seat and added earnestly, "But, honey, if you ever decide you're ready to make a play for Tom, you just say the word. I guarantee I'll figure out a way to get Natalie out of the picture, even if I have to marry her off to my short, nearsighted, very rich cousin Irving."

Liz smiled. "You've got yourself a deal."

Chapter 24

As Liz had suggested, Jeff had called Philip Barry to question him about the circumstances surrounding his resignation from Oakwood Junior High. When confronted with the hard facts about his termination, the teacher had not bothered trying to bullshit his way out of it.

"Yeah, you're right. Technically I was terminated. But I'd already typed my letter of resignation when I got their notice."

"Why didn't you tell me that before?" Jeff demanded.

"I guess I was a little embarrassed," Barry admitted. "Besides, I had already decided to leave. They just beat me to the punch. Does this mean you won't be needing me to come to court?"

"We'll probably still want you to come, but it might not be till the end of the case, as a rebuttal witness."

"Keep me posted. I would like to help you out if I can. Everything I told you about Brent was the truth. Scout's honor."

So Jeff was back pounding the pavement, trying to find someone other than Philip Barry who was willing to admit being aware of Brent Tompkins's bad character. So far his quest had resulted in his having more doors slammed in his face than a Fuller Brush man. He'd begun his search by attempting to contact the four boys Principal Richards had identified as Brent's closest friends. Not only did the families not let him anywhere near the kids, they didn't hesitate to read him the riot act as they ordered him off their property.

Josh Mahoney's mother: "I can't believe you're wasting your time trying to portray a nice boy like Brent as a common criminal. You should be ashamed of yourself!"

Chad Elliott's father: "Why don't you just admit you aren't able to find the real killer instead of trying to pin a bum rap on Brent?"

Taylor Huff's mother: "Attorney Versey warned us that you'd probably try to talk to Taylor. Why, I'm not letting you anywhere near my boy! You'd probably just haul him off to the jail for no reason, like you did Brent!"

Dillon Freeman's brother: "Beat it, cop, or I'll sic the rottweilers on you!"

Next, Jeff had tried to approach the families of the children whom Philip Barry said Brent had terrorized at school the previous year, with similar results. In each instance, the parents claimed that Barry had blown the incident out of proportion and what he viewed as Brent's harassing other students was merely good-natured horseplay.

In desperation, he paid a return visit to Joanne Johnson, hoping that Nate might be able to provide him with some additional leads. When Jeff arrived, Joanne was packing in preparation for her and Nate's spending the Fourth of July weekend with her sister in a Chicago suburb. Although she readily admitted him to the house and graciously ushered him into the kitchen, Jeff could tell that her attitude had changed markedly since his previous visit.

"How's Nate doing?" Jeff asked after sitting down and accepting Joanne's offer of a glass of iced tea.

Joanne filled a tall glass with ice cubes and poured the tea. She turned, walked toward Jeff, and set the glass in front of him, her face grim. "He's just devastated about what happened to Greg," she replied, taking a seat across from Jeff. "He's convinced Greg is going to go to prison for the rest of his life, and he blames himself for the whole thing."

"I'm sorry to hear that," Jeff said contritely. "If it'd be any consolation, you can assure him that nothing quite so dire is going to happen to Greg. He's not old enough to be tried as an adult, so even in the worst-case scenario, he's only looking at some time in a juvenile detention facility."

Joanne snorted. "I really doubt that would make Nate feel much better." She gazed out the window a moment, then turned back to face Jeff. "I hate to say it, but if I'd known it was going to be this hard on my son, I don't think I would've called you."

Jeff gave a slight nod. "I can understand that, but in time Nate will get over it—"

"It's not just Nate," Joanne cut him off. "I feel like the whole town is ready to boil over because of this thing. I can't go anywhere without hearing people talk about it. And it seems like the majority of people are dead against having those boys arrested." She rubbed her hands up and down over her neck in a nervous gesture. "I know this is irrational, but I can't help but think some of them know that it was Nate who first put you onto Greg, and I'm afraid we're going to be ostracized from Oakwood." She swallowed hard. "It's been difficult enough for us since Fred left, and now this . . ." Her voice trailed off.

"Look," Jeff said kindly, "I assure you no one will ever know Nate's role unless you choose to tell them."

"You're probably right, but I still feel like Judas Iscariot."

"You're being too hard on yourself," Jeff said.

Joanne shook her head sadly. "It's so hard raising children these days under normal circumstances, especially as a single parent. It was my idea to call the police, and now I have to live with the fact that my decision has caused my son tremendous pain. Try to put yourself in my place."

"I have a fourteen-year-old boy," Jeff replied. "And

a sixteen-year-old. And I'd like to think that even knowing how devastating this situation has been for Nate, that if one of my sons was in the same position, I'd do everything in my power to encourage him to do exactly what Nate did." He reached over and patted her hand. "Your boy is a hero. You should be very proud of him."

Joanne managed a small smile. "I am. I just wish there were something I could do for him. Or, for that matter," she added, "something we could do for Greg."

"There *is* something Nate could do that might help Greg," Jeff said.

"What's that?" she asked curiously.

"Tom Barker told us that the story Brent told Greg about wanting to kidnap Jeremy Barker to get even with Jeremy's father was a lie," he explained. "Brent probably made that up because he knew he'd have to give Greg some plausible reason to go along with his plan. A jury is going to have a much easier time convicting Brent if we can show what his true motive was. And if we can prove that Brent planned the murder in advance, for a much more sinister reason than just being chased out of Barker's yard, it would help put Brent away for a long time. It should also help Greg by showing he was just a patsy that Brent suckered into the scheme to do some of his dirty work."

Joanne frowned. "How could Nate be of any help?"

"I'm hoping he might be able to give me the names of some of Brent's friends. I got some names from people at the school, but none of those families will let me anywhere near their kids. Maybe Nate could supply some additional leads."

Joanne looked at him warily. "I don't know. Nate's already been through so much."

"I know this has been a difficult time for you," Jeff said, looking into her eyes, "but please . . . I wouldn't ask if it weren't important."

Joanne hesitated. "Well . . . all right. You can ask

him. But he may not want to talk to you, and I can't force him."

"I understand," Jeff said. "I'd appreciate it if you'd just let me try."

Joanne stood up. "I'll call him."

Moments later, Nate followed his mother into the room. Joanne took her former seat and patted the chair next to her. The boy dutifully sat down but stared down at his shoes, avoiding eye contact with Jeff.

"Hello, Nate," Jeff said softly. "It's good to see you again. How are you doing?"

There was no reply.

Jeff cleared his throat. "Nate, I understand how you must feel about what's happened to Greg, and I want you to know I'm very sorry about that. But I promise you Greg's gonna be okay, and I want you to know that I'm very proud of what you did."

There was still no response from the boy.

"The reason I stopped by today," Jeff went on, "is that I was hoping you might be able to help me out with one more thing. I was just explaining to your mom how you could do Greg a favor, too."

Upon hearing these words, Nate raised his head just a bit.

Seeing this encouraging sign, Jeff hurried on. "What I was hoping you could do for me is give me the names of some of Brent's friends so that I could talk to them—"

"No!" Nate shouted, his head snapping up so that he was staring Jeff straight in the face. "I won't do it! I already screwed up one friend's life. I'm not gonna screw up anybody else's!" He jumped up from his chair and raced out of the room.

"Nate!" Joanne called, but the boy paid no heed. She started to get up from her chair.

"Let him go," Jeff said, putting a hand on her arm. "It's all right. He's been through enough. We can't force him." He stood up and walked toward the front of the house.

"I'm sorry," Joanne said as they stood on the front steps. "I wish we could've been more help."

"It's okay," Jeff assured her. "Nate has been a tremendous help. I'll get the information I'm looking for eventually. I'll just have to keep digging."

Joanne nodded. "Good luck."

"Thanks," Jeff replied. "Have a good trip to Chicago." He glanced back at the house. "I think it'll be good for both of you to get away from Oakwood for a bit."

Having run out of leads and energy for the day but not wanting to go home just yet, Jeff swung by Sheriff Isaacson's house. Since a brief, childless marriage had dissolved years ago, the sheriff had remained a confirmed bachelor. He and Jeff shared the easy rapport of siblings. In fact, Jeff was much closer to Dan Isaacson than to his real brother, who lived in Michigan.

The rotund sheriff was in the backyard trimming a hedge with an electric clipper. "Hello, Jeff," Isaacson hailed him. "To what do I owe the honor of this visit?"

Jeff shrugged. "Nothing in particular. I'm just feeling a little down and thought maybe the sight of your smiling face might cheer me up."

"Son, you are as full of shit as a goose ready for slaughter." The sheriff switched off the clipper and wiped a sleeve over his sweaty forehead. "I'm just about done with this job. What do you say we go inside and quaff a coupla cold ones?"

"I'd say you won't have to ask twice," Jeff replied.

As they sat in the sheriff's super-air-conditioned kitchen drinking Miller Genuine Draft, Jeff explained his frustrations in trying to get Oakwood residents to talk to him about Brent. "I've had so many people throw me off their property I think I'm beginning to understand how Jehovah's Witnesses must feel," Jeff said, taking a long swallow of beer. "After a while a guy starts to get a complex."

"I thought you were a lot thicker-skinned than that," the sheriff chided.

"Usually I am," Jeff replied, "but these people are really starting to get under my skin."

"Sounds like a conspiracy of silence," the sheriff opined. "I'll bet if you could get some of them folks to open up, you'd find out that them Oakwood muck-ety mucks are hidin' all kinds of sinister things. The town's prob'ly a regular little Peyton Place."

"I wouldn't doubt it a bit," Jeff agreed. "I don't trust any of those rich bastards any farther than I can throw 'em." He took another swallow of beer and grimly stared off into space.

Guessing where Jeff's thoughts were, the sheriff asked, "How's your ma these days? I ain't seen her lately."

Jeff shrugged. "I don't know. Sometimes I think she's losing her marbles. She's so afraid she might run out of money before she dies. It's all she talks about lately. Well—that and how she thinks she might have a terminal disease."

"Is she ailin'?" the sheriff asked with concern.

"No," Jeff shook his head in disgust. "She's healthy as a horse. And she's pretty well set financially, too. It's all in her head. Julie's great with her—goes over there a couple times a week to try to calm her down, but I lose patience. I know I should visit more often, but lately every time I see her she says how much I look like my dad. Then she starts to cry and I sit there like an idiot, not knowing what to do."

"She never got over losing him, did she?"

"Not really," Jeff sighed. "It wasn't so bad when she was working part time, but since she retired she's got too damn much time on her hands and she just sits there and broods and talks about all the things my dad missed out on by dying young." He finished his beer and crushed the can in his fist. "And when she starts talking like that, it makes me remember, too."

"You see, the problem is your ma never really achieved closure after your daddy died. It woulda been so much more satisfying if that SOB who hit him had done some time."

Jeff nodded and reached for another beer.

"And now," the sheriff went on, "unless I miss my guess, you think history might be repeatin' itself. You're afraid these rich snots from Oakwood might get off scot-free, just like the guy who killed your daddy."

Jeff nodded again. "You oughta go into social work," he complimented his friend. "Yes, of course, the similarities between the two cases have crossed my mind a time or two. It'd sure help if I could come up with a motive for the killing, or at least show premeditation. A jury isn't going to want to believe a kid with a genius IQ who's gotten good-citizen commendations would kill just for kicks."

Isaacson took a big gulp of beer. "Never can tell. In my experience, you could never trust those Big Men on Campus. They're smart enough to fool people, but if you scratch the surface, nine times out of ten you'll find some real vermin. Think back a minute. Didn't you have somebody like that in your class?"

Jeff smiled at the memory and nodded. "Yeah. We sure did. Jack Kowalski. Tall, good-looking, A student, lettered in four sports, got all the best girls, voted most likely to succeed. God, I hated that son of a bitch."

"So what happened to him?" the sheriff asked. "I s'pose he's running a big corporation or workin' on Wall Street as one of them investment bankers or somethin'."

"No, as a matter of fact, he's dead."

"Really? How come?"

"He spent his junior year of college studying abroad, in Amsterdam. Got into some heavy-duty drugs while he was there. One night the fucker was high as a kite. Fell into a canal and drowned."

"No shit!" the sheriff exclaimed, guffawing heartily. "Well, what do you know? Maybe there is some justice in the world."

Jeff nodded and drained the rest of his beer. "I think there is," he said, grinding his teeth. "And if I have anything to say about it, there's gonna be justice for Brent Tompkins. When I'm through with him, the little bastard is going to wish he'd fallen into a canal."

Chapter 25

"Have you worked out a deal with Greg Saunders's attorney yet?"

Liz looked up and saw Harry standing in the doorway of her office, holding a sheaf of papers. It was a Monday morning in mid-July, and for the past week the two of them had been having a running battle over whether or not to offer Greg's lawyer a deal whereby they'd reduce the charges against Greg in exchange for a promise that the boy would testify against Brent. While Liz was in favor of waiting for Bennett to contact her, Harry wanted her to take the initiative on entering into a plea bargain.

A motivating factor behind Harry's uneasiness about the situation was the strong level of support that Oakwood residents were giving Greg and Brent. Soon after Liz filed the papers asking that Brent be waived into adult court, Harry had received a petition signed by one hundred people protesting the DA's handling of the case. While the petition was careful not to mention either Greg or Brent by name, it asserted that the charges against the thirteen-year-old Oakwood resident were "devoid of merit and brought solely for purposes of harassment" and that the effort to have the fourteen-year-old waived into adult court was "an abuse of prosecutorial discretion."

This had been followed by a barrage of letters and faxes demanding to know what basis the district attorney had for filing the charges against the boys. Liz had been deeply hurt by the protestations. These were her neighbors, for God's sake, and they were calling her professional judgment into question.

In addition, Liz had been receiving more nasty mail at home, each piece more vitriolic than the last. One letter had called her a stupid cunt. Another had referred to her as a Nazi pig. Although she promptly destroyed each diatribe as soon as she'd read it, the hatred embodied in the letters haunted her.

Most upsetting of all, though, was a call she'd received the previous day from Bob McMillan, telling her that he had just learned that Liz's long-coveted nomination to the Oakwood planning commission, which was to be acted upon later that week, had been tabled indefinitely.

"What the hell does that mean?" Liz had asked incredulously.

"I honestly don't know," Bob replied. "The commission's chairman was very vague."

"I'm being blackballed for having the audacity to prosecute Brent and Greg," she said bitterly.

"It does look that way, yes," Bob admitted. "But don't lose heart. I'm going to do everything I can to see that you get on that commission. And Esther went absolutely ballistic when she heard the news. She was ready to race down to the library to research how to make letter bombs so she could send them to all the commission members."

Liz had thanked Bob for his support, but when she hung up she was in tears. Her new life in Oakwood meant so much to her. Now it seemed it was all in jeopardy. And the source of all her troubles was this one case. The case of a lifetime. Probably the most important case she would ever handle. How ironic that she'd hoped prosecuting Jeremy Barker's killer would endear her to all Oakwood residents. Instead it was turning her into a pariah.

Liz knew her one chance of salvaging her reputation in the community would be to plea-bargain the charges against both boys. Harry was pushing hard for it, hoping to save his own political aspirations. While Liz had to admit that the thought of bailing out of this albatross was very tempting, she couldn't bring herself to do it. At least not in Brent's case. No matter what the consequences for her future life in Oakwood might be, Brent's case was going all the way to trial. Knowing how adamant Liz was in this regard, Harry had backed off on that front, at least for the time being, and was urging her to work a deal with Greg.

"Well," Harry prompted, "have you talked to Greg's lawyer?"

Liz shook her head. "I thought I'd wait till the end of the week to talk to Bennett."

Harry frowned, crossed the room, and tossed a stack of papers onto her desk. "Here's the latest batch of hate mail."

Liz pushed the letters aside. She already knew what they said, and they weren't going to change her mind.

"Greg's plea hearing is only ten days away," Harry said, settling into a chair. "The only way you can be sure of convicting Brent at trial is to have Greg testify against him. I'd strongly suggest wrapping up that part of the case now so you can focus on getting Brent waived into adult court."

Liz drummed her pen on the desktop as she mulled the situation over. She *was* a bit worried about the waiver hearing, largely because of a notice she'd received a few days earlier that a new judge had been assigned to the case. Versey had filed a request that a new judge be substituted for Louise Franchetta, and Roy Dunham had now been rotated in. Liz would have much preferred that the murder remain in Judge Franchetta's capable hands. Dunham, who had been on the bench three years, had a reputation for being soft on criminals.

If the substitution process had been available to the state, Liz would have invoked it, but in criminal matters only the defendant had that right. The only means the state had to challenge the judge assigned in a criminal case was to file a motion for recusal, asking the judge to excuse himself for cause. A hearing was then held, at which the state had to present evidence to show that the judge would not be able to act impartially in the matter. Generally the evidence offered was that the judge was a relative, close friend, or former business partner of the opposing party or for some reason had a monetary stake in the outcome of the case.

The process then devolved into a rather convoluted procedure whereby the judge himself got to decide whether he was biased. If he decided he wasn't— which is what happened 95 percent of the time—he remained on the case. While such decisions were appealable, it was very difficult to get an appellate court to rule that the judge should in fact have bowed out. There was no quicker way to piss a judge off than to question his integrity, so recusal motions were rarely filed, even when the facts might seem to warrant them. In Brent's case Liz had no basis for filing one, so she'd just have to stick with Dunham and hope for the best.

"I'm still hoping Bennett will make the first overture in discussing a plea bargain," Liz explained.

Harry shook his head. "It's a mistake to wait. I saw Bennett's motion asking the judge to suppress the statement Greg made to Detective Gardner. Frankly, I think he's got a decent shot at winning. And we both know if the statement is thrown out, your chances of getting a finding of delinquency on Greg are almost certainly out the window." He shifted in his chair and looked her square in the eye. "I would strongly advise calling Bennett. Now."

"Is that an order?" Liz asked evenly.

Harry held her glance for a moment, then shook his head. "No, it's not an order. Just some friendly advice." He got to his feet. "It's up to you whether you decide to follow it or not." He walked out of the office and closed the door behind him.

Liz sighed. She understood Harry's concern. With

his political appointment still in limbo, she knew he was hoping for a quick resolution of the case. They were still seeing each other sporadically, although her interest was waning—and she secretly suspected that his was as well. In spite of that, she still had warm feelings for the man. He'd remained true to his word that he wouldn't interfere in her handling of the case, and she would hate to do anything that would kill his chances of getting the federal job he so coveted.

She took another sip of coffee as she debated whether she should bargain with Greg now rather than later. Jeff was dead-set against it. He'd had no luck trying to find someone other than Philip Barry who would be able to shed some light on Brent's character, and it was obvious that he didn't handle failure very well, since his mood had been growing increasingly darker every time she talked to him. When she mentioned that Harry was strongly in favor of an immediate plea bargain for Greg, Jeff hit the roof.

"Absolutely not!" he bellowed, his eyes flashing. "How can you even think of such a thing this early on?"

"You know we need Greg's testimony," she replied.

"There will be plenty of time to deal later," he shot back. "This makes us look weak. And, hey—don't forget, I still might find you some other witnesses."

"I wish you'd hurry up and find them," she said. "I can't wait much longer."

"Bitch, bitch, bitch," he grumbled. "I'm doing the best I can."

"I know that," Liz said quietly. "But if you don't find anything, I've got to have other contingencies."

Now she walked over to the window and stood there quietly enjoying the view. The summer heat had continued unabated, and many people were taking advantage of the lake's cooling water. She sighed and shook her head. The other thing holding her back from calling Bennett was Tom.

Since the night of her discussion with Esther, he

had been increasingly in her thoughts. She found herself looking forward to his calls. He was unfailingly pleasant, although they rarely discussed anything other than business and he gave no indication that he was interested in a more personal relationship with her. From their recent calls Liz had learned that Tom was having a hard time coping with the notion of reducing the charges against Greg.

"Do whatever you think is best," Tom had said reluctantly, "but I have to tell you it hurts me to think that both of them aren't going to get the maximum penalty for what they did."

The support his neighbors were showing for the two boys hurt him, too. "I just don't understand," he'd said sadly when she read him the names. "How would they feel if their child had been murdered? Why do they have to be so damned judgmental? Can't they put themselves in my place?" Unfortunately, Liz had no answers for him.

She stared out the windows another minute, then shook her head decisively. Harry was right. Brent was the prime target here, and she needed Greg's testimony to put Brent away. Returning to her desk, she picked up the phone and dialed Bennett's number.

"Well, well, Ms. Stanfeld, what can I do for you today?" Bennett asked pleasantly when he came on the line.

"I was just looking at my calendar, and I noticed that Greg Saunders's plea hearing is scheduled for next week," she said conversationally. "It occurred to me that we might both be able to save ourselves a lot of extra work by coming to an agreement on the charges."

"I guess that depends what you have in mind," Bennett replied. "Give me your best offer, and I'll take it up with my client."

"I'd be willing to reduce the first-degree murder charge to reckless homicide, provided Greg agrees to testify against Brent."

Bennett laughed, a deep, throaty sound. "That's a good one, Ms. Stanfeld. Have you ever considered a career in stand-up comedy?"

"Well, if you don't like my offer, why don't you tell me what *you* had in mind?" Liz volleyed back. "It might make the process move along a little faster."

"Fair enough," Bennett replied. "Drop the murder charge entirely and we'll plead to kidnapping."

"What?" Liz exclaimed. "Why should I do that? I can definitely nail Greg on some degree of murder. By agreeing to help Brent with the kidnapping scheme, Greg became a party to all other crimes that followed."

"I wouldn't be so sure of that," Bennett said. "Frankly, I think I have a solid shot at getting Greg's confession thrown out. And even if I don't, I think we'll be able to make a very persuasive argument that he was forced to participate in the entire scheme against his will, because of the coercive, almost Machiavellian tactics of an older, more intelligent and physically threatening boy."

"Greg went along with the kidnapping part voluntarily," Liz persisted. "And once he did that, he opened the door to whatever else happened."

"You've heard my offer," Bennett said firmly. "If you drop the murder charge, we'll plead to kidnapping and Greg will testify against Brent." He paused a moment, then added, "Oh, there is one more thing: you recommend straight probation, no custodial time."

"This is preposterous!" Liz hissed. "Why should I let Greg off that easily?"

"Because, Ms. Stanfeld," he replied, "you need my client's cooperation a hell of a lot more than we need your deal. Although I'll admit the Saunders family would like to be spared the embarrassment of having to go through protracted proceedings to clear their son's name, they'll endure them if they have to, and I'm confident Greg will emerge relatively unscathed. You, on the other hand, sorely need Greg's testimony in order to ensure that Brent gets his just deserts. All 'round, it appears to me that I'm in the catbird seat."

Liz was so angry she could feel the veins on her neck sticking up. What Bennett said had a ring of truth, but she sure as hell wasn't going to give him the satisfaction of saying so—at least not yet.

"Why don't we both give this some more thought and touch base again at the end of the week?" she said in as calm a voice as she could muster.

"That's fine," Bennett replied easily, "although I'll warn you that I've already done all my thinking on the subject."

"I'll be in touch," Liz said.

"I have no doubt about that," Bennett responded.

Liz slammed down the receiver and sat there fuming. Damn it! This wasn't the kind of deal she'd had in mind. True, she did feel sorry for the Saunders family and she knew Brent was the real culpable party, but it still went against the grain to let Greg off with a mere slap on the wrist. She walked out into the office's common area to get a fresh cup of coffee. Returning to her office, she stood at the window and looked out at the lake, sipping her coffee.

She was still standing there when Jeff suddenly burst in and plopped into a chair. "Honest to God," he said, shaking his head. "I'm at a frigging dead end. I've tried everything. I've used my poor Southern boy routine. I've played it like Joe Friday. 'I need the facts, ma'am. Just the facts.' I've even threatened a few of the nastier ones with obstruction of justice. And I still haven't come up with a goddamned thing." He tipped the chair back. "We really need to talk to Greg. I'm convinced he's the key to the whole thing."

"Funny you should mention Greg," Liz said, finishing her coffee. "I had a talk with his attorney a little while ago." She recounted the conversation and Bennett's offer.

"What?" Jeff let the front chair legs come crashing to the floor with violent force. "No way, José!" he shouted. "He has to do *some* time, even if it's not much." He jumped up and started pacing in front of her desk.

"I understand how you feel, but Bennett does have a point. Without Greg's testimony we're up the proverbial creek without a paddle."

Jeff swung around to face her. "This is really a cop-out!" he said incredulously. "Why would you go along with it?" He paused a moment, then his face hardened. "This is your boyfriend's idea, isn't it?"

"Don't call him that!" Liz snapped back.

"Why not?" Jeff taunted. "Oh, I get it. The other people in the office don't know about the two of you, do they? I suppose that's smart. Otherwise, folks might think you two are rocking the desk every time you're in here alone together."

"Look," Liz shot back, ignoring his jabs at Harry, "I really don't see that we've got much choice. Unless you're suddenly able to come up with some other witnesses who saw the whole thing—in which case I'll gladly tell Bennett to go to hell."

Jeff ran his hand through his hair. "When do you have to get back to Bennett?"

"I need to get this firmed up by the end of the week."

Jeff nodded. "That gives me four more days. Promise you won't cut any deals until we've talked again."

"All right," Liz agreed, "but from the way things look, it's gonna take a miracle."

Jeff started for the door, then turned back. "When I stop in later this week, maybe we can run through my testimony for the waiver hearing. 'Course, it should be a piece of cake. Judge Franchetta heard most of it the last time."

Liz frowned. "Didn't I tell you? Franchetta got substituted out."

"She did? Who've we got?"

"Dunham."

"Oh, shit!" Jeff exclaimed. "Not that old woman!

Not only will he not waive Brent into adult court, he'll probably invite the little bastard home for tea and crumpets after the hearing. Can't you figure out a way to get rid of him?"

Liz shook her head. "The only way to do that would be if we could somehow show he is biased. Maybe while you're out there getting the Oakwood community to spill its guts about Brent, you could dig up some dirt on Dunham, too," she added sarcastically.

Jeff glared at her. "I just might do that," he said curtly as he turned and stormed out of her office.

Chapter 26

Liz gently fingered an orange-hued lily petal in the center of the arrangement of cut flowers on her desk. The weeks of hot, humid weather were getting to be damn oppressive, but her garden was thriving. She brought in an armful of new flowers every couple of days. She let go of the flower and glanced at the clock. It was ten-thirty on Friday morning. When she'd talked to Jeff the previous afternoon, he had reluctantly conceded that if she hadn't heard from him by eleven she should go ahead and finalize the deal with Greg's attorney. She'd wanted to phone Bennett first thing this morning, but Jeff had convinced her to hold off a few more hours, to give him one last chance to try to find a witness willing to bad-mouth Brent. As Liz watched the clock's second hand make its methodic march around the dial, she wondered if by some miracle Jeff would be able to pull it off.

Just when Liz had thought she and the detective had reached an accommodation, they now seemed to be at cross-purposes again. He had called her every day to tell her she was soft and didn't have what it took to be a good prosecutor. He'd also warned her that if she went through with it, her conscience would bother her for the rest of her life. While to his face she'd shrugged those statements off, deep down she did have some misgivings about letting Greg off that easy. However, she kept reminding herself that Brent's waiver hearing was a mere three days away, and she wanted to be able to walk into Judge Dunham's courtroom buttressed by the knowledge that when the trial came, Greg would be there to testify for them.

She had talked to Tom Barker the previous day and had prepared him for the distinct possibility that they'd be cutting deal with Greg. While Tom had clearly been less than thrilled with the news, at least he had been tactful in voicing his reservations.

"You're not thinking of making a deal with Brent, are you?" he'd asked with concern.

"Absolutely not," Liz had responded at once. "I'm not giving an inch on thos charges."

"Good," Tom had said with obvious relief. "I don't think I could bear it if he got off the hook."

"Don't worry," Liz had assured him. "He won't."

"I'll be so glad when this is all over," Tom had sighed. "I'd thought once the arrests were made I could at least start to put my life back together, but I feel just as anxious as ever."

"I know how hard this must be for you," Liz had commiserated. "Just hang in there."

"You probably think I'm a pest, calling you so often," Tom had apologized, "but it helps for me to talk things through with someone."

"You call as often as you want," Liz had encouraged him. "That's what I'm here for." She had blushed slightly as she realized how much she enjoyed their frequent talks.

Now, as she waited rather impatiently for the minutes until eleven to tick by, Liz glanced at the waiver petition and jotted some notes on a legal pad as to arguments she wanted to make at the hearing.

- There is prosecutive merit to the charges contained in the delinquency petition.
- The offenses charged were committed in a violent, aggressive, premeditated, and willful manner.
- The juvenile's motives and attitudes are similar to

those often seen in adult defendants in criminal court.

- The juvenile is extremely physically and mentally mature and is not developmentally disabled.
- The nature of the juvenile's needs and the need to protect the public render the resources available within the children's court inadequate and unsuitable.

When she finished writing, she allowed herself to steal one more glance at the clock. It was five to eleven. Oh, hell, she thought. Jeff wasn't going to come through. She needed to get this over with. She picked up the phone and dialed.

"Good morning, Ms. Stanfeld," Bennett said pleasantly as he came on the line. "Have you had the opportunity to do some more thinking about our earlier discussion?"

"Yes," Liz answered tersely. "Although frankly I have some misgivings, we will accept your proposal."

"An excellent decision on your part," Bennett said. "Is it acceptable to you if we keep the hearing date scheduled for next week and put our agreement on the record at that time?"

"That would be fine," Liz replied. "As you probably know, Brent Tompkins's waiver hearing is scheduled for Monday. I'd appreciate it if you could advise your clients not to let the Tompkinses or their attorney know that we've made a deal. I'd like them to feel complacent just a little while longer."

"I understand," Bennett replied.

"I'd like to set up an interview with Greg to pin him down on a few things," Liz went on. "Why don't we do that soon after the plea hearing? Perhaps you could check with the Saunderes and find out what day would be good for them."

"No problem."

"Just one more thing," Liz said. "And this is off the record. We've been searching high and low for someone who can tell us what Brent's motive might have been for killing Jeremy. Has Greg said anything to you about it?"

"Just what he told the detective: that Brent wanted to get back at Mr. Barker for some past injustice."

"Hmmm," Liz mused. "We know for a fact that's not true. I wonder if we'll ever find out what was really behind it. Well, I guess I'll see you next week."

"It's been a pleasure doing business with you," Bennett said. "Good luck on Monday."

"Thanks," Liz murmured. "I'll need all the help I can get."

She hung up the phone, walked over to Harry's office, and knocked lightly on the door. He might as well be the first to hear the news that the agreement had been consummated. At least she was sure he would think she'd done the right thing.

"Come in," he called out.

Liz stepped inside and closed the door behind her. "I just finalized the deal with Bennett. Greg will plead to kidnapping and will testify against Brent at trial. In exchange, I'll drop the murder charge and recommend probation."

"Well done!" Harry said, nodding his head and smiling. "That's one less thing to worry about. Once young Tompkins is waived into adult court, perhaps you'll be able to come to some agreement with Versey as well."

Liz frowned slightly. She had no intention of ever reducing the charges against Brent. From the day she'd filed the original papers, she'd made up her mind she would settle for nothing less than a conviction on murder one and a sentence of life in prison. But seeing Harry looking more relaxed than he'd been in weeks, she didn't have the heart to tell him that. "We'll have to wait and see," she said lamely.

Harry glanced at his watch. "I'd better get rolling. I'm speaking at a Kiwanis luncheon in Mequon. Perhaps I can reach Senator Kilpatrick on the car phone.

I know he'll want to pass the news on to the other members of the selection committee." He shrugged on his gray suit jacket. "Keep up the good work," he said, giving her shoulders a little squeeze as he passed.

Liz went back to her office and sorted through some mundane paperwork. Shortly before noon, she retrieved her egg salad sandwich and can of soda from the refrigerator and returned to her desk. She would call Tom after lunch and tell him the news. Her pulse rate picked up as she realized how much she was looking forward to hearing his voice again. As she took the first bite out of the sandwich, the door to her office flew open and Jeff burst in.

"Stop the presses!" he exclaimed. "I got the dirt you wanted."

Liz swallowed the piece of sandwich without chewing it and nearly choked. "What?" she coughed. "You're too late. I made the deal with Bennett an hour ago. We had an eleven o'clock deadline, remember?"

"No, no!" Jeff retorted with irritation as he leaned over her desk. "Not that dirt. The dirt on Judge Dunham."

"What are you talking about?" Liz asked, her eyes narrowing.

"I just found out that a large number of Oakwood residents made hefty contributions to Dunham's campaign fund when he ran for judge three years ago, including Martin Tompkins, who gave seven hundred fifty dollars. I'd say that's definite proof of bias. Get out a motion for recusal."

Liz put the sandwich down and stared at him. "It's not that easy," she said warily.

"Why not?" Jeff asked irritably, as he continued to hover over her. "You said we needed to show bias. I found you bias. Case closed. File the damn motion."

"Would you please sit down?" Liz said firmly. "You're making me nervous." When Jeff plopped into the chair in front of her desk, she continued. "We need to show the kind of bias that would be likely to make it difficult for the average judge to be able to decide a case fairly and impartially," she said, thinking out loud. "In this day and age I don't think receiving a campaign contribution of seven hundred fifty dollars three years ago is serious enough."

"But that was one of the largest individual donations," Jeff persisted. "A couple of Dunham's relatives gave him more than a grand, but old Martin's check ranks right up there. Look," he said in a calmer tone, "if this were your run-of-the-mill case, I'd probably agree that it wouldn't pay to try to get the judge off the case, but here we're asking that a judge who both of us agree tends to be soft on criminals make a ruling that no other judge in the whole damn county has ever made. In my book, we owe it to little Jeremy to do anything we can to get a sympathetic judge handling that hearing. So I say file the motion."

"It was three years ago!" Liz repeated. "Candidates never handle their own money in elections. They have a treasurer do that for them. It's possible Dunham doesn't even know about Tompkins's donation—or doesn't remember."

"I'm sure he remembers. Dunham's not one of your Oakwood big shots. He's a poor boy from Lakeview, just like me. Believe me, he'd remember anybody who gave him seven hundred fifty bucks."

Liz clenched her teeth. "You know the procedure if I file a motion," she said. "Dunham makes his own determination as to whether he can be impartial. Judges almost always decide that they can be, and I'm just afraid that once we've called his integrity into question, he's really going to stick it to us when it comes time for him to make a ruling."

"Christ!" Jeff growled, as he jumped up again and began to pace. "You've got to start showing some balls here! It's bad enough that you sold out on Greg's charges. Don't fumble the ball on Brent, too."

"I have no intention of letting Brent get away," Liz

said firmly. "I understand where you're coming from, but I think the odds of success here are minimal, and we stand to lose a hell of a lot by getting the judge PO'd before we even start."

"But—" Jeff began.

"I said no," Liz interrupted in a stern tone. "I appreciate your suggestions and the very personal way you're taking this entire case, but I thought we'd agreed that we would respect each other's areas of expertise. This happens to be *my* area, and I say we're not filing any motion—whether you like it or not."

"I don't like it one goddamn bit!" Jeff barked at her, his face flushed. Swinging around, he stomped angrily out of the office.

Chapter 27

The temperature hit ninety-eight degrees the day of the waiver hearing, tying a record that had stood for more than eighty years. As he sat in Judge Dunham's courtroom waiting for the proceeding to begin, Jeff silently cursed Liz for insisting that he wear a suit. It wasn't even ten o'clock yet and here he was, already sweating like a pig. By the end of the day there would be nothing left of him but a big puddle on the floor.

How did women always manage to look so comfortable even in the most wretched weather? he wondered as he glanced over at Liz, who was looking cool in her mint green suit. It wasn't fair. Women had a higher percentage of body fat. By rights that meant they should perspire more, but somehow it didn't seem to work that way. He guessed it must just be one of those inexplicable mysteries of nature, like salmon swimming upstream or the swallows always returning to Capistrano on Saint Joseph's Day.

Jeff knew Liz was nervous. She had admitted it when they'd met in her office earlier that morning. Actually, what she'd said as she went over her notes one last time was, "I'm scared shitless. There's an awful lot riding on this hearing."

It was the first time she'd really let down her guard, and somehow it had pleased him. He liked people who displayed a little vulnerability. He knew he'd been acting like a jerk the past week, and he'd tried to put her at ease by saying, "Hell, it's just a hearing like any other. You're gonna knock Versey right out of the water." Privately, though, he wasn't so optimistic. He sure wished he'd been able to convince Liz to try to force the judge to withdraw from the case.

Jeff gave Liz another glance. While they were in her office, Washburn had come in, tersely wished them luck, and then mumbled something about being out of town the rest of the day. The spineless toad, Jeff had grumbled to himself. In case things went badly at the hearing, Liz would have to deal with the fallout alone. From the way Harry and Liz interacted, Jeff got the distinct impression there might be trouble in paradise. Then, a bit later, Tom Barker had arrived. As with the custody hearing, he was going to await the judge's ruling in Liz's office. Liz had seemed a little flustered around Barker, and Jeff wondered if something was going on between them. If so, he also wondered what had happened to the redheaded knockout Tom had escorted to the village board meeting. He guessed he'd just have to watch for further developments on that front.

Jeff casually turned his gaze toward the defense table. Looked like a three-ring circus over there. Versey was dressed in a black three-piece suit. He had brought two hapless young associates with him for this go-round. They were attired in matching gray pinstripes. Jeff watched them and snorted to himself. He didn't give a shit how much money young attorneys made. He wouldn't stoop to carrying a briefcase for the likes of Versey if it were the last job on earth. He'd scoop ice cream at Schoeps first.

Brent was sporting the nautical look, with tan slacks, a blue-and-cream-striped shirt, and a navy blazer. Apparently the theory was that he looked younger in that garb than in a suit. With Versey's flair for the dramatic, it wouldn't have surprised Jeff if they'd dressed him like Little Lord Fauntleroy and stuck a lollipop in his mouth. Brent was smiling and chatting with one of the associates as if they were all waiting to have their lunch order taken at the yacht club. Jeff grumbled to himself as he watched Brent lean over and share some private joke with the young lawyer. Didn't that kid ever get rattled? He'd probably be one of those who walked to the gas chamber singing zippidee doo dah. It was enough to make a guy wish that Wisconsin had capital punishment.

At ten o'clock sharp Judge Dunham's bailiff called court to session. The judge emerged from a door behind the bench and regally took his seat. Dunham was in his early fifties, about six feet tall and thin, with a pasty white complexion. His face was pockmarked. He must've had a hell of a case of the zits when he was a teenager.

"Good morning, ladies and gentlemen," the judge said in a rather high-pitched voice. "This is a waiver hearing in the matter of Brent Tompkins. May I have the appearances, please."

After Liz and Versey had stated their names for the record, it was Liz's turn to present her case. She gave a brief opening statement in which she described the senseless brutality of Jeremy's murder. "Your Honor," she concluded, "the state intends to prove by clear and convincing evidence that it would be contrary to the best interests of the public to hear the case in juvenile court. As my first witness, I'd like to call Miles Durfee, one of the Oakwood School District's guidance counselors." Durfee was in his midforties and on the short and stocky side. After going through the preliminaries about his background, Liz said, "Mr. Durfee, I'm showing you what has been marked as state's exhibit four, a copy of Brent Tompkins's school record. Have you had the opportunity to review this document?"

"Yes, I have."

"Referring to page two, would you please give us a summary of Brent's achievement and intelligence test scores and tell us how those scores compare with those of the average Oakwood student?"

Durfee ran through the list of standardized tests

that Brent had taken, from kindergarten through
eighth grade. In each instance. Brent's scores were in
the top one or two percentiles.

Jeff noticed that as Durfee testified, Judge Dunham
appeared to be listening intently and was taking copious notes. Maybe keeping the old fart on the case
hadn't been such a bad idea after all.

"Are you personally acquainted with Brent Tompkins?" Liz asked Durfee.

"Yes, I am."

"And how would you describe him, in terms of intelligence and maturity?"

"Brent is without a doubt one of the most intelligent students I've ever come in contact with," Durfee
replied without hesitation. "And though I am not well
acquainted with him, in the limited dealings I have
had, he has struck me as being mature far beyond
his years."

"Thank you, Mr. Durfee," Liz said. "I have no further questions."

Versay asked a few follow-up questions, but when
it became apparent he would be able to make no
points with the witness, he desisted.

Then it was Jeff's turn to testify. As he took his
seat, he tried to quell his feelings of nervousness. He
stared directly at Brent. Without so much as flinching,
Brent stared back.

"Let's focus first on the first time you met Brent,"
Liz said. "I believe it was June 25. How would you
characterize Brent's demeanor at that time?"

"He appeared to be very unconcerned even though
we were discussing a very serious event, the beating
death of a four-year-old boy. In addition, he struck
me as being a very cocky young man."

"Objection!" Versey sputtered. "What does he
mean by 'cocky'?"

"Perhaps you could clarify what you mean by that
term, Detective," the judge suggested.

"Sure," Jeff said easily. "I asked him if he liked to

watch action movies, and he looked at me like I was a lower life-form and said he preferred classics like *Citizen Kane.*"

"Do you normally see this type of behavior with juveniles?"

"No. Usually juveniles who are being questioned appear to be very nervous."

"When was the next time you came into contact with Brent?"

"On June 27, the day he was taken into custody."

"And how would you characterize his demeanor at that time?"

"Again, very smug, very self-assured."

"Did he say anything to you?"

"No," Jeff admitted, "but after he'd been read his rights and another officer was leading him out to the car, he walked past me and he stared me right in the face and appeared to be sneering at me."

"Is this typical behavior when a juvenile is arrested?"

Jeff shook his head. "Not at all. In my experience, most juveniles who are placed under arrest either become hysterical or are extremely withdrawn. I have never seen a fourteen-year-old conduct himself in such a manner."

"Detective, based on your observations, would you characterize Brent Tompkins as being mature for his age?"

"Absolutely. Extremely mature." Jeff looked at Brent again. The youth appeared to be smiling at him.

"Thank you. No further questions."

Liz returned to her seat, and Versey stood up and approached the witness stand. There were beads of perspiration on the big man's face, and the heat and humidity had made his few strands of hair stick together so it looked like someone had unrolled part of a spool of black thread on the top of his head.

"Detective Gardner, do you have any training in psychology or psychiatry?" Versey asked.

"No, I do not."

"Do you consider yourself an expert in human behavior?"

"Not from a clinical standpoint," Jeff admitted, "but in the past twenty years I've certainly had the opportunity to observe many people involved in the criminal justice system."

"I see." Versey pursed his lips. "How many homicide arrests would you estimate you have participated in?"

Jeff paused a moment to consider. "I'd say somewhere between forty and fifty."

"Do all people arrested for homicide behave in the same manner at the time of their arrest?"

"No."

"Would you agree that it's possible that a person arrested for murder would likely be under extreme stress and thus might manifest behavior inappropriate to the situation?"

"I suppose it's possible," Jeff conceded.

"So, isn't it possible that the behavior of Brent Tompkins, which you described as 'smug' and 'self-assured,' could very well be a type of hysterical reaction caused by the stress of the situation?"

"I don't think so," Jeff replied at once. This pompous ass wasn't going to put words in his mouth. "When Brent was told he was under arrest, he didn't flinch, his hands didn't shake, there was not the least sign of any facial tic. He didn't look any more concerned than if he'd been told we were taking him to a rock concert."

"But isn't it possible that his reactions were not what they seemed?" Versey persisted.

"It's possible I might win the lottery tonight," Jeff said, glaring at Versey, "but it's not very likely."

"I move that the previous response be stricken from the record as unresponsive," Versey exclaimed.

"Sustained," Judge Dunham ruled. "The witness

will please refrain from making any gratuitous comments. Mr. Versey, you may continue."

"I have nothing further, Your Honor," Versey said magnanimously.

The judge nodded. "Very well. Detective Gardner, you may step down."

Jeff returned to his seat next to Liz, poured himself a big glass of water, and downed it in one long swallow. Liz informed the court that she had no more witnesses. Versey made a motion to dismiss the waiver petition on the ground that the state had failed to make a prima facie showing that waiver was appropriate. The judge promptly denied the motion and directed Versey to proceed with his evidence.

Versey's first witness was a young Presbyterian minister from the Tompkinses church. Reverend Daniels testified that Brent was a regular churchgoer who, for the past several years, had helped teach a first- and second-grade Sunday school class. "How did Brent get along with these youngsters?" Versey asked.

"Extremely well," the reverend replied. "It's clear that Brent loves children. He has a real affinity for working with them."

Jeff reached for Liz's legal pad and scrawled her a note. "If the parents are smart, I'll bet there'll be a mass exodus of kids from that class." Liz glanced down at the pad and nodded.

"Have you observed anything else about Brent and his work with the children?" Versey asked.

"He loves to play games with the kids," the reverend said. "Hopscotch, hide-and-seek, whiffle ball. They all have a great time together, and the kids treat Brent like he's one of them."

Hopscotch? Jeff groaned to himself. This was really too much. In light of Brent's recent experience, maybe he could add some new games to his repertoire. Find the horsies in the woods would probably be a real favorite.

On cross-examination, Liz established that the minister had only really observed Brent working with the children three or four times and had had one-on-one conversations with him only a handful of occasions.

Versey's next witness was Lucille Schmerse, the math teacher Jeff had previously interviewed. As she took a seat in the witness box, her eye met Jeff's for a split second; then she quickly turned away.

Mrs. Schmerse dutifully explained how Brent had been a model student who enjoyed helping her carry things in from the car and sometimes assisted in correcting papers. "He was very eager to please," she said. "In that regard he was more like a younger student. By the time most boys get to junior high, they want to act all macho, like they're above helping the teacher out. But Brent wasn't like that at all."

When it was Liz's turn for questions, she asked how the teacher would rank Brent in terms of intelligence.

"He's a very smart boy," Mrs. Schmerse admitted.

"In fact, he has a genius-level IQ, doesn't he?"

Mrs. Schmerse ran her tongue around her lips. "Yes. I believe he does."

"And would you say Brent was more or less mature than the average student in your class?"

There was a slight pause. "More."

"Thank you," Liz said pleasantly. "No further questions."

Versey put on another teacher, who had substantially the same observations as Mrs. Schmerse. His final witness was Brent's mother.

Maureen Tompkins took her seat in the witness box with a wad of Kleenex clutched in her hand. Oh, great, Jeff thought. When all else fails, call the killer's mother and have her weep all over.

Mrs. Tompkins played her role well, tearfully explaining what a good son Brent was, how gentle and patient he was with his younger sister, how helpful he was around the house.

"There's been a lot of talk today about how intelligent Brent is, how mature," Versey said gently. "Is that how you think of him?"

"No," Mrs. Tompkins sobbed. "He's just a child. He's my little boy."

Jeff coughed loudly. This was priceless. If he hadn't been sure that he'd be cited for contempt of court, he would've loved to jump up and cram the crime scene photos down her throat and say, "Look at this! This is what your precious baby did. Isn't that enough to make a mother proud?" But instead he sat there, sweating and gritting his teeth, until mercifully Liz declined to cross-examine and Versey helped the weeping madonna back to her seat.

By this time it was one o'clock. Judge Dunham said, "Ordinarily I would break for lunch at this point, but if there's no objection, I would really like hear counsel's closing arguments first."

"Thank God," Liz murmured to Jeff as she got to her feet.

As Liz took a couple of steps toward the judge, Jeff could see that the heat was finally getting to her, too. Her face was flushed and her blouse and jacket stuck to her back. "Your Honor, the offenses with which Brent Tompkins has been charged are the most serious our law allows: the kidnapping and intentional homicide of another human being. You have heard some of the witnesses testify that this is Brent's first offense, that he has no prior juvenile record. While that is true, the state believes that far from serving to minimize the situation, that factor exacerbates it. I submit that a young person whose very first offense is first-degree murder is a very dangerous person indeed."

She paused to take a breath. "The evidence has conclusively established that Brent is a very intelligent and resourceful young man. Your Honor is also able to see that Brent is physically mature for his age. Finally, I submit that the juvenile system is not equipped to handle or rehabilitate a young man of Brent's caliber. The intelligence and maturity that lift him above the fray and indicate his suitability to respond to the charges against him in an adult forum carry with them the requirement of special rehabilitative needs that can better be met by the vast resources of the department of corrections, with its full complement of health care professionals and vocational workers. Your Honor, the state respectfully requests that you grant our petition for waiver of juvenile jurisdiction. Thank you." She turned and walked back to her seat, clearly glad it was over.

Versey blustered away for nearly half an hour, repeating key points of his witnesses' testimony over and over, ad nauseam. Brent had never been in trouble. Brent was a good boy. Brent was a helpful boy. Brent was a devout boy. Finally, in disgust, Jeff wrote on Liz's pad, "Brent is a murdering boy."

"Your Honor," Versey hammered on, "this boy celebrated his fourteenth birthday only two months ago. Just think, if the offense with which he had been charged had taken place ten weeks earlier, we wouldn't all be sitting here today in this heat. Why?" he raised his fat arms as if waiting for someone to respond. "Because the law states that juvenile court jurisdiction may not be waived in homicide cases unless the offense occurred on or after the child's fourteenth birthday. Brent Tompkins barely meets the age requirement for waiver. In spite of his intelligence, it is clear from the testimony presented that Brent is still very much a child. He has led a sheltered and protected life. To cast such a young innocent into the adult criminal system would be to throw him to the wolves. He would be utterly unable to cope. His life would not be safe."

The sweat was now pouring down Versey's face. "Contrary to what Ms. Stanfeld said, there *are* suitable facilities and services available within the juvenile system to deal with a boy of Brent's mental capacity, assuming of course that somewhere down the line there is a finding that he committed the offenses with which he is charged. Therefore, Your Honor, we request that you deny the state's petition for waiver. Thank you."

"Thank you, counsel," Judge Dunham said. "I will now take this matter under advisement. Please report back here at four-thirty to hear my decision."

Jeff and Liz went back to her office, where an anxious Tom Barker was still pacing back and forth. "What happened? What took so long?" he asked.

"Versey obviously doesn't subscribe to the notion of making a brief or concise presentation," Liz said, peeling off her suit jacket and tossing it over her chair. "The judge is making up his mind now. He's going to announce his decision at four-thirty." She looked at the two men. "I don't know about you, but I'm starving and I'd like to drink about a gallon of water. Why don't the three of us sneak out the back and go somewhere cool to get a bite to eat?"

"We can take my car," Tom offered. "It's parked out back."

They had a quiet lunch at an out-of-the-way restaurant Jeff recommended. "The place isn't much on ambience," he'd explained, "but the food's good and cheap, they keep it well air-conditioned, and I can pretty much guarantee none of the press hounds are going to find us there."

They lingered at the restaurant until nearly four, then returned to Liz's office. At 4:25, Liz motioned to Jeff. "We'd better get in there," she said, putting her suit jacket on again. Jeff reluctantly did the same.

"What do you think is going to happen?" Tom asked anxiously.

"I think it's gonna be okay," Liz said, giving his arm a reassuring squeeze.

Judge Dunham entered the courtroom with a somber expression on his face. Without any preamble, he began to read from a prepared text. Jeff involuntarily found himself holding his breath. "This matter is before the court on the state's motion for waiver of juvenile court jurisdiction in the matter of Brent Tompkins. Having heard testimony and argument of counsel, the court finds that the record establishes to a reasonable probability that a violation of criminal law has been committed and that Brent Tompkins probably committed it."

Jeff let out his breath. So far, so good, but now came the hard part. He inhaled again as Dunham went on. "The court further finds that Brent Tompkins is not mentally ill or developmentally disabled; that he has not been previously found delinquent; that he has no prior offenses or prior treatment history. The court also finds that Brent Tompkins is both physically and mentally mature."

Jeff exhaled again. You're on the right track, you old bastard. Now just keep going, he silently urged the judge.

Dunham was reading faster now. "The offenses with which Brent Tompkins has been charged are serious ones which were alleged to have been committed in a violent, aggressive, premeditated, and willful manner. Finally, the court finds that the services and procedures available for the treatment of Brent Tompkins within the juvenile system are inadequate." The judge looked at Brent. "Based upon the foregoing, it is the judgment of this court that the state has met its burden of establishing by clear and convincing evidence that it would be contrary to the best interests of the child and the public to hear this case in juvenile court. The state's motion to waive jurisdiction is hereby granted." He slammed his gavel down. "Court is adjourned."

The tension in Jeff's neck and back eased. He reached over and patted Liz on the arm. "Nice job!" he whispered.

"Thanks," she murmured.

As they stood up and began to make their way back to Liz's office to give Tom the good news, Jeff turned

back and stole a glance at Brent. His head was turned
in profile as he listened to something Versey was saying. The color had drained out of his face and his eyes
looked slightly glazed. Well, what do you know? Jeff
thought. Maybe the little bastard does have feelings
after all.

At that moment, Brent turned toward the back of
the room and his eyes met Jeff's. Jeff gave him the
coldest look he could muster. Brent's lower lip immediately began to tremble, and he quickly turned back
to his attorney. That's right, Brent, Jeff thought to
himself smugly. You just got a little taste of your own
medicine and you didn't like it much, did you? Well,
don't worry, kid, you'll get used to it. Because before
this case is over, there's going to be plenty more fun
in store for you.

PART THREE

Chapter 28

"I'd like you to tell me what happened that day, Greg," Harry said in a conversational tone. "Start from the time Brent called you."

It was a bright Thursday morning, three days after Brent had been waived into adult court. Liz and Charles Bennett had appeared before Judge Franchetta the previous afternoon to put their plea bargain on the record. Although the formal disposition of the matter wouldn't take place for several weeks, during which time a probation agent would meet with Greg and furnish the judge with a written recommendation, that process was merely a formality and for all intents and purposes Greg's bout with the law was over.

Although juvenile court proceedings were closed to the public and the law strictly prohibited anyone from disclosing the names of the youngsters involved, once a waiver to adult court had been signed, the juvenile received exactly the same treatment as grown-up defendants awaiting trial. Judge Dunham had scarcely brought his gavel down on Brent's waiver hearing when the media eagerly waiting outside of the courtroom had learned the boy's name and proceeded to broadcast it, along with an eighth grade photograph of the youth culled from the Oakwood Junior High yearbook.

This publicity had made the Oakwood contingent supporting Brent all the more vocal. By eight o'clock the next morning, the DA's office had received twenty faxes protesting the waiver and accusing Liz of "blackening the good name of all Oakwood residents" and "crucifying the sterling reputation of the community."

"Christ!" Liz had grumbled to one of the senior assistant DAs. "You'd think we'd arrested Mother Teresa."

"You'd better get used to it," her colleague had cheerfully advised. "My guess is this isn't the kind of group that's going to take this lying down. You know, Liz," the man had added confidentially, "when you were first assigned to this case, I'll admit I was more than a little miffed. No offense, you understand, but a bunch of us *do* have more seniority around here than you. But now—" The man raised his eyes heavenward. "You couldn't run fast enough to give me that dog. Best of luck," he said, patting her on the shoulder sympathetically. "You're sure as hell gonna need it."

The Oakwood group's latest ploy had been to bombard Senator Kilpatrick with mail demanding that the investigation into Jeremy's murder be reopened. With his political future hanging in the balance, Harry had decided it would be a good idea if he got a firsthand look at Liz's star witness before reporting back to the senator's representatives that the case was in fact under control.

Liz had asked the Saunderses to bring Greg to the courthouse for an interview. The group was sitting in the county boardroom on the top floor of the courthouse, with Jeff and the prosecutors on one side of the enormous maple table and the Saunders family on the other.

After Harry asked his question, all eyes focused on Greg. Sitting there between his parents, the boy looked so small and pale and frightened that Liz knew she had done the right thing by agreeing the plea bargain. It would have served no purpose to send this child to a juvenile detention facility for his limited role in Jeremy's death.

"Greg, answer the man's question," Teresa Saunders prompted gently.

Greg took a deep breath and began to tell his story. The ordeal had left him with a slight stutter, and the words came haltingly. The entire time he spoke, he kept his gaze focused on the table in front of him, refusing to make eye contact with anyone. When he'd finished, Harry asked, "Do you ever remember Brent talking about the Barkers before the day Jeremy was killed?"

Greg shook his head.

"Did he ever talk about wanting to hurt any other neighborhood children?"

Another shake of the head.

"Do you know what Brent did with the shovel he used to hit Jeremy?"

"He took it with him when we split up that day," the boy replied in a small voice. "I asked him later what happened to it, and he said he took care of it so nobody would ever find it."

"Probably sawed the handle into pieces and buried the whole thing someplace," Donald Saunders suggested.

"Could be," Liz agreed. "Greg, had you ever known Brent to be violent before that day in the woods?"

Greg hesitated a moment and turned to his mother, a questioning look on his face. "It's okay," Teresa Saunders said reassuringly, patting her son's hand. "Tell them whatever you know."

Greg swallowed hard and said, "A couple of times I saw him punch kids on the playground."

"Do you know if they were injured?"

"I don't think so."

"Was the incident with Jeremy the first time Brent had asked you to help him do something you knew was wrong?" Harry asked.

Greg remained silent. "It's all right," his mother reassured him again. "No one will be mad at you, no matter what you might say."

"That's right," Liz added. "We're just trying to get into Brent's head."

"I did some stuff before," Greg said in a contrite tone.

"Can you tell us about it?" Liz prompted.

"Once Brent had me steal a pad of signed hall passes out of a teacher's desk," Greg answered slowly. "And then I had to fill them out for Brent and some of the other older guys."

"Were there any other incidents?" Harry asked.

Greg continued to stare downward. "I took ten dollars out of a girl's locker and gave it to Brent."

"And I take it you never got caught for doing these things?"

Greg shook his head.

"Why do you think Brent asked you to do these things?" Harry inquired. "Was he testing your loyalty?"

"I don't know."

"Well, can you tell us why you did them?"

Greg ran his tongue around his lips and hesitated, trying to find the right words. "Everybody looked up to Brent. I just wanted to be his friend."

Harry nodded. "Did Brent ask his other friends to do things like that?"

"I don't know."

"Did you ever hear Brent and any of the other older boys discuss things they'd done wrong?" Jeff asked.

"Not really. They never said much when I was around. Sometimes they'd be talking or laughing about something and when I'd walk up to them they'd say stuff like, 'Guess it's time to shut up now. We wouldn't want the kid to hear.' "

"And you have no idea what they meant by those remarks?" Jeff asked.

Greg bit his lower lip and shook his head.

"Greg, we've been told that Brent's close friends are Josh Mahoney, Chad Elliott, Taylor Huff, and Dillon Freeman," Liz put in. "Is he closer to one of those boys than to the others?"

"Josh and Taylor are his best friends."

"Can you think of any other friends' names?"

The boy thought a moment. "Sometimes he hangs around with Jon Bradford and Dan Fast."

Jeff flipped through his pad of notes. "I stopped at both of those households and got the same cold shoulder as every place else in Oakwood that I've tried."

Donald Saunders spoke up. "I can't believe how heartless people can be when something like this happens," he said. "Several customers who have come into my dealership have made inane comments about the case. And we've already had a number of harassing phone calls at home. We're going to have to change our number."

Teresa Saunders leaned forward, her face grim. It appeared to Liz that she probably hadn't had a good night's sleep since Greg's arrest. "I don't know how we're going to be able to go on living in that community," she said, squeezing her hands tightly together. "Already I feel like we're being shunned because Greg told the police about Brent. I don't know how," she sighed, "but everyone seems to know it. I stopped at the meat market on Tuesday night and a woman I barely knew looked at me and said, 'Your son ought to be ashamed of himself,' I was so upset I couldn't even think of a response. I just turned around and ran back to the car." She paused a moment and took a deep breath. "I'm afraid for Greg's safety. And for Patrick's, too. After all, Brent did threaten to kill Greg if he ever told what had happened, and if that monster is capable of killing once—" Her voice trailed off.

"There's a hearing tomorrow to deal with the matter of continuing Brent's bail," Liz said quickly. "There's already a restraining order keeping him away from Tom Barker. I can ask the judge to extend it to keep him away from your family, too."

"Do you really think a court order is going to stop

him?'' Teresa asked, her voice quivering. "From everything I've heard recently, that boy's not afraid of the devil himself.''

"I can understand your concern,'' Harry put in soothingly, "but court orders are generally quite effective. And you can rest assured that the Tompkins family has every incentive to keep Brent walking the straight and narrow from now until the trial.''

"The sheriff's department can easily send some extra patrols past your house,'' Jeff added. "And I'm sure your local police would be happy to do the same. If you'd like, I'd be glad to speak to them about coordinating something between our two departments so your house gets lots of drive-bys. That should quash any thoughts Brent might have about retaliating against Greg or your family.''

"That boy is an animal,'' Mr. Saunders said gruffly. "A very dangerous animal. Tell me frankly,'' he said, looking directly at Liz. "Are you going to be able to put him away?''

"We'll do everything in our power to make it happen,'' Liz promised.

"But what if something goes wrong and he gets off?'' Teresa asked, her eyes widening in fear. "We'd have to leave the area. None of us would be safe.''

"You'll make yourself sick thinking about things like that,'' Liz counseled. "I'm confident we'll get a conviction.''

"But it all hinges on Greg, doesn't it?'' Teresa asked anxiously. "And that horrid attorney the Tompkins hired is going to bully Greg and try to break him down.'' Upon hearing his mother's words, Greg's pale complexion had turned even whiter.

"We'll have some practice sessions to get Greg ready to testify,'' Liz explained. "We can even go in the courtroom so he can sit in the witness stand to make him feel more comfortable. I guarantee he'll do just fine.''

After the Saunderses had taken their leave, Harry

turned to Jeff. "Your suggestion of having the sheriff's department step up patrols was a good one. I'd appreciate your following up on that."

Jeff pushed back his chair and stood up. "I'll go to talk to our patrol commander right now and also call the Oakwood gendarmes to coordinate some surveillance of the Saunders house. If Brent is crazy enough to be harboring any more murderous impulses, that should snuff them right out."

When Jeff had left the room, Liz turned to Harry expectantly. "Well, what did you think?"

Harry looked at her evenly for a moment, then said, "What I think is that this case is far from a sure thing."

Liz's mouth dropped open. "What do you mean?" she exclaimed. "I've got an eyewitness to the murder."

"Yes, you've got an eyewitness," Harry agreed. "A boy who's so scared he can't get three words out of his mouth without stuttering and who can't even look his mother in the eye, much less hold his own on cross-examination." He stood up and walked over to the window. "Paul Versey will make mincemeat out of him in five minutes."

"I'll admit Greg wasn't in very good form today," Liz agreed, "but we've got a lot of time before the trial. Jeff and I will work with him. He just needs a little coaching, that's all."

Harry made a low coughing sound and turned back to face Liz. "You don't really believe that, do you?"

"Of course I do," she replied indignantly. "Given a little time, I think he'll do just fine."

"And what if he doesn't?" Harry asked, looking her in the eye. "What if he totally freezes up on the stand and can't get his story out?"

Liz's face was flushed. "What are you suggesting?" she demanded. "That I offer Brent a plea bargain because there's a possibility Greg *might* freeze up at trial?" Her gaze narrowed. "Yes, I suppose it would be so much easier for you if you could report to senator Kilpatrick that this entire messy case has been neatly disposed of."

Harry's mouth was grim, but he ignored her last remark. "I did not mention a plea bargain," he replied calmly. "What I *am* suggesting is that you find something more: a motive why Brent killed the child, some evidence that he's been violent or abusive to small children in the past, or some other, more articulate friend who'll testify that Brent told him what he did to Jeremy."

"Jeff is still working on all of those things," Liz assured him.

"Well, I'd strongly recommend that the detective throw his heart and soul into the project," Harry said. "Because without it I wouldn't bet a plugged nickel on getting a conviction." He turned and quickly walked out, leaving Liz sitting alone at the large table, with a feeling of dread growing in the pit of her stomach.

Chapter 29

Liz was standing on a ladder shaping a tall stand of arborvitae in front of her house on a balmy Saturday evening when Esther called to her from the driveway. "Come down from there! I'm getting dizzy just watching you."

"I'll be done in a minute," Liz replied. "You can go in the house if you don't want to watch."

"I don't know why you refuse to get a yardman," Esther said moments later as Liz calmly climbed down, her clippers in one hand. "You could hurt yourself."

"This is a good outlet for me," Liz replied. "It's how I take out my frustrations about the Tompkins case."

"If you fall, you're going to look pretty silly trying the case wearing a full-body cast," Esther grumbled. "So what's the frustration of the day?"

Liz shook the bushes to knock the clipped pieces to the ground. "The entire case, as usual," she admitted ruefully. "I keep telling myself that it doesn't bother me that many people here in town hate me for what I'm doing, but that's a lie. It still hurts."

"Any more hate mail?" Esther asked sympathetically.

"A couple pieces. More of the same crap. Anyway, to compensate for getting the cold shoulder around here, I feel like I have to try this case as if I were fighting for my life. I feel such pressure, such a compulsion to win. That's a new feeling for me. When I was in private practice, I always prided myself on being able to keep my distance from the matters I was working on. I'd do the best job I could for the client and if I won, it was great and if I lost—well, I'd pretty much take it in stride. But this—" She brushed her hair out of her eyes and looked at her friend. "I think about it all the time. It's on my mind so much that lately I haven't even cared about food. Now for me, that's a radical change in behavior."

"I noticed that you're looking quite svelte these days," Esther complimented her.

"Hardly svelte," Liz said ruefully, patting her hips. "But I have lost four more pounds, and I'm beginning to detect the presence of hipbones under here someplace." She scooped up the debris that had fallen from the bushes, throwing it into a bushel basket.

"How did Brent's bail hearing go?" Esther asked.

Liz shrugged. "Okay. The court commissioner continued his bail at half a million, and I got him to enter a restraining order keeping Brent away from the Saunders family. Teresa is very concerned that Brent might try to hurt Greg, and I can't say that I blame her. Jeff told the village police and the sheriff's department to step up their patrols in the area, so don't get alarmed if you happen to notice a steady procession of cop cars driving past your house."

"Thanks for warning me," Esther replied. "Otherwise I might've thought they were coming to arrest Bob for insider trading."

Liz piled the remainder of the clippings in the basket and took them to the curb. "That Paul Versey is sure a treat to deal with," she said, as she walked back up the driveway and put her clippers in the garage. "He renewed his request that Brent be allowed to leave the state for two weeks to visit his grandmother in Cape Cod. Apparently the family has some fancy spread where they take a sabbatical every summer."

Esther nodded. "Brent's mother's family has mega-bucks. I think they have a summer place at Chatham."

"That sounds right," Liz agreed. "Anyway, does Versey ever have a flair for the dramatic." She rolled her eyes. "You should've heard him carry on. When I objected to his request, he made it sound like I was the most narrow-minded person in the world, trying to deny Brent his constitutional rights to life, liberty, and the pursuit of summers at the shore."

"So what happened? I hope the commissioner didn't buy it."

Liz waved her hand in a dismissive gesture. "No, he denied the request in short order. There's no way in hell someone charged with first-degree murder is going to be allowed out of the state. We'd have to begin extradition proceedings to get him back." She grimaced. "But leave it to Paul Versey to ask for the moon. I keep wondering what he's going to think of next." She wiped her hands on her shorts. "Let's go inside. I made some iced tea earlier." A short time later the two women were seated at the kitchen table, sipping their drinks.

"What's up next in the case?" Esther asked.

"There's a preliminary hearing next Tuesday where the judge decides if there's enough evidence to bind Brent over for trial," Liz explained. "Then Brent will enter a plea of not guilty and the case will be set for trial."

"Any idea when that'll be?"

"Probably September."

"That fast?" Esther asked with surprise. "Boy, I guess there is no rest for the wicked."

Liz took another sip of tea. "I'm nervous about it," she admitted.

"That's only human nature. After all, there's a hell of a lot riding on it."

Liz nodded and ran her index finger around the icy glass. "My main problem is that Harry is coming down hard to try to force me to offer Brent a deal. In that case there won't be a trial.''

"You don't mean a plea bargain?" Esther asked incredulously. "How could Harry even consider it?"

"Because he's convinced Greg is going to make a lousy witness. And unfortunately I don't really disagree with him on that," she added ruefully.

"So you're being strong-armed to reduce the charges?"

Liz sighed. "Not exactly. At least not yet. As Harry put it, he strongly suggests that we find some additional corroboration that Brent was the killer. Jeff's been working day and night trying to come up with something, but it doesn't look good. None of the families whose kids were friends of Brent's will talk to him.''

"So after all you've gone through to get Brent waived into adult court, you might have to back off. What a crock of shit!"

"I'm still hoping it won't come to that."

"Damn that Harry anyway!" Esther exclaimed. "I thought he promised you that you could have free rein with the case. How can he go back on his word?"

Liz shrugged. "He's in a sensitive position."

Esther made a face. "You mean because of the damn federal appointment?"

Liz nodded. "The committee's made no move to recommend a candidate to the president. I've been wondering if they're not holding off to see what happens with Brent's case."

"So Harry pressures you to make the case go away quietly, thinking that'll increase his odds of getting the job.''

"Something like that."

"That sucks!" Esther exclaimed. "After all, your handling of the case cost you something you dearly wanted: a seat on the Oakwood planning commission. Believe me, if I were you I would've sued the village board for every dime they had, but you took it on the chin and stuck to your principles and kept right on prosecuting the case. Why can't Harry show he's a mensch and do the same?"

Liz smiled ruefully. "It's his call. I'm going to do my best to stick to my guns, but he *is* my boss, so if push comes to shove and he says I have to offer Brent a deal, I suppose I'll either have to do it or resign from the case."

"How infuriating!" Esther clenched her jaw. "I know this is a really sore subject with you, but are you still seeing him?"

"Sort of."

Esther wrinkled her nose. "That's like telling me you're a little bit pregnant. Are you seeing him or aren't you?"

Liz sighed. "We haven't broken it off, but we've been keeping a respectful distance from each other the past couple weeks. That's another reason I've been a little uptight. It makes things a bit stressful around the office."

Esther gritted her teeth. "When are you going to unload that turkey?"

Liz grimaced. "Esther, please. He's not a turkey—"

"Oh, no?" Esther retorted. "What would you call someone who tries to get you to compromise your principles and uses your personal relationship as a ploy to do it?"

"I suppose now you're going to give me another pitch about why I should throw myself at Tom Barker?" Liz asked, her lower lip curling down.

"The thought did cross my mind," Esther replied.

"I know your intentions are good," Liz said, "but I'm still not sure if it'd be a wise move."

"Oh, it definitely would be," Esther said airily. "Trust me. I promise you'll thank me for it later."

"Trust you, eh? I think that's what the captain of the *Titanic* said just before he hit the iceberg."

Esther smiled. "Don't worry. I have no intention of letting you go down with the ship."

Chapter 30

Liz's call relaying word of Harry's desire to offer Brent a deal unless they found more corroboration of the boy's culpability had sent Jeff into overdrive. Having failed to gain entrée into their homes, the following day he paid visits to the workplaces of the fathers of the two boys Greg had identified as Brent's best friends to see if he could persuade, cajole, or bully the men into allowing him to speak to their sons.

Josh Mahoney's dad was a dermatologist working out of a posh clinic in north suburban Milwaukee. At nine in the morning, after announcing himself to the snooty nurse-receptionist, Jeff found himself in a waiting room filled with teenagers with acne, old women with liver spots, and a middle-aged man with a virulent-looking red rash all over the exposed portions of his body. At ten-thirty, after paging through the waiting room's supply of six-month-old issues of *Seventeen*, *Sports Illustrated*, and *Ladies Home Journal*, and checking back with the receptionist three times to make sure she had informed the doctor of his presence, he was ushered into the doctor's office by a dour-faced nurse in her thirties.

Dr. David Mahoney was a russet-haired, ruddy-cheeked man about Jeff's age. The walls of his office were covered with diplomas from Ivy League schools and mounted game fish. The doctor was seated at his desk, scrawling some notations on a patient's chart. He barely looked up as Jeff entered.

"Dr. Mahoney, I'm Detective Jeff Gardner," Jeff

announced as he sat down in the straight-backed visitor's chair in front of the doctor's desk.

"I know who you are," the doctor replied without breaking stride in his writing. "You were at our house a while back asking questions about the Barker murder." He finally looked up at Jeff with cold green eyes. "As you can tell from the looks of my waiting room, I'm a busy man. You've got five minutes to state your business and move on."

Jeff frowned. Good day to you, too, asshole, he thought to himself. "I admire a man who gets straight to the point," Jeff said with just a hint of sarcasm. "I have reason to believe that your son Josh might have some information about Jeremy Barker's murder, and I'm here to ask your permission to speak to him."

If the doctor was surprised by this statement, he gave no indication of it. "And just how did you happen to come by this information?" he asked.

"I'm not at liberty to say," Jeff replied.

The doctor shrugged. "In that case, I thought it was made clear to you when you visited our house that no one in my family has anything to say to the police."

"I do recall getting that message loud and clear, but I was hoping you might reconsider."

"Is my son a suspect? Do you have reason to believe he abetted the murder in some way?"

For a split second, Jeff considered lying, but then thought better of it. He slowly shook his head. "No."

The corners of the doctor's mouth turned up in the smallest grin. "In that case, I must repeat that my family has nothing further to discuss with you."

"You realize, Doctor, that there are laws against obstructing justice." Jeff's voice took on a hard edge.

"And I'm sure you realize, Detective, that there are also laws against harassment," the doctor replied in a harder voice. "I understand that Martin Tompkins plans to file a civil suit against the county just as soon as the trial is over."

Jeff shrugged. "That's his business, but if I were Mr.

Tompkins, I'd save my energy. It's my firm belief that after the trial he'll be so busy driving up north to visit his son in prison that he probably won't have time to worry about suing anybody." He got to his feet. "Thank you for your time, Doctor. If you should have a change of heart, you know where to contact me."

"If I were you, Detective, I wouldn't hold my breath."

Jeff had similar luck with Taylor Huff's father, an executive at a computer software firm. At the close of that interview, Jeff asked Huff if he knew Tom Barker.

"I've met him, yes."

"Then perhaps you can put yourself in his place for a moment," Jeff suggested. "After losing his wife a couple of years ago, he loses his only child. Stop and think. If that happened to you, wouldn't you want to get to the truth of why that little boy was murdered, even though gaining that knowledge might prove painful for other people?"

Huff paused a moment and pursed his lips before replying. "I understand what you're saying, Detective, but I have an alternate scenario to suggest. Put yourself in *my* shoes. I have a fourteen-year-old son, alive and well, who requires my help to stay that way. I sympathize with Tom Barker's loss and his predicament, but I'm afraid that doesn't change my answer."

"I didn't think it would," Jeff mumbled bitterly as he left.

The rest of the day's efforts had yielded similar results. Jeff arrived home early that evening, ravenous and in a foul mood. He walked into the house expecting to find Julie preparing dinner. Instead, the only sign of life in the dwelling was the incessant noise coming from Bill's stereo. Jeff grabbed a can of beer out of the refrigerator and yelled up the stairs. "Where's your mother?"

"What?" came the faint reply.

"Shut that damn noise off and come down here," Jeff ordered.

Moments later a tall, handsome boy of fourteen, with Jeff's curly brown hair and his mother's deep blue eyes, dressed in navy shorts and a white muscle shirt, stood in the doorway between the living room and kitchen. "Did you say something?" Bill asked.

"Yeah," Jeff replied. "I asked where your mother is."

"She's at work."

"Still?" Jeff asked, frowning. "She was on first shift today."

"She left a message on the answering machine," Bill explained. "Somebody got sick, so she volunteered to fill in."

"That's lovely," Jeff grumbled. Ever since Julie had applied for the supervisor's position, it appeared to Jeff that she'd been bending over backward trying to score points with the brass. This was the third time in two weeks she'd worked a double shift. He didn't particularly mind—if she really thought that busting her ass at that damn hospital was the route to success, that was her business—but on days like this when he was really out of sorts he missed having her there when he got home. She could always calm him down and help him see things in perspective. Not to mention the fact that she was one hell of a cook.

"I don't suppose there's anything in the fridge we could warm up for supper?" Jeff asked, peering into the refrigerator.

"Nope," Bill replied. "I already checked."

Jeff drained his beer as he considered his options. Alex was at work, too, so it was just him and Bill. He supposed he could make sandwiches or grill some burgers, but he ate that stuff every day at lunch. "What do you say we hit Pizza Hut?" he asked.

"All right!" Bill responded enthusiastically.

"I'll go clean up and change clothes and we'll head

out," Jeff said, standing up. "Were there any other messages on the answering machine?"

"Yeah. Grandma called."

"Which one?" Jeff asked, although he already knew the answer, since Julie's mother was much more apt to stop by in person than telephone.

"Grandma Gardner," Bill replied, rolling his eyes. "Who else?"

"Did she want anything in particular?"

Bill shrugged. "I dunno. Somethin' about wanting you to help her go over her will."

"Oh, no," Jeff groaned. "Not again." Every six months or so, his mother would get it in her head she was not long for this world and would want Jeff to help her decide how to divide up her earthly possessions. "I'll call her tomorrow," Jeff said, heading for the stairway. He'd had all the aggravation he could handle for one day. He wished he could find a tactful way to tell his mother that none of her kin gave a shit whether or nor she bequeathed them the lead crystal ashtray or the hand-hewn oxen yoke that had belonged to her grandfather.

"I've got to encourage her to find a hobby," he muttered to himself as he showered. Something that would get her out of the house and keep her mind off her troubles. Or better yet, he thought, as he toweled himself dry, maybe he could convince her to move to Michigan. After all, Jeff had been listening to her troubles on a daily basis for more than twenty years. It seemed only fair that her other son take the next twenty-year shift.

Chapter 31

A major storm was brewing in the Midwest, and Horicon County was under a tornado watch the day of Brent's preliminary examination and plea hearing. Liz facetiously wondered whether there was some connection between the area's unstable weather and the presence of Paul Versey in their midst.

The blustering, corpulent attorney had blown into Lakeview early that Tuesday morning in a shiny black Cadillac chauffeured by one of his associates. After pausing for a photo op on the courthouse steps, during which the gusty winds wreaked havoc with his few strands of hair, and gracing the media with a short statement proclaiming his client's innocence, Versey and his assistant had decamped to a small private room off the building's law library, where Brent and his parents were already waiting.

Jeff and Liz were sitting in her office drinking coffee when Tom Barker arrived via a back stairway. "You know, you guys really have to stop meeting like this," Jeff said in a breezy tone, still wondering if there might not be something going on between the two of them.

Liz gave him a dirty look, while Tom gave no indication he'd even heard the remark. "Will this take long?" he asked anxiously.

"At most half a day," Liz replied. She stood up, straightened the skirt of her navy suit, and slipped into her jacket. "It all depends on how long Versey spends cross-examining my witnesses."

"Don't worry," Jeff said, giving Tom's arm a reassuring pat. "This'll be a piece of cake. Just make yourself comfortable. We'll be back before you know it."

The presiding judge at the preliminary would be John Hemming, a thoughtful jurist in his mid-fifties. Because Brent's case was now in adult court, all proceedings were required by law to be open to the public, unless the judge found good cause to order closure. As Jeff and Liz entered the courtroom, they saw that it was nearly full of media and other thrill seekers. They took their place at counsel table and awaited the entry of the defense team.

They didn't have to wait long. Within moments a roar went up in the courtroom. Jeff turned and out of the corner of his eye saw Versey, dressed in black, leading the procession of his faithful up the center aisle. Brent, who was wearing brown slacks and a brown tweed jacket, followed close behind. Versey's young associate and Mr. and Mrs. Tompkins brought up the rear.

"Where do you suppose that guy gets his clothes?" Jeff whispered. "From the wardrobe department of a funeral home? All he needs is a black cape lined in red silk and he'd be ready to give Bela Lugosi a run for his money." Liz responded by kicking him lightly on the ankle.

Brent sat between his attorneys at the defense counsel table. As they waited for the judge to enter, Jeff stared hard at Brent. Once again, the boy appeared completely calm. Did he really think he was going to beat this thing? His mother was the only person who looked nervous. She gave her son a quick hug before taking a seat next to her husband in the front row of the spectator section.

Jeff's musings were interrupted by Judge Hemming, a short, gray-haired man, who called the proceeding to order. After the appearances had been noted, Versey got to his feet and bellowed, "Your Honor, before we get under way here, I would like to make a motion to have this proceeding closed to the public."

A murmur went through the press corps. As Liz glanced up at the bench, it was obvious Hemming was not pleased with the way things were starting out. "As you know, Counsel, there is a presumption that preliminaries are open proceedings. On what ground do you feel you are entitled to closure?" the judge asked sternly.

"Your Honor," Versey boomed, "just look around you. This case has become a media circus. I firmly believe it will be impossible for my client to obtain a fair hearing in this environment. The matter fairly cries out for closure."

The judge rolled his eyes slightly. "Mr. Versey, the only crying I hear in this courtroom is coming from you. Your motion for closure is denied. Let's move on. Ms. Stanfeld—"

"You Honor," Versey interrupted. "I move that the prosecution's witnesses be sequestered."

Jeff turned to Liz in amazement. "What's he doing?" he whispered. Sequestering witnesses at a preliminary was highly uncommon in Horicon County.

Liz shook her head. "I don't know," she whispered back. "Your Honor, the state objects," she said aloud. "The purpose of sequestration is to prevent collusion among witnesses. There is no reason for it here. The only witnesses I plan to call are Dr. Raoul Ramirez from the state crime lab and Detective Jeff Gardner from the local sheriff's department. These men are each already well aware of what the other is going to say, so there is no reason why they shouldn't hear each other's testimony."

"Your Honor," Versey persisted, "section 970.03 sub (6) of the Wisconsin Statutes gives the defendant the right to sequestration of witnesses. I demand to be heard on this issue—"

Judge Hemming waved his hand dismissively. "There will be no need for that, Counsel. In the interest of finishing this hearing within my lifetime, I am going to grant your request. Ms. Stanfeld, will you please see to it that your witnesses leave the room. They can wait in the jury room next door."

"What the hell is this?" Jeff whispered angrily.

Liz jabbed him in the side with her elbow. "There's nothing we can do about it," she said under her breath. "Just get out and don't make a fuss. Tell Dr. Ramirez to wait out in the hall. We'll be needing him shortly."

Jeff gritted his teeth and purposely pushed back his chair in such a way that it made a great deal of noise as it scraped across the floor. Shooting a nasty look at Versey's back, he reluctantly left the room.

After making a short opening statement, Liz called Dr. Ramirez to the stand. The forensic pathologist testified as to the findings he made during Jeremy's autopsy.

"What was the cause of death, Dr. Ramirez?" Liz asked.

"The boy's skull had been crushed as the result of repeated blows with a flat, blunt object."

"From your examination of Jeremy Barker, were you able to determine the time of death?"

"Yes. Judging by the stomach contents, he died early in the afternoon of June 11."

"Thank you, Doctor. I have no further questions."

The judge turned to Versey. "Cross-examination, Counsel?"

Versey shook his head. "No, Your Honor."

The judge nodded. "Dr. Ramirez, you are dismissed. Ms. Stanfeld, kindly call your next witness."

"The state calls Detective Captain Jeff Gardner."

It was obvious that Jeff was still fuming about being excluded from the courtroom when he took the stand. He glared openly at Versey as Liz deftly led him through his investigation into Jeremy's disappearance and death, culminating in Greg's confession of what he and Brent had done. He stared at Brent as well, but this time the boy wouldn't meet his gaze. When Liz had finished, she informed the court that the state rested.

The judge turned to Versey and inquired if he wished to cross-examine Jeff.

"No cross, Your Honor."

"Thank you, Detective," the judge said. "You may resume your seat at counsel table if you wish."

Jeff nodded at the judge, shot Versey another dirty look, and returned to his seat next to Liz.

Liz was surprised but pleased at Versey's decision not to cross-examine. After he had Jeff expelled from the courtroom, she'd expected Versey to spend a great deal of time attacking his credibility and attempting to demean his character. She sure didn't understand the attorney's strategy. Nothing the guy did seemed to make much sense. He must have something up his sleeve, but damned if she could figure out what it was.

Liz made a short closing argument, explaining the reasons why the court should bind the defendant over for trial. The judge denied Versey's request for the opportunity to make a final argument.

"There's no need for that," Judge Hemming said firmly. "I am ready to rule." He referred to a piece of paper in front of him. "The court hereby finds that the facts that have been presented here today, together with the reasonable inferences that can be drawn from them, lead a reasonable person to conclude that crimes of first-degree intentional homicide by use of a dangerous weapon and kidnapping have probably been committed and that the defendant, Brent Tompkins, probably committed said crimes. I hereby order the defendant bound over for trial." Turning to Versey, he said, "Is the defendant ready to enter a plea?"

"Yes, Your Honor," Versey replied.

"Very well," Judge Hemming went on. "How does the defendant plead?"

Versey slowly got to his feet and leaned forward,

his big hands resting on the counsel table. "Your honor," he boomed, "the defendant pleads not guilty—"

Liz scrawled "NG" on her legal pad and began to put the cap back on her pen. That was all she wrote for this hearing.

"—and not guilty by reason of mental disease or defect." Versey continued with a flourish before sitting down again.

Liz dropped the pen on the floor. A murmur of excitement ran through the courtroom. Jeff reached down under Liz's chair and retrieved the pen. As he handed it back to her, they exchanged astonished looks. Had they really heard right? Was Brent Tompkins really pleading insanity?

The buzz from the crowd grew louder, and Judge Hemming rapped his gavel sharply. "May I remind those present that this is a court of law, not Grand Central Station," he admonished sternly. "If you are unable to remain silent, I will order the bailiff to clear the room." The noise immediately subsided.

The judge was the only one in the room who showed no outward surprise at the plea. "The defendant pleads not guilty and not guilty by reason of mental disease or defect," he repeated calmly. He reached under a pile of folders on one side of the bench and pulled out several papers. "In light of the NGI plea, the court exercises its authority to appoint a mental health expert to examine the defendant." Glancing at the papers, he said, "Dr. Frederick Weinberg shall be appointed to conduct the examination and shall be required to submit his written report to the court and counsel within ten days of trial. Dr. Weinberg's fees shall be paid by the county. If the defendant or the state wishes to retain another expert, they are free to do so and they are required to exchange reports within three days of trial." He looked up at counsel. "Are there any other matters to come before this court?"

Both Versey and Liz replied that there were not.

The judge nodded. "In that case, court is adjourned."

Liz scooped up her file and beat a path for the door, with Jeff close behind. As they reached the hallway, reporters shouted questions at her.

"Ms. Stanfeld, would you care to comment on the defendant's insanity plea?"

"Were you expecting an NGI plea?"

"Do you think the defendant is mentally ill?"

Without breaking her brisk stride, Liz called over her shoulder, "The defendant has the right to plead any defense he believes he is entitled to. Whether or not he will be able to prove that defense is an entirely different matter that will be up to the jury to decide. I have no further comments."

As she and Jeff hurried inside her office and closed the door behind them, Tom looked up with surprise. "That didn't take long," he said. Seeing the perplexed looks on their faces, he asked anxiously, "What happened? Did something go wrong?"

Liz dropped her file on the desk and shook her head. "No, everything's fine. The judge bound Brent over for trial as we expected." She took off her jacket and hung it over her chair. "The plea Versey entered *was* a bit surprising." She took a deep breath and said, "Brent pled insanity."

"What?" Tom exclaimed, jumping out of his chair. "Why did they do that? You don't think he'll be able to get off by pretending to be crazy, do you?"

"It's just a ploy," Jeff said, walking over to the window. "They don't really believe the kid's off his rocker. Boy, look at those dark clouds," he added. "Maybe we should all head for the basement."

"But what if Brent can convince a psychiatrist that he *is* crazy?" Tom asked, at the moment clearly not caring if a tornado decimated downtown Lakeview. "He'd get off, wouldn't he?"

Liz shook her head. "They test the hell out of NGI defendants, and all their tests have a lot of control questions designed to pick up people who are lying, so I don't think Brent's got much of a shot at faking a mental disease."

"But Versey will hire his own doctor, right?" Tom persisted. "And if the guy is paid a hefty enough consulting fee, he just might be swayed."

"Maybe," Liz agreed reluctantly, "but Brent would still have to get past the court's expert, and we'll hire our own shrink too, so it seems pretty unlikely he's going to be able to fool three doctors. At least two of them should be able to see through him. Look," she said, staring into Tom's handsome face, "even if by some fluke Brent *were* found insane, he still wouldn't get off. That just means that instead of going to prison, he'd be put in a mental institution. And from what I've heard, prison is like a country club by comparison."

"But if he's found insane it means he's not responsible for what he did," Tom said in an anguished voice. "And he was responsible."

"I know," Liz said quietly. "And I intend to prove that. We'll start by hiring the very best doctor we can find to examine Brent."

"Who do you have in mind?" Jeff asked.

"I'm not sure," Liz replied. "I'll want to consult with some of the senior people in the office before making a decision."

"When will the case be set for trial?" Tom asked.

"Soon," Liz replied. "It'll be assigned to a judge in a day or two and that person will probably hold a scheduling conference right away."

Tom leaned against the wall and gave a small nod of acknowledgment. Seeing his distress, Liz got up, walked over to him and put her hand on his arm. "Don't worry," she said. "Brent will pay for what he did to Jeremy."

Even Jeff broke his long-standing rule of never promising something he wasn't sure he could deliver. "We'll nail him," he assured Tom confidently. "Sometimes rich people get breaks that they shouldn't, but this isn't going to be one of those cases. Believe me," he said fervently, "all the money in the world isn't going to be enough to get this boy off."

Chapter 32

Her mother's voice was starting to give her a headache, and Liz held the phone away from her ear to muffle the sound.

"Now don't forget that your father's birthday is the twenty-sixth," Mona Stanfeld reminded her daughter.

Liz signed. "When have I ever forgotten Pop's birthday?" she retorted irritably.

It was a late afternoon in early August, and Liz had already suffered through ten straight minutes of her mother's running off at the mouth on first one subject and then another. Her malaise was compounded by the fact that earlier in the day she had learned that Dr. Daniel Moss, her first choice of a psychiatric expert to examine Brent, had already been retained by the defense. She would now have to go with her second-string candidate, Dr. Evelyn Swayze. Dr. Swayze was highly respected in her field, but the thought that Versey had beaten her to the punch with Moss really rankled.

"I'm having a surprise dinner for him at Mader's that night," her mother prattled on. "You know how much he loves German food. Of course I had to tell him about it so he wouldn't schedule some silly office meeting or decide to work until all hours, but he promises he'll look surprised when he walks in and sees everyone sitting there. It'll be a small group, around twenty or so. Oh, I was so tickled. Wait till you hear this! Marlon called last night. He and Dorothy and the kids are going to be coming into town for the week. The last time I talked to him, he wasn't sure if they'd be able to make it. You wouldn't believe the long hours that boy puts in at his job. Of course, it sounds like it's paying off. He said he just got a huge profit-sharing check, and he and Dorothy have been looking at bigger houses. I'm so proud that both of my children are doing so well for themselves."

Liz rubbed the bridge of her nose. She'd long suspected that her father only pretended to be hard of hearing to avoid having to pay attention to her mother's incessant chattering. "I'm glad things are going well for him," she said weakly. "He deserves it."

"What do you think we should do about dessert at the birthday party? I thought instead of a cake it'd be fun to give everybody schaum torte. After all, it is one of Mader's specialties, and it's one of your father's particular favorites."

"Torte would be fine," Liz said agreeably, trying her best to bring the conversation to an end. "Look, Mom, I hate to cut you off, but I have to run home and change clothes and pick up Esther. She and I are going to a dinner and style show in the city. I'll call you later in the week and we can talk about some more of the party details."

"Do you think we should try to do something in the way of decorating?" her mother went on, oblivious to Liz's comment. "Maybe a couple of arrangements of fresh flowers would be nice, just a little something to brighten up the room a little."

As Liz opened her mouth to respond, the door to her office opened and Harry stepped inside, carrying several sheets of paper. Liz glanced up, grateful for the interruption, and started at the stricken expression on Harry's face. He walked slowly across the room and sat down in the chair in front of her desk.

"Something important just came up, Mom," Liz said in an urgent tone. "I promise I'll call you in the next day or two. 'Bye." She slammed the phone down and turned to Harry. "What happened?" she asked with concern. "You look like you've seen a ghost."

Harry handed her the papers he was holding. As she looked at the top page, her eyes widened and she sucked in her breath. "Oh, my God!" she exclaimed as she began to read.

RECALL PETITION

We, the undersigned, being persons registered to vote in Horicon County, Wisconsin, do hereby support the recall of an elected official, to wit: Harry S. Washburn, the duly elected District Attorney for Horicon County. The reason for the recall is our belief that said Harry S. Washburn has committed grievous errors of judgment in exercising the prosecutorial discretion vested in him by means of his office.

The pages contained the names of one hundred fifty persons, all with Oakwood addresses.

Liz looked back up at Harry. "Don't worry," she said reassuringly. "They'll never get anywhere with this. For the county clerk to order a recall election, they'd need the signatures of twenty-five percent of the people who voted in the last gubernatorial election. They're not going to be able to get that many. This is just some sort of scare tactic."

"I know that," Harry agreed in a low voice. "And so do they. But they don't need to get any more signatures. They've already accomplished what they set out to do."

"What do you mean?"

"They faxed a copy of this to Senator Kilpatrick," Harry replied tonelessly. "One of his aides just called to inform me that it was with the deepest regrets that the senator is withdrawing his support for my nomination as U.S. attorney."

Liz's jaw tightened. "Oh, Harry," she said softly. "I'm so sorry. I never thought it would come to this."

"Neither did I."

Liz looked back at the petition. "This doesn't make any sense. This represents only a minuscule number of voters. Why would the senator even pay any attention to them? There must be something more behind it."

"There is," Harry said tersely. "The senator's aide told me on the QT that the senator's wife is a shirttail relation of Brent Tompkins's mother, a third cousin or some such thing. It appears this decision was probably in the works all along. The petition was just the final nail in my coffin."

"But that's so unfair!" Liz exclaimed. "Why didn't the senator tell you that from the start?"

"That's politics for you," Harry said disgustedly.

"I wish there were something I could do—" Liz began.

"No," Harry interrupted. "Forget about the appointment. It's over. I don't want to discuss it. But there is something else I wanted to talk to you about." He paused awkwardly and looked down at the floor.

"What is it?" Liz asked, frowning.

Harry cleared his throat. "Liz . . . I think it would be best if we didn't see each other anymore—outside of the office, that is. I feel that it's affecting our working relationship, and I can't allow that to happen."

Liz's mouth dropped open, then she recovered and said tersely, "If that's what you want, Harry, it's fine with me. And I'm sorry about your appointment, but you know you're not the only one who's suffered as a result of prosecuting this case. I may have to move out of Oakwood when this is all over, but that's a chance I'm willing to take because I know in my heart that putting Brent Tompkins in prison is more important than my winning popularity contests. I'm only sorry that you obviously don't share my views."

Harry stared at Liz, then turned and fled the office without saying another word.

Liz sat at her desk, doing a slow burn. Unbelievable. *Harry* had dumped *her*. After all the support she'd given him and after weeks of putting her own reputation on the line for the sake of the case, Harry—Mr. Vanilla Pudding himself—had given her the boot. If she weren't so damn angry, the situation would be laughable.

She glanced up at the clock. It was nearly five. She sure as hell wasn't in the mood to go out and socialize with anyone, but she knew Esther would be waiting. Shaking her head in wonderment, she retrieved her purse from a desk drawer, then slowly got up out of her chair. So Harry was now history. Boy, was Esther ever going to crow about this!

"Oh, happy day!" Esther exclaimed as she and Liz sat on a heavily padded banquette outside the Hyatt Regency's grand ballroom, sipping glasses of wine. "No more Harry! That is the best news I've heard in ages." She touched her glass to Liz's. "Here's to exciting new beginnings."

"I don't know why you think a great celebration is in order," Liz said rather morosely. "I just got dropped like a ton of bricks. That's hardly an ego booster."

Esther waved her hand dismissively. "The important thing is that it's over," she said. "It doesn't matter who delivered the coup de grace." She got to her feet. "Let's get another glass of wine and then buy tickets for some of the raffle items."

They headed toward one of the portable bars, slowly working their way through throngs of well-dressed women who had each paid the local symphony orchestra league seventy-five dollars for the privilege of eating a first-rate meal and seeing a style show of fall and winter fashions from chichi stores in town. Suddenly Liz stiffened and clutched Esther's arm. "Isn't that Natalie Helprin over there?" she whispered, motioning to her left, where a red-haired woman dressed in a form-fitting green leather suit was holding court.

Esther glanced over and nodded. "She's showing some things from her store."

Liz groaned. She was in no mood for sparring with the ice queen. "Why didn't you warn me she'd be here?"

"Because I figured you'd refuse to come if you knew and I thought you were badly in need of an outing." By this time they had inched their way up to the bar. "Two glasses of chardonnay, please," Esther called to the bartender.

"Oh, God," Liz hissed under her breath. "She's coming this way."

Esther calmly handed Liz her drink and, with a big smile on her face, turned to greet her friend's nemesis. "Natalie!" Esther exclaimed as though she had discovered a long-lost friend. "How good to see you. I'm so excited about seeing what you've brought from your shop. You always have such yummy things."

Natalie gave her long hair a toss, causing her oversized gold and jade earrings to jangle melodiously. "Thanks," she said, giving Esther a phony smile. "I'm sorry, but I seem to have forgotten your name."

"Esther McMillan. And of course you know my friend Liz Stanfeld." Esther strong-armed Liz into turning around to face Natalie.

"Yes, of course," Natalie said in a less pleasant tone, as she eyed Liz up and down with a look of disdain. "I'm so glad both of you could make it."

"Tell me," Esther said, lowering her voice confidentially, "where do you find all those divine creations you sell? They are so unique."

"Why, thank you." This time Natalie's smile was genuine. "I like to promote new young designers. I do a lot of my buying in Europe. As a matter of fact, I'm leaving the day after tomorrow for a trip to Paris and Rome."

"Really!" Esther exclaimed, her eyes lighting up. "How exciting. Will you be gone long?"

"Two weeks." At that moment a middle-aged

woman came up and put a hand on Natalie's arm. "Sorry to interrupt, but the society page editor would like a word with you."

"We won't keep you," Esther purred. "So nice talking to you. Have a great trip." She gave a little wave as Natalie hurried off to meet the press.

"Honestly!" Liz grumbled. "Why would anyone wear a leather suit when it's an inferno outside?"

"This *is* a fall and winter show," Esther replied. "Say, Liz—" she began, turning to face her friend.

"Absolutely not!" Liz interrupted as she saw the wheels beginning to turn in Esther's head.

"I haven't said anything yet," Esther retorted, pretending to be hurt.

"You don't have to say anything," Liz shot back. "I saw you light up like a Christmas tree when you heard Natalie was going to be out of the country for two weeks. You've got some idea hatching in that devious mind of yours, and whatever it is, the answer is no."

"Lower your voice. People are looking at us," Esther said. She took her friend's arm and guided her to a quieter spot. "I just had a brainstorm," she said eagerly.

"No," Liz repeated.

"I'll have a small dinner party this Saturday and invite six or seven couples. You and Tom will be the only singles."

"I said *no!*"

"Look," Esther said earnestly, "the fates have dropped this wonderful opportunity in our laps. We can't let it go to waste." Seeing Liz's frown, she said, "The worst that can happen is you both have a nice dinner and some scintillating conversation and then you go home alone. I don't expect you to leave my house and drive to the nearest justice of the peace to elope. Of course, it'd be great if that did happen, but we won't hold our breath. That was supposed to be a joke," she added, seeing Liz's scowl deepen. "You know, your face is going to crack if you keep up that expression."

Although Liz didn't want to admit it, she was actually warming up to Esther's idea. She was furious with Harry and tired of thinking of nothing but the case. And while she had no intention of getting involved with Tom Barker, she did like him a lot, and it might be fun to make old Natalie jealous. "How do you know Tom will even agree to come?" she asked warily.

"He'll come if I have to hog-tie him and load him in my car," Esther replied fervently. "Okay, then, it's all settled. My house. Saturday. Seven o'clock. Oh, and try to wear something sexy. Do you fit into that red silk dress you wore that time we all went to the yacht club? Every man in the place was falling down ogling you in that outfit."

"I can't wear that!" Liz protested. "It's much too low-cut."

"It's been ninety degrees almost every day this whole damn summer," Esther replied. "What's wrong with dressing cool?" The corners of Liz's mouth curled down.

"Listen, kid," Esther said seriously, "the whole idea is to get Tom to see you in a new light, as something more than just a stuffy attorney. I hate to say it, girl, but I have to believe that one of the reasons Peter is now married to Amanda is that he couldn't take his eyes off her jumping around in one of those skintight aerobics outfits. Well, that's the image you can portray for Tom if you wear your red dress."

"The idea of the dinner party is goofy enough," Liz said, "and *if* I come—and I haven't decided yet that I will—there is no way in hell I'm going to wear that dress." She raised a finger to cut off Esther's protests. "My mind is made up on this. No matter what you say, I cannot be swayed. I will not wear the red dress, and that's final."

Chapter 33

"Don't take me off the Barker case, Dan!" Jeff pleaded, as he leaned forward, his palms on the sheriff's desk. "Just give me one more week. If I haven't come up with anything by then, you can reassign me wherever you want."

Although Jeff hadn't worked on the case exclusively since Greg confessed, he had continued to devote significant amounts of time to it, in between his other assignments. But now, because of the lack of progress, Sheriff Isaacson had just informed the detective that he was pulling him off the investigation completely.

"Just seven more days," Jeff continued earnestly. "The trial's been set for September 22, and Liz really needs me to come up with some dirt on Brent. Please, Dan. Do it as a favor to me."

The sheriff shifted uncomfortably in his chair and slowly shook his head. "I'm sorry, Jeff," he said sadly. "I'd sure like to help you out, but I'm afraid I've already given you all the leeway I can. What with Anderson's back goin' out on him, Riley and Boltz need help workin' those two armed robberies and that rape case."

"Can't you shuffle somebody else around? Why can't Wilson or Jenkins be reassigned temporarily?"

"They're both rookies," the sheriff explained patiently. "The trail is still warm on those three cases, but you and I both know that in order to have a snowball's chance in hell of solvin' any of 'em, I gotta assign somebody with experience to help Riley and

Boltz out. And now that Anderson's laid up, I'm afraid you're it."

"Goddamn it, Dan, there's somebody out there who knows something!" Jeff exclaimed, pacing back and forth in front of the big man's desk. "In another week I might just be able to shake something loose."

"You won't let go, will you?" the sheriff said with a sigh. "You've already shook every tree in the whole damn town. You've got to face it, son. There just ain't nothin' loose around there."

"I won't know that for sure unless I keep trying," Jeff said stubbornly. "Look, Dan," he said in a calmer voice, "Harry Washburn is putting pressure on Liz to reduce the charges unless I find some corroboration that Brent's a lowlife. I can't let that happen. That's why I need more time."

"What happened to the kid that ratted on Brent— the Saunders kid?"

Jeff grimaced. "He's a sad case. I've stopped by to see him a couple times. I was there yesterday, as a matter of fact. He's so uptight about going to court that it's pathetic. I've tried to give him pep talks, tell him testifying won't be so bad, but I'm afraid he's not gonna be a very good witness. *I* know he's telling the truth, but he's so scared I'm not sure the jury is gonna believe him. That's why you've gotta let me stay on the case. I'm positive there's someone else in Oakwood who can help us!"

"That may well be, but I don't think you're ever gonna find 'em," the sheriff said ruefully. "Think about it, Jeff. Why should any of them fancy Oakwood people rat on one of their own boys? There's not a damn thing in it for them, and they've got a hell of a lot to lose. You and I have both been around long enough to know that the Good Samaritan story is just a myth. People don't give a damn about the greater good. Ninety-nine point nine percent of the time folks will act to save their own skins—and their families'. Don't you think if somebody was gonna come forward, they would've done it by now? I do. I'm sorry, son, but I think it's time you faced up to the truth and moved on."

Jeff gritted his teeth and looked his friend in the eye. "I know all that," he admitted, "but this case has got under my skin like nothing else I've ever worked on before. I want to make sure that little bastard Brent Tompkins rots in prison. I want to see for myself that sometimes the system does work and that rich people can't always buy their way out of trouble."

The sheriff looked him in the eye, then said quietly, "Son, no matter what you might think, putting Brent Tompkins in prison is not going to avenge what happened to your family twenty years ago."

"I never said it would," Jeff protested.

"You don't have to say it," the sheriff replied. "I've known you long enough to be able to see which way your mind is goin'. And I can't say as I blame you. What happened with that guy that killed your dad had a big impact on you. It's only natural you'd see some similarities here, with that Tompkins kid hiring a fancy lawyer from the city and all. But the way you're carrin' on here just is not healthy." He leaned back in his chair. "You can't let all that anger build up inside you. The way you've been actin' lately reminds me of that summer we first met? Remember? Your dad had been killed that spring. You'd dropped out of college and were workin' for old man Wilkersen, fixin' cars. You were helpin' coach that Little League baseball team. I was coachin' that year, too. I remember watchin' you on the field and thinkin' to myself, 'Holy Christ, that boy has got more anger in him than anyone I've ever seen. If he don't find some outlet for all that anger, he's going to hurt somebody real bad. Either that or he's gonna hurt himself.' That's why I asked you to consider filling out an application to work here at the department. You remember that?"

Jeff settled into a chair in front of Isaacson's desk

and snorted. "Yeah, I remember. As I recall, I told you to fuck off."

The sheriff chuckled. "You did say that at first," he agreed. "It took you about six months to come see me about a job." He looked at Jeff intently. "You know, you never did tell me what finally changed your mind."

Jeff put his head back and closed his eyes for a moment. Opening them again, he took a deep breath, then exhaled. "You really want to know what happened?"

Isaacson nodded.

Jeff pursed his lips, then said quietly, "I just about killed myself, that's what happened. I'd been at one of the taverns south of town drowning my sorrows. I was in no shape to drive home, but in those days people didn't make such a big deal out of driving drunk. Hell, even the cops weren't very vigilant about arresting people for OWI. On top of being shit-faced, I was driving too fast. About halfway home, I couldn't make a curve and flew off the road."

He paused and swallowed hard, remembering. "It was the damnedest ride of my life. I missed hitting a big oak tree by about two feet. It was a miracle, but I walked away with a few bruises, and the car only had some scratches. I walked to a farmhouse and called a buddy to come pick me up. It wasn't until I got home that it hit me: I was no better than the son of a bitch who'd killed my dad. After that I did some serious thinking about the direction my life was taking and decided I'd better make some changes while there was still time. That's when I came to see you." He swallowed hard again. "Nobody knows that story except Julie."

"That's a powerful story," the sheriff said. "I always wondered what brought you to us. Not that it mattered any. I could see right from the start that this was the right place for you to be. You took to police work right away. You're smart, you're tenacious, and you're a good judge of character. You can smell when somebody's tellin' the truth and when they're not. Yessir, I do believe fate led you to your proper calling."

"The job's been pretty good to me," Jeff agreed. "Up until now, that is. I think I'm gettin' burned out. Maybe I've just been doing it too long. Could be it's a sign that it's time for me to get into a different line of work."

"What the hell else would you do with yourself?"

"I don't know offhand," Jeff admitted, "but maybe I should start giving it some thought."

"Whoa, boy," the sheriff got up, walked around the desk and put a hand on the younger man's shoulder. "Not so fast. Have you forgotten you're my hand-picked replacement to take over my job when I retire?"

Jeff snorted. "You love your job, Dan. You and I both know they're gonna carry you out of here feetfirst."

"No, they're not," the sheriff replied. "I'm only gonna run for one more term. Then I'll be fifty-five and I'm gonna hang it up."

"And do what?"

The sheriff shrugged. "I've been thinkin' I might just move down south, to Mississippi or maybe Arkansas. I'd fit right in. Lots of good ol' boys like me down in that part of the country."

Jeff furrowed his brows. "How're you gonna afford to retire at fifty-five? You been playin' the ponies or something?"

"I've been putting a little money aside for my old age," the sheriff replied. "Besides, the way I hear tell, with the pension I'll be gettin' a man can live like a king in Arkansas." He clapped Jeff soundly on the back. "So I don't wanna hear any more talk outa you about gettin' into a different line of work. I'm countin' on you to take over when I'm gone. I gotta make sure the county's left in good hands."

Jeff managed a small smile. "I'm not quite ready to hang it up yet," he said. "I have some unfinished business to take care of."

"So we're back to the Barker case now, are we?"

Jeff nodded.

The sheriff sighed. "I've got no choice but to order you to help Riley and Boltz with their cases. The county board would have my ass in a sling if I tried to justify paying a man to keep beatin' a dead horse."

"Yeah, but you and the county board don't have any say over what I do on my own time," Jeff said, a plan forming in his mind.

The sheriff frowned. "That's true enough, but Riley's and Boltz's cases are gonna occupy a lot of hours out of every day. How do you plan to fit in some moonlighting?"

"Maybe I'm an insomniac," Jeff replied eagerly. "My wife's been working double shifts lately. I might as well do the same."

"You realize we could both get in hot water if somebody finds out," Isaacson said. "The deputies' union would not take kindly to your doin' work without gettin' paid for it."

"I'm not gonna be doing work," Jeff reminded him. "I'm just gonna be driving around, shooting the breeze with people."

The sheriff grinned slyly. "All right, boy. Go to it. Just so you understand those other cases are your first priority. Oh, and try not to broadcast what you're up to. I don't wanna hear any flack from the other men."

Jeff grabbed the big man's hand and pumped it hard. "Thanks, Dan. You won't regret it," he said fervently. "Like you said, I need to find a way to direct some of my anger. And believe me, doing whatever I can to make sure they put that kid away is the best outlet there is."

Chapter 34

"I don't think this was such a good idea." Liz frowned as she stood in front of the full-length mirror in Esther's foyer. It was early Saturday evening. Reflected in the mirror was the infamous red silk dress, plunging provocatively in front to reveal a tantalizing glimpse of cleavage. Its cinched-in waist accentuated Liz's recent weight loss, and a generous slit up the right side displayed a long expanse of leg.

"My stomach is feeling a little queasy," Liz went on, as she self-consciously tried to pull the gaping bodice of the dress together with one hand. "I think maybe I should go home."

"Don't be ridiculous," Esther replied, touching her friend lightly on the shoulder. "You look wonderful, and you're going to have a smashing time. What do you think, Bob?" Esther called as she spotted her husband in the upstairs hallway. "Doesn't Liz look great?"

Bob McMillan started down the stairs. He stopped in his tracks and gave a low wolf whistle as Liz came into view. "Wow!" he exclaimed. "Liz, you're an absolute knockout!"

"See, what did I tell you?" Esther chided. "Now, will you please stop acting as though this party were a form of torture?" She headed toward the kitchen.

"I'm serious, Esther," Liz said soberly, following her friend down the hall. "I don't know if I'm up to it and besides, I have no business making a play for a man who's a key part of the most important case I've ever handled."

Esther turned and put both hands firmly on her friend's shoulders. "I know you're a little nervous," she said. "But you're making far too much out of this party. You've been working very hard, and you deserve to have a relaxing evening in the company of some interesting people, one of whom just happens to be a very attractive man who's involved in your big case." When Liz continued to look skeptical, Esther added, "Look, if you're not enjoying yourself by the time dessert is served, you can excuse yourself and go home with my blessings. But please stick it out until then. Is it a deal?"

Liz thought a moment, then nodded slowly. "Deal."

"Great!" Esther exclaimed, giving her a big hug. "Now, come keep me company while I fuss with the flowers."

In the McMillans' spacious white kitchen, their housekeeper and a caterer were putting final touches on trays of cocktail canapés. Esther began rearranging one of the large displays of cut flowers on a counter. "So," Liz said, as she picked up a black olive stuffed with bleu cheese and popped it into her mouth, "are you going to tell me how you managed to get Tom to agree to come?" Esther had called the previous evening with the triumphant news that *everyone* on the guest list had accepted, but she'd refused to give Liz any details.

Esther looked up from the flowers. "Well—" she hesitated a moment, then grinned devilishly. "I guess there's no harm in telling you. I knew a personal visit was in order because it's too easy to beg off from a phone call or a written note. So on Thursday night, I dressed up the kids in their cutest outfits and we walked over to his house. The car was in front of the garage, so I knew I was in business. I buzzed him on the security system, told him who I was, and he came right out." She scrutinized that flower arrangement, nodded slightly to herself, and turned her attention to the next one.

"Tom opened the gate, and we all walked up the driveway. He couldn't have been nicer. I made small talk for a couple of minutes and was just leading up to telling him about my impromptu little neighborhood party when Cameron fell down on the cement and skinned his knees and started to cry." Esther paused and smiled at the memory. "I wish you could've seen it. It was so cute. Tom picked him up and asked him if he was hurt. There were big tears running down Cammy's cheeks, but he shook his head and said he was okay. I could just see Tom melting right before my eyes. I hurried up and finished explaining about the get-together, and he said he'd love to attend. His only concern was that some of the people coming might be sympathetic to the Tompkinses. I assured him that I wouldn't have any of *those* people in my house, and that was that." She smiled snugly.

Liz shook her head in amazement. "Honestly, Esther. You should be ashamed of yourself, using your children as props. Did you happen to mention that I was coming?"

Esther pursed her lips. "Come to think of it, I didn't. I guess it must've slipped my mind. I told him there would be about fifteen people, which is true, and I mentioned a few couples' names, but he didn't ask for a complete guest list and I didn't volunteer one. I think taking him by surprise is the best strategy." She glanced up at the clock. It was six-thirty. "I told people to come at seven, so we have a little time yet. You're still looking much too nervous. Would you like something to drink? Some white wine maybe?"

Liz smiled. "Do you have anything stronger? I'm really feeling self-conscious."

"Sure. Name your poison."

"Bourbon, straight up," Liz replied without hesitation. "I have butterflies in my stomach the size of buffalo. Maybe I can drown them."

By seven-fifteen the other six couples had arrived and were milling around in the solarium, drinking and nibbling on the hors d'oeuvres. Liz, after sipping on the bourbon, was feeling a bit more relaxed. "I'll bet he's not even coming," she said to Esther crossly as the two women met at the shrimp and crab bowl. "He probably smelled a rat. You made me get dressed up in this clown suit for nothing."

"He'll come," Esther assured her. "He's just fashionably late." At that moment they heard the doorbell peal. Esther smiled. "There. You see. He's here."

Liz looked apprehensive. "There's still time for me to duck out the back."

"You'll do nothing of the sort," Esther said, putting a restraining hand on Liz's arm. "You stand right here and look alluring. Bob will be bringing him in in just a minute."

Liz set down her plate of food, walked over to the bar, and picked up a glass of wine. She then sauntered casually toward the patio doors at the rear of the room that looked out on the backyard. She stood by herself and kept her back toward the door, pretending to be admiring the landscaping as she heard Bob introduce Tom to some of the other guests.

"And of course you already know our lady in red," Bob said.

Liz took a sip of wine and tried to act nonchalant as she turned to face the two men. They were about six paces away. A look of startled recognition came over Tom's face. "My God, Liz!" he said, smiling. "I didn't recognize you at first. What a great dress!"

Liz had to admit Tom was looking very handsome. He was wearing a pair of black pants, a white shirt, red floral tie, and a loosely woven black tweed linen jacket. He was holding a glass filled with what looked like scotch and water. As she watched him smiling at her, Liz could feel some of her nervousness subside. "Thank you," she said, smiling back at him. Maybe this wasn't going to be so bad after all. Over Tom's shoulder she could see Bob McMillan wink at her as he faded back into the crowd.

"So, are you a friend of Bob and Esther?" Tom asked, taking a sip of his drink.

Liz nodded. "We go way back—to when we all lived on Lake Drive in Milwaukee. Esther and Bob moved out here about five years ago, and Esther was the one who talked me into coming here when I was looking for a new place last year."

"Had you lived in the city long?"

"About ten years."

"Really? What prompted you to move?"

Liz looked up at him and after a moment's hesitation said, "I was going through a rather messy divorce and decided some lifestyle changes were in order." Once the words were out, she realized with surprise that this was the first time she'd been able to mention her divorce without feeling the least bit of regret or remorse.

Tom nodded solemnly. "When something devastating like that happens, switching gears is sometimes the best medicine." He took another sip of his drink and gazed out at the gardens. "Lately I've been giving some serious thought to moving back into the city. It'd be closer to my work, and there doesn't seem to be much left for me here."

Liz briefly wondered if she, too, might need to move back to the city. She fervently hoped not. "This probably isn't the best time for you to be making major decisions," she counseled. "Things might look a lot different after the trial." For both of them, she prayed silently.

Tom shrugged and nodded ruefully. "You could be right," he agreed. "I've never been a big fan of winter, but this year I am very much looking forward to its coming. It seems like this summer has already lasted long enough for three lifetimes."

"The end is in sight," Liz assured him. "You just have to be patient."

"That's never been my strong suit," he admitted.

"Mine either," Liz said. "But I guess we really don't have much choice, do we?"

"Come on, everyone," Esther's cheerful voice called. "Grab yourselves another drink and let's start moving into the dining room. Manuel has got some of the world's best grilled chicken shish kebab waiting for your enjoyment."

Both Tom and Liz had finished their drinks. "Care for another one?" Tom asked, taking her empty glass.

"Why not?" Liz replied. She'd already had more than her quota of alcohol, but surely one more glass of wine couldn't hurt.

Crafty Esther had seen to it that Liz and Tom were seated next to one another. More wine was served with dinner, and by the time the individual portions of English trifle were being served, Liz was feeling downright mellow, her thoughts of making a hasty exit long forgotten. Tom was interested in many subjects—travel, local history, food, even gardening—and conversation flowed easily. Liz had been concerned that they would fall into the trap of talking about the case, but so far the subject had received only passing mention.

Tom showed no interest in talking to any of the other guests and remained by Liz's side all evening. All too soon the group was standing outside on the patio, sipping sherry and saying their good-byes. "This was a very pleasant evening," Tom said as he finished his sherry, a hint of surprise in his voice. "I almost declined Esther's invitation, but now I'm very glad I didn't."

"I'm glad, too," Liz said sincerely. "I had a very nice time. You're good company."

"So are you," he said with a smile. He looked at his watch. "I'd better be going. My former brother-in-law is trying to get me to take up golfing, and we've got an early tee time tomorrow."

Liz nodded. "I'll talk to you next week," she said

evenly, although she couldn't help but feel a twinge of disappointment that her evening with this fine, caring man was at an end.

"I'll look forward to it. Good night, Liz."

"Good night, Tom."

He turned to go, then unexpectedly turned back, leaned down and kissed her lightly on the lips. He smiled at her look of surprise, then quickly took his leave.

Feeling slightly tipsy, Liz stood there quietly, looking up at the dark, starry sky, replaying the events of the past several hours in her head.

She was glad Esther had badgered her into coming to the party. It had been a lovely evening, and she'd had a wonderful time, but by next week the night would be just a fond memory and it would be back to business as usual. Natalie would be home from Europe. Preparation for the trial would continue; Liz and Tom would go back to being just lawyer and client; and that would suit Liz just fine. She looked up at the sky again and sighed. Or would it?"

Chapter 35

The following Wednesday morning, Liz was standing behind her desk, leaning over to check a reference in a statute book, when she heard someone clearing his throat. Looking up, she saw Jeff standing in the doorway. "I hope you're not planning to go to court looking like that," he said. "The Judge might hold you in contempt."

Liz frowned, not catching his drift. Jeff pointed. "Somehow I don't think Horicon County is quite ready for assistant DA's who dress like Madonna."

Glancing down, Liz saw that the pin that had been holding the bodice of her aqua shawl-collared dress had come undone, exposing the lacy white bra she wore underneath. "Christ!" she swore, clutching the fabric together and reinserting the pin. "What are you doing here?"

"Aside from enjoying the view," he replied with a leer, "there was a hearing in my armed-robbery case, so I thought I'd stop in and see how you were doing." He moved into the room and plopped into a chair. "Did I catch you at a bad time?"

"No," Liz replied, sitting down. "As a matter of fact, your timing is impeccable. The mail just arrived, and I received two things relating to our case." She dug through a stack of papers in front of her and pulled out a single sheet of paper. "First of all, Judge Andrews denied Versey's request for a change of venue. It looks like Brent will have to find a jury of his peers right here in the county."

"You don't seem too thrilled," Jeff commented. "I thought that's what you wanted."

Liz sighed. "I'm still not sure how I feel on that issue. I mainly opposed the motion on the ground that anything Versey wants, I don't, but who knows? Maybe we would've been better off elsewhere. After all, there *is* some fairly strong sympathy for Brent here, at least in some quarters."

"Yeah," Jeff grumbled, bouncing his right heel up and down on the floor. "Even my kids seem to think Brent's getting railroaded. Lucky for us that teenagers can't serve on juries."

Liz smiled. "I've been giving some thought to what type of juror we should aim for. I think we'd probably do best with people between thirty and fifty who don't have kids. As you said, young people might identify with Brent, while people our age with families might be reminded of their own children and feel sorry for him. And older people might not be willing to believe that someone that young could do something so awful."

Jeff nodded. "That sounds logical. And you'd better stick with non-Oakwood people. Us hayseeds are more apt to want to sock it to a spoiled rich kid. His own kind will probably bend over backward to protect him. I mean, look at the recall petition they filed on your boyfriend."

Liz frowned.

"Ex-boyfiriend?" Jeff asked.

Liz ignored his question and picked up a manila envelope. "I also got a tape from Dr. Swayze of her interview with Brent and a summary of the various tests she conducted on him."

"Let me guess." Jeff put his fingertips to his temples and closed his eyes as though he were attempting to divine the contents of Dr. Swayze's report. "The doctor has never encountered anyone in her entire career who is as batty as Brent Tompkins, and she can't understand for the life of her why you're even thinking about putting the county to the expense of a trial because no juror in his right mind is going to find the kid sane." He opened his eyes. "How'd I do?"

Liz rolled her eyes. "Fortunately, not even close." She flipped through the pages of Dr. Swayze's report. "Actually, this is rather interesting. The doctor concludes that Brent is highly intelligent and without a doubt was able to conform his conduct to the requirements of the law at the time of the offense, but in her opinion he is almost totally lacking in conscience. That is, he appears to lack the internal policing device that keeps most law-abiding citizens on the straight and narrow. She says this doesn't mean he lacks the mental capacity to distinguish between right and wrong—objectively, he is well aware of the difference. However, subjectively, he appears to have no need to act on it." Liz looked up. "What do you think of that?"

Jeff shrugged. "It sounds like the doctor supports our theory that Brent is one bad hombre. Did she ask Brent any specific questions about the murder?"

"Yes. It's on the tape. I was just going to listen to it." Liz popped the cassette into a tape player and pushed the Play button. Moments later a soft, feminine voice could be heard.

"Good morning, Brent. How are you feeling today?"

"Very well, doctor," Brent answered congenially. "How are you?"

"I am fine. Brent, as you probably know, I am going to be asking you some questions about Jeremy Barker's death. It is my duty to inform you that any statements you make that might be against your interest may not be used by the prosecution during the guilt phase of the trial. Do you understand what that means?"

"Yes, I do."

"Very well, then. Let's begin. How long have you known Tom Barker?"

"I wouldn't say I actually know the man at all. I

believe he moved to the village about five years ago, so I have no doubt been aware of him for that length of time."

"But you do know who he is?"

"Yes."

"Were you also acquainted with his son, Jeremy Barker?"

"My answer would be the same. I was aware of the deceased's existence."

"Prior to June 11 of this year?"

"Prior to the event in question, yes."

"By the term 'the event in question,' I take it you are referring to Jeremy's death."

"Yes."

"Have you ever spoken to Tom Barker at any time?"

"Perhaps, once or twice, just in passing."

"When was the last time you spoke to Tom Barker prior to June 11?"

"I don't recall."

"Have you ever had any disagreements or arguments with Tom Barker?"

There was a pause. "You could say that, yes."

"Can you elaborate on that?"

There was no response.

"Do you like Mr. Barker?"

"No," Brent replied in a loud voice.

"Why not? Did he do something to upset you?"

"Yes. He belittled me and treated me like a child."

"Explain, please."

Brent sighed. "I don't want to. Let's talk about something else."

"All right. Had you ever spoken to Jeremy Barker prior to June 11?"

"I don't recall ever speaking to the deceased."

"Did you speak to Jeremy Barker on June 11?"

There was a pause. "No."

"Did you ever talk about the Barker family with any of your friends?"

"Which friend did you have in mind?"

"Any friend."

"I would imagine you're referring to Greg Saunders." There was a smirk in Brent's voice.

"Do you consider Greg a friend of yours?"

"Not really."

"Why not?"

"He and I don't have much in common."

"Oh?" The doctor's voice indicated surprise.

"No, his tastes run to more childish pursuits than mine."

"And what are you particular interests, Brent?"

"I have many interests. I read a lot. Lately I've been doing some reading about psychiatry. Tell me, Doctor, do you believe the theories of Freud or Jung have more relevance in today's society?"

"Let's get back to my original question, if we may. Did you ever talk about the Barkers with Greg Saunders?"

"Neighbors do tend to talk about one another, don't they?"

"That still doesn't answer my question." The doctor was beginning to sound a bit exasperated.

"Did Greg tell you we talked about the Barkers?"

"As a matter of fact, I have never spoken to Greg."

"Well, if you do, here's a word to the wise: You shouldn't believe everything Greg tells you. Not by a long shot."

"And why is that?"

"Because Greg has some problems."

"Really. What kind of problems?"

"He has a problem telling the truth."

"You're saying Greg is untruthful?"

"I'm saying he sometimes has difficulty distinguishing the truth from fantasy."

"Is that so? Do you ever have that problem?"

"I don't know. Do you?"

"We're not here to talk about me."

"But I'll bet you'd be a much more interesting subject than I am. Doctor, are you a fan of Nietzsche?"

Jeff leaned over and punched the Stop button on the recorder. "I've heard enough," he said disgustedly. "What was all that crap about referring to the murder as 'the event in question' and not wanting to refer to Jeremy by name?"

Liz shrugged. "Beats me. Maybe that's Brent's way of proving he's insane."

Jeff shook his head. "It proves the kid's a smart-ass, but it sure as hell didn't sound like he's nuts. What were the results of the tests the doc gave him?"

Liz flipped through the report. "She says she got the feeling that Brent was manipulating his answers to some of the standardized tests. She says he scored one hundred fifty-nine on the Stanford-Benet IQ test, and based on her interviews with him, she believes that is accurate. She goes on to say she's far less certain that his scoring on the MMPI—that's the Minnesota Multiphasic Personality Inventory—is a true reflection of his personality—"

"The Minnesota Multiphasic," Jeff interrupted. "Isn't that the test where they ask you about fifty different ways if you have diarrhea?"

Liz rolled her eyes and continued reading. "The test has a fair number of control questions designed to catch examinees who may be attempting to obtain a false reading, and although there's no sure way to prove it, her feeling is that Brent was somehow familiar enough with the concept and format of the examination to successfully answer the control questions while at the same time giving false responses to other key inquiries."

"Is that admissible at trail?" Jeff interrupted.

"What?"

"The doctor's conclusion that Brent is untruthful and manipulative."

"None of this is admissible at the guilt phase of the trial," Liz explained. "If he's found guilty, then at the insanity phase the doctor can tell the jury that based on her years of experience in the field it's her belief that Brent wasn't giving truthful answers on the tests."

"But you can't have her testify about his untruthfulness at the guilt phase?"

Liz shook her head.

"But it'd sure help our case if a doctor told the jury Brent is a compulsive liar."

"Sorry," Liz said. "That's the way the evidence code works." She again flipped to another page of the report. "There are a couple of other interesting comments here. The doctor said Brent appeared to be extremely well versed in psychological jargon and while he could have just picked that up from reading about the subject, she wondered if perhaps he had undergone analysis at some point in his life."

Jeff frowned. "Did he?"

Liz shook her head. "He said not, and the background report filled out by his parents corroborated that. But Dr. Swayze also interviewed both parents, and she said she had the feeling they were not being completely truthful with her. She especially felt that Mrs. Tompkins might be hiding something."

"That wouldn't surprise me a bit," Jeff said. "From the first time we met them I've thought they were covering something up. Like I've said all along, I'd be willing to bet there are more dark episodes lurking in that boy's past, if I just knew where the hell to look."

"You might be right," Liz agreed, "but if we haven't found anything by this time, I'm afraid the missing puzzle pieces are going to stay missing."

"Never say never," Jeff said vehemently, turning around to face her. "I might just surprise you and pull a rabbit out of a hat."

"And I might wake up tomorrow looking like Cindy Crawford," Liz retorted, "but it's not likely. I'll tell you what," she said, tucking her hair behind her ears. "If you come up with the missing piece to the puzzle, I'll buy you dinner anyplace you want."

"Anyplace?" Jeff's eyes lit up."

"Well, let's say anyplace within a hundred miles," Liz qualified her offer. "I'm not about to fly you to Paris."

"Oh, darn," he said, snapping his fingers. "The thought of spending the night with you was getting me all excited."

"I'll bet," she replied dryly. "If you want to collect a free meal, I suggest you channel some of that excitement into the case."

"Boy, you really know how to motivate a guy," he said heading for the door. "Madam, I shall return."

"You always do," Liz called after him. "Kind of like a rash you can't shake."

Chapter 36

Jeff pulled down the Chevy's sun visor to block the glare of the early evening sun as he drove home from work. It was late August, and the monsoon-like conditions that had enveloped the region for most of the summer had finally abated. The day had been warm and dry and clear, just the kind of weather Jeff favored, the kind that made him glad he lived in Wisconsin rather than someplace like Florida, where it was so humid that you walked around most of the year feeling like you ought to wring your clothes out.

Today, though, the weather wasn't enough to lift Jeff's spirits. In fact, he was more depressed than he'd been in quite a while. The three cases Isaacson had assigned him to had been closed, but now there was a car theft ring and a couple of instances of counterfeit twenty-dollar bills being passed at local businesses that demanded his attention. Deputy Marv Anderson, the department's second-ranking detective after Jeff, was out of commission following back surgery, so Jeff had been keeping particularly busy.

His surreptitious moonlighting in the Barker case had turned up nothing, so he knew there was no point in even asking the sheriff to let him officially get back on the case. Though he knew it was irrational, Jeff counted the inability to uncover some new evidence as a personal failure, and as the time before Brent's trial grew shorter, his feelings of inadequacy increased.

His dark mood had only deepened after a meeting he and Liz had had with Greg Saunders earlier that afternoon to begin preparing the boy for trial. Although Greg's stutter had improved somewhat over the summer, it hadn't abated entirely, and Greg was still very apprehensive about testifying.

While Greg's parents waited in a nearby room, Liz and Jeff spent an hour in her office explaining to the boy what would be expected of him at the trial. In later sessions they would go into the courtroom and have Greg sit in the witness box, but for starters Liz had felt the boy would be more comfortable in a less intimidating setting.

"Before we begin," Liz told Greg, "I want you to understand that when Brent's lawyer asks you questions, he's not attacking you personally. He's just doing his job, which is to raise doubt in the jurors' minds, if he can, about what really happened the day Jeremy was killed. I want you to listen carefully to his questions and take your time answering them. Please don't blurt out any answers right away because if his questions are improper, I'm going to need time to object to them, and it gets a little tricky if you've already answered, because then if the judge rules in my favor, he'll have to instruct the jury to disregard your answer, but once they've already heard it, it's hard for them to pretend they didn't. Do you understand that?"

Greg nodded solemnly.

"Good," Liz said. "Now let's run through some questions. What is your name?"

Greg looked at the floor and mumbled his response.

Liz pursed her lips and said gently, "There's a microphone in the courtroom, but you're going to have to speak up a bit so the judge and the jurors can hear your answer. And I know you're shy, but do you think you could try looking at me when you respond? You don't need to look at anyone else in the courtroom if you don't want to, but please try hard to look at me. It'll make it easier for everyone to hear you. Okay? Good. Let's try it again. What is your name?"

"Greg Saunders." This time the answer, although delivered in a low voice, was at least audible.

"Where do you go to school?"

"Oakwood Junior High."

"What grade are you in?"

"Eighth."

"Are you acquainted with Brent Tompkins?"

Greg nodded his head.

"I know it probably seems like there are a lot of rules to remember," Liz said softly, "but you need to answer every question out loud so the court reporter can record what you say. Now, are you acquainted with Brent Tompkins?"

"Yes."

"Did you have any contact with Brent Tompkins the morning of Tuesday, June 11?"

"Y-yes."

"What was the nature of that contact?"

"He c-c-called me." Greg was growing more flustered and his stutter was becoming more pronounced. Liz glanced over at Jeff. He nodded slightly. Liz said, "I think that's enough for today. You're doing just fine, Greg. We'll get together again next week and go through some more questions."

"The most important thing to remember, sport," Jeff said, "is to always tell the truth, no matter what you're asked. If you do that, everything will be just fine."

Greg swallowed hard. "Are you going to be at the trial?" he asked Jeff.

"I sure will," Jeff replied. He didn't care if a serial killer was at work in Horicon County in late September. Come hell or high water, he was going to be in that courtroom every damn minute.

That news seemed to cheer the boy a bit, and he left looking slightly less anxious.

"He's going to need more practice than I'd thought," Liz said ruefully after the Saunderses had departed. "I didn't want to start working with him too soon because I thought he'd get stale, but now I wonder if we shouldn't have started weeks ago."

"We'll get him ready somehow," Jeff assured her.

"He likes you a lot," Liz said. "I think it'll really help put him at ease if you could manage to be here for our other practice sessions."

"I'll be here," Jeff promised. "Even if I have to take vacation days or sick leave to do it."

Jeff pulled the car into the garage and walked into the kitchen, feeling an overwhelming longing for companionship. The house was dark and still. The boys were at football practice, but Julie should've been home by now. Damn it, he thought. She must be working another double shift. Her work load was really starting to get up his nose. She'd had two interviews for the supervisor's job and had recently been told she was one of three finalists vying for the position. Jeff hoped the hospital brass made their decision soon so things could get back to normal at the Gardner household.

Feeling like an orphan, he took a can of Pepsi out of the refrigerator and went into the living room to watch the six o'clock news. A perky weather lady had just come on the screen, promising three more days of clear skies and balmy temperatures, when Jeff heard Julie's car in the driveway. Moments later the door between the garage and kitchen slammed, and he could hear the sound of a package being set on the kitchen table.

"I thought you were probably working," Jeff called out to her. "Did you stop for groceries? What are we having for supper?"

"I stopped for a couple of things," Julie called back. "What do you feel like eating?"

"I don't know. Did you bring home anything good?"

"Why don't you come see for yourself?"

Jeff flicked off the TV and walked to the kitchen.

The kitchen table was bare. Julie was bending over something in the sink. Jeff frowned. "Did you put everything away already? You couldn't have bought much."

Julie swung around to face him, holding a bottle of champagne. "I bought the essentials," she said with a big grin. "Here," she said, handing him the bottle. "Give me a hand. I can't get this damn thing open."

It took Jeff an instant to figure out what was going on. "You got the job!" he exclaimed, as he grabbed her around the waist and swung her off her feet.

"Careful. That champagne was expensive, so don't drop it," she scolded. "Yes, I got the job. I found out just as I was leaving. I can't believe they decided this soon. I was sure they'd keep me hanging for at least another two weeks."

"That's great news!" Jeff said, kissing her. "I'm very proud of you." He deftly popped the cork while Julie got two glasses from the cupboard. "At least one member of the household is moving up, careerwise."

Julie held out the glasses. "Well, what are you waiting for? Aren't you going to pour?"

Jeff looked up at the clock, then grinned slyly. "What time do you think the boys will be home?"

"I don't know. Probably not for at least an hour. Why?" She looked up at Jeff, then caught his meaning. "Oh," she said, moving close and kissing his chin. "More than enough time."

"Definitely," Jeff said, kissing her back. "Come on. It's been much too long since you and I drank champagne in bed. And later on, we'll go out for steak and tails. Unless we decide we'd rather not get up," he said, tightening his hold on her, "in which case you can have a rain check for tomorrow night."

"I think I like that last option best," Julie said, pulling him toward the stairway.

The meeting with Greg had left Liz feeling down. She found herself wishing she could talk to Tom. Since

Esther's party she had been calling him more frequently, always in the guise of discussing the case. He never seemed to mind. Today his secretary informed Liz that Tom had gone home early and asked if Liz would like to leave a message. Liz said it wasn't important, that she'd try again in the morning.

On the drive back to Oakwood, though, she began to toy with the idea of dropping by his house. The closer she got to home, the more taken she was with the idea. There was nothing improper in dropping in on a neighbor who also happened to be a client, she reasoned as she turned into Oakwood Hills. She really could use some company, and she was certain he would want to hear about her session with Greg.

As she turned onto Tom's street she could see that his front gates were open. Surely that was a good omen, she thought. But then, as she pulled into the driveway, she saw a white Saab parked next to Tom's black Lexus, and her heart immediately dropped. Somehow, without being told, she knew whose car it was. Natalie. Shit! she cussed to herself. So much for good omens.

As she pulled the van up next to their cars, trying to decide if she should drive back out again, hoping they hadn't seen her, Tom appeared at the front door. She resolutely killed the engine and got out. "Hello, Liz," Tom said, shaking her hand warmly. "Would you like to come in?"

As Liz followed him down the hall, smoothing out the wrinkles in her blue linen dress, she noticed that Tom was dressed casually, in jeans and a blue and white T-shirt. When they reached the family room, she spied Natalie, wearing red shorts and a low-cut red and white top, her long hair pulled back into a ponytail, lounging on one of the couches. Liz suddenly felt fat and overdressed.

"Please, have a seat," Tom said. "Natalie just dropped by," he explained. Liz primly sat down on an overstuffed chair. Tom seated himself on a matching chair opposite her. "So," Tom said, "what can I do for you?"

Acutely aware that Natalie was glaring at her, Liz cleared her throat and briefly explained her meeting with Greg. "I'm going to be working with him intensively between now and the trial," she said, "but I just wanted you to know that he's not going to be the best witness."

"The poor kid," Tom murmured. "What an ordeal this must be for him."

"Tell it to us straight," Natalie said in a caustic voice. "Can you guarantee that the jury is going to convict Brent?"

"I can't guarantee anything," Liz heard herself snapping back. "This isn't like buying a truckload of dresses, where the manufacturer agrees to take them all back if you find a flaw." Her eyes were blazing. Although she knew she should shut up, she found herself continuing angrily. "We're talking about a jury of twelve people. Flesh-and-blood human beings, with all the foibles inherent in our species. I guarantee that I'll do the very best I can to ensure that Brent Tompkins gets the punishment he deserves, but beyond that, we just have to believe that the process will work the way it's supposed to."

"That's all we ask," Tom said quickly, trying to make peace. "We trust you to know how best to present things to ensure a conviction."

Liz stood up. "I have to be going," she said.

"I'll walk you to the door," Tom said, also getting to his feet. He looked distinctly uncomfortable.

As they started out of the room, Natalie's voice once again rang out. "Well, if you ask me, Tom, it sounds like the case is going down the tubes. You and I will just have to put on our thinking caps. Maybe we can come up with some good strategy, even if she can't."

Liz resisted the impulse to turn back and punch the bitch in the mouth.

"I appreciate your stopping by," Tom said when they reached the door. "And I'm sorry about—" His voice trailed off. "Natalie doesn't have much experience with the legal system."

Liz nodded. "It's okay. I'll talk to you next week."

As she drove home, Liz soundly berated herself for ever having decided to stop at Tom's house. It had been a shitty day and she'd been feeling lonely and had wanted some company. Instead she'd made herself look like a fool. She sighed. There were still a couple of hours of daylight left. When she got home she was going to skip supper and go out and work in the yard. Maybe that would make her feel better.

As she pulled into the driveway and began to reach for the garage door opener, she sensed there was something wrong, but just what it was didn't register immediately. Then, as she drove closer, it became all too clear. Emblazoned on the garage door in huge black spray-painted letters were the words "GET OUT OF TOWN YOU FUCKING BITCH."

Liz shut off the ignition and stared at the words for a moment. Then she put her hands over her face and sobbed.

Chapter 37

Liz was sitting at her desk the Thursday after Labor Day reviewing some police reports that had just been delivered regarding the theft of two new Dodge mini-vans off a local dealer's lot when her phone rang.

"Liz Stanfeld," she answered.

"Good morning, Ms. Stanfeld," a deep voice said. "This is Paul Versey. How are you today?"

Liz's eyes narrowed. "Just fine," she answered warily.

"I'm glad to hear it." Versey paused and cleared his throat. "I wanted to—" he stammered uncharacteristically. "This is—I'm calling to let you know that we are withdrawing our insanity plea."

Liz grabbed a sheet of paper and eagerly scrawled a note as Versey continued. "I am sending a letter to Judge Andrews today informing him of this fact, with a carbon copy to you, but I wanted to do you the courtesy of letting you know as soon as possible so you can adjust your trial preparations accordingly."

"I appreciate the call," Liz said. "If you don't mind my asking, was there something in particular that prompted your decision? I must say, this is rather unexpected."

"Yes, well . . ." Versey continued to sound flustered. "I'll admit it came as a bit of a surprise to me, too. The truth of the matter is our psychiatric expert, Dr. Moss, withdrew from the case this morning."

"Oh?" Liz asked with surprise.

"Yes, to tell you the truth, I'm not quite sure what

was behind his decision. I'd been led to believe things were going well. The doctor had just completed interviews with Mr. and Mrs. Tompkins when I got a rather terse message from him saying he would not be able to help us out. In any event, we will now be proceeding to trial strictly on the plea of not guilty."

"Well, thanks for calling," Liz said. "Good-bye."

She hung up the phone and sat there a moment, tapping her pen lightly on the desktop. That was certainly good news. The only possible explanation for Dr. Moss's defection was that no matter how much money he received for his testimony, the doctor was just as convinced as Dr. Swayze had been that Brent was completely sane.

Liz wondered if she should call Tom. While she was certain he'd be thrilled with the news, her encounter with Natalie the week before had somewhat altered her opinion of Tom. After all, any man who would hang around with a bitch like that was a bit suspect.

While she debated whether or not to call Tom, she tried to reach Jeff. He had been the first person she'd called the night she discovered the spray painting on her garage. Although she had the feeling that she'd interrupted him in the middle of something important at home, he came right over. As she expected, he found no clues as to who might have done the deed, but after scolding her for not informing him about the hate mail she'd been getting, he calmed her down and stayed and kept her company well into the night. She had the door repainted the next day and was trying to put the incident out of her mind. But the nastiness had had one positive result: Liz now considered Jeff a true friend.

Jeff wasn't at the department. Now what? Oh, hell. Regardless of her personal feelings, Tom deserved to be kept abreast of any developments in the case. She picked up the phone again and resolutely dialed his number.

Tom's secretary came on the line. After Liz had

identified herself, the woman said, "I'm sorry, Ms. Stanfeld, but Mr. Barker is out of town. I don't expect him back until Monday."

Out of town. Another excursion with Natalie, perhaps? "I see," Liz said in her most professional voice. "Would you please ask him to call me when he returns?"

"Of course, Ms. Stanfeld. I'll see that he gets the message."

Liz hung up the phone, then got up from her desk. She had a feeling that Versey's call was a good omen about the course the trial was going to take. She wanted to share it with someone.

Harry was on the phone when she poked her head into his office. He motioned for her to come in. She took a seat in front of his desk as she waited for him to finish his call. From all outward appearances at least, Harry seemed to have gotten over his disappointment at not getting the federal prosecutor's job. Even though Liz had never been very good at remaining friends with old flames, she hoped that Harry might turn out to be an exception. Although they were no longer seeing each other socially, in the office he continued to express confidence in her ability and her judgement.

"You're looking awfully cheerful this morning," Harry said as he replaced the receiver. "What's the good word?"

Liz filled him in on Versey's call. When she finished, she was surprised to see that Harry was frowning.

"Did Versey broach the subject of a possible plea bargain?" Harry asked.

"No," Liz replied. "Neither one of us mentioned it."

"Doesn't that seem odd to you, particularly since he just backed off of an important defense? Wouldn't you think he'd now be looking to cut a deal?"

"I thought we had agreed a plea bargain was not warranted," Liz said. "Especially since Greg has seemed more confident in the last two sessions Jeff and I had with him. Don't tell me you're having a change of heart?"

Harry signed. "No," he said, shaking his head. "Just don't let Versey sucker you into feeling complacent," he cautioned.

"Don't worry," she assured him. "Now that the insanity phase of the trail is gone, I'm feeling much better about the case."

"Good," Harry said, managing a wan smile. "I just hope your confidence isn't misplaced."

When Jeff called her back later that day, he expressed considerably more enthusiasm about the withdrawal of the insanity plea. However, he was convinced that Dr. Moss's decision to withdraw from the case had some sinister underpinnings.

"What exactly did Versey say?" he asked.

"I've already told you," Liz replied. "Something about the doctor having just interviewed Brent's parents."

"Anything else?"

"No."

"Hmmm," Jeff mused. "The parents must be the key to this whole thing. What could the doctor have learned from them that would make him pull out of the case?"

"I don't know," Liz admitted. "All I care about is that this will simplify the trial and increase the chances that Brent will be convicted."

"There's got to be more to it than that," Jeff persisted. "Shrinks don't usually drop a paying client like a hot potato. I'd bet anything that one of the parents revealed something so distasteful about Brent that the doc couldn't in good conscience stay on the case."

"Like what?"

"I don't know. Maybe that Brent has killed four other little boys and buried them in the cutting garden."

"Honestly!" Liz exclaimed.

"I can feel it! There's something there."

"Maybe so, but there's also such a thing as doctor-patient privilege," Liz reminded him. "Dr. Moss can't divulge anything he learned in the interviews. And it's not likely Mr. or Mrs. Tompkins is gonna tell us. So even if there is something bad about Brent that we don't know, I'm afraid it's going to stay hidden."

When Liz got back from lunch the following Monday, there was a message on her desk that Tom had returned the call she'd placed four days earlier. Must've been a lengthy out-of-town stay, she thought as she picked up the phone. She wondered bitterly if he and Natalie had had a good time.

Tom came on the line immediately, and Liz filled him in on Versey's withdrawing the insanity plea. "I have to tell you I've been feeling much more upbeat about the case ever since I got that call," she said. "And I'm feeling even better about it today because Jeff and I just had another session with Greg, and he's doing much better. I think he's going to be a good witness."

"That's great," Tom said, but his voice seemed to lack enthusiasm.

"And as long as I've got you on the phone," Liz continued, "why don't we set up a time for you to come in so we can go over your testimony? How would next Monday be? Say around nine?"

"That'd be fine," Tom replied.

Liz hesitated a moment, then said, "You sound a little distracted today. Is everything okay?"

"Yeah. Fine." Liz could hear him exhale, then he corrected himself. "Actually, I've been a little spacy the last week."

"Oh?" Liz said carefully. "I'm sorry to hear that. Is it anything you want to talk about?"

"I broke up with Natalie."

Liz's mouth dropped open, then she broke into a grin. What super news!

"We went to Chicago over Labor Day," Tom explained, "and we had a big fight—a continuing series of fights, actually—about a whole bunch of things. So, more or less by mutual agreement, we decided to stop seeing each other. I think it was absolutely the right decision, but it's still been kind of tough, with everything else that's going on."

Liz was so caught up in her own thoughts, it took her a moment to realize that Tom had stopped speaking and was now waiting for her to say something. "Ah, yes," she cleared her throat to buy some time in an effort to come up with something intelligent to say. "I can understand how you must feel, but the important thing is that you think you made the right decision. You have to go with your instincts, even though it's sometimes hard." As soon as she'd finished, she made a face. So much for trying to sound intelligent.

"Yeah, well, like I said, I'm sure it's for the best. I guess I just need a little more time to sort some things out."

"You know what they say: time heals all wounds." Oh, God. She was going from bad to worse.

"You're probably right," Tom sighed. "Anyway, I'm glad to hear the case is going well. I'll see you next Monday at nine."

"Great. And if you have any questions in the meantime or if, you know, you just feel like talking to someone, I'm a pretty good listener." There. That was better.

"Thanks for the offer. I just might take you up on that sometime. Good-bye."

" 'Bye."

Liz hung up the phone, feeling so light that she was sure she could leap out of her third-floor window and float to the ground if she had a mind to. So Tom broke up with Natalie. Well, well, well. Who would have guessed it?

She sat there briefly, savoring the moment, a self-satisfied grin on her face. Then an urgent thought sprang into her mind. "I have to tell Esther!" She reached for the phone. Oh, hell, she thought. Esther and her mother were in New York for several days of shopping and plays. They wouldn't be back until Thursday.

Liz frowned. No, this news would definitely not keep that long. She picked up the phone and dialed New York information. "Operator, I'd like the number for the Plaza." As Liz jotted down the number, she smiled to herself. Suddenly the whole world seemed rosier. Rather than dreading the start of the trial, she welcomed it. It would mean she'd have daily contact with Tom. And now that that red-haired shrew was out of the picture, well—anything was possible.

PART FOUR

Chapter 38

After a weekend of heavy rain, the first day of the trial dawned warm and clear. Liz hoped that the change in the weather was a good omen.

She arrived at the office early to go over her notes on jury selection one more time, wearing the black Chanel suit Peter had bought her when she'd made partner at her old law firm. Although she'd had to admit that the outfit made her feel sophisticated and just a bit decadent, she'd also feared it gave the impression she was flaunting her wealth, so she'd only ever worn it a handful of times, and then only to events where she'd been sure other women would be similarly attired. For the past couple of years the problem of finding an appropriate place to wear it had been moot, since it hadn't fit. But last week, when on impulse she had slipped into the skirt and discovered that the zipper once again slid up as though the garment had been made to order, she just knew she had to wear it today. It made her look sleek and stunning, and more important, it gave her an air of confidence. For this second attribute she was especially grateful since, in spite of the fact that she knew she had a strong case, she was still nervous.

Jury selection was scheduled to begin at nine o'clock. Jeff arrived shortly after eight, carrying a styrofoam cup of coffee from Stop-n-Go. "You look great," he complimented her as he sat down and set the cup on her desk. "New outfit?"

Liz shook her head. "I decided if Versey could wear

two-thousand-dollar suits, so could I," she said fliply as she ran through a checklist of exhibits.

Jeff frowned. "You're kidding. That getup didn't really cost two thou."

"My ex-husband bought it for me," Liz explained. "It was one of his last kind gestures before we split up."

"Jesus!" Jeff exclaimed, shaking his head in amazement. He had purchased a new suit at Kuppenheimer's earlier in the year and had hated to shell out two *hundred* dollars. "If I gave a woman a suit that cost two grand and then broke up with her, I'd demand custody of the damn thing," he grumbled. "Or at least visitation rights."

Liz shrugged. "Believe me, Peter was so eager to trade me in on a newer model that he didn't squabble over trifles like my clothing. Did you get things squared away so you'll be able to be here for the whole trial?"

Jeff picked up his coffee cup and nodded. "Good old Dan," he said, smiling. "I was all set to take vacation, but he said, 'Son, it's both your civic and moral duty to attend the entire proceeding,' and he reassigned all my cases for the duration." He took a sip of coffee. "That caused some bitching at the department, but I really don't give a shit. There's no way in hell I was gonna miss one minute of this."

"I'm glad you'll be around," Liz said. "It'll mean a lot to Greg." She paused a moment, then asked, "Do you think he's ready?"

"Yeah, I do," Jeff replied without hesitation. "I thought the last couple of sessions where we worked with him in the courtroom went real well. I think he's gonna do just fine."

"Me, too," Liz said. It was the truth, but she sure wished she could stop her heart from palpitating.

"You haven't had any more excitement around your house, have you?" Jeff asked casually.

Liz shook her head. "The extra patrol car drive-bys you arranged must've done the trick."

"Any more mail?"

"No."

"Good. I think you've probably heard the last of whoever was pulling those pranks."

"I hope so," Liz said fervently. "It bothered me more than I cared to admit. And thanks again for coming to my rescue that night. I was in pretty bad shape when I called you."

"Don't mention it. Rescuing damsels in distress is one of the nicer parts of my job."

"Good morning," Tom Barker said as he walked in the door, straightening his tie. Liz looked up at him and smiled. She had spoken to him on the phone several times since the conversation in which he'd told her he'd broken up with Natalie, and a week ago they had met in her office to prep him for his trial testimony.

During the meeting, Liz had fluctuated between feeling self-conscious and wanting to throw herself at him, but she had managed to exercise restraint. Even Esther, who earlier couldn't wait to see Liz involved with anyone other than Harry, had cautioned her to take it slow. "Don't even think about making a move now," her friend had warned. "You've got to have your wits about you to get through the trial. But once that's over, hell, I'd hit him with both barrels." Liz was giving serious thought to following up on that suggestion.

"The parking lot's already full," Tom said, shaking his head in amazement as he gazed out the window. "I had to park out on the street about two blocks away."

Liz nodded. "The media are taking up so many seats in the courtroom that there's only going to be room for fifty or sixty spectators. People were lining up at seven so they'd be sure to get in."

Tom stepped back from the window, balled his

hands into fists, and tapped them lightly against his legs. "I'm nervous as hell. I sure wish it was over."

"It will be before you know it," Jeff said encouragingly. Then he added, "Don't sweat it, pal. The case is in great hands."

"I know that," Tom said, giving Liz a look that made her melt. "I guess I'm just a little apprehensive about testifying . . . and about seeing Brent, too," he admitted. "It's going to be very emotional."

"You'll do fine," Liz assured him. "Just try to relax."

Harry Washburn stepped into the office. "Good morning, Detective, Mr. Barker," he said rather stiffly. "Liz, I just wanted to stop by to wish you good luck."

"Thank you," Liz said. Several days earlier, Harry had renewed his suggestion that Liz think about offering Brent a plea bargain. She had rejected the idea out of hand, and although Harry had not pressed his point, she could tell he had a been a bit miffed. Frankly she didn't care what he thought anymore. If he'd wanted the case handled differently, he should've accepted her offer to resign when the charges against Brent were first filed.

"I'll probably sit in on some of the testimony, although I don't intend to watch the entire trial," Harry went on. "But if you want to run anything by me, I'll be in the office all week. Don't hesitate to ask if I can help with anything."

"Thanks," Liz said rather coolly.

Brent, his parents, and his attorneys were already in the courtroom when Liz, Jeff, and Tom arrived. Brent was dressed in gray slacks and a gray tweed jacket. He was sporting a new short haircut. As Liz watched, the boy leaned over to say something to Versey. The attorney's response caused Brent to flash a broad smile. It was unbelievable, Liz thought, how a boy his age on trial for murder could act so blasé. In fact, of the entire defense contingent, only Mrs. Tompkins looked nervous. As she sat stiffly at her husband's side, the woman continually fidgeted with the buckle on her blue dress, clasping and unclasping it.

It took two full days to select a jury. Judge Gilbert Andrews, a tall, sinewy man in his late fifties, began the process by asking each prospective juror a series of questions, starting with whether they had heard or read anything about the case. If a person responded affirmatively, the judge would inquire whether what they had heard had caused them to form an opinion as to the defendant's guilt. If they said they *had* formed an opinion, the judge would dismiss them.

While most panel members survived this phase of the questioning, to Liz's surprise, a significant number of people said they would have difficulty convicting a fourteen-year-old of intentional homicide. After fourteen out of the first eighteen called had been dismissed for this reason, Liz began to wonder whether they'd be able to find enough people out of the available pool to hear the case. Otherwise, Judge Andrews would be forced to send his bailiff out to shanghai folks off the streets of Lakeview to fill the remaining slots.

Finally, by late Tuesday afternoon, after questioning one hundred people, they had their jury: five women, seven men, and two alternates, one of each sex. Although Liz hadn't been able to completely avoid jurors with children or grandchildren about Brent's age, overall she was happy with the makeup of the group. Only one juror was from Oakwood, a female accountant in her forties who had moved to town in the spring and said she didn't know any of the parties and had heard very little about the case.

At nine o'clock Wednesday morning, Judge Andrews called on Liz to make her opening statement. She picked up a small stack of three-by-five cards and moved to the lectern that had been placed in front of the jury box. She took a deep breath. The case of *The State of Wisconsin v. Brent Tompkins* was officially under way.

"Ladies and gentlemen," she began slowly, attempting to make eye contact with each juror. "Jeremy Barker was a four-year-old boy who had his entire life ahead of him. He had a good home and a loving father. He was a bright, inquisitive little boy who brightened the lives of those around him and was brimming with great promise for the future. Sadly, there will be no future for Jeremy because his life was cruelly and intentionally snuffed out by the defendant, Brent Tompkins."

She paused to let the jury take a good look at Brent. She turned to look at him too and saw that he was sitting quietly, his hands folded neatly in his lap, his eyes gazing impassively into space. Liz turned back to the jury. "The evidence will show that after engineering a scheme to kidnap the boy by luring him into the woods, Brent Tompkins hit Jeremy over the head with a shovel. The first blow knocked him to the ground and rendered him unconscious, but Brent's viciousness and cruelty didn't stop there. He continued to hit Jeremy over the head again and again. The child's skull was completely shattered. When he was certain the boy was dead, Brent carried him deeper into the woods and, with the same shovel he had used to kill him, he dug a hole, placed Jeremy's body inside, and covered it up with dirt."

She paused again and looked at the jurors. They were all listening intently. "Ladies and gentlemen, Jeremy's death was not an accident. It was not a case of roughhousing gone awry. It was instead an intentional act of murder, planned and executed in cold blood by Brent Tompkins. I submit that after you've heard all the evidence, you will have no alternative but to find the defendant guilty of all charges. Thank you." As Liz turned and walked back to her seat, she glanced at Tom. There were tears in his eyes.

As was his prerogative, Versey reserved the right to make his opening statement at the beginning of the defendant's portion of the case.

The remainder of the day was taken up with background witnesses. Deputy Ronald Hasslett described how he and his tracking dog had searched for and ultimately located Jeremy's body. Liz had Hasslett identify several photographs of the body, and the pictures were then distributed to the jury for their perusal. Glancing casually toward the jury box, Liz could see that the photos were having the desired effect. Several jurors made faces as they looked at them, and one woman gasped out loud.

Next, Liz called two investigators from the medical examiner's office, who testified that they had personally overseen moving Jeremy's body from the crime scene to the morgue and that no one had disturbed the body during that time. They were followed by Dr. Ramirez, who explained the findings he had made as a result of Jeremy's autopsy.

The day's final witness was Jeremy's nanny, Darlene Powell. Liz was glad to see that the woman appeared to have recovered from the breakdown she'd suffered after the little boy's death. She had moved to Madison to be close to her daughter and had recently begun taking care of a professional couple's twin girls. In response to gentle questioning from Liz, Darlene described how she had come to live in the Barker household when Tom's wife became ill, her care of and devotion to Jeremy, and the events that had taken place the day he disappeared.

"What did you do when you realized Jeremy was missing?" Liz asked.

"I ran through every room in the house, calling his name," Darlene replied. "When I couldn't find him, I searched the backyard and ran up into the woods, screaming his name at the top of my lungs."

"Did you find any trace of him?"

"Not a thing," the woman said, fighting back tears. "He had vanished. I never saw him again."

"What did you do then?"

"I ran back to the house and called the police and Jeremy's father."

"Thank you, Mrs. Powell. I have no further questions."

The judge adjourned for the day, and Jeff, Liz, and Tom met back in her office.

"I think things are going really well," Jeff said. "Hell, Versey's hardly opened his mouth to cross-examine."

"He's probably saving all his energy to pick on Greg," Liz muttered.

"I've been watching the jury, and they seem to be riveted," Tom offered.

"Better get a good night's sleep," Jeff advised her. "Tomorrow's going to be a big day."

Liz nodded. She was only too well aware of that fact. She would start the day's session by calling Tom to the witness stand. And after that, Greg would have his long-awaited day in court. The anticipation of that event sent a nervous shiver up her spine. "I'll see you both tomorrow," she said, gathering her file up in her arms and heading for the door. She hoped a long soak in the tub and listening to some soft music would ease her jitters. The next day's agenda would make or break her case. There would be no room for screwups.

Chapter 39

Liz spent a restless night.

She had an old, recurring dream that haunted her whenever she was under stress. She was back in law school and an exam was being given in one of her classes. She'd thought she was well prepared, but when the test was handed out she looked through it and discovered to her horror that she didn't know the answer to even one of the questions. She glanced around to see if by some chance she was in the wrong room, but no, she recognized the other students and apparently none of them shared her predicament. They were all busy filling their essay books with their answers. The harder Liz stared at the questions, the more panic-stricken she became.

Just as she was about to bolt from the room in terror, she woke up, drenched in sweat, her heart pounding. She looked at the clock. It was three-thirty Thursday morning. She got up for a drink of water and then crawled back into bed, but sleep eluded her. At five-thirty she decided it was a lost cause. She got up, drank several cups of coffee, and nibbled on some toast, trying to exorcize the demons that were tormenting her.

By the time she arrived at the courthouse at seven-thirty, she was feeling better. She met briefly with the Saunderses in her office and gave Greg a few last words of encouragement. Jeff had offered to stay and keep the family company until it was time for Greg to testify.

Tom and Liz arrived in the courtroom simultaneously. She gave his arm a reassuring pat and took her seat.

Tom strode confidently to the stand when called, but as he sat down, Liz noticed that his face was pale. For a moment it appeared that he was struggling to keep from looking at Brent. Finally, he did glance over at the boy. When he saw Brent staring at him, Tom's whole body immediately tensed. He swallowed hard and looked away. Brent seemed to be smirking. Liz gritted her teeth and shot him a cold glance.

Liz had Tom tell the jury about the tragedy of his young wife dying and how that ordeal had brought him even closer to his son. He identified a photograph of Jeremy that had been taken a week before the child's death. It showed the little boy dressed in swimming trunks and standing proudly in front of the pool, the very spot from which he had been enticed.

"When was the last time you saw Jeremy?" Liz asked.

"It was about seven-thirty the morning of Tuesday, June 11."

"What was he doing?"

Tom stared into space for a moment, remembering. "He had just gotten up. He was still in his pajamas and was sitting at the kitchen table. It was a hot day, and he told me that he was going to go swimming later that morning, and he asked me what I was going to do."

"What did you tell him?"

"I said I had to go to work, and I told him how lucky he was that he could stay home and loaf all day."

"What did Jeremy say to that?"

Tom ran his tongue around his lips. "He said, 'Hurry home, Daddy, and then we can loaf together.' "

"Was that the last time you saw your son?"

Tom nodded. "It was the last time I saw him alive." His voice began to crack, and he cleared his throat. "The next time I saw him, he was in the morgue."

Liz swallowed hard and found herself blinking back tears as she said quietly, "Thank you. No further questions." She retreated hastily to her seat and poured herself a glass of cold water. Glancing at the jury box, she saw two women wiping their eyes.

"Mr. Versey, cross?" the judge asked.

Versey shook his head. "No questions, Your Honor."

"Thank you, Mr. Barker, you may step down," Judge Andrews said. "Ms. Stanfeld, you may call your next witness."

Liz greedily took another couple of gulps of water before getting to her feet again. "Your Honor, before I do that, I would like to read the jury a stipulation entered into between Attorney Versey and myself."

Judge Andrews turned to Versey. "Any objection, Counsel?"

"No, Your Honor," Versey replied magnanimously.

"Very well, Ms. Stanfeld," the judge said. "You may proceed."

Liz cleared her throat and faced the jury. "The witness you are about to hear was initially charged in a juvenile delinquency proceeding with the same counts for which the defendant, Brent Tompkins, is now on trial. As a result of a plea agreement, the witness was found delinquent on the kidnapping charge and is currently on probation. As part of the state's agreement to drop the first-degree intentional homicide charge, the witness agreed to give testimony against Brent Tompkins in this case." She paused, took a deep breath, and said, "At this time the state calls Gregory Saunders."

Jeff had been stationed at the back of the courtroom, ready to usher Greg in when he was called. A hush fell over the room as the boy, dressed in black pants and a white shirt, slowly walked up the center aisle and stood in front of the court clerk, waiting to be sworn in. It was apparent that many of those in attendance were aware who Greg was and were anxious to hear what he had to say.

"Do you swear that the testimony you are about to give will be the truth, the whole truth, and nothing but the truth, so help you God?" the clerk asked.

"I do," Greg replied in a small but clear voice.

"Have a seat, Greg," the judge instructed kindly. Greg sat down and nervously folded his hands in his lap.

As Liz had instructed, the boy turned his body toward the jury box so he could avoid inadvertently making eye contact with Brent. Liz was thankful she'd given this directive, since she noted that Brent was staring straight at Greg.

"Would you please state your name for the record?" Liz said.

"Greg Saunders."

"How old are you, Greg?"

"Thirteen."

"Are you acquainted with the defendant, Brent Tompkins?"

"Yes."

"When did you first meet him?"

"About five years ago. That's when we moved to Oakwood."

"At some point did you become better acquainted with Brent?"

Greg nodded. "Last year, at school. I was in seventh grade and he was in eighth. Sometimes I'd hang around with him and his friends."

"Did you consider Brent your friend?"

"Yes."

"Greg, I'd like to call your attention to the morning of June 11. Can you tell us what you did that day?"

The boy explained his phone call with Brent, the rendezvous in the woods, and Brent's unveiling of the plan to kidnap Jeremy Barker. Then Liz carefully led Greg through his role in luring Jeremy out of the yard by promising to show the child horses in the woods, to Brent's suddenly striking the little boy with the shovel, to carrying the corpse to the gravesite and finally burying it. Through it all, Greg remained calm and his stutter manifested itself on only one or two occasions.

"After Brent had buried the body, did he say anything to you?"

Greg nodded.

"What did he say?"

In a voice so low that Liz had to strain to hear it, Greg replied, "He said if I ever told anyone what had happened, he'd kill me, too."

"I don't think the jury heard that," Judge Andrews said. "Perhaps the court reporter could read it back."

The courtroom was absolutely still as the reporter looked at her notes and repeated in a loud, clear voice, " 'He said if I ever told anyone what had happened, he'd kill me, too.' "

Liz smiled to herself in satisfaction as she saw the jury respond with frowns, clenched jaws and angry looks directed toward Brent. "Thank you, Greg," she said. "I have no further questions."

Judge Andrews looked at the clock. "It's nearly twelve o'clock. This seems to be a good time to break for lunch. We will reconvene at one-thirty."

Liz and Jeff whisked Greg and his parents back to her office, where they were both effusive in their praise of the boy. "That was just great, Greg," Liz exclaimed. "Absolutely first-rate."

"She's right, sport," Jeff agreed. "The jury just loved you. See, it's not so bad, is it?"

"I'm still worried about Versey's questions," Teresa Saunders said anxiously.

"Greg's going to do just fine," Liz assured her. She turned to the boy and said, "All you have to do is answer his questions the same way you did mine. Be brief and to the point and above all, be truthful. If you do that, you won't have any problem. You trust me, don't you?"

Greg looked up at her, swallowed hard, and nodded.

"Atta boy," Liz said, giving him a smile. "Now, let's go grab a bite to eat." She patted him on the back. "It'll be all over before you know it."

After the judge called court back into session and the jurors took their seats, Greg was recalled to the stand. In spite of Liz's reassurances, it was obvious that the boy was extremely nervous. His hands were folded in his lap, and he was squeezing them together so tightly that his knuckles were white. As before, he was seated so that he was facing away from Brent.

Versey's cross-exam started out innocuously enough. "Good afternoon, Greg," he said pleasantly. "How are you today?"

"Okay," Greg replied in a weak, quivering voice.

"I'm glad to hear that," Versey said. "Now Greg, before we get started, I'd just like to remind you that this morning you took an oath promising to tell the truth in this proceeding. Do you remember that?"

"Yes," Greg nodded.

"Good. Now if I remember correctly, you said you've known Brent Tompkins for about five years, is that right?"

"Something like that," Greg agreed.

"Brent is a year older than you and a year ahead of you in school, isn't he?"

"Yes."

"I believe you also testified that you considered Brent your friend, is that right?"

"Yes."

"When did this friendship develop?"

Greg paused a moment to consider. "Last year, I guess," he said somewhat hesitantly.

"When you were in seventh grade and Brent was in eighth?"

"Yes."

"Is it fair to say that prior to last year you didn't

really consider Brent your friend; he was just somebody you knew from the neighborhood?"

"I- I guess so."

Liz caught Greg's eye and smiled. So far he was
doing just fine.

Versey nodded. "What types of things would you
do together?"

"Ah, mostly go to each other's house to watch movies or listen to music. Sometimes hang around together
at school."

"When the two of you shared these activities you've
just spoken of, which one of you would initiate the
suggestion that you do them together, you or Brent?"

Greg gave a small shrug. "Ah . . . it depended.
Sometimes it was me and sometimes it was him."

"I see," Versey said, stroking his chin thoughtfully.
"Did any other boys ever participate in the things you
did with Brent?"

Greg paused a moment, then shook his head.
"Not really."

"Brent had a lot of other friends at school, didn't
he?"

"Yes."

"A lot of boys from his own class?"

"Yes."

"Did Brent ever include you in any of his activities
with those other boys?"

"I don't know," Greg hesitated. "I guess not."

"Did it upset you to be excluded?"

"No." Greg's expression was wary and his stutter
was worsening.

"It didn't bother you not to be included in things
Brent and his friends did?"

"Not really."

"You never got angry at Brent for not inviting you
along when he did things with other boys?"

"No."

Versey paused to pour himself a glass of water and
take a long drink before continuing his questioning.

As he finished the water, he made a smacking sound with his lips. Liz watched Greg's expression grow more fearful. Then, smiling pleasantly, Versey said, "Greg, do you recall that last November Brent invited five or six boys to stay overnight at his house?"

Liz could see Greg's eyes widen. "Yes," he replied somewhat hesitantly.

"You weren't invited to that sleepover, were you?" Greg shook his head. "No."

"Did that bother you?"

"No."

"Do you recall what your reaction was when you found out you weren't invited?"

Liz watched Greg swallow hard a couple of times before replying softly, "I don't remember."

"You don't remember," Versey said in a loud voice, "or you don't want to tell us?"

"Objection!" Liz said. "Argumentative."

"Overruled," Judge Andrews responded. "You may answer the question," he directed Greg.

"I don't remember," Greg said again.

"Isn't it a fact that when you found out you had not been invited to the sleepover, you screamed at Brent and punched him in the stomach?" Versey went on.

"I don't remember." Greg's stutter worsened.

"You don't remember," Versey repeated sarcastically. "Well, let's test your memory of another incident. Do you recall that in March of this year you and Brent were on the school playground when you learned that Brent had invited several of his friends to accompany him and his family to Chicago for a weekend?"

"I guess so."

"And isn't it a fact that when you learned you were not among the boys invited, you became so incensed that you repeatedly kicked a tree and broke your toe?"

Greg's face was white, and he was breathing hard now. "It was an accident."

Versey plowed on. "Isn't it a fact that you knew Brent never considered you his friend? You tried to force your way into his group but he didn't want you. Isn't that true?"

"Objection," Liz said. "The question is argumentative."

"Overruled," the judge called out. "Please answer the question, Greg."

"No." Greg shook his head.

"And isn't it a fact that in spite of Brent's continued rejections, you refused to take no for an answer and kept on hounding him?"

"No."

"And isn't it also a fact that the more you hounded him, the more he rejected you, and the angrier you got with him?"

"No!"

In his effort to defend himself, Greg inadvertently swung around to face Versey. Too late he remembered that his movement would put him eyeball to eyeball with Brent. As Liz looked on in horror, she saw Brent staring defiantly at Greg. The younger boy involuntarily drew in his breath and emitted a low wail.

"Your Honor!" Liz jumped to her feet in an effort to divert Greg's attention. "Counsel is badgering the witness with this line of questions," she said. Glancing over at Greg, she saw that thankfully the tactic had worked. The boy was now watching her. "Furthermore," she went on, "this inquiry has been asked and answered."

"Sustained," the judge agreed. "Mr. Versey, move on."

"Greg," Versey said in a softer tone, "Before you came here today, did you practice going over your testimony with Ms. Stanfeld?"

Greg stared at Liz. When she nodded, he replied in a whisper. "Yes."

"How many practice sessions did you have?"

Greg hesitated, then squeaked, "Four or five."

"Thank you," Versey said. "No further questions."

"In that case, this witness may be excused," the judge said. Greg sat completely still, as though he were unable to budge from his chair. The judge leaned down toward him. "You can go now, son," he said kindly. This remark seemed to jar Greg back to reality. He slowly got up and unsteadily walked toward the back of the room where his anxious parents were waiting.

The judge turned to Liz. "Ms. Stanfeld, you may call your next witness."

Liz took a deep breath. "Your Honor, we have no further witnesses. The state rests."

The judge nodded. "In that case, Mr. Versey, may we hear your opening statement, please?"

Though she tried to pay attention, Liz scarcely heard a word of Versey's remarks. She was too busy berating herself: for not prepping Greg thoroughly enough, for promising the Saunderses that Greg would make it through cross-examination unscathed, for being foolish enough to think Versey might go easy on the boy. She glanced over at Brent and saw him staring at his attorney, the expression on his face one of unmistakable admiration. She clenched her jaw, praying that Greg's poor performance didn't mean Brent would have a chance at getting off.

Versey had finished his opening. "Thank you, Mr. Versey," Judge Andrews said. "You may call your first witness."

Liz sighed, wondering which witness Versey would use to start out his case. Probably one of the independent crime scene experts he'd hired to try to refute the exact time of Jeremy's death. She was looking forward to some boring crime scene talk. She'd had enough tension for one day.

It was with disbelief and horror that Liz listened to Versey purr, "If it please the court, the defense calls Brent Tompkins."

Chapter 40

A hush fell over the courtroom as Brent walked confidently to the witness stand. Liz groaned to herself as he swore to tell the whole truth and nothing but. That boy wouldn't know the truth if it bit him in the ass.

She had to admit he cut a fine figure sitting there, his hair styled in a neat razor cut, his gray suit expensive and fashionable. No question about it, in a few years teenage girls would consider him a real heart-throb. Liz was still hoping that if she did her job properly, the lad would spend his reckless youth in a place that was decidedly not coed.

After going through the preliminaries of Brent's background, Versey turned to a discussion of Greg.

"You heard the testimony given by Greg Saunders, did you not?"

"Yes." Brent's voice was clear and confident, his expression sincere as he spoke directly to the jury.

"I'd like to clarify a few statements Greg made. Did you consider him your friend?'

Brent shook his head. "No."

"How did you think of him?"

"As a younger boy who lived in my neighborhood."

"Were you aware that Greg thought you were friends?"

Brent shrugged. "He was always wanting to hang around me. I felt kind of sorry for him, because I don't think he had very many friends, so sometimes I'd humor him."

"But you never felt you were friends?"

"No."

"Besides the fact that you felt sorry for him, was there any other reason you sometimes let Greg Saunders hang around with you?"

"Yes. He had a rather violent temper, and I figured it was easier to let him pal around with me once in a while rather than risk having him blow up."

Liz frowned and furiously scrawled notes on a legal pad to help her formulate questions for cross-exam.

"Can you give us some examples of Greg's temper?"

Brent recounted the two incidents Versey had referred to in his questioning of Greg.

"So on each of these occasions Greg became violent and abusive when he learned you had not included him in outings you had planned with other boys in your class?"

"That's right."

"Brent, I'd now like to turn your attention to the morning of June 11. Do you recall that day?"

Brent's face became solemn. He swallowed hard and nodded. "Yes."

"What happened that morning?"

"I was home alone when Greg called and wanted to know if I had any plans for the day. I didn't, so I asked what he had in mind. He said he had a surprise and wanted me to meet him in the woods."

"Did he say what the surprise was?"

"No."

"Did you meet him?"

"Yes."

"And what was the surprise?"

Brent paused and again swallowed hard. "He told me he wanted to play a trick on Tom Barker by kidnapping Barker's son Jeremy."

Liz's mouth gaped open as the defense strategy became apparent. The lying little bastard was going to use Greg's story but reverse the roles.

A murmur ran through the courtroom. "Order in

the court!'' Judge Andrews commanded, rapping his gavel sharply on the bench. The crowd fell silent.

"Did Greg say why he wanted to play a trick on Mr. Barker?" Versey went on.

Brent nodded. "He said Mr. Barker had chased him off his property a couple of weeks before and had called him a bastard."

"I see," Versey said thoughtfully. "So in retaliation Greg decided to get even by kidnapping Mr. Barker's son?"

"Yes."

Liz shifted in her chair and looked toward the back of the room where Greg was sitting with his parents. Teresa Saunders had her arm around him, and the boy had his head buried in his mother's shoulder. It looked like he was sobbing. Liz's heart went out to him. She wished she had advised the Saunders family to leave the courtroom immediately after Greg's testimony.

"What role were you supposed to play in Greg's scheme?" Versey continued.

"None, really," Brent replied. "I was just supposed to be a witness."

"A witness?" Versey asked quizzically.

"Yes. You see, I believe Greg thought the reason none of the other boys from my class liked him was that they considered him sort of a sissy. And Greg seemed to feel that if he did some manly act, like kidnapping a little boy, the older guys would think more highly of him. I was just supposed to be a witness, so I could corroborate that the kidnapping had actually taken place when he later recounted the incident to the other boys."

"Did you try to talk Greg out of this scheme?"

Brent sighed. "I know now that I didn't try as hard as I should have. I remember telling him it was a dumb idea, but he started to get very upset and yell at me, so I decided to play along with him, at least for a while."

"Did you think any harm was going to come to the child?"

Brent shook his head adamantly. "Absolutely not. Greg assured me he was just going to keep the boy in the woods for an hour or so, just long enough for the family to get scared, and then let him go."

"How was the plan carried out?"

"Greg had a pair of binoculars along, and we took turns watching the Barker house. The nanny was out by the pool with the little boy. Around noon a UPS truck pulled up to the gate, and we saw the nanny go inside. That's when Greg made his move. He ran down through the lawn and said something to the little boy—I'm not sure what it was—but whatever he said worked because the little boy ran back up through the lawn and into the woods with Greg just as fast as he could go."

"What happened when they got to the woods?"

"Greg told Jeremy that I was his friend and we were going to go for a walk. He told me to hold Jeremy's hand and walk ahead of him, so I did."

"Then what happened?"

Brent paused and his chin began to tremble. "Greg was walking behind us, and the next thing I knew he'd hit the little boy over the head with a shovel."

Liz was so incensed she could hardly concentrate. If the prison system had a theatrical department, Brent would be a natural.

"Had you seen him carrying a shovel?"

"No," Brent said, swallowing hard. "But he got to the woods before I did, so he must've had it hidden someplace."

"What happened after he hit Jeremy with a shovel?"

"The little boy fell to the ground, and Greg hit him over and over again." Brent's voice was breaking.

Liz groaned. This was really too much. Bring on the violins.

"What were you doing during this time?"

"I was just totally stunned, you know, like I was in a trance. I remember trying to move, but I couldn't."

"What happened next?"

"Greg handed me the shovel and said, 'Here, make yourself useful. Carry this.' So I carried the shovel and he put a plastic bag over Jeremy's head so he wouldn't get blood on his clothes. Then he picked Jeremy up and carried him off into the woods. We walked quite a ways before Greg put Jeremy down. Then he grabbed the shovel from me, dug a hole, and buried Jeremy in it."

"Did he do anything else?"

Brent nodded. "Yes. He had a pair of men's eyeglasses with him. He threw those about fifteen or twenty feet from the body and said, 'That's evidence that will put the police on the trail of somebody who deserves to be arrested.' "

"Do you know whose glasses they were?"

"No."

"What did Greg do then?"

"He picked up the shovel and said he'd take care of it so nobody would ever find it."

"Anything else?"

Brent ran his tongue anxiously around his lips. "He said, 'You saw that killing means nothing to me. Well, the same thing's going to happen to you if you ever tell anybody what happened.' "

"And then you split up and each went to your respective homes?"

"Yes."

Versey paused a moment, then said, "Brent, sometime after the murder, you were questioned by Detective Jeff Gardner, were you not?"

"Yes."

"And did you tell Detective Gardner the story you've just told us?"

"No."

"Why not?"

Brent sniffled. "I was afraid what might happen to me if I told."

"You mean you were afraid Greg might follow through on his threat and kill you?"

Brent nodded. "Yes," he said, tears running down his cheeks. "And I guess I was afraid for Greg, too. He's really not a bad kid. I didn't want him to go to jail."

"Thank you, Brent," Versey said. "I have no further questions."

Judge Andrews looked at the clock. "It's after five. I'm afraid I have an appointment out of town this evening that precludes us from running any later today. We will resume at nine tomorrow morning with cross-examination of this witness. Until then, court is adjourned."

While normally an attorney will protest mightily when denied the opportunity to cross-examine a witness immediately after direct exam, Liz was exceedingly grateful for the break in the proceedings. She needed time to get her thoughts in order. Unfortunately, she was afraid one night wouldn't be enough to figure out how to counteract Brent's powerful performance.

Dodging her way through reporters and rudely refusing to answer any of their questions, Liz made a beeline for her office. Tom and Jeff joined her moments later.

"Jesus Christ! What a circus!" Jeff exclaimed as he slammed the door behind him.

"The jury's not going to buy Brent's story, is it?" Tom asked with concern.

"I don't know," Jeff replied warily. "They were sure listening to him awfully intently."

Liz gritted her teeth. "I'm just going to have to do the best I can to discredit him on cross." Turning to Jeff, she said, "You'll be a good rebuttal witness, and Philip Barry can help us, too, although the facts that he didn't get along with any of the other teachers and got a notice of nonrenewal from the school board are going to hurt his credibility." The former Oakwood teacher who'd had problems with Brent was scheduled to fly in from Seattle that weekend.

Liz sighed. "I wish we could recall Greg to the stand to counter what Brent said, but I'm sure he'd fall apart completely and that would only make things worse." Turning to Jeff, she said, "Run next door and ask the court reporter if she can get us an immediate transcript of Brent's direct exam. I was trying to take copious notes, but I might've missed something."

"Will do," Jeff said, immediately heading out of the office.

"Is there anything I can do to help?" Tom asked anxiously.

"Yeah," Liz muttered as she flipped through her file. "You can start praying."

Chapter 41

"Ms. Stanfeld, you may proceed with cross-examination of this witness."

Liz's head was pounding. She had worked long into the night working up the questions she would ask Brent, but she still didn't feel adequately prepared.

Her attempts to poke holes in Brent's account of Jeremy's murder got her nowhere. Brent had that script committed to memory and never deviated from it. She soon abandoned that tack and tried to challenge his depiction of Greg as angry and volatile.

"You testified to two occasions on which you claim Greg became violent. In both of those instances, his anger was directed at your not including him in some social function you'd planned with other boys in your class. Is that right?"

"Yes," Brent replied, looking directly into her eyes.

"Were these the only occasions on which you saw Greg become angry?"

"No, there were others."

"Could you describe some of those?"

Brent paused a moment. "There are really so many that it's hard to pinpoint individual ones."

"Please try," Liz said sweetly.

Brent took a breath and stared into space for a moment. Then he looked back at Liz with a slight smile. "All right. I've thought of a couple. Once he hit another boy who cut in ahead of him in the lunch line, and another time he accused someone of stealing his watch and really blew his stack."

"I see," Liz said, pursing her lips. "Do your recall the names of the other boys involved in either of these incidents?"

"Mmmm . . . no, I'm afraid I don't."

I didn't think so, Liz thought. "Well, then, do you recall if there were any other witnesses to either of these events?"

Brent shook his head. "I'm afraid I don't. These things happened some time ago, and I guess at the time I wasn't paying attention to who else was present."

"But you're sure the events did take place as you've described them?"

"Oh, I'm positive."

"Since you apparently held this view much of the last school year—that Greg had a violent personality—did you ever speak to a teacher about your concerns?"

"No."

"Is there a reason for that?"

Brent shrugged. "I didn't want to get Greg in trouble."

"But if you truly thought he was violent, didn't it occur to you that you should tell someone?"

"I guess I thought his anger was mainly verbal," Brent explained. "I never believed he was capable of doing what he did."

"If you didn't consider Greg your friend, why were you so eager to comply with his request that you meet him in the woods the day Jeremy Barker was killed?"

"As I already explained," Brent said patiently, "I didn't have anything to do that day. I guess I was feeling a little bored. It was real hot out and a walk in the woods sounded like a good idea, so I agreed to meet him. I didn't know what he had in mind."

"But after he told you what he had in mind, why didn't you leave?"

"Because he started to get really angry. He was

yelling at me and his face was turning red. I just decided to go along with him."

"Did he threaten you into staying?"

"No," Brent admitted.

"Were you fearful for your own safety?"

"Well—" Brent hesitated. "As I said, he seemed very upset. I guess I didn't know what he might do."

Liz paused and looked carefully at Brent. "I'd say you must be four or five inches taller and forty pounds heavier than Greg. Didn't you think you could defend yourself or subdue him if a fight developed?"

Brent shook his head, a look of bewilderment on his face. "I just didn't know. Sometimes when people become violent, they take on almost superhuman strength."

"I see," Liz said with mock patience. "Well, then, if you were concerned he might hurt you, why didn't you leave when Greg ran down through the Barkers' yard? Surely there would have been enough time for you to escape then."

Brent threw up his hands in a gesture of futility. "I wish I could tell you why I didn't leave then. Believe me, I wish I had left. I don't know why I stayed, but that decision will haunt me the rest of my life."

"I'm sure it will," Liz murmured under her breath. "Why didn't you try to intervene after Greg hit Jeremy the first time?" she asked.

"I wanted to," he said, his voice rising. "I knew I should do something, but I couldn't seem to move."

"Was Jeremy still alive after the first blow?"

Brent sighed. "I don't know. He wasn't moving."

"But it's possible he was still alive?"

Brent swallowed hard. "Yes, it's possible."

"You knew there was a chance the boy was still alive, but you did nothing," Liz said slowly, letting it sink in for the jury. "I have no further questions."

Judge Andrews turned to Versey. "Counsel, you may call your next witness."

The remainder of the day was filled with the mundane witnesses Liz had expected Versey to use to start out his case: investigators and forensic people hired by the defense, whose rather boring testimony challenged in a number of insignificant ways the findings of the state's technical witnesses. However, none of these people really disputed the conclusion that someone had bludgeoned Jeremy Barker to death sometime on the afternoon of Tuesday, June 11.

Late that afternoon, as one of the witnesses was dismissed, the judge again turned to Versey. "We might have time for one more witness, provided the testimony isn't expected to take more than an hour."

Versey got to his feet. "Your Honor, there will be no further witnesses. The defense rests."

"Very well," Judge Andrews said, "My normal procedure is to hold court on Saturdays. However, this weekend I am obliged to attend a family funeral in Minnesota. For that reason, court is adjourned until Monday morning at nine, at which time the state will present its rebuttal." He rang his gavel down, signaling the end of the first week of trial.

Back in her office, Liz plopped down into her chair and put her head down on her desk.

"What do you think?" Tom asked anxiously as he and Jeff joined her moments later.

Liz looked up at him. "I don't know," she said honestly. "I'd like to be able to tell you that the jury believed Greg instead of Brent, but I just don't know. Let's face it," she said, looking from one man to the other, "Greg didn't come across particularly well."

"I'll be able to testify that Brent's a liar," Jeff said fiercely as he leaned against the door frame. "And Phil Barry will say Brent was bad news when he had him in his class."

"Yeah," Liz agreed, "but I'm not sure that's going to be enough." She got up and walked over to the window. "Maybe it's just because I'm exhausted, but to tell you the truth, right now I'm afraid that come

Tuesday, Brent and his family might just be able to take that vacation to Cape Cod they missed out on this summer."

"I just wish I could've gotten somebody to come forward and say that this wasn't the first time Brent did something awful," Jeff said, chastising himself. "There must be somebody out there that I missed."

"You didn't miss anyone," Liz reassured him kindly. "You talked to every man, woman, child, dog, and cat in Oakwood. Nobody there had anything bad to say about him." She turned around and walked back to her desk and sat down again.

"That's it!" Jeff exclaimed, his eyes lighting up.

"What's it?" Liz asked sharply.

"Nobody in *Oakwood* had anything bad to say," Jeff said, rushing over to Liz's desk.

"What are you getting at?" Tom asked, a puzzled look on his face.

"I need to go to Cape Cod," Jeff said eagerly.

"What for?" Liz asked incredulously. "This is a hell of a time to decide you need a vacation."

"I know it's a long shot," Jeff continued excitedly, pacing back and forth in front of Liz's desk, "but it's the only hope we have left. I don't know why the hell I didn't think of it before. Remember how Versey made such a fuss at those hearings about Brent needing permission to go to the Cape to visit an aged relative and how it was some big family tradition to go there every summer?"

Liz nodded.

"Well, why wouldn't it be possible for Brent to have gotten himself into trouble there on one of his earlier visits?" He rubbed his hand over his chin. "Maybe the missing puzzle piece we've been searching for is somewhere on the Cape. Now all I have to do is figure out where the Tompkinses' relative lives."

"Chatham," Liz said quietly. "My friend Esther told me it was Chatham. But this is crazy," she went on.

"The odds are probably one in a million that you'll be able to find anything."

"I've got no odds at all if I stay here," Jeff retorted. "I might as well spend the next two days out there trying to come up with something." He looked up at the clock. It was five-thirty. "I wonder if I can still get a flight out tonight."

Tom, who had been standing there quietly all this time, now spoke up. "I'm going with you," he said.

Jeff frowned. "I don't know if that's such a good idea."

"We'll be able to cover twice as much ground," Tom said. "I've been told I'm pretty good at talking to people. You just tell me what to ask and I'll go to it."

Jeff's look told Tom he was still skeptical.

"Look," Tom said, raising his voice. "I have a vested interest in this. My son's murderer might walk off scot-free unless we come up with something. You might just as well accept the idea that you're going to be stuck with me because I guarantee I'll come out there on my own whether you want me to or not."

Jeff gave Tom one more hard glance, then nodded. "All right. You're on." He looked around Liz's desk. "Where's your phone book? We'll need to find out about flights."

"Let me take care of that," Tom said. "I have an excellent travel agent. She'll make all the arrangements. We'll need a hotel and a rental car, too."

"Okay," Jeff said. He turned to Liz. The blood had drained out of her face, and her eyes were wide. "What's the matter? You look like you've seen a ghost."

Liz shook her head. "I just don't want any of us to pin our hopes on something that's not there."

"Hey," Jeff chided, lightly touching her chin. "Isn't hope what life's all about?"

Chapter 42

Jeff and Tom arrived in Chatham, Massachusetts, around three in the morning. They had caught the last Midwest Express flight from Milwaukee to Boston and then hopped aboard a twin engine Beechcraft that Tom had chartered, which transported them to the Barnstable Municipal Airport. There they picked up their rental car and drove the last leg of the journey, to the Chatham Bars Inn, an opulent oceanfront resort.

After snatching a few hours' sleep, they grabbed a quick breakfast at the hotel and set out for the police station. Chatham, an aristocratic old village situated at Cape Cod's knobby elbow, had a population of around five thousand. With a healthy percentage of its residents coming from old money, the town had managed to escape the sometimes tasteless development and commercialism that had run rampant elsewhere on the Cape.

From phone calls he had made before leaving Wisconsin, Jeff had learned that Brent Tompkins's maternal grandmother was named Edith Asherton and that she owned a home on Old Harbor Road. He had also thought to bring with him several enlargements of the photo of Brent that the local papers had been running along with their stories about the trial.

Being the last week in September, it was already off season in the Cape, and the downtown area was nearly deserted. Tom and Jeff discovered the local constabulary in a neat two-story brick building just off

Main Street. A fresh-faced young officer in his thirties was manning the front desk. "Can I help you?" he asked in a thick Boston accent. His badge identified him as Bob Monroe.

"I'm a police detective from Wisconsin," Jeff explained, showing his ID. "My friend and I are trying to track down any information we can about a family named Tompkins that vacations here every summer."

"Tompkins," Monroe repeated thoughtfully. "Doesn't ring a bell."

"Mrs. Tompkins's mother is a woman named Edith Asherton," Tom put in.

"Oh, sure," Monroe said, an immediate look of recognition coming over his face. "Everybody knows the Asherton place. It's one of the biggest houses in town. Most people who have houses that size live in them all year," he explained. "But not Mrs. Asherton. She just uses it as a summer place. It's empty right now. I heard she's already gone back to Cambridge."

"Do you remember ever seeing this boy in town?" Jeff handed him the photo of Brent. "He's Mrs. Asherton's grandson."

Monroe studied it, then shook his head. "No. Can't say that I have. Was he here recently?"

"No, not since last year," Jeff replied. "Would you be able to tell us if anyone named Tompkins ever got a citation of any kind?"

The young officer looked over his shoulder to where two older men could be seen talking in a back room. "This is really against procedure," he said confidentially, "but what the hell." He typed the appropriate code into his computer and waited for his search to be completed. "Only thing we got on a Tompkins is a speeding ticket issued to a Martin Tompkins on July 11 last year. He was doing fifty-five in a thirty mile-per-hour zone. Gentleman paid a hundred-eighty-dollar fine."

"You have no record of a Brent Tompkins?" Tom asked.

Monroe shook his head.

"Have any assaults been made on small children the last couple of summers? Maybe an incident that was never solved?"

Monroe shook his head again. "No. This is a pretty quiet town. I've worked here at the department ten years, and I'm sure if there had been an attack on a kid I'd know about it."

"Thanks for the information, anyway," Jeff said as he and Tom turned to go.

"My pleasure," Monroe replied. "Sorry I couldn't be more help."

"Now what do we do?" Tom asked when they got back out to the sidewalk.

"Go door to door, canvassing as many businesses as we can. Show people Brent's picture and ask questions. Keep a running list of each place you go into and every person you talk to so we don't waste time backtracking. Let's start here in the center of town. I'll work north and east and you head south and west." He looked at his watch. "Let's meet back here at four and go over what we've found."

"Okay." Tom started to head out.

"Hey." Jeff caught him by the arm. "Just one more thing."

"Yeah?" Tom turned back.

"Don't be too disappointed if we come up empty. We're literally hunting for a needle in a haystack here."

Tom looked at him gravely. "I know that. But I want to be able to say that we did everything we could."

Jeff nodded. "Me, too." He clapped Tom soundly on the back. "Happy hunting."

They both pounded the pavement until they had blisters. They talked to shop owners, innkeepers, bartenders, waitresses, fishermen, realtors, and garbage men. While many people they talked to knew Mrs.

Asherton, only a handful knew her daughter and fewer still ever remembered seeing the handsome, well-built boy in the photo. Of that last group, none could recall the youth ever misbehaving in any way.

After reconnoitering at four, Tom and Jeff decided to push on. While Tom continued making his rounds on foot, concentrating now on private residences, Jeff took the car and headed for the outskirts of town on the theory that a strong, adventurous boy like Brent might well decide to walk two or three miles in search of kicks.

From time to time throughout the long day, Jeff found himself struck by the beauty of the area. The pristine beaches, the waves crashing against the shore, the narrow streets, the well-maintained houses—all combined to make it one of the loveliest places he had ever visited. A drive past Mrs. Asherton's house confirmed that the old lady must indeed be loaded. With the fog rolling in, the sprawling clapboard residence high atop a bluff overlooking the sea looked like something out of a gothic novel. Imagine being rich enough to have a house like that for a summer place, Jeff thought, shaking his head ruefully. And here he was, trying to scrape together money for a new furnace. No doubt about it, the class system was definitely alive and well in the U.S.

Tom and Jeff finally returned, exhausted, to the hotel, meeting in the restaurant at eight. "I have newfound respect for people who go into police work," Tom said, taking a big swallow of his scotch and water. "I thought my job was tough, but compared to this it's a walk in the park."

Jeff smiled wryly. "You realize that the fact that you have a personal stake in the outcome does add to the stress level."

"I know that," Tom said. "So what's your excuse? Unless I'm mistaken, your stress level is pretty damn high, too."

Jeff pursed his lips and thought of his father. "I

don't know. I guess maybe you could say I have a personal stake in this, too.''

The waiter came to take their orders.

"We'll both have the broiled lobster," Tom said before Jeff had a chance to speak up. "With new potatoes and Caesar salad. Oh, and could we also get a bowl of your seafood chowder to start?"

"Very good, sir." The waiter headed back to the kitchen.

"I was just gonna order a steak sandwich," Jeff said. "Did you see the price of the lobster?"

"Fuck the price!" Tom said sharply. Then he added in a softer voice, "This is my treat. I appreciate everything you and Liz have done. I'm just glad I've got the chance to do something for you in return."

"Hey, I'm just doing my job," Jeff said as the waiter brought the chowder. "But since you brought it up, I might just have an idea what you could do for Liz—"

"What?" Tom asked.

Jeff took a sip of his drink as he pondered what torture Liz would devise for him if she ever got wind of this conversation. Oh, what the hell. Might as well live dangerously. He set down his glass. "After the trial is over, I think you should ask her out."

Tom paused, his spoon in midair. "What makes you think she'd be interested?"

Jeff shrugged. "Just a hunch. You do whatever you want to, but if I were in your shoes, I'd sure give it a shot. In my book, she is one classy woman."

"There's no doubt about that," Tom agreed. He hesitated a moment, then said, "You know, I think I like your suggestion. I just might ask her—after the trial."

Jeff nodded as though he didn't care one way of the other, but inside he was beaming. "I don't think you'd be sorry," he said.

Tom smiled. "Neither do I."

After sleeping like dead men for nine hours, they followed the same game plan the next day. Many businesses were closed on Sundays, and most of those that weren't didn't open until noon, so they both focused on canvassing private residences. At least they weren't running into the wall of silence he had encountered in Oakwood, Jeff thought gratefully as he moved from house to house. True, he hadn't come up with any useful information yet, but at least people gave him the opportunity to ask his questions and politely said they were sorry but they couldn't help him rather than threatening to call their lawyers to get a restraining order keeping him off their property. Maybe all those stories about New Englanders being unfriendly were just bunk.

Jeff and Tom met for a quick lunch at one. Their flight from Barnstable to Boston was at seven. They knew they were running out of time. "Got any bright ideas?" Jeff asked.

"Let's take the car and head out of town a bit," Tom replied. "You went toward Orleans yesterday, right?" Jeff nodded. "Well, why don't we go the other way? Let's take 28 toward Harwich Port."

In the next three hours they stopped at a multitude of homes and business establishments with the same lack of results. It was after four o'clock, with their energy and enthusiasm seriously waning, when they walked into a small grocery store called Maggie's Place. The only customers there were a couple who were having a rather heated discussion over what brand of frozen pizza to buy.

Jeff approached the plump, dark-haired, middle-aged woman behind the sole cash register. "Are you Maggie?" he asked genially.

"That's me," the woman replied. "Maggie Sturgis. What can I do for you gents?"

"Have you ever seen this boy?" Jeff asked, displaying Brent's photo.

Maggie's expression immediately became wary. "Why? What's he done?"

"I just want to know if you ever remember seeing him," Jeff said patiently.

Maggie ran her tongue around her lips, stared hard at the photo, and then looked back at Jeff. "I asked you what he's done," she said, her voice shaking.

Jeff glanced over at Tom, then said, "He's been accused of murdering a small child in Wisconsin. He vacationed around here with his family the past few summers. We're trying to find out if he ever got into any trouble."

At the word "murder," the woman's face grew ashen. "Do you remember him?" Tom asked quietly.

Maggie swallowed hard, then nodded. "You wait here," she said. "Let me get my daughter." She came out from behind the register and hurried to the rear of the store, where she disappeared through a doorway. Moments later she reappeared. A slender young woman in her early twenties dressed in tight jeans and a red flannel shirt was walking hesitantly behind her.

"This is my daughter, Vickie," Maggie explained.

"Hello, Vickie," Jeff said. "I'm Jeff Gardner, and this is Tom Barker."

"Hi," Vickie said shyly, pushing her long brown hair behind her ears. She looked at the men warily.

"Show her the picture," Maggie said.

Jeff handed the young woman the photo. Vickie held out her hand to receive it, but the instant she saw Brent's face, she let out a gasp and covered her face with her hands. The picture dropped to the floor.

"What's wrong?" Jeff asked anxiously. "Do you know him?"

Vickie made a whimpering sound, then nodded.

"How do you know him?" Jeff persisted, picking up the photo."

Vickie dropped her hands and opened her mouth, but no words came out.

Her mother came to her rescue. "Vickie knows him because last summer that monster tried to kill her little boy."

Chapter 43

After Maggie had sent the pizza customers on their way, she hung the CLOSED sign on the door and the four of them went upstairs to the family's meager living quarters. There Jeff and Tom met a shy, brown-haired five-year-old named Sam Sturgis. After his grandmother had sent the boy off to play in his room, Vickie told her story.

"It was July 11," she explained in a soft voice. "In the late afternoon. I was alone in the store. My mother had left the day before to visit a sick relative in California." She paused and ran her tongue nervously around her lips.

"Would you like a glass of water, honey?" her mother asked kindly.

Vickie nodded. When the older woman brought the water, Vickie gratefully took a couple of big swallows before continuing. "Sam was out playing by the pier. I was in the back of the store. The screen door was open, and I thought I heard him cry. I ran outside and that's when I saw the boy in your picture."

"What were Sam and Brent doing?" Jeff asked gently.

Vickie took a deep breath. "Sam was laying face-down on the beach. Brent was standing over him. He was holding a piece of plank in his hands. It looked like he was about to hit Sam with it."

"What did you do then?" Jeff asked.

"I ran over to Sam, screaming as loud as I could. As soon as Brent saw me, he dropped the plank and ran off. Sam was unconscious. I was so scared," she said, twisting her hair nervously. "I picked him up and saw right away that he had a big bruise on his forehand. I rushed him to the hospital. He woke up on the way there. The doctor did a CAT scan. He told me Sam had a slight concussion and that he wanted to keep him overnight for observation." She paused and took another drink of water.

"Tell them what happened then," her mother urged.

Vickie nodded. "While I was waiting for them to transfer Sam to his room, I went out to the lobby. I was going to call the police. When I got to the lobby, there was a man waiting for me. He told me his name was Martin Tompkins, and he asked if he could talk to me outside. I said okay. When we got outside, he said his son, Brent, had told him there'd been an accident involving my little boy. He said he was very sorry and wanted to know how Sam was. I said he had a concussion but the doctor said he'd be okay." She paused for a moment, remembering.

"Then what happened?" Jeff asked softly.

Vickie nervously twisted the tail of her shirt and continued. "At first Mr. Tompkins seemed like he was real shook up about what had happened. He kind of stared off into space, like I wasn't even there, and started mumbling a lot of things about Brent."

"What did he say?"

Vickie frowned. "All kinds of stuff. How he and his wife had been living in Boston and had wanted a child so badly but didn't think they could have their own, so they adopted Brent. He was over a year old when they got him, and he'd been abused and neglected by his real parents. The Tompkinses had problems with him right from the beginning. He was mean and had tantrums and caused them so much trouble that for a while they thought of not going through with the adoption. But they didn't have the heart to send him back to a foster home, so they kept him, thinking if they gave him enough love he'd eventually straighten out."

"Oh, my God," Jeff said under his breath. He'd long suspected the Tompkinses were harboring some dark secret, but he'd never imagined it would be something like this.

Vickie continued. "Mr. Tompkins said they took him to the best psychiatrists in Boston, but none of them could help him. There was something about the fact that he never bonded with his real parents that caused him to never develop a conscience like most people have. The family moved to Wisconsin when Brent was three and they never told anyone there that he was adopted. Shortly after they moved, Mrs. Tompkins got pregnant, and after their daughter was born Brent seemed to improve a little but then he got worse again. They didn't want anyone in Wisconsin to know about his problems, so every summer they'd come to the Cape for a long vacation so Brent could go through some kind of radical therapy in Boston. Mr. Tompkins said all of that had been a waste of time and money because nothing they did could change Brent."

"Then what happened?" Jeff prompted.

Vickie drew in a deep breath. "Then Mr. Tompkins seemed to snap out of it. He stopped talking about Brent and got a hard look on his face and he said he'd give me fifty thousand dollars on the spot if I agreed not to go to the police."

"He did *what*?" Tom asked incredulously.

Vickie's chin began to tremble. "He said Brent was ready to swear that he saw Sam accidentally fall of the pier and hit his head on a piling and that nobody would believe me if I tried to say otherwise. I didn't know what to do. I was so confused. I knew Mr. Tompkins was rich. How could I ever prove that Sam didn't hit his head? If I went to the police, it'd be my word against the Tompkinses, and who was going to believe a twenty-one-year-old unwed mother who didn't even finish high school?" She brushed tears from her eyes and took another drink of water before continuing.

"My head was spinning. The doctor had said Sam would be fine in a few days. Fifty thousand dollars was more money than I'd ever see in my lifetime. I thought about all the things I could do for Sam with that money, and I told Mr. Tompkins I'd accept his offer. He pulled out his checkbook and wrote me a check right on the spot." She shook her head in amazement. "I couldn't believe it. He was no more concerned than if he was buying a new shirt."

"Tell them what else Tompkins said to you," Her mother said, scowling.

Vickie took a deep breath, then exhaled. "He said if I ever went to the police, he'd be back and he'd not only want his money back, he'd also take our store away from us. I said I understood. Then he shook my hand and he left."

"She couldn't get hold of me until the next day," Maggie Sturgis said, taking up the narrative. "I was livid. I told her she was naive and that she'd just taken 'hush money.' From the description she gave of Brent, I said I'd noticed the kid hanging around outside the store for the past couple of weeks. I came back from California right away and tried to talk Vickie into contacting a lawyer, but she insisted on sticking to her bargain. Luckily, the doctors were right and Sam is fine. And he has no memory of the event, thank God. In the past year, I think Vickie has pretty well convinced herself that maybe the incident did happen the way Tompkins described it. She put the money in an account in Sam's name, and we thought we'd heard the last of the Tompkins family." She paused and looked intently at Jeff and Tom. "That is, until today when two strangers with Midwestern accents wandered into our store."

"Will you come back to Wisconsin with us?" Jeff asked Vickie urgently. "We need you to testify about what Brent did to Sam."

A fearful expression immediately came over Vickie's face. "I can't," she cried. "I promised I wouldn't tell. I'd have to give the money back, and Sam needs that for his future. Mr. Tompkins might even try to hurt Sam. I can't go with you."

Tom reached into his wallet and pulled out a picture. This is the child Brent killed," he said quietly, handing Vickie the photo. As she studied it, he added softly, "That was my son, Jeremy."

Vickie let out a low moan and her brown eyes grew wide. "He was four years old," Tom continued, "and Brent Tompkins beat him over the head with a shovel until the back of his skull was completely smashed in. "Please," Tom said, looking into her eyes. "Please help us make sure that Brent Tompkins doesn't ever get the chance to hurt another little boy."

There was a long pause. Vickie looked at her mother. The older woman gave a small nod. Vickie took a deep breath. "All right," she said in a weak voice. "I'll do it."

"Thank you." Tom reached out and hugged her tightly.

Jeff looked at his watch. "We're going to have to hustle, folks, or we'll miss our plane."

Jeff called Liz from the airport. "I don't believe it!" she exclaimed when she heard the news. "So that's why the Tompkinses were so eager to have the judge let Brent go to the Cape to visit his grandma. They didn't want him to miss his yearly primal scream therapy." She heaved a big sigh of relief. "You have no idea how happy I am to hear from you. I've been worried sick that you wouldn't find anything and Brent would walk."

"Well, you can relax now," Jeff said. "I think we're home free."

"Nice job, Detective Gardner. If you were here, I'd kiss you."

"If I were there, I'd let you," Jeff said, smiling. "On

second thought, maybe you should extend that offer to Tom. He turned out to be quite a detective, too. Not to mention a hell of a good guy."

"I've known that for quite some time," Liz said quietly.

"I had a feeling you did," Jeff replied.

Chapter 44

At a hearing in Judge Andrews's chambers the next morning, Versey fought like a banshee to keep the jury from hearing Vickie's testimony.

"The state did not list this woman as a potential witness," he bellowed. "The defense is entitled to notice."

"This is newly discovered evidence, Your Honor," Liz countered, brushing a piece of hair off her black suit. "It was mere happenstance that Detective Gardner located Ms. Sturgis in a small town a thousand miles from here. There is no way the state could have known of her existence before now."

"There is no proof my client was responsible for her child's injuries. Perhaps he did hit his head in a fall," Versey went on.

"The hospital where he was treated faxed me a copy of his medial record," Liz said, waving the document in front of the blustering lawyer. "The emergency room physician says the boy suffered a blunt force trauma to the back of his head consistent with being struck with a flat object," she told Versey. "The doctor's notes specifically state that his injuries could not have been sustained in a fall."

"The evidence should still be excluded," Versey shot back. "The state is attempting to show that the defendant is predisposed to commit assaults on children. That is clearly not allowed under the evidence code."

"You are mischaracterizing my intentions," Liz replied. "I know full well that I can't tell the jury that they should find Brent guilty of killing Jeremy solely because he might have assaulted another child. However, I am entitled to introduce the evidence to show motive, preparation, or plan."

"It would be unfairly prejudicial to my client to allow it," Versey persisted.

Judge Andrews held up his hands, signaling an end to the arguments. "I sympathize with your predicament, Mr. Versey," he said. "There is no doubt the evidence is highly prejudicial. However, the incident in Massachusetts happened only a year ago, so it is not remote in time. It also closely resembles the assault on Jeremy Barker. Hence, I concur with Ms. Stanfeld that it does tend to show a motive, plan, or scheme on your client's part, and I will allow Ms. Sturgis's testimony."

"In that case, Your Honor," Versey continued, with obvious agitation, "With all due respect, I would ask that you limit this woman's testimony to her observations of my client and preclude her from testifying about her dealings with Brent's father."

"I object!" Liz said hotly. "Martin Tompkins's payoff is a crucial part of Ms. Sturgis's testimony."

Versey opened his mouth to counter, but again the judge cut him off. "No, Mr. Versey," he said firmly. "My ruling allowing Ms. Sturgis to testify covers *all* aspects of her story. You'll just have to do the best you can to discredit her on cross and if that doesn't work, hope that the court of appeals might decide I made the wrong decision and grant you a new trial." He glanced up at the clock. "Now, I'd suggest that we get this show on the road. We've already kept the jury waiting half an hour, and as you both know, an impatient jury can turn into an unpredictable jury when it comes time for them to deliberate. I'm sure neither one of you wants that."

"Your Honor—" Versey spoke up once more.

"Yes, Counsel?" the judge asked, his eyebrows knitted together in irritation.

"May I please have ten minutes to speak to my clients?"

The judge sighed, then nodded. "All right, but not one minute more."

As the two attorneys made their way out of the judge's office, Liz caught Versey's sleeve. "Did you know about Vickie Sturgis or about Brent's past psychological problems before today?" she hissed under her breath.

Versey turned, swallowed hard, and shook his head. "On my oath, I did not."

Liz searched his face, then nodded. She believed him. "Detective Gardner and I have been wondering if the reason Dr. Moss withdrew from the case was that either Mr. or Mrs. Tompkins told him about Brent's past?"

Versey shook his head. "I don't know. I suppose it's possible."

Liz nodded again. "I wouldn't care to be in your shoes right now."

"Nor I," Versey murmured as he walked out to face the Tompkinses.

When Judge Andrews called court into session ten minutes later, the room contained some new faces. Harry Washburn and Sheriff Isaacson were seated in the spectator section, as were Esther and Bob McMillan. Martin Tompkins was conspicuously absent. His wife was there, wringing her hands in her lap. Her cheeks were tearstained. But it was Brent's demeanor that gave Liz the most sublime satisfaction.

Brent looked in a state of near collapse. His usually ruddy complexion was ashen. While his gray suit was neatly pressed and his white shirt crisp, his habitually erect posture was stooped. His ubiquitous smirk and defiant gaze had been supplanted by a quivering chin and downcast eyes. That's more like it, Liz nodded to herself. It's about time the kid started to act like someone who's on trial for murder.

Liz had decided to save Vickie for her last witness. That way she could make Brent squirm as long as possible, as he anticipated what was to come. She began the morning session with Jeff's testimony.

The detective repeated his oft-told story about his investigation of the case and his questioning and arrest of Greg and Brent. Versey came out swinging on cross.

"Have you ever arrested someone for a crime and later found out that person was innocent?"

"Yes," Jeff answered easily.

"So you're not infallible, then?"

"I daresay no one is infallible, sir. Not even you." A murmur of laughter went through the crowd.

"Prior to my client's arrest, you were investigating at least one suspect from Lakeview, were you not?"

"Yes."

"I see." Versey paused. "Detective Gardner, isn't it true that you wanted to solve this case so badly that you jumped at the chance to arrest my client rather than pursuing other possible suspects?"

"It's true, Counselor, that I jumped at the chance to arrest your client, but that was because I was and still am absolutely convinced that he is the person who murdered Jeremy Barker. Under the circumstances, there was no need for me to continue my investigation."

Versey flushed. "No further questions," he muttered.

Philip Barry, a well-built man of thirty with shoulder-length brown hair, told of Brent's escalating bad behavior the year he had been in the teacher's class. "Mr. Barry," Liz said, "from your acquaintance with Brent Tompkins, did you form an opinion as to his reputation for truth and veracity?"

"Yes," Barry replied.

"And could you tell us what that was?"

"I wouldn't believe a word he said."

Liz also asked Barry about his disenchantment with

the Oakwood School District and the school board's decision not to renew his contract. "Moving to Wisconsin was the biggest mistake I ever made," Barry admitted candidly. "I was lured by the shiny new facilities and the high salary, but from day one it was clear I didn't fit in. I wouldn't have stayed on even if the board had begged me."

"Thank you," Liz said, nodding. "No further questions."

"You have a chip on your shoulder about the entire Oakwood community, don't you?" Versey asked.

"I wouldn't say that," Barry replied, looking Versey right in the eye, "There were some nice people in Oakwood and some students that I was proud to get to know."

"But you don't count Brent Tompkins among them?"

"No, sir. I do not."

"Isn't it possible that the bad blood between you and the school district has colored your recollection of your relations with Brent?"

"Absolutely not," Barry answered without hesitation. "Every word I said was the absolute truth."

At that point Versey decided to abandon his questioning of the witness.

When Liz returned to the courtroom after the lunch break, it appeared that the mood in the defense camp had sunk even lower. Brent's father was still noticeably absent. His mother was sitting several rows further back from the spot she had occupied during the rest of the trial, as though she had made a conscious decision to distance herself from her offspring.

Brent was seated between Versey and the young associate, his head down, his hands clenched into fists in his lap. When the jury began to file into the room, the associate gave Brent a sharp jab in the ribs. At this signal Brent snapped out of his lethargy enough to sit up straight and stare fixedly in front of him.

"Ms. Stanfeld," the judge boomed, "kindly call your next witness."

"The state calls Vickie Sturgis."

A murmur of curiosity went through the courtroom as the door from the hall opened and Vickie walked resolutely up the center aisle. Who was she? Why had her name never come up earlier in the trial? What could she possibly have to say?

The urgency of departing from the Cape the previous evening had left Vickie only minutes to pack. Even if she'd had the luxury of more time, her wardrobe contained little that would have been appropriate for court appearances. Thanks to an emergency loan from Liz's friend Esther, Vickie was now dressed in a conservative black long-sleeved dress with a white collar and cuffs. Two pearl barrettes held her long hair back off her face.

As Vickie stood in front of the witness box and swore to tell the truth, Liz glanced over at Brent. He looked as though he was trying to curl up in a fetal position. His feet were resting on the rungs of his chair. His elbows were on his knees. His head was down and his eyes appeared to be closed. Liz gave a quick look back at Mrs. Tompkins. She was holding herself so stiffly she looked as though rigor mortis had set in.

Vickie took her seat in the witness box. She sat up straight, with her hands folded primly in front of her. After briefly going through Vickie's background, Liz asked, "Do you have any children?"

"Yes," Vickie answered in a quiet voice. "I have a son, Sam. He's five."

"Would you please tell us what happened to Sam on July 11 of last year?"

"He had a concussion."

"How did you become aware that Sam had been injured?"

"I thought I'd heard him scream. I looked out the

back door of my mother's grocery store and saw him lying facedown on the sand, near the pier."

"Did you see anyone else nearby?"

"Yes."

"Who did you see?"

"Vickie ran her tongue around her lips. "I saw a teenage boy standing over Sam. He was holding a board over his head. It looked like he was going to hit Sam with it."

"Is the boy you saw standing over Sam present in this courtroom?"

"Yes," Vickie said softly.

"Would you point him out, please?"

Vickie took a deep breath, then raised her arm and pointed her right index finger straight at Brent. "He's sitting over at that table, between those two men. He's wearing a gray suit."

"Let the record indicate that Ms. Sturgis has identified the defendant, Brent Tompkins," Liz said.

The reaction in the courtroom was swift and intense. Liz heard several jury members gasp. Spectators turned to one another and exchanged astonished looks and words.

"Order in the court!" Judge Andrews commanded, banging his gavel on the bench. "If anyone wants to jabber, I suggest they leave the room at once!" The noise slowly subsided.

"What did you do when you saw Brent Tompkins standing over your son?"

"I screamed and he ran off."

"Then what did you do?"

Vickie explained her mad dash to get Sam to the emergency room, the CAT scan, Sam's regaining consciousness, and the doctor's happy prognosis.

"Did you notify the police about what had happened?" Liz asked.

"No."

"Why not?"

"I was going to," Vickie explained. "While Sam was

being transferred to his room, I went to look for a phone to call the police. But when I got out into the hospital lobby, a man was waiting for me."

"Did the man identify himself?"

Vickie nodded. "Yes. He said his name was Martin Tompkins."

Liz could feel the jurors glancing over to where Tompkins had been sitting. Several of them were frowning. Where was he? their faces seemed to say. "Why did Mr. Tompkins want to talk to you?"

"He said his son, Brent, had told him there had been a misunderstanding, that I thought Brent had hurt Sam."

"What did you say to that?"

"I told him I'd seen Brent standing over Sam with a board, looking like he had just hit him and was going to hit him again. Mr. Tompkins said that Brent claimed he just happened to be walking by and that he'd seen Sam fall off the pier and hit his head."

"What was your response?"

"I didn't know what to think. I was confused and I was very upset."

"Did Mr. Tompkins say anything else?"

"Yes. He said Brent was adopted as a small child and that they'd had a lot of problems with him and that he'd been through intensive therapy to help him deal with his anger but that it hadn't worked."

"Anything else?"

Vickie nodded. "Yes. He asked me if I was married, and I said I wasn't. Then he told me he knew I could stir things up and cause trouble if I called the police. He said his wife's mother was elderly and that it would kill her if there was any bad publicity. He said if I'd agree not to call the police, he'd make things right for me and Sam."

"Did he explain what he meant by that?"

"Yes. he said he'd give me a check for fifty thousand dollars on the spot if I agreed not to talk to the police."

Another murmur went through the crowd. Again Judge Andrews banged his gavel and called for silence.

"Did you accept Mr. Tompkins's offer?" Liz asked gently.

Vickie swallowed hard. "Yes." Her voice was now little more than a whisper. "Like I told you, I was tired and confused. The doctors had told me Sam would be okay. All I could think about was how the money would help Sam have a better life. So I told him he had a deal and he sat right down and wrote me a check."

"Did Mr. Tompkins say anything else?"

"Yes. He said if I ever did talk to the police, he'd come back and want all the money back, plus he'd see to it that my mother and I lost everything we had."

"Thank you, Vickie," Liz said, giving the young woman a smile. "I have no further questions.

"Mr. Versey, cross?" the judge asked.

Versey slowly got to his feet. "Your Honor," he said quietly, "I have no questions for this witness." He took his seat again.

The judge addressed Vickie. "Ms. Sturgis, you may step down." As Vickie gratefully left the witness box and walked out of the room to where Jeff was waiting, the judge turned to Liz. "Ms. Stanfeld, you may call your next rebuttal witness."

Liz stood up. "Your Honor, the state has no further witnesses."

The judge nodded. "Mr. Versey, does the defense have anything further?"

In a defeated tone, Versey replied, "No, Your Honor."

"Very well," the judge said. "In that case, let's take a ten-minute break, after which we will hear closing arguments."

Knowing that the powerful impact of Vickie's testimony was still fresh in the jurors' minds, Liz kept her argument brief. "Your primary role as jurors is to

judge the credibility of the various witnesses who testified here. In the course of this case you heard two
versions of the events that occurred the day of Jeremy
Barker's murder that are diametrically opposed to
each other. Greg Saunders told you that the defendant, Brent Tompkins, beat Jeremy Barker over the
head with a shovel until he was dead. Brent Tompkins
told you that it was Greg Saunders who killed Jeremy.
Vickie Sturgis told you that a year ago in July she saw
her young son Sam lying unconscious on the beach
while Brent Tompkins stood over him holding a piece
of board in a menacing fashion. You will recall that
Ms. Sturgis's testimony was not rebutted.

"When Mr. Versey and I have finished our remarks,
Judge Andrews will be instructing you on the law you
are to apply in deciding this case. He will tell you that
the fact that Brent Tompkins was involved in the assault of another little boy does not automatically mean
he is guilty as charged in this case. You are, however,
entitled to believe that Brent Tompkins's role in causing Sam Sturgis's injuries is indicative of a plan,
scheme, or motive on Brent's part."

She took a deep breath and for the last time made
eye contact with each juror. "Ladies and gentlemen,
I submit that the evidence demonstrates that on June
11 of this year Brent Tompkins went to the Barker
home with intent to kill Jeremy Barker and that he
carried out that intent. I further submit that when you
think back on everything you've heard during the
course of this trial, you will have no alternative but
to find Brent Tompkins guilty of kidnapping and first-
degree intentional homicide. Thank you." She returned to her seat.

Versey's closing was so subdued as to be almost
nonexistent. Liz wondered if, knowing all hope was
lost, Versey was perhaps trying to do Brent the only
favor he could by setting himself up for a claim of
ineffective assistance of counsel that Brent's new lawyer could raise on appeal. He spoke of Brent's child-

hood and his exemplary school record. He mentioned neither Greg nor Vickie Sturgis. He did not look directly at the jurors. He concluded by saying, "Brent Tompkins's fate is now in your hands. I am confident you will use the power that has been vested in you wisely."

When the jury had been given its instructions and had retired to begin its deliberations, Liz, Jeff, Tom, and Vickie rushed to Liz's office. "How long do you think they'll be out?" Tom asked anxiously.

"Not long," Jeff predicted confidently.

"Did I do all right?" Vickie asked nervously.

"You were wonderful!" Liz praised her. "That was the most dramatic testimony I've ever heard."

"I can't begin to thank you for coming back here with us," Tom told the young woman.

"Once you'd told me what Brent did to Jeremy, I had to come," Vickie replied. "I couldn't have lived with myself if I hadn't."

The jury was out only ninety minutes, a negligible amount of time in a first-degree homicide case.

"Will the defendant please rise," Judge Andrews instructed when the jury had filed in.

As though he were operating in slow motion, Brent pushed himself to his feet.

The judge turned to the jury. "Have you reached a verdict?"

"Yes, Your Honor," the middle-aged man who had been chosen to act as foreman, replied.

"How say you?" the judge inquired.

The courtroom collective held its breath.

The foreman read from the sheet in his hand. "In the Matter of the *State of Wisconsin* v. *Brent Tompkins,* on the charge of kidnapping, we, the jury, find the defendant—guilty."

Brent's chin dropped to his chest.

The foreman continued. "On the charge of first-degree intentional homicide by use of a dangerous weapon, we, the jury, find the defendant—"

Brent swayed from side to side as if his legs were made of rubber. Versey put one hand on the boy's arm to support him.

"—guilty."

Brent slumped into his seat.

Liz didn't realize she had been holding her breath until she found herself exhaling. Her heart began to pound wildly. They'd done it!

Jeff clenched his hands into fists and broke into a wide grin. Atta girl, he thought, beaming at Liz. Score one for the good guys.

"On behalf of Horicon County and the parties, I would like to thank you for your diligent service," the judge was saying to the jury. "You are now dismissed." The jurors filed out of the room.

Turning to the defense table, the judge said, "I will set sentencing for three weeks from today pending the preparation of a presentence report that will address the question of what date should be set for the defendant's parole eligibility. In the meantime, the defendant is remanded to the immediate custody of the Horicon County Sheriff's Department." He rapped his gavel down on the bench. "Court is adjourned."

Two uniformed deputies whom Jeff had stationed in the room moved forward at once and took Brent off to jail. His mother made no attempt to embrace him as he was led past.

Versey waved off reporters' questions. Before he and his young associate beat a hasty retreat out of town, he handed Liz a note saying that she and Jeff had been right. Mrs. Tompkins had inadvertently blurted out the story of Brent's assault on Sam to Dr. Moss. After hearing that Brent had a history of assaulting youngsters, the doctor had made the decision that he could not in good conscience proceed with the insanity defense.

Liz spent the next three quarters of an hour giving interviews. The exhilaration she felt from winning the case far overpowered the fatigue brought on by the strain of the trial. She knew that tomorrow she would have to begin the process of reevaluating her life and deciding whether her future lay in Oakwood or elsewhere. But tonight she was going to bask in the glow of a job well done.

When she finally made it back to her office, she discovered it was full of her colleagues and other well-wishers. Jeff had sent someone out for several bottles of champagne. "Here's to the best prosecutor in the state of Wisconsin," he toasted Liz when everyone had a glass in their hand.

"Hear! Hear!" everyone seconded.

"I hate to drink and run," Jeff said to Liz when he'd downed his glass, "but I have to get Vickie to the airport and then I have to go to a retirement party for someone my wife works with at the hospital."

"Oh." Liz looked at him over the top of her plastic glass. "That's too bad. I was hoping I might be able to pay off on that dinner I owe you."

"Don't worry. I have every intention of collecting on that bet," he assured her. "I'm still doing some research to find the most expensive restaurant in a hundred-mile radius. But in the meantime," he said, looking meaningfully over at where Tom was standing, talking to Esther and her husband, "I know somebody else who would probably love some food and a sympathetic ear tonight."

"Do you really think so?" Liz asked. She looked over at Tom. The expression on his face was a combination of joy at the jury's verdict, fatigue brought on by the strain of the past months, and confusion as to what direction his life would now take. She caught his eye. He smiled, genuinely happy to see her. Liz felt her face flush.

"Go for it," Jeff said, giving her a little shove. "You both deserve to have someone nice in your life."

Liz reached up and kissed him on the cheek. "It's been a pleasure working with you, Detective." Then she added softly, "Your dad would've been so proud of you."

Jeff felt a lump form in his throat. "Thanks," he said, giving her a hug. "Now get out of here before I embarrass both of us by saying something mushy."